The Defendant

Colin A. Mayo

PART ONE: THE INVESTIGATION

PART TWO: THE TRIAL

PART THREE: THE VERDICT

POSTSCRIPT

FOR THE FALLEN

"Oh, what a tangled web we weave, when first we practise to deceive!"

Sir Walter Scott, 1808

"People weighted down with troubles do not look back; they know only too well that misfortune stalks them."

Victor Hugo, *Les Misérables*

Foreword

It is very rare for me to read a novel and be hooked by it. But *The Defendant* was one I couldn't put down. The writer exposes a nightmarish situation that many people in prison find themselves in. And perfectly details the steps that must be taken when you find yourself accused of a serious crime. He captures the feelings of finding yourself in prison, and the daily trials of dealing with an uncaring system when you also have to sort out a defence to the accusations.

The only penalty for murder in this country is life imprisonment. If you are accused of murder, then it becomes all or nothing for you – guilty means a very long stay in prison. And, even when you're eventually released, you will be on life licence for the rest of your natural, liable to be recalled to prison without even recourse to a court.

This is a book that should be read.

Noel 'Razor' Smith
Author of *The Dirty Dozen*.

PART ONE: THE INVESTIGATION

Chapter One

" " Have you ever met Anne-Marie MacDonald?"
The police officer was standing in the front room of my ground floor flat; I'd not pulled the curtains across to blank out the cold, dark winter night and outside I was aware of cars passing by, their tyres splashing on the wet road and their hazy headlights refracting off the moisture. I was momentarily blinded as James' fast-moving red Mazda MX-5 screeched to a halt on the wet gravelled parking area at the front of our large, shared house; it bathed the front room in a white halo of brilliant halogen.

"No," I said – and that was my first mistake.

"But you were in Pryzm nightclub on Saturday, 15th November?" the officer asked.

"Yes," I said. "I was there."

"Who with?"

"Friends," I said.

The police officer smiled superciliously. He was about my age but slightly taller and a lot broader. He wore a stab vest with a crackling mouthpiece over his heart and a belt laden with the tools of the job: cuffs, pepper spray, the radio and an extendable baton. He stood legs apart as if he had taken ownership of a section of my living space. "Richard, it may be helpful to give some names."

I looked at the short, brown-haired PC who stood next to him; she caught my gaze and gave me a quick half smile – conspiratorial? They had introduced themselves as Tanner and Price, it was almost like the name of a hardware shop. I was unsure of who was who.

I thought about that Saturday night. Who I'd been out with? It was the usual crew, Mark, Dave, Suggo, Matty but I hadn't been with them, not really, I was an outsider, on the fringes. I listed names – real names, as well as addresses. The officer noted them down in a flip-up notebook.

"Well, I'm sure my colleagues will be speaking to them in due course, this is just routine at present. What time did you leave the club?"

I shrugged. "Early, 12.30, perhaps 1am."

"Were you with anyone?"

"No."

The officer smiled knowingly – I wondered if he, or his colleagues, had reviewed the CCTV over the nightclub door and seen me leaving with my arm around a brunette girl in a short, black satin skater skirt and high-heeled ankle boots. The same girl the internal CCTV would no doubt have shown me kissing and dancing with earlier in the evening. I wondered if this visit was far from routine at all. I wondered what the police knew. I wondered what had happened to Anne-Marie and if she was actually the same girl I'd been with – surely there could not be two Anne-Maries? Our copulation had not got as far as surnames so 'MacDonald' was new to me. Neither of the police officers were giving much away. I was aware that I was being watched by the officer who hadn't spoken. Closely. Body language. Soft cop, hard cop, although up to that point they'd both been pretty soft but, as my short-haired, large guest said, it was 'only routine'. Or was it? Someone at work had mentioned a 'woman's death' – it had been all over social media. Out of curiosity I had driven back past Anne-Marie's terraced house, on my way home from work. I had seen a police officer standing outside, and white and blue zig-zag tape across the front gate. The scene had sent shivers down my spine, but I felt the best thing to do was try to put it to the back of my mind and just carry on as normal.

"What about your friends?" the officer asked. "What time did they leave?"

What about my friends? Mark – the womaniser – had, as usual, gone off earlier in the night with a pretty blonde in a tight red sequinned dress and, as for the others, they were getting drunk at the bar; belatedly I'd followed in Mark's slipstream.

"They were still there, except Mark who'd met a girl he knew and left with her."

The truth was I didn't have clue if he knew her or not, but he knew so many women it seemed likely.

"So, you left on your own?"

"I think I said that."

The officer raised his eyes and smiled. His colleague was still burning my cheeks with her vibrant hazel eyes. I felt myself doing all the things body language experts say are signs of lying; scratching my nose, loosening my tie and collar, moving from foot to foot. The thing was, and this sounds absolutely pathetic now, but I was anxious to go to my writers' circle which met every Monday night in a meeting room at the local library.

"I just want to clarify if you'd had a drink?" the police officer enquired.

"Not really, I was driving."

"How much approximately?" he pressed.

I shrugged. "A pint… maybe two."

I didn't drink and drive, anyway, I'd had to get up early to take Debbie and her son out for the day. I'd agreed to take them to an aircraft museum. To think on that happy Sunday the only thing I had been worried about was my infidelity but by Monday evening things had just got a whole lot worse. Yet at that stage, I was not really sure how bad they were. Debbie was not the jealous sort at all and had no issues with me seeing my friends although she distrusted the womaniser, Mark ('you should stay away from him – he's a bad influence on you') and she thought Suggo was a juvenile, crude idiot ('I don't see what you see in him, he's an immature caveman who thinks farting is funny'); Matty and Dave were 'alright' according to Debbie's checklist but 'drank too much' but I was a nice guy. I'd always been a nice guy. I'd been a nice guy at school. An average 'nice guy'. I was a 'nice guy' at work too – an unambitious 'nice guy'. That was me, Richard Andrew Turner, known, since school, as 'Rat'. Mr Nice Guy. To think, as I walked around that aircraft museum and held Debbie's hand and occasionally kissed her cheek, the only thing that had concerned me was that I'd got away with being unfaithful. Again. And maybe my denials to the police that Monday evening, when I came home from work, were partly based on a desire to keep the truth from Debbie. Yes, I'd gone out with my friends that Saturday night but I had cheated on my girlfriend too.

For some reason I put my hand inside my suit jacket pocket and took out a pen, an expensive silver affair that my sister Kate had given me for my last birthday – I like writing, right? Though most of it was done on computer. I opened and shut it so it clicked as if I was using one of those counters, counting the number of people entering a club. Hazel Eyes didn't miss a beat.

"Is that the pen you used to write down Anne-Marie's telephone number?"

God, that struck me hard. I felt myself blush. If Hazel Eyes had been on a body language course, she'd have read me from cover to cover like a bleeding comic but the irony of it was I'd not written anything down, I'd had no need to. My mouth felt dry.

"What… what has happened to this girl?" I asked, trying to change the subject.

"Anne-Marie?" the first officer asked as if we were now talking about someone completely different.

"Yes, Anne-Marie."

The officer looked at Hazel Eyes and raised his eyebrows and smiled. He folded his notebook and placed it back inside his pocket and then slid his hands inside his stab vest as if he were trying to keep them warm.

"She's been involved in an incident," he said, before adding, "we need to establish the full circumstances."

The colour must have drained from my face for Hazel Eyes said, "Do you need to sit down, Richard?"

I knew what they were thinking; *why he is he bothered about someone he doesn't even know?*

But the word that was ricocheting through my head was: murder! Murder! Murder! I was a suspect in a murder case – fuck, cunt, bollocks, bastard! Fuck me, that was a hard concept to get my tiny little mind around but I was innocent. They must know that! But I knew I

6

must be a suspect. I was a suspect. I swallowed hard, my mouth felt dry, I knew I was sweating. Anne-Marie was dead. The police were in my front room. There could be no other explanation. I felt a prickling sensation run through my whole body.

"I see," I choked. "I guessed something serious must have happened; well, you wouldn't come around here if she'd been caught shoplifting, would you?"

It was my attempt to gain some semblance of control. Inject my pathetic humour into the discourse. It didn't work.

"No, I don't suppose we would," Hazel Eyes said; her gaze never left me. "What did you get up to yesterday?" she asked.

I told her about the trip to the museum with Debbie and her son.

"Can we have her details?" she requested.

"Why?" I felt desperate.

"It's just routine. We probably won't need them but it saves us coming back later," she explained.

I reeled off Debbie's address and phone number as Hazel Eyes scribbled in her notebook.

"We'll be off now. If we need to speak to you again, we'll be in touch," her colleague said. And I knew what he meant was 'when' – 'when' we speak to you again, not 'if' but 'when' – Richard Andrew Turner, known as Rat, was a suspect in a murder investigation.

After the police had gone, I collapsed onto my three-seater brown leather sofa to the left of the front door; it was opposite the TV and I was vaguely aware of the silent *One Show* on BBC1 (the police officer had asked me to turn the TV down when he'd entered my rented flat). My head was filled with muddled, confused and colliding thoughts.

I have to act normally, I told myself. *I have to, I've done nothing wrong.* But I had. My eyes were drawn to the small pine desk to the left of the television where my computer was situated; beside it a printer sat on a wooden set of three drawers. In the second one down was an envelope stashed with cash. *I've got to get rid of that fucking money*, I told myself, *I've got to get rid of that money!* I glanced up at the silver-rimmed clock – black numerals on a white face – it was on the wall above the computer. 6.30pm. The writers' circle started at 7pm. I quickly got up and walked to my bedroom and got changed out of my work suit. With shaking hands, I carefully hung up my jacket and trousers and put my shirt in the wash basket and then I pulled on jeans, a T-shirt and a thin red jumper. To be honest, part of me wanted to lie on the bed and just flake out but I knew I had to keep going. My heart was pumping so fast I could feel my blood gushing through my veins. I tried to calm myself; I knew I had to carry on, I had to act normally.

Once changed, I took a black leather jacket from the wardrobe and put that on, then taking a pair of leather gloves from the pockets of another coat I put them in the pockets of my leather jacket and pulled a scarf around my neck. Finally, I left the bedroom and went to the printer. I had already run off a short story I planned to read at the writers' circle that night: it lay on top of the printer. I picked up the story and put it inside a black folder, then I opened the second drawer. There was the envelope bulging with cash. Used notes. I didn't know how much money there was but it was one hell of a lot. I thought of Debbie, that engagement ring, I thought of that trip to Paris on the Eurostar and then I thought of Hazel Eyes and PC Snot (as I'd christened him with my writer's hat on) who'd just visited. If they laid their hands on that little wad of joy, I'd be staring down the barrels of a 'whole life tariff' as they say in the criminal justice trade. No question. Quickly, I put on my gloves and took out the envelope. To be honest I'm not sure why I did this because my dabs were all over the envelope and I had used some of the money the day before when I had taken Debbie and her son Dylan to the aircraft museum. I had paid the admission fees and bought lunch in the restaurant and a present, a toy plane, for Dylan. The museum trip had been enjoyable with Debbie laughing as I'd spent what seemed like hours trying to explain to her eight-year-old son that 'once upon a time' planes had propellers (or technically I think they are called airscrews, don't propellers propel from behind as the name suggests?) and flying planes was a bloody dangerous affair as the engines often used to 'conk out' mid-flight.

"No, they did not always have jet engines, Dylan!"

Debbie had tugged on my arm.

"You're so patient with him," she had said and kissed my cheek. "You'd make a wonderful dad."

Hint, hint!

I stood with the drawer open looking at the envelope, then I picked it up and ran my leather-clad thumb through the notes trying to make a rough calculation of the number of tens, twenties and fifties there were (there were even some Euros, bizarrely). Then I took a couple of twenties from the centre and put them in my pocket. Next, I placed the envelope in my folder between the pages of my short story. With a deep sigh I took my door keys off the coffee table, picked up an umbrella by the door and left my apartment.

Juliette, who lived with James in the room above mine, was just coming home from work, laden with shopping bags.

"Hi, Richard," she said breezily, "just off to your writers' circle?"

"Yes," I replied.

"I've always fancied writing," she said; she tended to say this to me every time we met. "I've got *sooooo* many stories whizzing about my head, I should write them down, but I just never get the time."

"You should come along," I said. "A writers' circle's good for motivation."

"Maybe," she said (she always said this too). She and James were a similar age to me and both professionals. They were saving up for a house and a wedding – one was out of their league so they were banking on a big 'Big Day' but I didn't know when. They tended to be fairly quiet although I did hear them padding across the floor and the occasional argument, Juliette's voice being the louder. Due to the configuration of the flats, which meant my bathroom was next to the bedroom at the back of the flat and their flat was identical, sometimes at night, it would sound to me as if James or Juliette were pissing on my head when they went to the toilet (always flushing as well which was annoying) but other than that they were fine – like me, they had lived in their flat for about six or seven years.

So, I stepped out into the cold, wet November night with my file under my arm and the umbrella over my head. I walked across the drive, over the road and down a path with high fences, gardens and houses by the side. Then I crossed a road and walked down another alleyway which brought me out between the back of shops and onto the pedestrianised high street. Immediately on my right was the Lord Rochford pub which had been a post office when I had first moved into the town. It was, as always, offering a special 'meal night' and was one of the pubs where I occasionally ate on my own, if I couldn't be bothered to cook.

I paced quickly to the library which was at the far end of the pedestrianised zone. As soon as I left the house, I felt a lot calmer; the cold, damp air was invigorating and I had the anticipation of meeting my writing friends. One of my Monday night 'treats' was to visit a fast-food restaurant en route, and enjoy a burger and fries whilst reading though whatever short story I planned to subject the group to that night. However, the police visit had curtailed that pleasure – it would have to be reserved for the end of the evening. So I marched with purpose to the library, trying to forget Anne-Marie and the police visit and everything else connected to it and that included the money. I found a council bin – one of those round concrete affairs with pebble-dashed exteriors – and, holding the umbrella in one hand, I rested my folder on it. Then I opened the folder up and, with shaking, trembling hands tipped the envelope into the bin. Job done. There was nothing to connect me to Anne-Marie bar CCTV, DNA, forensics and whole lot of other stuff, but you know what I mean and, for the record, my short story – once read – was also binned. I walked past the near empty, trendy Crazy Horse pub and arrived at the modern library building.

Claire, a girl I had once dated, was standing outside finishing a roll-up. She stood under an over-hang so she was shielded from the slanting rain. We had always got on well and went into the library together talking about the short stories we were going to read and an excellent Jimmy McGovern drama that had recently aired on TV called, ironically, *The Accused.*

"I wish I could write like that," I said. "His writing is so powerful."

"He's a writer with a social conscience," Claire stated.

Claire was big on 'social consciences'; if you had one you were a good person, if you didn't you weren't. During the brief three or four months – perhaps longer – that we'd dated she clearly felt I fell into the former category and when we moved from lovers to friends, I remained a person in her eyes who had a 'social conscience'. When she'd critique work at the writers' circle, she would often use a phrase like, 'to me your character hasn't got much of a social conscience and therefore I can't build any empathy or sympathy with him or her' – it was a typical Claire-ism. Another Claire-ism was 'moral compass' as in 'your character lacks a moral compass' or she'd say it about a politician – it was always an insult, it always meant Claire did not hold said person in high regard. To be 'in' with Claire you had to have a 'social conscience' and your compass needed to be pointing in the right direction.

We passed the dark-blue-uniformed security guard and walked up to meeting room 3. We sat down next to each other at the long pine table facing the desk where the secretary and chair were seated, the room being set out in a horseshoe shape. The circle was very well organised and there were about thirty members of which about twenty, including Claire and me, came every week. The members were mixed ages, though they tended to be fifty plus, and a lot were retired. The gender balance probably leant towards the female. As there were only a few of us in our thirties or younger, we had formed a little inner circle, which I'd dubbed The Writers Revolutionary Committee, and we'd regularly adjourn (please God stop me from using legal terminology!) at the end of the evening to a friendly little pub called The Queen of England where we would discuss literature, TV, theatre and generally gossip and pick holes in other members of the group and their stories.

Being at the circle that particular Monday was a great release; for a few brief hours I felt I could forget about the police visit and Anne-Marie MacDonald. But it was still there like a dark shadow in my mind. At least I'd got rid of the money – or most of it. What was left I'd use for my fast-food meal at the end of the night and for petrol on Tuesday morning.

"You coming for a drink, Rich?" Kevin, one of the Revolutionary Committee, asked me (I'd not shared my nickname, Rat, to anyone at the circle, having made the mistake of sharing it at work where it'd caught on fuelled by ex-colleague, Mark's, frequent use of it – where Mark went others followed.)

"No, I need to phone Debbie," I said.

"Oh, he's all loved up," Claire joked with a devious twinkle in her eye.

I laughed. "I've got to tell her something."

"Exactly – how much you love her!" Claire bantered.

We were walking down the stairs by this time and Claire was rolling a cigarette with one hand, something that had always impressed me.

We reached the bottom and walked back out into the wet November night.

"You can come for just one," Claire pleaded, grabbing my leather jacket.

"I've not eaten either," I said. "I'd better go."

So, I said goodnight to the small group, who trotted off down an alleyway on the right of the library and disappeared amidst the darkened shops. I jacked my umbrella up, turned in the other direction and walked off into the town, back along the pedestrian zone. I stopped on the way for my burger and fries, paid for with a twenty-pound note from the envelope.

I arrived home and let myself in. I left the umbrella by the door and then took off my jacket. I quickly ate my burger and then phoned Debbie.

"I thought you'd have gone down the pub?" she said.

"No, I had a visit from the police earlier."

"The police? Why? What's happened?" There was a note of panic in her voice.

"You know I went to the Pryzm Saturday night with the boys?" I said.

"Of course I do! You were wasted when we went around the museum on Sunday."

"Well, someone died, in suspicious circumstances."

"Who?"

"Some girl."

"You didn't know her, did you?" Debbie asked.

"No, no, of course not."

"So, what are you worried about then?" Debbie, ever practical, said.

"I'm not," I said.

Then suspicion rose in Debbie's voice. "So, the police are interviewing everyone who was in the nightclub on Saturday night?"

"I guess," I said, "or maybe they've looked at CCTV and are concentrating on those who left about the same time."

"Umm, possibly, you didn't speak to her, did you?" Debbie asked.

"Me? No! I was with Suggo and that lot."

"You didn't see her? You don't know what's happened and why the police are interested?"

"No, no of course not. I've not got a clue why they came around. It's just routine."

"How did they get your name and address?" she asked.

It was a good question and one I'd been asking myself.

"Dunno," I said.

"You're not covering for that Mark, are you? I've always told you he was a bad lot. Men who sleep with women like that, well they can't be trusted, all he'll ever do is cheat. Cheats never change. They're always looking for the next challenge, the next conquest."

I gulped. "No, Mark met someone else, I don't think it was this girl."

"But you don't know who the girl was, do you? It could have been."

"No, I don't and you're right, Mark was chatting to a few girls and one could have been this girl that's died, maybe that's why they're talking to me – the cops, I mean, it makes sense now."

Debbie was quiet. "Richard, I don't want you getting into trouble, you mean so much to me and to Dylan, so, so much, I just wish you'd stay away from Mark; I know you're a loyal friend but please tell the truth and don't cover for him. Tell the police all you know even though you may think you're being disloyal to Mark."

"If I knew anything I'd tell them but I don't! I've told the cops that. No idea who she is and why they've come around. Hopefully they won't be back."

And that was my second mistake. A timely confession to a hopefully forgiving Debbie might have saved me a whole bundle of trouble. But I had a shovel and I was digging... digging... digging like a man possessed, desperate to escape forces which seemed to be closing in on him but at the same time making matters one hell of a lot worse. I didn't know it then but I was a marked man.

Chapter Two

Needless to say, I'd met Anne-Marie in the Pryzm nightclub and if the police were now telling me her surname was 'MacDonald' so be it – it was one and the same. I knew it, the police knew it and social media knew it too. I didn't do a lot on social media but my WhatsApp group – originally entitled 'The Boys' (I wasn't responsible for that one), which included Mark, Suggo, Matty, Dave and a few others had sent around updates saying my name was being linked to the victim on Facebook and some other social media sites. Great.

That fateful Saturday night I'd nominated myself as a driver as I was due to meet Debbie the next day and take her and Dylan to the aircraft museum. I hadn't wanted to be hung over or drink too much so I'd given a lift to Mark, Dave and Suggo. We'd met Matty in the Crazy Horse bar where we'd enjoyed a few drinks and some banter. The air had been peppered with the aromas of perfume and aftershave and hair spray and everywhere you looked there was an anticipation of a good, good time. The night time was filled with young people out to enjoy themselves which meant drinks flowed. Young women, spray-tanned and hair-sprayed, vied for attention as they stood around in groups chatting and laughing and drinking Jaeger Bombs and shorts or necking bottles. The beer was flowing from the pumps and the barmen were handing over bottles of Desperados and Corona Extra and Stella and Bud which were being necked by the thirsty before debit cards had flashed across card machines. The Horse throbbed with excitement and anticipation.

The mirror behind the bar reflected the bottles of spirits, the triangular optics and the backs of blue T-shirted bar staff. The Horse was one of those loud, large bars with a wide open wooden floor with seats and tables around the edge. The management wanted groups to stand to get more customers into the space available and on a Friday and Saturday night that meant there was little room to move. When we had arrived, the floor was already sticky with spilt beer. We had a convention; driver didn't need to buy a round or go to the bar – until we hit the club - which suited me just fine. Matty, as the first to arrive, did the honours coming back with a snooker-rack-shaped treble-pinter with a bottle in each jacket pocket. Suggo, as usual, was telling crude jokes like a comedian on speed. I was half listening and half looking around, seeing what was happening. Mark was the same. He wore a black blazer, button-up shirt and chinos. He smelt of a powerful aftershave – that one Johnny Depp advertises, I forget what it's called now. He was tall with it. I noticed an attractive brunette in tight PVC leggings look at him. Smile. Raise her eyebrows. He had a reputation. A reputation that gave him credence and confidence. He was a great guy to know, a useful guy to be seen with. Why he liked me I don't know; we were hardly in the same league when it came to women, but I was quietish, easy to get on with, I didn't mind driving, I dressed pretty well, I spent money and I guess I wasn't an embarrassment. Mark would not be seen with anyone who was 'an embarrassment' which is why he steered clear of the potty-mouthed Suggo. Mark could handle himself too which is a necessity for a womaniser – by the law of averages there's always going to be an absent boyfriend or a jealous ex. Fighting had never been my thing and I tried to avoid altercations, although it has to be said my bad temper had got the better of me a few times. Finally, I guess Mark liked the fact I was interested in him. I liked to listen to him, his words of womanising wisdom, he fascinated me. He had what I could never have, he had achieved what I could never achieve. I guess he was what I wanted to be.

Mark and I were similar heights, both over six foot, but whereas Mark was well-built, due to some gym work, I was as skinny as a pipe cleaner. As well as being the same height he was the same age as me – thirty. I'd once sported an earring but that had long since been removed whereas Mark still had a gold stud in one ear and, well, I had a slight mullet. My explanation was that I kind of liked all those '80s footballers, like Chris Waddle and Glen Hoddle, you see on YouTube so I'd paid a bit of homage to them. However, if I'm being honest, it was because my dad had one in the only photograph I had of him when he was young. The photo was old, worn and bent but it was of him standing on the pitch at Millwall's former ground, The Den on Cold Blow Lane. He was dressed in a Ben Sherman T-shirt, drain pipe Levi jeans and his polished, black eighteen-hole Doc Marten boot rested on a football. I guess he was mid-twenties. He looked handsome and smart and was smiling as if he didn't have a care in the world. God knows what he was doing on the pitch and who took the photo. I had found it in the loft at my mum's house along with a signed Millwall shirt, a football and some programmes which I'd taken back to my rented flat. If Mum had seen the picture, she would have destroyed it. I know some people laughed at the mullet, took the piss, but it was me; individualistic, slightly apart from the crowd. It was who I was. I felt, through no fault of my own, that I didn't really fit in so, by the time I had reached thirty, I had stopped trying. I was an outsider. Unlike Mark. He was very much on the inside.

Mark's game was easy. He stood with a foot in two camps. The lads, Suggo, Matty, Dave and me, out for a drink and a good time and the lasses – the predator on the perpetual 'pull'. The former was 'cover' for the latter. He wanted to make out he was laid-back, spontaneous, not bothered and so every now and again he would slip back into 'lad company'; keep his head down, pretend not to be interested in his surroundings whilst all the time his watchful eye did nothing but scan and seek out like a probe with an in-built homing device. I liked listening to him, I guess I was jealous, correction I *know* I was jealous, but Mark was good. It was the confidence, the charm, the easy 'take it or leave it' attitude. I'd learnt a lot from him but lacked his natural ability. He could deliver subtle compliments, which almost went unnoticed, and he could build rapport, he had that talent. He had that magical thing called charisma whereas I had none. I was boring, average, nothing special, choose your own description (you certainly will by the end of this, if you get that far! I can guarantee that!)

So, Mark and I stood talking. He took an interest in you and when you spoke to him you felt he was giving you the full eyeball but I knew, as we all knew, that unless you were female he was only half interested. Men didn't interest him. Not one bit. He wasn't much for male talk – football and the like, he was fascinated by women. He genuinely liked women, he was captivated by them, they intrigued him and he took an interest in them, what they were wearing, what perfume they wore (how many times have I heard him say *'umm, who is wearing that lovely scent?'* when standing at the bar as a 'way in') in other words Mark had the full metal jacket and there were no fucking creases in it.

"So, how's it going, Rat?" he said as he raised a beer bottle to his lips and showed off a sparkling gold bracelet which drifted down his wrist.

"Not so bad," I said. I told him about the company where I worked; he had been employed there too, so we knew the same people. As I don't want to be identified, for pretty obvious reasons, let's call the company Zorin Logistics after Zorin Industries, James Bond *A View to a Kill*; theme tune performed by the sublime Duran Duran, so good they named them twice.

The job was admin and, to be honest, pretty boring but I enjoyed working at the company; there were a lot of young people and the social life was good. Mark had got a job with Zorin when he had been eighteen whilst I'd been to a university in the Midlands where I'd studied a Film and Media Studies degree. I'd got a job there, aged twenty-two going on twenty-three, temporary at first (from my point of view) whilst I looked around for the mythical 'graduate level job' but seven years later I was not looking anymore. I had little in the way of ambition and the offices were just across the M4 so it was not far to drive, it suited me just fine.

Mark mentioned some girls, asked if they were still there, then reeled off names like football players. I wondered, after each, whether they had been his conquests. Neither of us had liked the manager, Williams, who had hated Mark and disliked me: we'd been pleased when he had left and had bonded in mutual antipathy.

"Sarcastic bastard," Mark said.

I agreed. "It's better now with Helen – she's a lot fairer and she's really nice too. You can trust Helen and she doesn't shout at you or put you down."

"Umm, I liked Helen," he said.

Mark had gone to work in advertising in London but slowly he had started working from home more which he didn't enjoy; he missed the bonhomie of office life, the chatter, the travel on the train and the tube, which had expanded his lothario net. How he did it I just do not know but many a time he'd recount stories of how had 'pulled' on the commute. Even so, Mark was one of those lucky people who just sailed through life. He had no experience in advertising but had become friendly with the father of one his many ex-girlfriends. The father was a director, or at least high up in the advertising company, and he had taken Mark under his swan-like wing. He had pulled a few strings for him and got him a job he a) wasn't qualified to do or b) had any great aptitude for - the fact he'd done it for over five years said more about the company he worked for and Mark's incredible ability to quietly promote himself than anything else. Although, in fairness he was one of these people who had an engaging and self-deprecating manner. He often said to me he knew 'fuck all about advertising' and 'didn't have a fucking clue how he'd managed to hang on to the job for so long' with its high salary and substantial perks. For me there was never such largesse from Lady Luck. Never such gifts from life. My life was a fuck up. A car crash. And that was before all this.

"The world is full of bullshitters, Rat, and the bigger bullshitter you are the further you will go in life, it's as simple as that," Mark always said.

So, that night, we chatted for a while and then the others joined us. Rounds were bought but not for Mark and me (Mark told me once that one of the secrets of his success with women was that he didn't get drunk or drink too much).

After a few more drinks we left. The black-suited, rotund bouncer who stood outside The Crazy Horse mumbled a 'goodnight' and we walked along the pedestrian zone, past the shut up, grille-fronted, unlit shops, along the side of the library and then out of the centre and back onto the main road. It was a clear, cold, bright night, and the dark sky was speckled with droplets of oyster white stars. As a group we crossed the busy main road, forcing cars to stop for us – we were a gang in motion. We passed the side street where I had parked earlier and walked up to the Pryzm nightclub which was on the edge of town, situated on the corner of a roundabout. Of course, I texted Debbie as we queued up to get in: told her where I was and that I hoped she was having a good night in front of the TV watching some crime drama on Netflix and… of course, that I couldn't wait to see her on Sunday. Later, still in the queue, I texted her to tell her I was missing her too in reply to her message with the same sentiment. Ironically, I'd met Debbie (again) in the same club we were just about to enter. The first time I'd met her I'd been on a training course a couple of junctions up the M4. I had been getting my bag out of the boot of my car when a white Citi Cab minicab had pulled into the entrance of the car park. A woman had got out and walked towards the training centre. She had been wearing knee-high black boots, a filmy, purple-patterned skirt and a black jacket. My eye had lingered on her and, as I had shut my boot, she had been next to me. She had smiled and said a cheery, 'Hiya'. Unfortunately, she had been on a different course (we were at a training centre with multiple training rooms); but I saw her again during the break and smiled at her and later I asked her if she had been enjoying the course. She said it was 'OK, a bit boring' – about a month later she had been out with some friends in the Pryzm and I had introduced myself properly.

Mark smiled at my message. Put his arm around my shoulders. Squeezed.

"You soft bastard, Rat," he said playfully punching me in the stomach.

"Got to keep her sweet," I said. "I really like her, she's great company."

"How long's it been?"

"A year, I guess," I said. "She puts no pressure on me."

"No," Mark said. "I can see that."

And then we were in, down the murky, neon-lit corridor and into the heart of the pulsating nightclub. The music throbbed in welcome, and the perfume, aftershave and hairspray of the Crazy Horse was replaced by the smell of sweat, one of the less spoken about by-products of the smoking ban. The nightclub was large with a circular, pit-like dance floor with brass rails surrounding it. Around the outer edge were high tables and equally tall stools. There were two bars – one stretching across the far end, opposite the entrance corridor and a smaller one on the other side. That one was quieter but closer to the dance floor and usually, in the early hours, was the bar of choice for smooching couples who had just met. Further back were soft red velveteen seats in booths.

Matty, Dave and Suggo found their way to the closest bar, the long one in front of the entrance where the majority went. The three of them got on well. Mark and I were the outsiders. They, Matty, Suggo and Dave, that is, often went out for a drink together, or played snooker, during the week whereas Mark normally had a female friend to see and I was with Debbie or else I went to my writers' circle. Writing had been a pastime of mine since I had been a teenager. I had joined a writers' circle and done a writing course whilst at university, studying my Film and Media Studies degree and it had carried on from there. The reality was I had wanted to study English and become a journalist, but I'd failed my English A- level so I had scraped into a poly-versity (one of the ex-polytechnics) with two D's. I'd got in through clearing which I considered a great achievement. My secondary school hadn't been great and few of its alumni went to university, so it was a feather in my baseball cap. As to writing, I'd been fortunate enough to have a few pieces published online in various student emags whilst at the university, been runner-up in a competition and had even had a short story published in a national magazine for which I had received the princely sum of £150. In addition, I had had a few letters published in magazines and newspapers (fillers as they're called in the trade) and earnt a little money from that. So that was me that Saturday night, out with my friends, an understanding girlfriend who had a young son, a job in logistics which was far from taxing and a very nice rented flat or apartment as the Americans say.

Mark and I tried to chat up a few girls without success, then he got talking to two girls: a blonde in a red sequined dress and her dark-haired friend who wore tight black leather trousers and a black sparkly top. I was slow to talk to her, feeling uncomfortable and not knowing what to say and then, when I did, this friend made it clear she 'had a boyfriend' and 'wasn't interested' so I went off. I spent some time with Suggo, Matty and Dave but they were talking about people I didn't know about, who drank at a pub I didn't care about, so I walked off and wandered around on my own. It was getting late and Mark had seemingly found love in the arms of the blonde girl who had her arms around him and was staring into his deep, dark eyes. I stood on the edge of the dance floor watching him admiringly: they danced check to check, as he stroked her bare arm. I smiled as I recalled one of Mark's many pieces of womanising wisdom.

"Don't let yourself get dragged onto the dance floor, Rat – don't let them know you can't dance until it's too late." Followed by, the fact it was, "OK if was the end of the night and everyone's just swaying."

Mark clearly didn't always obey his own maxims. A few minutes later he took his newfound friend by the hand and led her back towards the entrance. I went to the toilet to relieve myself, queued for a while, splashed on someone else's aftershave and then went back to my observation post at the far side of the dance floor.

And that's when she approached me. Anne-Marie MacDonald. She came up behind me and took my arm.

"Hey, handsome, don't stand there looking like a little boy lost! Come on, let's dance!" she said.

The next thing I knew she had hold of my hand and dragged, no, let's be honest here, led, me to the dance floor. So, I was on the dance floor and snatching bits and pieces of conversation in between the intense noise of the club. She knew the words to the songs, swung her hips and arms in tune to the music and she danced, like a party girl out for a good time. Lifting her arms high in the air and snaking her hips. High on something if not life. Now when I look back, I think of things I should have noticed. The red flags. The absence of friends, the fact I'd seen her talking to two suited, muscled up, gym goons earlier in the evening, talking hard, talking about something, I remember her shaking her head. Yes, I remember that, or at least I think I remember that, maybe my subconscious had detected danger but at the time my focus was on the black satin miniskirt, the wide PVC belt, the lovely, shapely legs encased in thin, dark nylon. She wore a black nylon blouse which was frilly and open and exposed a white bodycon vest beneath. Her hair was brownish blonde and wavey and lacquered and smelt heavenly, mixed as it was with her Yves St Laurent scent. She placed her arms around my neck in the same way the blonde girl had pawed Mark, and I felt aroused, as she kissed me with her cherry red, glossed lips.

"How old are you?" she asked.

"Thirty." (I never discovered she was twenty-four until after she died.)

"Nice age," she said for some unknown reason. "How did you get here?" was her next question.

"Drove."

She couldn't hear so I had to repeat myself.

"Good, I like a man with wheels." She made a steering wheel motion with her hands and laughed. Infectious, playful.

Then she released me and was off and dancing again. Concentrating on her hopping feet and the black, high-heeled ankle boots she wore. Almost ignoring me. Pretending we were not together but then she was back and she kissed me again. On the lips. Then French. I smelt her perfume, her soft skin against my cheek. In a strange moment of prophesy, I said,

"I would give my life for just one night with you."

Anne-Marie laughed. "Have you got a block of cheddar in your pocket?"

"No, why?"

"That's the cheesiest line I've ever heard."

You see I was no Mark; I could not pull off compliments. But she laughed again and put her arms around my neck, and then she kissed me deep and hard and then it was another dance and then we were leaving, hand in hand. Without a word. The language of love, of passion. Unspoken.

She collected her coat from the cloakroom: a thick, waist-length tartan affair, and she struggled getting her arms into the sleeves.

"It's getting a bit nippy out there," she said as she put it on and for the first time, away from the music, I picked up the tiniest wisp of an east coast Scottish accent.

We walked along the dark corridor, led by strip lights in the floor like airport landing lights, and then we were out in the cold November night. The tuxedo-clad bouncer said 'goodnight' and as he did so he handed out a card – an invitation to the club on Wednesday night with the appeal of half price admission and cut-price drinks during a 'Happy Hour' that would last for two. I didn't take one, but Anne-Marie did.

I put my arm around her shoulder and we walked across the carpark. Suddenly the chill seemed to alter Anne-Marie's mood; she stopped talking, she appeared to be looking around, she seemed, dare I say it, nervous, anxious. I thought at the time that maybe she didn't want to spend the night with me (but wanted a lift home) and didn't know how to break the bad news. I liked Anne-Marie. I liked her playfulness, her spontaneity. I thought of Mark; how would he persuade a recalcitrant partner? But the thing with a reputation is that it goes before you like a flag bearer before a marching army and in Mark's case every girl would know how a date with him would end. In bed. With me it was different, I was nice guy, Richard Andrew Turner, remember?

"I thought you were parked in the carpark," she said as we hit the street.

"No, I got blocked in once and had to leave my car till the morning, I'm on a side street, come on." I guided her back along the pavement to my blue Hyundai. It wasn't much of a car but it was all I could afford for part cash, part loan after my first, too expensive hire purchase car, a mustard yellow Audi TT which I adored, had been repossessed. I'd bought it to create a bit of an image but I had ended up deeper in debt.

The Pryzm was away from the town centre, not far but far enough after a boozy night out. I knew Matty, Dave and Suggo would get a minicab when they saw I had left without them. I always parked between the town, with its bars and pubs and the night club. So, we walked; I liked the way the satin of Anne-Marie's skirt stuck to her thin, dark tights as she strolled along beside me with a confident, purposeful stride - her high-heeled ankle boots paced the ground easily. I felt aroused again. I took her small hand in mine, felt her loose ring on her finger. We went up a side street and finally reached my car. I pressed the key. She climbed into the passenger side with one last backwards stare towards the main road. As soon as she was seated the vanity mirror came down and she pretended to be looking at her mouth. The card given to her by the doorman rested on her lap. Her handbag was on the floor.

"I thought I had lipstick on my teeth," she said as she fastened her seat belt.

I put my own safety belt on and turned the ignition; the car dials illuminated in translucent blue. I've always liked the look of cars at night, the instrument panel all lit up with promise. The engine started, a soft purr. I moved away from the kerb.

She picked up the Pryzm advertising card absentmindedly and drew it across her fingers.

"Ouch," she said. "Paper cut."

I noticed a spider web line of red across the top of her finger.

"There's some plasters in the glove compartment," I said.

She pulled it open, moved my glasses, closed it.

"Nothing there," she said.

"There is, you haven't looked properly." I sounded like my mother.

"Don't worry, I won't bleed to death," she said as she sucked her finger.

I was now unsure how the night would end. Anne-Marie appeared to be getting cold feet.

As I indicated to turn right, I noticed that a car, a minicab, was behind me. I could see Anne-Marie looking in the vanity mirror which she had not flicked back. She shook her head as I pulled out and the white cab did the same.

"It's a minicab," I said.

"I know, Citi Cabs, I used to use them all the time."

The cab was still behind us.

I suddenly felt unsure. "They're not following us, are they?"

Anne-Marie laughed. "No! What made you think that?"

It was my turn to laugh. "The fact they're behind us."

"I don't think so," Anne-Marie said. "He's probably just picking up a fare."

She gave me directions, but the conversation was stilted. She told me she rented a room in a house owned by a friend from 'up north' who had gone home to see her parents that weekend. I asked her what she did for a living.

"Not a lot at the moment. I buy and sell on the internet to get by. I'm looking for something permanent."

"What do you sell?"

"Clothes mostly."

"Like an influencer?"

She laughed, "Not likely," and then added softly and with a touch of melancholy, "I couldn't influence anyone to do anything."

I drove under the M4 and then right at a roundabout and back on myself (I probably didn't go the most direct route but Anne-Marie's directions left a bit to be desired). I passed some side streets with the cab following us all the way. I turned right and then, finally we arrived at Church Street, a road of 19th-century terraced houses where Anne-Marie lived. When I indicated and turned left up her road, the cab drove on. Her house was in the middle up a slight incline. It was a high-density residential area and Church Street was lined with parked cars, making the street in effect one car-width wide. I parked where I could find a space, nearly opposite her house but on the other side of the road. We got out of the car and walked across the street together. The house was a two-bedroomed affair with a snub-nosed front garden. Anne-Marie walked up the short drive clutching her black handbag to her chest. She took out a solitary key, opened the door and let herself in, I followed. I noticed a bell jingle.

"What's that for?" I asked, seeing a bell tied to the inside door handle.

"Oh, there's been a lot of break-ins," she said.

"Ever thought of a burglar alarm?"

"No, we're OK with the bell, thank you very much," she said closing off the conversation.

The house was cold and uninviting. No lights had been left on, but Anne-Marie didn't seem to mind. She pushed open a door on her right which led to the living area. The curtains had not been pulled and the full moon threw a shadow of pale, blue-tinted, gossamer radiance across the room. I was immediately struck by the smell of dope. The house was untidy. There was a worn red throw over an equally worn settee and an old television on a stand opposite: it was in the far corner by the front window. The sofa was at a slight angle to the kitchen door, I guess so it was directly facing the TV. A scratched coffee table sat by the two-seater sofa and there was an old armchair in the corner to the left of the sofa. There were two ashtrays filled with reefers and cigarette butts on the coffee table along with numerous national lottery slips, partly completed but with letters down the sides and initials, along with multiplication signs and numbers circled: someone obviously spent time studying the lottery 'form'. I noted a lack of photographs and personal touches. The place seemed temporary somehow, it reminded me of the student houses I'd visited at university, places I'd always avoided living in due to my Howard Hughes-ian obsession with cleanliness. So, because I was a tidiness freak, perhaps due to my OCD, I'd never shared any house with my student brothers and sisters, preferring my own company and my own room, which was yet another reason why I had never been accepted into any group. It was another part of the 'Turner the Outsider' sculpture; yet another reason I didn't really 'fit in'.

Whilst no lights had been left on at the front of the house, the uncovered kitchen light had been and carelessly showed an array of dirty dishes on the surfaces. It looked as if more than one person had eaten or one person had not washed up for days, weeks, possibly months.

Before Anne-Marie had even taken her coat off, she said,

"I'm desperate for the loo, make yourself at home."

She then left the living room, leaving the internal door wide open, and scurried upstairs in her pixie boots without placing her heels on the stairs, her handbag pressed tightly to her chest.

Whilst Anne-Marie was upstairs, I texted Debbie.

Home. Love you, looking forward to seeing you tomorrow… today!

When Anne-Marie returned, after some time, the coat was gone and she had a blue plaster on her finger – I wondered why she had been so long but didn't like to ask. I took in the satin skater skirt, fringed against her dark nyloned legs. I noted she'd reapplied her lipstick and brushed her hair. Anne-Marie smiled as she placed her handbag on the coffee table.

"Usually take your handbag to the loo?" I half joked. I was feeling slightly belligerent, I thought Anne-Marie was leading me on. I wanted sex but thought I was going to get the brush-off; oh, to have the confidence of Mark.

Anne-Marie turned serious. "I needed my phone – I'm expecting a text, nosey."

She walked past me and into the untidy kitchen.

"Want a coffee?" she called. Then she laughed as if she had told a joke. I thought it was because of the subtle double entendre.

The mood had changed, the atmosphere was cooler but still just about on the warm side of frozen.

I said, "Yeah, thanks," but I didn't really want one.

"It's cold, isn't it," Anne-Marie said and shivered mechanically, but it was as if she were making conversation as she made no attempt to turn on the heating or gas fire.

Standing in the front room, I could see the white of a Citi Cab car outside, I was unsure if it was the same one that had 'followed' us.

"I think that might be that minicab again," I said.

"Minicab? Where?"

Suddenly Anne-Marie was at my side looking out the window, holding a chipped mug in her hand which she was drying up. The car moved on.

"They after you?"

"No, but they say I owe them money," Anne-Marie said by way of explanation.

"Hard to owe a minicab company money, I'd have thought."

"I had an account, I used to use them a lot, I can't drive, you see."

"And they're after you?"

"Possibly."

She stepped back into the galley kitchen. This time I followed her and stood just outside the door. The kettle was on. It stood next to a knife block which was under a wall-mounted cupboard, and further up was a microwave. She placed the mug down she had been drying up and opened the cupboard looking for a jar of coffee. The cupboard was just to the left of the sink. The sink was below a sash window. I moved further into the room and stood at the door, resting against the jamb. And that's when I saw it. The money, I mean. A dirty white envelope bulging with notes. It was on the left side of the cupboard with a jar of sauce propping it up. I couldn't believe it and opened my mouth to say something when she closed the door. Quickly. I'm not stupid, no, correction, of course I'm fucking stupid. But let's just say I'm not naïve. I knew it was drugs money. Somehow Anne-Marie was involved in drug dealing. It was a shame because I liked her, she had some indefinable quality, a playfulness, a zest for life which I liked in a woman. If I could find one fault with Debbie, she was apt to be a tad serious, a tad sensible. OK, I liked that, and she was a good influence on me. No question. But I also liked a bit of spontaneity and Anne-Marie had that. She was unpredictable. I guess 'free spirit' is the phrase I'm looking for.

She poured boiling water into the two cups, adding milk from a carton which she took from the fridge.

"Do you want sugar?"

"Yeah, one, please."

She went back to that cupboard and took out a sachet, the type that you pick up in cafes and restaurants. There was a small pot filled with them. Once again, I glimpsed that bulging envelope, there was no mistaking it. Money. Lots and lots of money. She closed the door, ripped off the top and poured the sugar in. She passed me a red mug, sipping hers as she did so. Then she followed me out of the kitchen. I sat down on the low sofa. Anne-Marie placed her cup down, smoothed her black skirt and sat beside me, perching on the edge. She placed her flattened hands between her legs, stretching her short skirt. She was quite elegant in her way. Feminine.

"What do you for a living?" she asked. She seemed genuinely interested.

I told her as she took her pixie-like ankle boots off and pushed them under the coffee table.

"So, you have a good job, don't you?" she said, with a hint of that delightful, easy-on-the-ear east coast Scottish accent. She picked up her mug and held it like some arctic explorer trying to warm their hands. I noticed the chipped black nail varnish, the shortness of her nails.

"It's OK, steady, can't afford anywhere but the place I rent is nice."

I sensed a wistfulness, as if it was something she would like too. A normalness. I asked her about her job again and her house mate. She told me she was called Lisa or 'Big L' but she was evasive. She said she had 'gone up north' to see her 'folks' and wouldn't be back till 'late Sunday'. She stared at the TV even though it wasn't on. She was someone who seemed to change from being playful to serious very quickly.

We sat in silence for a few minutes. I was unsure what to say. I glanced at the pile of lottery tickets.

"Some one likes playing the National Lottery, do you ever win?" I was going to add something about the money in the kitchen cupboard but stopped myself.

Anne-Marie seemed irritated by the question. By way of an answer, she put her mug down and shuffled the coupons up. She placed them on a shelf below the coffee table.

"Aye… well… nay… not really. It's Lisa, she plays," she said, picking up her mug again.

It was a lie of course. It was all lies.

"You ask a lot of questions, don't you?" she added, and she wasn't joking, or playful.

I shrugged. I couldn't pick up on the signs. I didn't know what to do or say so I played with my mullet, a nervous habit of mine.

Finally, Anne-Marie giggled girlishly.

"You're very slow, Richard," she said. She put her cup down on the coffee table again only this time she leant back in the sofa. She was small in stature and when she inclined, she virtually collapsed into the corner.

"I'm sorry," I said. I was just so crap at the whole relationship thing. The truth was I was useless with women. One way or another I'd always fucked it up. I put my coffee cup on the pine table and moved closer to her: we started to embrace. All my earlier doubts drifted into the ether. Anne-Marie was a passionate kisser. She started to undo my shirt as I eased my hand under her blouse, felt her small, pert breasts through the bodycon top. We kissed and caressed for some moments and then broke off.

"We'd be more comfortable upstairs." She pointed to the ceiling as if I didn't know where 'upstairs' was and then, with a swish of her satin skirt she got up. She took the two mugs and placed them in the kitchen sink bowl, she then walked around the sofa and out of the door.

I followed her to an untidy bedroom which was at the front of the house. I noticed the curtain was sagging off the plastic rail, and a triangle of moonlight partially lit the cluttered room. The thin curtain could not absorb the orange of a streetlight, directly outside the window. It mixed with the white of the moon to give the room an ethereal glow. The double bed was strewn with clothes which Anne-Marie bundled up and carelessly placed on the floor. A white wardrobe door was open and various jackets, cardigans, tops and skirts were hanging off hangers. There were so many clothes the wardrobe positively bulged and I feared it would collapse at any moment. There was a pair of new black, high-heeled boots in an open Prada box on the floor, I noticed other designer boxes too: Gucci and Dior and Jimmy Choo and Tommy Hilfiger. I thought about what she told me about buying and selling on the internet, perhaps it was true after all. On the bedside table an alarm clock, with two bells on top, ticked relentlessly. I wondered who her mysterious northern friend, Lisa, was and what she did. I wondered how the two friends could afford to live if they both had transient incomes. I wondered if they had boyfriends. Certainly, there didn't seem much evidence of any men living in the house, but it had the appearance of one in which people entered and left. It was not like Debbie's cosy home, which smelt of washing powder and had photographs of Dylan everywhere. Then there was my own tidy abode. Anne-Marie and Lisa had placed no stamp on the house. It was like a hostel, that was it, a hostel. I guess I was having those thoughts as we got undressed, which we did independently. I carefully placed my clothes on the floor. I stood before her naked.

"I like that lurching lion tatt on your arm," Anne-Marie said softly. "Are you into wildlife?"

I laughed. "No, I'm a Millwall fan, a few of us got them done when we were teenagers."

She looked confused.

"Millwall are nicknamed The Lions," I said, adding, "football."

She murmured an, "oh, I see."

"I'm not a big footie fan though, not really," I said for no obvious reason. "It was just a laugh, a dare."

By then she was completely naked too. The lacy red bra she had been wearing was carelessly discarded on

45

the floor. She pulled down the crazy zig-zagged yellow and black duvet and sat down on the bed completely naked, as she tweaked my semi-erect cock.

"Are you pleased to see me, Richard?" she joked.

Then she pulled me down on top of her – there was no talk of contraception and moments later I was penetrating her good and hard and enjoying the freedom of illicit sex. Anne-Marie was passionate and moaned and groaned with each penetrating shaft. I thrust into her deep and long and for one brief moment felt alive and in the present. I thought of Debbie and that turned me on even more; the thought that the following night I would be fucking my girlfriend too. It was wrong but it felt so right for sex is sadism and love is masochism. When we had finished, I turned over.

"That was good," she said. "I've not been fucked in an age. God, I feel horny tonight. You're slow to get going but when you get started you know how to fuck, baby."

I laughed. I felt like Mark. I knew in some bedroom, in some house or flat, somewhere in the city that pert blonde girl in the red sequined dress he had left with would be experiencing the delights of the local lothario and it felt good. Good to be in his macho league. Good to join him at the party. Good to have a story to recount next time we meet up. A great story to WhatsApp 'The Boys'.

Minutes later, as the clear, full moon shone even more brightly through the partially pulled curtain, Anne-Marie eased herself on top of me and started to rock back and forth, back and forth on my stiff cock. I grabbed her pert breasts and played with her erect nipples as she arched her back, opened her mouth and panted: the abrasive rubbing of pubic hair against my skin continued until we both climaxed.

After, we chatted for a while; she seemed relaxed, cheerful, playful again and then she turned on her side and went to sleep, I lay awake thinking, about Debbie, about Mark, about Anne-Marie. And I remember thinking, *thank fuck, it's a one-night stand and she doesn't want to see me again*. Finally, I too dozed off.

I was awoken by a sudden thud. Then another. I lay awake but there were no further noises and I dismissed them as the neighbour or outside in the street. I was suddenly aware of the fact I had a headache and my mouth felt dry: a consequence of being in an airless, dry, noisy nightclub. I got up and went to the toilet, which was next door to the bedroom. I peed without flushing so as not to awaken Anne-Marie (I was all too conscious of flushing toilets at night because of James and Juliette who lived above me and flushed their toilet at least twice a night). After, I decided to look in the bathroom cabinet for a paracetamol. I didn't notice it at first, it was on the top shelf and the pills I needed were on the bottom but there it was, a condom half filled with white powder. I picked it up and squeezed it. Well, I'm no expert but I knew, or thought I knew, that it was cocaine. I put it back, closed the cabinet door without taking a pill, and went back to bed but I couldn't sleep. At about 4.15am – according to Anne-Marie's large bedside clock – I got up, found my clothes on the floor, took them out on to the landing and dressed there so as not to wake Anne-Marie. Then I padded downstairs. I reached the hall and was about to leave.

My slip-on shoes were by the door where I'd left them. I looked at them for a few seconds. Then I thought of that money. That money. That money. That money. I had huge debts, the money was drug dealer money, there was no doubt about that. It was dirty money. It was untraceable money. I wanted to take Debbie to Paris. To propose. I wanted to pare down my debts. The lounge door was open. It was a clear, cloudless, moonlit night and the light shimmered and skimmed across the threadbare lounge carpet and into the kitchen: almost creating a 'yellow brick road' of white for me to follow. I padded slowly into the room, unsure of whether I should remove the money or not. My heart pounded. I felt a shiver run down my spine. Sex with Anne-Marie had given me confidence, self-belief. I moved towards the kitchen, entered it. My pulses pumped. I'd never done anything like it before in my life. But it would be stealing from criminals, what was wrong with that?

I took a deep breath. I stood in the galley kitchen by the sink. In front of me was a window, and outside it was as black as the ocean depths due to a high yard wall separating the terraced house from its neighbour. I imagined eyes, bright and penetrating, peering in at me through the window. I jumped, startled by a noise. No one there. My conscience. I was shaking. I moved to the left. My hands quivered like newly fired arrows into a target. I took a deep breath and opened both the cupboard doors. I put my left hand on that envelope bulging with money. I squeezed it, felt the notes between my fingers. I was almost hyperventilating. I imagined Anne-Marie bursting into the front room and catching me. The scene that would follow. But all was quiet. I waited a few seconds and then I took the envelope out of the cupboard. I quickly unbuttoned my shirt and dropped the money inside. I did up the awkward shirt buttons with fumbling, shaking fingers. I could feel the envelope against my stomach. Cold and hard and heavy. I closed the cupboard doors gently as I listened for noises. My senses hyper-alert to every night-time sound; the car driving past, the cat meowing, the bark of a dog. I stole back across the moonlit front room and into the hall. I slipped on my shoes and opened the front door slowly, softly, my hand over that blasted, pointless bell and then I was gone.

The cold of the early morning suddenly hit me, it was like walking into a freezer. I only had my shirt on and the cloudless, star-studded night meant a deep frost was stirring. As I walked back to the car, I could already see a thin layer of ice shimmer on the windscreen and the side windows of my Hyundai. I got in and started the engine, rubbing my hands together to keep warm. I turned the heater on full blast but the air was fridge cold. My eyes felt tired and sore so I took out my disposable contact lenses and dropped them into the foot well on the passenger side. Then I took my glasses from the glove compartment, and put them on. I was always prepared like that, I always had to have my glasses and plasters and some other things in the glove compartment, something Debbie (and Mark) found amusing. The screen had still not cleared so I took a scraper from the backseat, opened the door and climbed partially out. That's when I saw them: a black or maybe dark blue car parked further up the road, a Beamer – BMW. At first, I thought the driver must be a resident but as I looked more carefully, I saw a man with a beanie style hat in the driver's seat, watching me. Two men in fact. And they were not getting out of the Beamer. Slightly scared, I got back into my car. The screen still hadn't cleared and I'd just cleared a tiny bit, a slit in fact, what's termed a 'tank commander' in ice-scraping circles. Even so, I put my car in gear and drove home.

The streets were quiet but I drove carefully. I could feel the bulky envelope against my warm stomach, a constant reminded of my theft. Eventually, I came to a stop on the stony drive of the shared property where I lived. I unlocked the communal front door and then my door, which was immediately on the right, and went into the front room. Exhausted, I put the money in the drawer by the computer and put my clothes in the wash. I left my trousers over the sofa as they had beer down them and needed to go to the dry cleaners. Then I put my completely dead phone on charge, cleaned my teeth, drunk some fresh water, had a couple of paracetamols and collapsed into the bed – having set my alarm for 8.30am.

What a night!

The next day I pocketed some cash from that bulging envelope and drove around to Debbie's house; she couldn't drive so she caught the bus to work, which meant I drove whenever we went out, unless we took a minicab if we both fancied having a drink. She lived in a housing association property on the edge of town, a grey brick, ex- council house. It was actually quite a spacious, three-bed affair which she had shared with her ex. They had acquired the house when Debbie had been expecting another child but she had subsequently miscarried. Twice.

I pulled up outside and hooted the horn. Dylan ran up to the car excitedly followed by Debbie wearing tight blue jeans; a white jumper and a brown jacket. A scrunched scarf was around her neck and her shoulder-length dark hair fell about the collar of her coat. She got in and kissed me on the lips.

"Did you miss me last night?" she asked. I caught a whiff of her Daisy perfume and her fresh-smelling hair.

"Of course, Debs," I said. "You know I get lonely without you."

"You didn't get up to anything, did you?" Debbie asked, squeezing my thigh. Tighter. "Did you?"

"Like what?"

"You know."

I yawned; God I was tired. "Of course not! That's Mark's game, not mine! You're the only woman for me."

"Yeah, right!" She pulled the seat belt over her large breasts. "You think I came up with the fairies, you do."

In turn I squeezed her leg playfully, put the car in gear and drove off. The aircraft museum, which might have been in Cambridgeshire, was about seventy or eighty miles from where we lived so it took about an hour and a half to drive there. En route I chatted to Debbie and Dylan and tried to keep my tired eyes on the road.

"I hope we're not keeping you up," Debbie said as I yawned again.

Dylan laughed.

"Sorry," I said, "I didn't sleep well."

"A likely story! Well, that'll teach you for going out with the boys and not having a cosy night in with me," she chided.

Debbie had been on her own for five years, so she was very much used to her own company. She was very independent and extremely placid. She worked part-time as an administrator and secretary in a busy office. Her husband had left her for another woman he had met at work (he was a delivery driver and had met a receptionist) but despite that she was remarkably stoical and not at all jealous or questioning. In fact, she told me once she was quite glad her husband had left her as she much preferred bringing Dylan up on her own as she had more independence: she felt she had married far too young. Dylan had only been three when his dad had walked out (four years younger than me when mine had left) and since then she'd not dated much but on one of the rare occasions she had gone out with friends, we'd met for the second time in the Pryzm nightclub: the first being on that training day a few months earlier. That had been just over a year ago.

I really liked Debbie, we got on well, perhaps I loved her, I don't know, certainly I was thinking in terms of asking her to marry me. She didn't mind me going out with friends and she liked coming around to my clean and well-furnished flat when she could get a friend to babysit or Dylan's friends' parents didn't mind him sleeping over. When she came to my flat, I'd cook her a meal, we'd watch TV or a movie or we'd do other stuff.

After a tiring but traffic-free journey I finally drew up in the museum's spacious car park. Whilst gathering up her handbag from the footwell Debbie noticed the Pryzm advertising card on the floor. She picked it up.

"What's this?"

"Oh, the bouncer was handing them out as I left," I said.

"Unlike you to leave litter in your car, Rich, oh, there's blood on it!" She winced.

"I got a small paper cut from it," I said.

Debbie scrunched it up.

Fortunately there was a bin close by and she dropped the card into it as we walked towards the museum entrance.

"There, I've thrown nasty card that cut your finger away," Debbie joked in a mumsy type voice. I was just glad she'd not asked to see the cut which had miraculously healed with a Christ-like touch. I smiled, mostly with relief that I'd steered a course through potentially choppy conversational waters.

We continued our walk across the car park to the museum, hand in hand. Dylan danced around behind and in front and at the side of us. When I'd bought my Audi TT (mustard yellow. remember!) I was super conscious of door knock scratches so I had always parked away from other cars (which had often prompted Claire, whom I had been dating at the time, to say we needed to call a taxi to get us across the carpark): I had continued the habit when I had purchased my Hyundai.

I used the cash from the envelope to pay for the admission at the museum and we then walked around the aircraft displays whilst I impressed Dylan with some bits and pieces of randomly obtained knowledge. Something I've always had a talent for (if you can call it that) is the retention of useless and not so useless information. The strange thing is I can remember facts but not events and things that have happened to me in the past, not clearly anyway. Then we had something to eat in the museum's overpriced restaurant before heading home.

"Do you want to come in?" Debbie asked when I pulled up outside her house.

I shook my head. "I think I need to go home and get my head down," I yawned.

"Come on," Debbie insisted, grabbing my arm. "Don't be such a wimp. You didn't see me last night – come in and spend some time with me. You're always out with the lads on a Saturday."

It wasn't strictly true, but she had a point. I suppose I felt guilty about the night before so I did go in. We sat on the sofa and had a cup of tea and chatted whilst Dylan played computer games. It was difficult making love with an eight-year-old about, which was one of the reasons why Debbie liked to come to my flat, but even so we ended up kissing passionately.

It was quite late when I left Debbie's house, maybe 10pm, perhaps later. I got home, got undressed and collapsed into my own bed. I slept well. I'd got away with it. Again. Later, when I reflected on that Sunday, I thought that spending time at Debbie's house had been a good thing: if I had gone straight home and had a nap, I would have undoubtedly woken up, and at some point in the evening, counted that stash of money and maybe moved it – put some in my wallet, some in my bedside cabinet and left some in the drawer. As it was, I went home and went straight to bed and slept until Monday morning. Overslept in fact. I didn't think about the money again until I was at work, and almost as soon as I got home PC Snot and Hazel Eyes kindly paid me a visit.

So, the following morning, Monday, I got up for work feeling refreshed and in a remarkably good spirits after my weekend. The house where I lived contained four separate flats. There was a small exposed porch and then you went in through a very big blue wooden front door with two locks, mortice and Yale; the door was one of those spring-loaded ones that comes back on itself. Once inside, on the left there was a table where sorted post was left, once someone had picked it up off the doormat. I often did both jobs being closest to the front door. Next to the table was flat two, so nearly opposite mine, then there were stairs which took you up to the other two flats.

My flat was immediately on the right, number one, maybe two or three paces from the front door. You went in and down a short hallway, and then immediately on the right was a large window overlooking the drive. In the hall there were some coat hooks and shoes on a rack and a narrow walk-in cupboard with shelves which contained a pre-paid electricity metre and an ironing board, an iron, a tent, stove and camping equipment and some other bits and bobs. In the corner of the front room was a TV: this was at the far end of the window and beside it a small, pine storage unit. Next to that there was a desk with a HP computer on top, with a clock on the wall above it and a tray with post and stories to the side. There was also a holder of pens and a rubber lion, arms folded, wearing full Millwall kit and with its football boot on a ball that my dad had given me when I was a kid. Next to the computer desk was a pine set of drawers with a HP Envy printer on top. The wallpaper was flowered and yellow and white – not my choice of course, but the large, gold framed picture of an old-fashioned sailing ship docked in an inlet at dusk, which I had bought at a charity shop, was mine and so was an artist's impression of Millwall's Den, their former ground, which was above the printer. Next to this was an old, dark oak bookcase, full of books, which I'd also bought from a charity shop (most of the books and the case). On top of that were three photographs: one of me with Debbie and Dylan when we'd been camping in the

New Forest, one of my sisters Kate and Donna and my mum and, in the middle, my graduation photograph. Opposite was a brown, three-seater leather settee with cushions with a small, square coffee table in front of it – the flat was too small to entertain a table or chairs.

The living area led through to a very small, open-plan kitchenette, so next to the bookcase the work surface started. There was a fridge underneath, then the next bit was exposed with a chrome stool underneath. Well, that's where you'd have found me having my breakfast that Monday morning. There was a small radio on the side which I listened to in the morning and further down the work surface a microwave, toaster and a kettle. There were cupboards above. Moving along was the electric cooker, then the sink at the far end with a window looking out onto the rear garden. There were cupboards underneath and a washing machine to the right, no dishwasher. Next along was a water boiler. Moving around the kitchen in an anti-clockwise direction was the door to the bathroom: the toilet was straight ahead and the bath parallel to the back wall with a high frosted window which opened out onto the communal back garden. There was no door to the small back garden which meant you had to go out the front door and around the side of the property (which I normally did) or down the hall and through an old store room at the rear of the property and use the rickety backdoor. At the opposite end of the bathroom was a small airing cupboard. Coming back out and into the kitchen again there was a shallow, built-in storage cupboard. Next to which was the door to the bedroom, where a double bed dominated, the headboard at the bathroom end. Two bedside cabinets were beside it with a brown wardrobe at the foot of the bed (another charity shop purchase) with a case on top (in which I stored linen) and a wash basket to the side. The room was quite small and had no window, hence I tended to keep the bedroom door open at night.

So that Monday I made myself a pot of tea, you know those small pots for one with the teapot and cup? Well, I had a yellow one with blue edging. I tipped cereal into a bowl, poured on milk and sprinkled on some white sugar and ate ravenously. After I'd eaten, I sat down at the PC and checked my bank account and then my emails. Then I checked my WhatsApp messages on my iPhone from Suggo, Dave, Mark and Matty: one had been sick through drink; one had had a dance and a snog; one had left early on his own and two had found love – Mark and Rat-boy! Boy, was I keen to add my adventures to the WhatsApp banter and typed away excitedly telling them all tales of love and adventure! Yet another mistake.

Chapter Three

I'd always got on well with my line manager, Helen Glover. For some reason she liked me, so after the previous manager, Williams, had left, I'd stopped looking for other jobs. I really liked working for Helen and the working environment. Helen made me feel good as much as the sarcastic bully Williams had made me feel bad and, although she didn't say it, she knew that Williams had bullied Mark and me and she was sympathetic to our cause, especially mine as I didn't stand up for myself. OK, the job wasn't much, I was an administrator in a logistics company which meant I organised, or rather helped organise, the distribution of packaging to supermarkets, to famous to mention. The depot was further up or down the M4 depending on how you looked at it. My role was to book and manage shipments, generate transportation lists, liaise with the depot regarding deliveries and organise miscellaneous deliveries and resolve complaints. As well as that I did some Excel spreadsheet work on KPIs (Key

Performance Indicators), delivery targets and the like with graphs and all that bumph that managers love. It was technically a post you could do with GCSEs or equivalent and a NVQ in the relevant field but I'd nudged into Zorin Logistics with a Film and Media Studies degree (and wasn't the only graduate interviewed) but, as I say, it suited me. I'd been there just over seven years and had settled into a routine. Like a lot of jobs experience was key and after a couple of years I'd got the hang of it. Although I'd never have any sympathy for the bully Williams, I'd have to be honest and say when I'd started I'd been pretty useless.

Another factor for me in staying at Zorin was that I had a fantastic social life: I had a girlfriend, I had friends and was a member of a vibrant writers' circle. I liked where I lived as it was close to town and there was a decent pub called the Beehive just around the corner from me on Herschel Street, which was the next road up from where I lived on Petersfield Hill. I would occasionally go there on my own if I was bored with the TV and being in the flat by myself (they also did meals too if I didn't fancy cooking; their chilli con carne was to die for). My main ambition in life was to write a book – a thriller (but certainly not this one, God, I would give my eye teeth *not* to have written this pile of shite!). Anyway, on the Tuesday after the police visit, I knocked on Helen's door and asked if I could have 'a word'; she said she was busy but later she came over to my desk and took me into her office.

"You're not going to tell me you're leaving, are you, Richard?" Helen asked. She sat back behind her desk and, as she did so, she folded a very long, belted grey cardigan around her, covering her tight black top.

"No, no nothing like that," I said.

I went on tell her an almost true account of Saturday night and about the police visit the previous evening. Helen looked at me for some time without saying a word. I could see she was disappointed. She knew Debbie as I had introduced her at a wedding we'd attended together during the summer: we had sat on the same table and they had got chatting. Helen, who was a divorcee with no partner, and had liked my girlfriend, they had had a lot in common. She scratched the palm of her hand with a varnished, well-manicured purple nail.

"What do you suggest I do?" I asked.

Helen took a deep sigh. "Tell the truth. Tell the police what you've told me. Make a clean breast of it. Honesty is always the best policy. Better still, you like writing, write it down so you can get it clear in your head and take it to the police station, so you don't feel anxious. I can appreciate the pressure you feel under when you're suddenly asked questions and you don't know what to say so you lie unintentionally. It's easy to do; you think you have to say something, so you panic. So, write it down, Richard. Don't leave anything out. The police will be impressed by how diligent you are. I would then go back to see the police, with a solicitor, and hand in your statement. Don't talk to the police without a solicitor being present."

"Thanks, Helen, that's great advice," I said. I was about to stand up.

"Look, I can see you're worried, Richard but you're innocent so you're not going to get into any trouble. You've just been caught up in a horrific coincidence. I could say something about how you've treated Debbie, but I won't as I can see this incident with the police has really shaken you up – I'm sure you'll draw your own conclusions." She raised her eyebrows. "Don't let Debbie down."

"No, I won't." I tried to laugh. I rubbed my temples. "God, I wish I could turn back time – I wish I'd never met that stupid girl. What a sodding nightmare."

"That's a song, isn't it?"

I laughed. I had a reputation for knowing songs, which was probably something I had inherited from my dad who had been a part-time DJ and had an encyclopaedic memory of the Jurassic music period i.e. music from the '50s through to the '70s... perhaps a little '80s and '90s. "Turn back time? Yeah, Cher."

Helen got up and walked over to me; she placed her hand on my shoulder.

"Don't worry, Richard. You say it was just a routine visit by the police. I imagine, once they've thoroughly checked the CCTV and read your statement, then you'll no longer be a suspect. They're so clever nowadays with DNA and forensics in a day or two they'll have realised it couldn't have been you."

"Thanks, Helen," I said. "I feel a lot better; I'll do what you've suggested. I'll write a statement. They caught me on the hop on Monday and I panicked. I feel better now."

So that night when I came home from work, I got changed out of my suit into casual clothes, and before I'd prepared my dinner I sat down at the computer and started to type out a statement explaining my actions since Saturday evening. As Helen had suggested, writing it out was better as it allowed me to go back and add details I'd forgotten. It was clear to me that if Anne-Marie had died in suspicious circumstances then the drivers at Citi Cabs needed to be questioned. It was just a cruel coincidence that Anne-Marie had died close to the time I had been at the house, if indeed she had, for as far as I knew she could have died at any time on the Sunday.

I was typing away on my computer when I saw through the window the headlights of a car drive up and park and then heavy footsteps outside on the gravel. Next thing there was a ring on my doorbell. I walked to my front door and then the communal front door. Although I could buzz it open, I was so close it was always easier just to go out and let visitors in. I was already starting to feel anxious, hot and flustered. I knew it was the police again: this time it was a detective and a different police officer.

"Mr Richard Turner?" the police officer said.

"Yes."

The detective flashed his warrant card.

"I'm DCI Hinton, the SIO – that's the Senior Investigating Officer – on the MacDonald case. We'd like you to make an appointment to come down to the station for a voluntary interview about your whereabouts on Saturday night and the early hours of Sunday morning. We need to eliminate you from our enquiries."

My heart started to race like a sprinter doing the one hundred metres at the Olympics. My hands felt clammy; once again the police had stolen the initiative from me. I gulped, let the front door swing open and stepped back inside my flat.

Hinton was a small man, mid-fifties, slight build with a vaguely stooped appearance, with a voice an octave lower than the normal male register but he was very softly spoken: he carried himself with an air of confidence and self-assurance. He held a black leather folder under his arm which was marked, scuffed and dirty.

"An appointment?" I exclaimed. It was like going to the bloody dentist!

"Yes," Hinton said. "It's how we work these days. We'd like to talk to you as soon as about Saturday night, nothing heavy, just clear up some details; could you come with us now for instance?"

"But I'm…I'm…I'm…I'm just writing a confession," I stammered. "Explaining what happened!"

By this time, I had backed into the flat with Hinton matching my backward steps. The large uniformed police officer loomed behind him, full of menace and presence.

The detective, hand in jacket pocket, walked past me and further into the room without being asked; he had seen my computer and open Word document.

"Oh goody, we'll take a look at that," he said. "Can you print it off for me?"

"But I've not finished it yet."

"Don't worry, you can fill in any blanks at the station," Hinton said.

I printed off the page, my hands shaking uncontrollably as I tried to operate the light mouse. When I had finished I handed the piece of A4, printed on both sides, to the DCI who placed it in his zip up folder.

"Are you doing anything now? There's a car outside. Best to clear the air and put it all to bed so to speak. I'll bring you straight home afterwards."

As Hinton spoke, he walked around the flat, his beady little eyes peering everywhere and at everything. I thought about warrants and my legal rights but I didn't know what they were or what to say. I just felt shit scared. The PC stood at the door like a guard, as if he were trying to stop me from escaping from my own home.

"Pleasant place you've got here, do you own it?" Hinton asked.

I laughed. "No, generation rent, I'm afraid." I tried to make a joke. "I've got as much chance of owning my own place as you boys have of finding Lord Lucan."

Hinton gave a hint of smile. "Yes, it's tough for youngsters, isn't it?"

He stopped and looked at the bookcase and then the silver-framed photographs on top. "Nice though, you keep it tidy. Live here alone?"

"Yes."

"But you've got a girlfriend?" Hinton said.

"How do you know that?"

"That photograph – the woman with a child – 'bout your age – next to those three lovely ladies."

"My mum and sisters."

"Yes," Hinton said. "I guessed as much. And that's you on your graduation day, what did you study?"

"Film and Media Studies."

Hinton gave a tight-lipped smile. "My stepdaughter's at university studying forensic psychology, she wants to follow in my footsteps."

"She'll be good at identifying them at least," I said, trying to make another crass joke.

Hinton gave that same tight-lipped, half smile; a smile of politeness rather than humour. "Indeed."

He looked around the flat some more, glanced into the kitchen and then, without further comment said,

"Anyway, what's it to be? Taxi with me or under your steam tomorrow or another day? We could write a letter but then it's all a bit formal and takes a bit of time – you know what the old snail mail is like these days? Takes a week for the first class. May as well get it out the way, eh?"

"Sure," I said. "Sure thing. Makes sense. Voluntary you say?"

"Yes, voluntary, purely voluntary, get up and leave if you wish."

"Just give me two ticks."

I wished Hinton and the police officer would just get out of my messed-up life, leave me in peace! I wished I could go back to 'normal' – I wished, I wished, I wished. I wished my car crash life was just not such a fucking car crash. It sounds really rubbish but I actually felt like crying.

Instead, I went to the toilet and had a pee and tried to compose myself and then, for reasons I can't explain I combed my hair and opened the bathroom cabinet and dabbed on some Paco Rabanne aftershave. I imagined Hinton's eyes roving over my apartment's interior like bloody CCTV cameras. When I'd finished in the bathroom I went to my bedroom and took my black leather jacket from the wardrobe. My head was in a haze, I just couldn't believe what was happening to me. Since the first police visit, I seemed to have a permanent dull headache and could feel my impish, pulsating heart through my thin T-shirt. My eyebrow had taken on a permanent tick.

Finally, I picked up my bunch of house keys which were on the breakfast bar, and walked out behind Hinton and the police officer, closing and locking the front door behind me. The car was a red Vauxhall Astra, the new model. Hinton opened the back door and I got in. The car smelt fresh and clean. The police officer sat next to Hinton in the front. Hinton drove. I felt like a child with his parents. The PC's radio crackled and he turned it off or down. After a few minutes Hinton and the police officer started talking. Hinton asked him when his shift finished and if he wanted to stay in 'uniform'. I was ignored. The officer even asked if Hinton had a 'lot on at the moment'.

Hinton said, "No, apart from this, very quiet. Getting ready for the Christmas rush."

They both laughed at that. Then, as we approached the station, the PC turned in his seat and faced me, his stab vest creaking under the weight of all the paraphernalia he carried.

"Have you ever given a voluntary interview before, Richard?"

I shook my head.

"OK, it'll be under Code C of PACE – that's the Police and Criminal Evidence Act, 1986. What that means to you is that you'll be cautioned and the interview will be recorded. It also means you have the right to a solicitor; do you want one?"

I thought of Helen's words. "Yes, please."

The officer turned back in the seat, moving awkwardly due to his heavy vest. He looked ahead. "We'll arrange one."

My head was filled with confused thoughts: why would it be recorded if the interview was voluntary? Could I change my mind? Say I wanted to go home? I rubbed my hands together. My leg was shaking.

The car pulled up on the road outside the station and they took me in through the tinted glass entrance. There was a heavily pregnant Eastern European woman wearing a long multicoloured dress and denim jacket sitting on the seat opposite the hatch talking rapidly on her mobile phone. The PC tapped some numbers into the keypad beside the door and it buzzed open.

"After you," he said, holding the door open. It closed behind me. Hinton gestured to the custody sergeant, and I walked over to a Perspex screen.

"He's here for a voluntary, the MacDonald case but we need to arrange a solicitor."

The bald sergeant took a sharp intake of breath and made a hissing sound like a boiling kettle. He rubbed a pen back and forth across the top of his ear.

"Could be difficult, Miss Cody's just gone in with another client."

"What about Ding-Dong, I thought she was on duty tonight?" Hinton asked.

"Miss Bell? She's got a client too – some homeless guy who started throwing his weight around, as well as a few chairs and beer glasses in the Lord Rochford. We've had quite a busy night."

"OK, see what you can do."

"I'll phone through to Miss Bell's firm, see if anyone else can come out."

Hinton turned to me. "You don't have a solicitor on speed dial, do you, Richard?"

I shook my head.

"No, I thought not. You're not a regular. Alright, we'll see what we can come up with. Would you mind waiting outside please, Richard?"

The door was buzzed open and I went back outside and sat on a cold, hard plastic seat. The Eastern European woman was giving someone both barrels as she now stood with her hand on her enlarged hips. I massaged my temples and played with my mullet. I was

71

desperate for the toilet though I'd only just gone back at the flat: nerves, I guess.

I don't know how long I waited but the Eastern European woman had disappeared through the inviting dark tinted exit to the murky outside. Eventually Hinton came out with his scruffy folder under his arm. He sat down on the seat beside me.

"Sorry to keep you waiting, Richard. We're having trouble locating a Duty. It's your choice, of course, but I've been through your statement." Here he opened his folder and revealed my printout which now had spidery blue writing in the margins and arrows pointing to various sentences. "It's very good. Very clear and concise. I could see from your bookcase you enjoy creative writing and you've put together a very coherent statement." He paused. "You've really thought about it and put together something that could save us all a lot of time – it's a pity really that we interrupted you before you'd finished it. You did intend to hand it into a police station, I take it?"

"Yes, yes, of course, what else would I do with it?"

Hinton clicked his teeth as if it were a naïve question. "Yes, yes, well, as I say it's very good. Excellent in fact."

It felt like I was at the writers' circle and they were praising one of my short stories. I felt a bit more relaxed, maybe it wouldn't be as bad after all. Hinton continued.

"There's just one or two points of clarification. My colleague DI Drake and I would just like a little more meat on the bones as it were, if that's alright with you? As I say it's your choice."

I felt relieved. Maybe, as Helen had predicted, the police realised I was innocent, I was a witness more than a suspect. A witness was good. I'd take that all day long.

"OK," I said.

Hinton closed his folder. "Great, brilliant." Hinton got up. "Would you mind stepping this way, Richard?"

I followed him to the door. He tapped in a code and the door buzzed.

"After you, Richard."

I walked back up to the front counter.

"Right, we have to book you in," the custody sergeant behind the front desk said.

"Why?" I asked.

"'Ealth and safety – we need to know who's on site." The custody sergeant was probably in his late fifties. He asked me to confirm my name and why I was attending the police station. Then he repeated that the interview would be under caution and recorded and as such I had the right to have a legal representative. Did I want one?

"No," I now said.

He typed my answer into the computer. He then took a note of my date of birth and address and entered them onto the screen. The officer who had accompanied DCI Hinton stood at the internal door.

"Can you take everything out of your pockets, Richard?" he requested. With shaking hands, I took my mobile phone and wallet out of the pockets of my trousers and jacket as the sergeant held out a clear bag for me. I added some loose change, comb and car/door keys too. I was even asked to remove my watch.

Then he came over to me and asked me to hold up my arms. He had put on some blue latex gloves. He went over me with a wand and then patted me down.

"Why…why…why… do you need to do all this?" I asked, mid-search.

"We don't want people entering the station carrying knives or other weapons, Richard," Hinton said.

"Or bombs… we don't like getting blown up."

This was from a fairly tall blonde woman wearing a white collarless cotton blouse and black trousers. Her shoulder-length hair had a large silver clasp on the back. She stood in the corridor that led to the interview rooms, with a folder in her hand and a lanyard around her neck.

The officer then walked off through another door leaving me with Hinton and the blonde woman, who introduced herself as DI Alison Drake.

I followed Hinton to an interview room with Drake behind me. I sat down on a metal chair with a grey cushioned seat. The room was windowless and sparse. To the left of me was Neal recording equipment with all sorts of monitors and dials on it. My heart started to race. I bent forward with my clammy hands on my knees, like a footballer in a team photo. Hinton sat in front and to my left, by the machine and Drake on the right: my chair was positioned between the two. Hinton played around with the machine which made a few electronic pops and whistles then said, "ready?"

I nodded.

He smiled. "You'll need to talk to us, not nod, Richard, OK?" He paused, "Alright – for the tape…"

Drake laughed, "Dave, you're so old-fashioned! Richard, this interview will be recorded onto DVD and then you'll be given a copy."

"Thanks," I said.

"OK, for the DVD," Hinton began again. "It's Tuesday, 18th November at 7.07pm and we are about to interview Richard Andrew Turner in regard to the death of Anne-Marie MacDonald. I'm Detective Chief Inspector Hinton, leading the investigation."

"And I'm Detective Inspector Alison Drake. Are you alright to proceed with a voluntary interview, Richard?"

I nodded then remembered Hinton's words. "Yes."

"OK, here we go then." Hinton said.

Hinton moved in his chair and made himself comfortable. He took my A4 paper from his folder and hovered over it with a pen. Alison continued.

"Look, Richard, you're not under arrest, but it is a PACE interview and that means you are entitled to legal representation, it also means you can terminate the interview, which will be recorded, at any stage and ask to leave. Is that clear?"

I confirmed it was.

"We just want to establish some facts, is that alright?" Her voice was husky as if through smoking; she seemed friendly though, and I knew they were just doing their job.

I nodded again. "Yes," I said.

Hinton looked up; he had just finished reviewing my brief statement. Again. I noticed Alison had a copy too, which rested on a pad with a pencil on top.

"Thanks for preparing this, Richard, it's very helpful," Hinton said.

"Are you sure you don't want a solicitor?" he asked. "We could do this another time."

I thought of Helen's advice. If I made another appointment, it would mean sleepless nights and more worry, I just wanted to get it over with as quickly as possible and move on with my life.

"No, no," I said. "Let's get on with it."

"Good stuff. That's the spirit. Right, for the benefit of the recording do you mind if I read out your statement? Please stop me if you want to elaborate, add anything or correct something but I think it would be a good starting point."

"Fine."

I sat back in the chair and listened to Hinton's monotonic, deep, quiet voice drone through my words.

It was as if it was about someone else, like a piece of fiction I'd concocted. I corrected or expounded a few things but the statement was a somewhat shorter version of the one I have recorded here (minus the money of course). When he had finished, he said,

"Are you're happy with this statement?"

"Yes."

Hinton drew out his pocketbook and flicked over the page. "Oh, before I forget, would you mind signing this?"

It was like a fan asking for some actor's autograph.

"Sure," I said. I looked at what was written: *I've just finished writing a confession* and the time and date.

"You did say that, didn't you?" Hinton said. "When we arrived, I mean? You said 'I've just finished writing a confession' that's right, isn't it?"

"It was a slip of the tongue."

Hinton shrugged, smiled. "Look, it's something and nothing, Richard. In the police we have to document everything. It's for us as much as you. We can't do anything without dotting the 'I's' and crossing the 'T's'; police work is not what it was, everything has to be recorded nowadays."

"That's for sure," Drake laughed.

I signed the notebook.

"Good," Hinton said as he closed and pocketed it. "On Monday night you told PC Tanner you'd never met Anne-Marie MacDonald, why was that?"

"I dunno," I said. "I'd cheated on my girlfriend, I didn't want her to find out. I panicked, I felt scared, I wanted to go to my writers' circle."

"Indeed," Hinton said. He liked that word. "So even though, at the time, you didn't know *why* PC Tanner and PC Price were asking you questions about Anne-Marie MacDonald and Saturday night you felt it better to deny everything?"

"It wasn't like that. There was stuff going around social media about a woman who had died on Church Street; I knew that was where Anne-Marie lived. I drove past the address on the way home from work to check it out. I saw the white and blue chequered police tape and realised something serious had happened."

"So, during a routine enquiry you suspected that Anne-Marie may have died?" DI Drake intervened.

"Yes."

"Any other reason for not being honest?" she asked. She smiled, motherly. God, could my heartbeat get any faster? Put me on a blood pressure machine and it would have exploded, I was constantly tapping my foot as if I had St Vitus dance.

"Well, as I said, I didn't want my girlfriend, Debbie, to know." I looked down at the table. "I felt bad about cheating on her."

"Indeed," Hinton said.

"Why would she have known about that?" Drake asked. "If it was just a routine enquiry?"

I shrugged. "I don't know."

"Look, Richard, we are investigating the suspicious death of a young woman and you might be a key witness. Did you think about that?" Hinton said.

"No," I said.

"But you feel now you should be up front?" Hinton whistled out the word 'front'.

"Yes," I said.

"Why would it have been a problem to tell PC Tanner and PC Price the truth though? I mean regarding your girlfriend?" Hinton pursued.

"I dunno."

"Did you think they would drive around to her house and tell her you'd cheated on her?" Hinton persisted, sitting back in his chair and wrapping his jacket around him.

"No, I guess not."

Drake chipped in. She leant forward and placed her hands together forming a triangle. "Look, Richard, can I level with you? This is a murder investigation. That means it is very serious. Very serious indeed. We're not interested in your romantic assignations. What we need from you is honesty. It would have helped if you had been honest with PC Tanner and PC Price when they visited last night. It wastes police time otherwise. The police can only operate effectively with the full support and co-operation of the general public."

That was me told. I felt like a naughty schoolboy. "I'm sorry," I said.

Hinton was more conciliatorily. "Well, at least you've being co-operative now and have written this which is very good, plenty of new information. Let's go through it in detail, shall we?"

He looked at my A4 testimony. "You mention Citi Cabs and a driver who appeared to be following you and the fact that Anne-Marie presented as being concerned when you mentioned seeing a cab outside her house. She said something about an issue she had had with the company – an unpaid debt. We'll look into that." He paused. "Where did you park when you went out on Saturday?"

"On King Edward Street."

"And the driver followed you from there?"

"From the junction when I turned out, yes."

"What time did you leave the club with Anne-Marie?"

"About 12.30am… maybe slightly later."

"What way did you travel back to Church Street?" Hinton asked.

I wasn't sure so Hinton got an old A-Z out of his folder and showed me some possible routes.

"Yes, I think that's right," I said to one.

"Let's see if we can get the name of that driver?" he said to DI Drake.

Alison moved my statement to one side and wrote 'Citi Cabs' on her pad in pencil.

"You also mention this dark BMW."

Still with the A-Z on the table Hinton took some plain A4 paper from his folder and drew a rough map.

"Anne-Marie lived on Church Street." He then drew lines at either end. "This is High Street West and the street at the other end is Latimer Road." He drew a small box about a third of the way up Church Street and then wrote '32' in it. He turned it around. "Where did you park?"

I showed him. "Almost opposite."

He drew another box and wrote 'R' in it.

"And the BMW?"

"Further up the street." Again I showed him; again, he wrote on his makeshift map.

"So, about ten houses up? You passed the BMW as you drove off – I assume you went towards Latimer Road?"

"Yes."

"You didn't see the occupants?" Hinton asked.

"No, my side window was frosted up and the windscreen was still a bit iced up. I thought one was wearing a beanie hat when I scraped the windscreen but I couldn't see faces."

"No dashcam, I assume?"

"No."

"Check out doorbell cameras," this was to Drake. He made a quick calculation, "from about 46 to 54 – both sides – see what you can get."

Again, Drake jotted it down on her pad.

"Right, you talk about meeting Anne-Marie and you went back to her house. You say it smelt of weed."

Alison chuckled. "Positively reeked of the stuff."

Hinton continued. "Then after you'd had sex, and she'd fallen asleep, you say you woke up and went to the bathroom and looked for a paracetamol but saw cocaine in a condom in the bathroom cupboard, is that right?"

"Yes."

"How did you know it was cocaine?"

"It was white powder, I guessed she was a drug dealer or something."

"Indeed," Hinton said.

I saw Drake write 'bathroom cupboard' on her pad and a question mark.

"Oh... I almost forgot.... you say in this statement that she mentioned her housemate, Lisa, would not be back till late Sunday afternoon, is that right?" Hinton said.

"Yes."

Hinton turned my testimony over and read through the second side. "OK, nothing more from me, unless there's something else you wish to tell us, Richard?"

I'd not written down the last bit, about the events before leaving the house. I'd been deep in thought about it when Hinton and the PC had arrived. How to explain it? That was the question. I needed to say something. I took a deep breath. I'd thought about it a lot and knew what I needed to do.

"Look, I didn't finish that statement." I put my left hand to the back of my head and tugged my mullet. "Before I left the house I went into the kitchen."

"You went into the kitchen?" Hinton repeated. He looked at me with his small, dark probing eyes. "Go on."

"I said I had a headache, well a thirst too, I was desperate for a drink. I opened some cupboards just to the left of the sink and looked for a glass."

"Did you find one?" Drake asked. She sat pencil poised. Engrossed. There was no sound in the room apart from the Neal recording device and my pounding heart.

"No."

"What did you see in the kitchen cupboard, Richard?" Hinton asked.

God, I was sweating, I rubbed my hands on my trousers repeatedly. "Nothing, well I say that…" I laughed falsely. "The coffee jar… obviously, a pot of sugar sachets, condiments, sauces, tins, packed with stuff it was. Lots of those Knorr powder sauces from what I recall."

"Did you open both cupboard doors, Richard?" This was Drake.

"Yes, yes, I think so."

"But you didn't find a glass?" Hinton probed.

"No."

"So, what did you do?" The DCI asked.

"I rinsed the mug I'd had coffee in earlier and poured water into that and had a drink."

As you may have gathered, I've always had a peculiar ability to read upside down and I saw DI Drake write the words 'taps' and 'cupboard doors' and underline them both two or three times. Only she didn't write 'taps' she wrote 'tapes', and it was that spelling mistake that aroused my curiosity.

"Then you left?"

"Yes."

"Did you wear shoes or stockinged feet, socks in other words, when you entered the kitchen?" Hinton said.

"Socks."

"How long do you think you were in the kitchen, Richard?" Hinton queried.

I shrugged. My foot was tapping and I knew I was sweating. Hinton and Drake seemed to be peering into my inner soul. "I dunno, no more than a couple of minutes, I'd have thought."

"How long did it take you to get back to your flat?" he asked.

"About ten to fifteen minutes," I said.

"You drive slowly," Hinton said, "you were less than three … maybe even two miles away."

I shrugged. "Well, I'm careful, I keep to the speed limits."

Hinton leant forward, raised an eyebrow. "Even at night?"

"Speed cameras never sleep. I've only ever had one SP30."

Hinton almost laughed. "Well, you're a more careful driver than me," he said.

"And me," Drake added.

"Anyway, thanks for that, Richard." Hinton held up my statement. "It's been useful."

Alison Drake now moved forward in her chair and spread her arms across the table, her hands clasped in front of her. Her white blouse completely covered the A4 pad: it was Hinton's turn to write.

"Now, I'm going to ask some questions which may seem a bit left field but bear with me, Richard. When you had sex with Anne-Marie did she, at any point resist or indicate she was reluctant?"

"No, no, not at all, I'm not a rapist!"

"No one is saying you are, Richard, we're just trying to establish the facts. So, she was willing. You say in your statement you had sex twice, who initiated the act?"

"She did, I'd say."

"And did she suggest anything a little out of the normal? I mean bondage, S&M, anything of that nature?"

"Fuck me, we'd only just met!" I exclaimed.

"Do you like that sort of thing though, Richard? Being dominant? Being in control?" Drake asked. "Sex games? Asphyxiation?"

"God no, no, not at all," I said and here I tried to crack one of the infantile jokes that used to get me into trouble at school; it was sign of nerves but they weren't to know that. I put on a stupid, high-pitched voice and said, "there's only one position for me, sir, said the missionary."

Hinton looked at me as if I was completely deranged. He had a point. Drake ignored me.

"When you were with Miss MacDonald, was she wearing a wrap?"

"How do you mean?" I asked.

"At any time during the night did she wear a cream-coloured satin dressing gown or wrap with black edging and a black tie?" Drake asked.

"No."

"Are you sure?" Drake repeated.

"Yes."

"So, whilst you were with her, she never put on a wrap or dressing gown?"

"No."

"And you never saw a black tie or band that would do it up?"

"No."

"OK, thank you," DI Drake said.

Talk about confused! It was like trying to make your way home through a thick fog.

Hinton took over the line of questioning. "You've told us about Citi Cabs and the Beamer, did you see anyone else?"

I shook my head. "No."

"Did Anne-Marie give the impression she was scared? A violent ex or something?"

"No," I said. "But the drugs in the bathroom cupboard may be a clue."

"They would be if they were still there," Hinton said.

"Well, that tells you that someone else was in the house after I left," I said.

Hinton fixed me with an unblinking stare. "Indeed. We don't doubt the truth of what you've told us, Richard."

"I've told you everything I know. I swear to God I did not kill Anne-Marie." I thumped the table. I was starting to panic. I felt overwhelmed. "I did NOT kill Anne-Marie!"

"Indeed," Hinton said softly. He glanced at DI Drake.

"Well, you've clarified a few points," Alison said, "don't go anywhere, we may need to talk to you further."

She picked up her pad and Hinton gave a message to the recording equipment and turned it off.

I felt rooted to the chair. My buttocks were stuck to the soft cushion. I physically could not move, my body was so tense.

"Can...can...can I ask," I stuttered. "Debbie... my...my... girlfriend, you won't involve her, will you?"

Drake stood by the table looking down on me, the pad across her chest. "We're not in the business of sharing information between interviewees but we may need to speak to her, yes."

"B...but... but why?" I stammered. I felt myself flush. The situation was getting out of control. *Poor Debbie*, I thought, she didn't deserve it. "She wasn't even at the nightclub. Why interview her?"

"We may need to establish some more facts," Alison said.

"But it's nothing to do with her!" I exclaimed. I felt my stomach churn.

"We'll be the judge of that, Richard," Hinton said. "We're taking statements from a number of people. It's an ongoing and fast-moving investigation. We're talking to a lot of people at present and we're following up a number of leads and you've just given us a few more so thanks for that."

"We like work, don't we, Dave?" Alison said.

"We do indeed," Hinton replied.

I thought of Mark, Suggo, Matty and Dave. They'd all be getting the policemen's knock too. If they hadn't already. It was all a mess. A great big, fucking mess.

"Let's run you home," Hinton said, taking his keys from his pocket. "And thanks for doing a voluntary. It makes it easier in the long run."

I followed them both along the corridor and back to the reception area. Drake veered off to the left through the door which led to the police station's inner sanctum. It was the door the police officer had gone through earlier. The custody sergeant handed over my personal belongings, which were now in a tray. I pocketed my wallet, keys and the other bits.

"Didn't I have a watch?" I asked.

The custody sergeant shook his head and then scratched the back of his hand with the end of a pen.

"Only what's in the tray. What was it like?" he asked.

"Hugo Boss, silver strap, black face."

The sergeant looked around the counter and disinterestedly peered into some other trays and clear bags.

"Nothing here."

Hinton was standing at the door waiting to go. He beat a tattoo with his car key on his hand.

"Are you sure you were wearing a watch?" the custody sergeant asked.

I couldn't remember. I couldn't think straight.

"Maybe not," I said. I followed Hinton out to his Astra. This time I sat in the front. We didn't speak.

I guess the interview had lasted about an hour, perhaps longer. I'd said what I had to say and I had come clean-ish. The money was a real bummer, why had I been so foolhardy to take it? All I knew was that I needed to keep that quiet. When we arrived back outside my flat on Petersfield Hill, Hinton said,

"If you think of anything else, just give me a call," as he handed me his card. It all felt very ordinary but of course it wasn't. This was a murder investigation. This was mega-serious. I felt numb; my head was filled with random, jumbled thoughts. I stumbled across the gravel drive in a daze and unlocked the front door and then my door. I collapsed on the sofa and took some deep breaths to calm myself.

Then, taking my mobile from the pocket of my leather jacket I pressed Debbie's number. It was so nice to hear her reassuring voice. She confirmed the police had been in touch and wanted her to give a statement.

"But why, Rich, I just can't understand it. It doesn't involve you and I wasn't even there!"

"I know it doesn't make any sense but I'm a suspect, God knows why, apparently some money went missing as well." The mobile was shaking in my clammy hand.

"What, from her handbag whilst she was in the nightclub?" Debbie asked.

"Maybe, I don't know… anyway… it's for the best if, when you give your statement to the police, you don't mention I paid cash for the museum…" I paused. "Or on second thoughts they've probably caught me on CCTV paying cash so just say you owed me some money. Say you gave me some cash in the car which I then used to pay for the museum admission and the meal…"

"But why, Rich, I'm getting frightened. This is so, so unlike you. What's going on?" Debbie was on the verge of tears.

"Look, Debs, don't worry about it. It'll all turn out alright in the end. It's just routine but you know what the fucking police are like! Anxious to make a quick arrest and they don't care who they fit up as long as they can just close the case down. Nowadays fighting crime is a tick box exercise – the cops are just a bunch of bean counters."

"But they have fingerprints and DNA and CCTV and all sorts of clever stuff to make sure they get the right person."

"They do but if they can't catch the criminal, they pin it on whoever was around at the time – the next available suspect. It happens all the time."

"No, it doesn't."

"It does, Debs, you're naïve about how the police work. The cops fit people up right, left and centre. There was a chap in Bristol, a landlord, I think. One of his female lodgers got murdered and the cops tried to fit him up because of his shock of white hair and eccentric manner. There was big outcry about it in the papers. I swear to God it's true."

"But your name's on Facebook. People are saying you're the person that left with this girl, you didn't sleep with her, did you?"

"No, of course not, but that's probably where the police have got my name... Facebook and social media."

"Do you think so? It's just social media? Be honest with me, Rich. Tell me the truth. I can't stand all this." She started crying. "I need to know. Please, please Rich, tell me the truth, did you meet that girl or not?"

I took a deep breath. I'd been trying to avoid this conversation since Monday night when I'd had the pleasure of meeting PC Snot and Hazel Eyes. I thought about Debbie's interview with the police. Better from me than Hinton. Now I was in the shit. Big time. Talk about digging my own grave!

"Look, Debbie, it wasn't what you think, she came on to me, she wanted to dance, she led me on. One thing led to another."

"Oh, Richard!" I could hear Debbie's panting, sniffling tears. "How could you?" she shrieked. "I can't believe it! Rich, how could you? How could you do that to me?" Her voice rose like a loaf of bread in an oven. I hated confrontation. I hated people being upset. All my life I had tried to avoid arguments. It was a trait I had inherited from my mum who had feared my dad and had tried to placate him whenever he was in a foul mood or drunk – which was most of the time.

"I'm sorry, Debbie," I said. "I'll make it up to you. Take you to Paris… and Dylan too, I'm sorry…I'm so, so sorry…"

"You bastard! You cheating, lying bastard!" she screamed, hitting some really high-pitched notes. "How could you? And I thought we were so, so close. You said you loved me."

She sobbed for a bit and then she bellowed, "you fucking bastard."

She almost couldn't speak, she was so angry, and then the floodgates really opened and I was crying too.

"I thought I could trust you! I thought you loved me!"

Dylan must have entered the room and asked why she was crying for I heard her say (I must say with a good deal of motherly composure),

"Nothing, darling, don't worry, Richard and I have just had an argument…. That's all…(*sob*)… no, it'll be OK… (*sniff, sniff*) we're not splitting up…."

Then she must have realised I was still on the phone because she shouted, 'fucking bastard' again and 'terminated the call' for want of a better phrase.

Chapter Four

After a long, sleepless night, most of which I'd spent watching television or on my computer (thank God for 24-hour TV and online gambling) I phoned my manager, Helen, in the morning and told her I wasn't coming in to work. I explained that the police had visited again and this time I had undertaken a voluntary interview at the station – without a solicitor being present. I could tell she didn't think that had been a good idea. I also told her that Debbie had an appointment with the police to give a statement. Helen wondered why. My heart started to race. It was a question I asked myself all the time. It indicated to me that I was the Numero Uno suspect and just to use a French phrase – I was in *la merde*. Big time.

"I need some time off," I said. "I just can't concentrate. I feel sick with worry. I just keep turning the events of Saturday night over and over in my head."

Helen was understanding. In total contrast to how a conversation with my former manager, Williams would have been. Not that I would have been so open with him, I would have just phoned in sick but with Helen I could be honest.

"Take the rest of the week off," she said. "I'll say you're taking some leave; you need to try to sort this out, Richard. Have you told Debbie yet?"

That was something Helen had been insistent upon when I'd spoken to her the day before.

"Yes, she didn't take it too well."

"Umm," Helen hummed. "I'm not surprised. Well, I hope you can sort yourself out and if you need any help just phone me."

She gave me her home and mobile numbers. That was why I'd not left Zorin Logistics, or at least not tried to get another job. Helen was a fantastic manager and a really nice person. A good boss is worth their weight in gold. When I'd left uni, I'd lived at home for a while whilst I'd been looking for a permanent position. At the time the effects of the 2008 credit crunch were starting to bite and jobs were hard to come by; everyone, it seemed, was making cuts. Anyway, I had managed to get a temporary job on a 12-month contract at a large company in South East London. It was an admin role which included organising meetings and taking minutes. The boss, Rick Lambert, (I dubbed him 'Rick the Ranker') had disliked me just as much as Williams had later. God knows why I had that effect on managers. The thing was he hadn't appointed me and had wanted someone else (I think he had been on leave or sick or something when I'd come in for the interview); anyway, Lambert had it in for me from my first day. He was always criticising and finding fault, especially with my poor minute-taking. He clearly wanted me to leave but because I'd been appointed through HR and thrust upon him, he couldn't get rid of me without a complicated capabilities procedure. The next best thing was to bully me into leaving and that's what he did from the start. Every morning he would greet me with the 'welcoming line', 'are you still here, Turner?' The only positive was that it did spur me on in terms of applying for other jobs and to pass my driving test which I felt would be a great asset. The thing with Rick the *R*anker was he even disliked the fact we had the same name, Rick being a diminutive of Richard. Unbefuckinglievable, but true. Then I'd found a permanent position and jumped from that temporary frying pan into the sarcastic permanent fire of Williams so my working life had started off with two mega-awful bosses. Once again, I say unbefuckinglievable.

After I got off the phone to Helen, I went around the flat thinking about links to Anne-Marie and what I could do to help myself get out of the terrible, terrible mess I was becoming embroiled in, partly through my own stupid, stupid mistakes and decisions. I tried to take stock. My clothes from Saturday night had been washed and I'd taken my trousers to the dry cleaners. I liked my flat to be clean and tidy and always kept it neat, in part as a result of my mother who was always cleaning and insisted on our house being tidy but mainly due to my OCD. I had two older sisters who my mum favoured, so as I got older, I used to help around the house, vacuuming, cooking the dinner, cleaning and such like to get in her good books. Although she would praise me, she never showed me the deep affection she showed my sisters, she never laughed with me like she did with them, never shared jokes and stories, never sat in the kitchen chatting… but I digress. As my flat or apartment was small it didn't take a huge amount of effort on my part to keep it tidy and it was something I found Debbie, and other women who had visited over the years, seemed to like.

Anyway, that Wednesday morning I looked around the flat and then on my phone. There were no incriminating messages; apart from the unwise Monday morning WhatsApp message and the texts to Debbie as well as texts and WhatsApp messages from Matty and Suggo which I had not replied to. There was no point in deleting them as that would look suspicious and they were on other people's phones as well.

There was nothing on the computer apart from the statement which the police had seen. Although I must admit that, during my sleepless night, I had done a few internet searches on police procedures. I wiped the search memory but we all know that nothing is ever really deleted from a computer, don't we? Fortunately, the money was no more (or so I thought). The small amount I'd taken from the envelope had been used to pay for the museum, the museum restaurant, a present for Dylan, the burger on Monday night and petrol on the Tuesday morning so that had gone or been converted into change. I wasn't a criminal, not really, but I knew I had to think like one to get the cops to back off.

I kept thinking about what Debbie had told the police, or would tell them, because I didn't know the time of her interview. I imagined a police officer would visit her at home in the morning when she had taken Dylan to school and then she would go on to work. Her hours worked around the school day – except on a Friday when she did a longer day and Dylan went to a friend's house after school. Of course, I could no longer call her to find out what she had said and I wondered if she would have told the police about my phone call to her the previous evening and what I had said about the money. However you looked at it I was in deep, deep trouble. If I had come clean to Debbie beforehand, and not the night before she was due to give her statement, perhaps I might have been able to make amends. Just maybe I could have got on better terms with her, sent her flowers, told her how much I loved her, shown remorse – but there was no time for that now. I paced up and down my flat, anxiously trying to think of any small things the police could use against me. I knew they would be looking for inconsistencies in my statement and the statements of Matty, Mark, Suggo and Dave as well as Debbie. The problem was I just couldn't think straight, I felt 'panicked', nervous, on edge, numb, emotional: I just wanted to get out of the appalling fucking mess I'd managed to get myself into. I didn't know who to turn to. Part of me wanted to run away. Pack a bag, drop it in the boot of my car and get the hell out. But how far would I get with ANPR and CCTV? And then wouldn't I look even more guilty? I was trapped.

The doorbell rang. It was 3.30pm on Wednesday afternoon. I'd seen the two police vehicles pull up on the drive – a car and a van. I was half expecting it. I knew they would come for me. Like water draining from a bath, I was being drawn inextricably towards the plughole and oblivion like some Kafkaesque nightmare in which there was no escape. Only darkness. Endless all-embracing, fucking darkness.

I answered the door to DCI Hinton, DI Drake and the officer who had visited the previous night. Hinton spoke,

"Richard Andrew Turner we are arresting you on suspicion of the murder of Anne-Marie MacDonald somewhere between 3am and 7am on Sunday, 16th November. You do not have to say anything. But it may harm your defence if you do not mention when questioned something which you later rely on in court.

Anything you do say may be given in evidence. Do you understand?"

"Yes," I replied. "Can I get anything?"

"No," Hinton said. "We will be carrying out a full search of your flat. If you have any requirements or needs you need to let the custody sergeant know."

The police officer asked me to hold my hands out and he locked cuffs onto my wrists. Just at that moment my mobile phone rang. The officer took it from the pocket of my jeans and turned it off. Then I was led away to the police car parked just outside the door. A white CSI (Crime Scene Investigation) van had drawn up and police, in blue paper overalls, masks and hoods, were waiting for us to leave before they commenced a search of my flat (one thing I had gleaned, from my internet research, was that once arrested the police could search your premises without needing a warrant). I imagined the neighbours watching. I felt like shit.

They took me back to the same local station. This time the car drove into the underground carpark and I was taken down a long, cream-coloured brick corridor. There seemed to be a lot of pipework. The corridor was lit by bright lights, some workmen moved some paint pots as I came past and one of them looked at me suspiciously: the place smelt of fresh paint. I was taken upstairs and marched up to the custody sergeant. I was searched and my mobile phone, wallet, loose change, keys and belt were surrendered and placed in a clear plastic bag which was marked with my name and details. Hinton informed the sergeant about the reason for my arrest. The sergeant then approved it and read the charge against me and informed me of my rights. He asked if I had any dietary requirements and if I wanted to see a solicitor, I said I did. Then they took my photograph, fingerprints, and a DNA swab. Finally, I was led away to a white or cream-coloured cell with a high reinforced glass window with a grille over it. A metal ledge protruded – this was my bed; it had a purple, plastic mattress on top. In the corner was a stainless-steel toilet which jutted out of the wall. The heavy door had a grille in it. I was placed inside, and the door was slammed shut and locked.

I'm not sure what time it was when they came to collect me, but I know they had been waiting for a solicitor to arrive (and perhaps, in an effort to get more evidence from my flat and car, they had not phoned to request one straight away, in fact I am sure that was the case). The solicitor was of Indian heritage and wore a pale blue pin- striped skirt suit. She was probably about my age; she was already in the interview room when I was led in. Also present were the arresting officer, DCI Hinton and DI Drake.

"Can I have a few minutes with my client?" my brief said. I came and sat down beside her, and she introduced herself as Hemal Patel. She had shimmering, straight black hair which reached to her waist and she was stork-leg thin. She unzipped her case and gave me her business card prior to removing a pen and pad.

"Right, I've had a brief look at the case and DCI Hinton has filled me in as well. My suggestion is you go 'no comment'. At this stage, they are just fishing but from what I can gather the evidence is all circumstantial."

"OK," I said – and that was yet another mistake. We discussed the case for a few minutes, and I went through the events of that fateful night. Ms Patel said she would make a brief statement at the beginning of the interview. Finally, Hemal told Hinton we were ready and he and Drake returned to the interview room. The electronic equipment was once again engaged and Hinton stated the date, time and who was present in the room.

Ms Patel stated that I had nothing to add to the written statement and to the voluntary interview I had given the day before.

"My client feels he was very helpful to the police on Tuesday evening. He explained his actions in some detail with a written statement and then provided verbal clarification of any points you felt needed further substance or had not been fully covered. He has nothing to add to these two statements, one written and one verbal."

But that wasn't good enough for Hinton.

"Did you kill Anne-Marie MacDonald?" Hinton asked, getting straight to the point. His mood had completely changed from the previous evening. There was no more 'Richard', no more friendliness.

"No comment."

But they didn't give up, of course they fucking didn't! And what follows here is a sample of some of the questions that I remember being asked.

"What were you wearing on Saturday night when you were in the Pryzm nightclub?"

"No comment."

A photograph was produced of me leaving the nightclub with Anne-Marie MacDonald.

"Do you recognise either of the people in this picture?" Hinton asked.

"No comment."

"Just for the record one of the individuals in the photograph has been identified as Anne-Marie MacDonald, the victim. A number of witnesses have said the other person is you, do you know why they might say that?" Hinton asked.

"No comment."

"Would you agree that male looks remarkably similar to you? He is about the same height and he even sports an '80s style mullet which is not dissimilar to your own," Hinton stated. "And he is wearing a white shirt."

"No comment."

"A white fibre has been found on the door jamb of the kitchen of number 32, Church Street, is it from that shirt?"

"No comment."

"You have already admitted that you went back to Anne-Marie's house, did you at any point lean against the kitchen door jamb?" Hinton asked.

"No comment."

"When we get the results back from forensics do you think it will show a match for your shirt?"

"No comment."

"Do you wear disposable contact lenses?" Drake interjected.

"No comment."

"Disposable contact lenses have been found in the footwell on the passenger side of your car, are they yours? Drake asked.

"No comment."

"Did you take your contact lenses out before you entered Anne-Marie's house?" Drake pressed.

"No comment."

"When did you take your contact lenses out and put on your glasses?"

"No comment."

"We have a statement from Debbie King, who I believe is an ex, or current partner of yours, stating that you like to play sex games involving bondage and spanking, is that correct?" Drake asked.

"No comment."

"In those games Ms King reports that you were the dominant party and sometimes grabbed her by the neck, is that true?" Drake asked.

"No comment."

"Do you know why Miss King might say you grabbed her by the neck?" Drake persisted.

"No comment."

Then it was Hinton's turn.

"Did you attempt to steal a large sum of money from Anne-Marie's property?" he asked.

"No comment."

"Did Anne-Marie confront you during the act of theft?" Hinton asked.

"No comment."

"When Anne-Marie confronted you did you draw a knife from the knife block and attempt to scare her?" Hinton asked.

"No comment."

"Come on, Richard," Drake eventually said. "If it were an accident, we may be able to help you; just tell us what happened in the kitchen and front room of 32 Church Street in the early hours of the morning of Sunday, 16th November."

"No comment."

And so, it went on and on and on, the pair spinning me by firing question after question with my solicitor sometimes intervening.

Finally, I was taken back to the cell. I was given a ham sandwich and a cup of tea brought in on a plastic tray. I lay on the bed, deep in thought. I'd been wearing my daily disposable contact lenses for a long time and had told the custody sergeant I needed my glasses from the flat. They didn't appear. Later in the evening I took my lenses out at last and flushed them down the toilet. Then, yet again, I asked for my glasses.

"They're been taken away for forensics, boss," the burly officer said through the grille.

"But I can't see," I said. "I need my fucking glasses! I can't fucking see!"

"You don't need to see anything, boss. Let me describe the cell to you? There are four off-white walls. A door. A bed to the right of the door with a khazi at the end of it. That's all you need to know." He slammed the grille shut. I lay down on the bed and put my arm over my eyes and cried. Why was my life so fucking shit?

I didn't sleep at all what with all the banging on the cell doors, people shouting and general worry about the total fucking mess I was in. My solicitor, Ms Patel, had told me they could hold me for up to thirty-six hours; twenty-four hours initially and then they could apply for a twelve-hour extension to a Chief Constable or something which was always granted in serious cases like suspicion of murder.

So the next day, after breakfast of porridge, I was interviewed again - fortunately someone had gone to my

106

flat and collected a spare pair of glasses. Hemal was again my solicitor, and again she advised a 'no comment' interview even though a range of different questions were put to me. This time they focussed on the following day – the trip to the museum which I'd paid for in cash as referenced by a nice piece of very clear CCTV. There was also CCTV from the fast-food restaurant on Monday evening which showed me buying a burger and fries with cash, as did CCTV footage from a petrol station forecourt the following day when I'd filled my car up with petrol. Just to make Hinton's life easy for him I had revealed I'd visited McDonald's and a Texaco petrol station when I had given the voluntary the night before.

"Do you still have the money you stole from Anne-Marie's property?" Hinton asked.

"No comment."

"You seem to have used cash at the museum, the fast-food restaurant and the petrol station, where did that cash come from?" Hinton asked.

"No comment."

"Do you think, when we have finished searching your property, it will reveal any money taken from Anne-Marie's address?"

"No comment."

"Did you kill Anne-Marie when she confronted you in the front room and saw you had stolen her money?

Money she knew she had to hand over to drug dealers?" Hinton asked.

"No comment."

"How much money did you steal from Anne-Marie's house; did you have time to count it?" Drake asked.

"No comment."

"The kitchen knife that was taken from a knife block in the kitchen, which we believe was used to stab Anne-Marie, has gone missing, where is it?"

"No comment."

And so it went on. Endless, endless, endless questions. Finally, I was taken back to my cell. Later in the day I was 'released under investigation' (RUI). I guess the police didn't feel the need to extend the agony for a further twelve hours since I was not going to answer their questions.

Various items were not returned as they were of 'forensic interest': these included my glasses, my mobile phone, my wallet and the trousers I'd worn Saturday night which the cops had kindly collected from the dry cleaners on my behalf... oh, and my car. I was asked to sign a form acknowledging that the police had said items in their 'safe' custody.

When I returned to my flat it looked pretty normal except the computer was missing, leaving loose wires on the desk. I realised they had also taken some other things which seemed pretty random to me, like the shirt I'd worn Saturday night and washed and ironed – well,

I had been desperate for something to do! The slip-on shoes I'd worn on the night, my black leather jacket, my gloves, various books from the bookcase, my diary and other bits and bobs. There was some evidence of grey powder from dusting but the murder hadn't taken place in the flat so I think it was in relation to the money and possibly the other items the police said had been taken from the victim's house. Also, I guess they were looking for any signs of blood in the flat. The officer who dropped me home asked me to sign another form listing what had been removed from the flat and again I was given a copy.

Juliette from the flat upstairs was working at home so she came down to see me under the guise of 'are you alright?' but, of course, she wanted to know what the hell was going on. I gave her a brief outline. She said the police had been through the flowerpots at the front of the house, the garden and the storage room at the rear of the house.

"What are they looking for, Richard?" she asked.

"I dunno," I said – but I did. It was the money… and possibly the murder weapon.

When she'd left, I phoned Helen and told her what had happened and then I phoned my solicitor (or at least Ms Patel's firm) who told me to 'sit tight' and not to talk about the case to anyone and definitely not to 'do' any social media (without a mobile phone and computer that was hard). Then I phoned Mark on my land line. He was at work but left the office to speak to me. He was in a stairwell and I could hear the echoes of footsteps as people walked past. Mark said my name was 'all over' social media and people were using the word 'murderer' to describe me. Social media trolls are spitting vile: '*if the cops don't nail that bastard I will – Turner is a dead man walking*' and a Just Giving page set up for Anne-Marie. Mark knew more about her than I did; she was twenty-four, apparently, and lived with Lisa who was twenty-eight. Lisa had discovered her body on Sunday afternoon in the front room when she had returned from a visit to Hull to see her parents.

Without technology I felt a bit lost, so my appetite whetted by Mark's comments I walked back to the local library, where our writers' circle was held every Monday. Instead of going up to the meeting rooms, I went to the counter and asked to use a computer. The librarian gave me a slip of paper with a code on it and I accessed the internet. I had a look at the local paper which had the Anne-Marie murder on its front page – the piece actually didn't say very much…

"We are working at pace to establish what has happened and we would ask for those with information to come forward," Hinton had said, "I know many people will be concerned about this incident, and I would like to offer our reassurance that we have a large number of officers dedicated to our investigation. We appeal for those with CCTV, smart doorbell or dashcam footage from the area on or around Church Street and surrounding area as well as King Edward Street and the Pryzm nightclub on the night of Saturday 15th November and early morning of Sunday 16th November to get in touch. We are particularly interested in tracing the owners of a dark blue or black BMW, Series 3 saloon which was parked on Church Street during the early hours of Sunday morning, facing towards High Street West. Anyone with information about that car or who has any information about the victim should get in touch.'

The piece ended with that old police chestnut that a 'man in his thirties had been arrested on suspicion of murder and released on police bail.' (Although technically that was not the case).

Well, that was reassuring, give Hinton his due, they hadn't just focused on me. I was interested in the model of the BMW – I didn't know it, that meant someone else had seen it or it had been picked up on doorbell footage.

Further into the piece family and friends were fulsome in their praise for Anne-Marie.

The internet was of more interest: like me Anne-Marie had been brought up in a one parent family, like me she had two older sisters, like me she had been to a local academy school but she seemed to have drifted out of education aged sixteen, whilst I'd gone to a sixth-form college until I was eighteen. I had achieved two Ds at A-level, which was better than my sisters who were similar to Anne-Marie inasmuch as they had not achieved much in the way of qualifications. I discovered that Anne-Marie had indeed come from Scotland, Leith near Edinburgh to be precise, and had moved down to London for a job but had found herself in a house on the M4 corridor with her friend, Lisa. What she worked as, and what she had done previously, was all a bit of a mystery. Her jobs were variously described as 'bar staff', 'telesales', 'shop worker' – although she did appear to have a wide circle of friends. It was sad to read, but of course, what I knew and what wasn't really being reported was that Anne-Marie had somehow got caught up in a drug dealing racket.

Chapter Five

Perhaps a week passed by, I don't know, I think it was 22nd November, when events took a turn for the worse but in truth my mind was so muddled, I couldn't think clearly and I'd lost all track of time. I couldn't eat much and I seemed to be in constant mental fog from which sleep was no release. The word 'murderer' had been daubed on the communal front door in red paint. I mainly went shopping in the early hours or bought provisions from small convenience stores.

Then there was Debbie; she was apologetic but ended the relationship,

"It's Dylan, he's getting bullied at school," she told me on the phone – yes, we really had started talking again. I didn't blame her, I had cheated on her after all. She also informed me that the police had interviewed her again and were particularly interested in the museum trip and how I had funded it. Fortunately, she had kept to her story that I had lent her some money and she had returned it to me in the car park before we had entered the museum.

"I don't know everything that went on that night but I know you didn't kill *that girl* and I would hate to think of you being locked up for a crime you didn't commit," Debbie said. "You know I'll always support you."

That was a huge relief as it had been one of countless things that had been troubling me.

When you're under suspicion for a serious crime you just want to get your life back to how it was before. I suppose it's a little bit like being involved in a road accident when you know you're partly or solely to blame. You think *why the fuck did I look at my phone? Or why did I pull out when that car was going so fucking fast?* I guess its Post-Traumatic Stress Syndrome. You know you've made a fuck up but you also know other people have made the same mistake without any consequences. I just wanted the whole nasty incident to come to an end. I knew, or I thought I knew, that Citi Cabs were the key to the whole affair. Anne-Marie had been worried by their presence, one car had followed us and another minicab had stopped outside her house: possibly it was the same car. Therefore, on 22nd November, I walked to their office to confront them. By this time I had been signed off sick by the doctor due to stress and anxiety but being alone in my flat wasn't doing my mental health a whole lot of favours.

As I walked into the Citi Cabs office there were two Asian men playing pool and a youngish white woman in the kiosk leaning over a copy of the *Daily Mirror*; she had a streak of blonde in her brown hair. I walked up to her. She looked me up and down eyeing me with a good deal of suspicion (or was it my imagination – I'd got to a stage where I thought everyone recognised me from social media and pointed the proverbial finger). I asked to speak to the manager - she clearly thought I had a complaint so she asked me what it was about. I told her I could only tell the manager.

"I think he's busy," she said, but even so she walked through a door and a few minutes later a tall, potbellied man with a glistening bald head came around the side. His eyes were deep set and dark, almost as dark as his scraggy beard.

"I'm Mr Iqbal, how can I help you?" he said. His voice was quiet and he mumbled as he spoke.

"Can we talk in private?"

"No, we talk here."

I told him about Anne-Marie, asked him why one of his cabs was following her on the night of Saturday 15th November. The two guys stopped playing pool; it was if the whole room went quiet. Then the phone rang with another booking and the girl answered it.

"I tell you, you need to get out of here, mate, and away from these premises. I know who you are and you are in big, big trouble, mate. You can't go around pinning the blame on me or my drivers. You're the bad one, now get out!"

The two men approached with pool cues. I started to beat a hasty retreat.

"Get out or I call the police," Iqbal said.

I turned. "But you guys know the truth of what happened at 32 Church Street." I was almost desperate.

"No, we know nothing. You killed her, mate, now come on, get out of here."

I started walking back but suddenly my way was blocked by two pool cues forming a barrier like two swords criss-crossing.

"Jenny, call the police," Iqbal called.

"Why?" I asked. "I've not done anything. I just want to know the truth about Anne-Marie, she said you were chasing her for debts."

For the first time Iqbal smiled. "She never used our cabs, mate, we wouldn't let her."

"Then why did she say she was scared because she owed you money?" I asked.

The 'swords' came down. Iqbal seemed to relax. The other two taxi drivers were smiling too.

"You didn't know her very well, did you, mate?" Iqbal said.

"No," I admitted. "Not very. Why?"

"She was up to high jinks, mate. We wouldn't let her in our cabs."

"Not if she paid double," one of the pool players chipped in.

The three men laughed.

"You're in big trouble, mate, now leave us alone."

I turned and left the building. I was more confused than ever. I had thought that Citi Cabs held the key to Anne-Marie's murder but it seemed they didn't or if they did, they weren't telling me.

Citi Cabs' office was on the corner of London Road, at the far end of the pedestrianised zone, not far from my flat due to a path that weaved between houses and the shops. I went out and turned left through the pedestrianised zone, my hands deep in the pockets of my Crombie coat. I felt tired and confused but I decided to venture into the McDonald's restaurant I visited every Monday on the way to the writers' circle. I went up to automated menu display and put through my order: a meal deal consisting of a triple cheese burger, drink and fries, then I stood around waiting whilst 'number 57' was processed. As I did so I watched the carousel screen advertise a new burger, British beef and job vacancies. The restaurant wasn't busy but I got the feeling people were looking at me, or maybe I was just being paranoid again. There was a mother sitting at a table eating a burger with her two primary school-aged children; a couple of teenage girls were looking at their phones, a black lad was cleaning the surfaces with a cloth and spray. Even so I couldn't wait to leave and get back to the sanctuary of my home. I took the brown paper bag and walked back through the pedestrianised zone and up the step path to Petersfield Hill and the house where I lived. The word 'murderer" had been washed off but there were egg stains on the window which I hadn't noticed before. Fortunately, the road where I lived was fairly quiet most of the time, it only really became busy during the rush hour as it was a cut through or 'rat run'. Not a lot of pedestrians walked by and the footsteps of anyone walking up the drive sounded on the gravel.

I went inside, drew the curtain and turned on the television just for the company. It was a dark day but still late afternoon, perhaps about 4pm. I made myself a cup of tea and sat on the stool in the kitchen watching the TV and eating my burger and fries – I decided to save the orange drink which was part of the meal deal for later. I'd just finished my dinner when there was a knock on the door. The police. Hinton and another officer. This time they had come to arrest me… again.

Once more those stiffened black plastic cuffs were placed on my wrists and I was hauled away to the waiting police car. I was in the depths of despair. Since that night with Anne-Marie my life had been thrown into utter turmoil and anguish. I felt desperately sorry for her housemate, Lisa, and her family and I hoped the police would catch whoever was responsible but whilst they were questioning me, they weren't looking for the real murderer or if they were they were no closer to catching him.

The police car stopped at the junction at the top of Petersfield Hill and then turned right onto London Road. It then drove over the M4. It was a fairly short distance to the police station: basically, to the left and at the back end of town where the library and the Pryzm nightclub were situated. The car pulled into the underground car park beneath the station. It was the third time I had been taken to that underground car park.

I was led up to the custody suite where I was searched again and surrendered my personal effects. The custody sergeant was seated behind a clear screen. He stood up and read the charge and my rights from a computer. I was again told I was still under arrest for suspicion of murder and that I would be held until being formally charged in the magistrates' court the following day. My heart started to pound. Right from the start I thought there would come a point when the police investigation into me would cease and I would be 'discharged' – if that's the right word – as a suspect, but I just seemed to be wadding deeper and deeper into the mire.

"Look, I need to see a solicitor," I said. "I need to make another statement. You need to know the truth; I need this to stop, for fuck's sake, it's doing my head in."

"OK, we like the sound of that. A brief can be arranged," the custody sergeant said.

I was placed in a cell whilst they waited for the duty solicitor to arrive at the station. About an hour or so later – it was difficult to know the time with no watch or clock (not that I had one since my Hugo Boss watch had been 'lost' in the police station earlier) – my solicitor arrived and I was taken to the interview room to meet her. It was a different solicitor this time, Hannah Stavonsky from a local firm called Breakspear & Venables. She had straight brown hair which fell to her shoulders and she wore a light grey, brushed trouser suit. On the table in front of her was a purple zip-up folder. I told her I had not been happy with the two 'no comment' interviews and I wanted to answer the questions in full as, now I was clearly going to be formally charged, I wanted to clear my name. We talked for a while about the case, the evidence against me and what I had done previously. She was quite impressed that, apart from one relatively minor incident, I'd not been in trouble with the police before.

"Do you realise the police may use anything you say against you? If there's any contradictions or inconsistencies in your story, it'll be used in court?"

"I understand that," I said. "The thing is I typed out a statement and then gave a voluntary interview without a solicitor being present and I want to correct a few things. They have that interview so they will use that against me. I'm just sick of all of this. I just want to clear my name and get out of here."

"Do you have a copy?" Hannah asked.

"No."

"Alright I'll get one from the Senior Investigating Officer, you said his name was DCI Hinton, didn't you?"

"Yeah."

Hannah got up and went outside, and a few minutes later she returned with a clean copy of my statement.

"Let's go through it, shall we, and see what you said and what you want to add," she suggested.

So, we sat huddled together going through what I'd written. It felt a bit like being seated next to my manager Helen as she looked over some figures I'd compiled for her. By that time, I had my computer back (after all there was nothing on it of significant interest although, through my recovered search history, they had managed to get some more circumstantial evidence against me) and, in addition, I had noticed that my statement had been deleted. They had also returned my wallet, cash and car but not my glasses, which were expensive and tinted, as well as some items of clothing and some books and my diary.

Once we'd gone through the statement Hannah said, "Are you ready for them to come back in?"

I said I was.

"If you don't know just answer 'no comment', the worst thing to do is try and guess or give inaccurate or misleading information which the police investigation contradicts. You will give them something to latch on to. And don't provide too much information, the rule is to only answer the question you're being asked honestly and then stop. Don't ramble on, don't elaborate, don't say any more than you feel you want to or you need to. Is that clear?"

I said it was. I thought about all the 'inaccurate' and 'misleading' information I had already provided to the police – I'd certainly made a rod for my own back. Talk about a naïve fool! One of the reasons I wanted to make a fresh statement was because I was aware of what Drake had written on her A4 pad, namely 'cupboard' and 'taps' or, due to a misspelling, 'tapes'. It was obvious what the words meant, 'check for fingerprints' and whilst my dabs were on the kitchen cupboard doors, they weren't on the taps. I needed to explain why not.

I remembered that the taps were a few inches apart and my story was going to be that the shirt I was wearing was too long in the sleeve (due to my skinny arms and quite tall physique it was difficult to get shirts shorter in the arms and longer in the body) and when I'd gone to turn on the tap the cuff had gone over my hand and momentarily covered it. I had then let the water run so I'd only touched it once more to turn the tap off. I had tried this at home, with another identical shirt, during the days following the first police interview when I had been trying to think of anything that could link me to the murder. It was plausible although it would not account for the complete absence of any finger-marks and, if believed, it could be misconstrued as an attempt to avoid leaving them.

The other thing I wanted to explain was my use of cash after 15th November, which had been raised in my last 'no comment' interview. Debbie had supported my story that she had repaid me some money she had borrowed from me, so I wanted to ensure I made the police aware that was indeed the case.

At last, we were ready and DCI Hinton came back into the room. With him was DI Alison Drake. It was strange because Hinton had never told me his first name although I had discovered it was 'Dave' due to him being addressed as 'Dave' by Alison. DI Drake had introduced herself as 'Alison Drake' when we'd first met but I guess Hinton was old school.

Hinton started the recording equipment. He said a bit for the recording apparatus, time, date who was present in the room, and then he drew my statement from his folder. I wanted to just add bits to my existing statement but once again Hinton stole the initiative. He said he would rather I made a fresh statement.

"Let's go back to the night of Saturday, 15th November," he said, taking a deep breath. "Talk me through your evening from the time you left your flat and drove around to collect your friends."

So I explained again, how I had driven around to Mark's flat (which he owned, of course) and then to the rented house which Suggo and Dave shared with two others. I had parked up on King Edward Street and then we'd met Matty in a bar in town called the Crazy Horse. Later we'd walked out of town to Pryzm nightclub which was located on the corner of a busy junction, a few streets away from the pedestrianised area.

"And how did you meet Anne-Marie MacDonald?"

Again, I explained our meeting, how she had approached me in the nightclub. Hinton kept glancing at the statement I'd made previously but I knew I was keeping quite closely to it – after all it was the truth. So, we went through it in detail: the guys I'd seen her chatting to in the nightclub earlier in the evening, the minicab that had followed us and how I had subsequently arrived back at her house.

"We noticed in your car, which we took away for forensics, there were old contact lenses on the floor, are they yours?" Hinton asked.

"Yes, daily disposables."

"And when did you take them out?"

"When I left Anne-Marie's house."

"Not as you went in?"

"No."

"Are you sure?"

"Of course, I'm sure."

"You weren't wearing glasses when you entered her house?" Hinton insisted.

"No."

"So how do you explain traces of her blood on your glasses?" Hinton questioned.

I explained the flyer from the Pryzm nightclub, the papercut. Stupidly I'd not included it in the first written statement which had ended just before I had entered the kitchen, and to be honest I'd forgotten about it, it had seemed so trivial.

"Right, you are now in the house with Anne-Marie, what happened next?" Hinton quizzed.

"We went into the front room. I saw the Citi Cab out of the window and told Anne-Marie and she came to the window too, she seemed pretty frightened. She said she owed them money. Then she asked me if I wanted a cup of coffee. I said I did. She went to the kitchen and opened up some kitchen cabinet doors and took out a jar of coffee."

Whereupon I noticed a white envelope bulging with cash – is what I didn't say.

"You saw her do that?" Hinton asked, trying to catch me out.

"Saw? Good God no! Heard. I was sitting on the sofa by that time."

"So, the whole time she was making the coffee you sat on the sofa?" Hinton queried.

I rubbed my neck, feeling the hair ends of my mullet with my clammy hands. I felt hot, nervous. My foot tapped constantly. Jesus, it was nerve-wracking but I knew I had to stay strong. I needed to be focused.

"Yes, yes, sitting on the sofa."

"You didn't go into the kitchen?" Hinton pressed.

"No."

"You didn't stand at the door and look into the kitchen?" Hinton quizzed.

"No."

"Then what happened?" Hinton asked.

"She made me a cup of coffee, I got up and walked to the kitchen door to collect my cup."

"There's a fibre from your shirt on the kitchen door frame," Hinton said. "How do you explain that?"

"I guess I may have leant on the door jamb when I collected the coffee... Anne-Marie called to me and asked me to take my mug... I guess she didn't want to carry two."

"We have reason to believe that there may have been a considerable amount of money in the kitchen cupboard. Did you see it?"

"No."

"Did Anne-Marie mention it?"

"No."

"What time did you retire to bed?" Hinton asked sarcastically.

"I don't know, maybe half an hour later."

"You know Debbie King?" Hinton asked.

"Of course, yes, she is... was my girlfriend."

"Well, she describes games of a sexualised nature you'd play together – with you being the dominant

party, bondage and such like – is that so, Mr Turner?"
Hinton asked.

I shook my head; I could not believe Debbie would
have told the police something as personal as that.

"It was mild stuff."

Drake fixed me with a long stare. "It's still a sex
game with you as the dominant party. Did you play a sex
game with Anne-Marie?

"No, no, of course not."

"Did it get out of hand? Did she get annoyed? Did
you perhaps argue?" Drake took over the questioning.

"No!"

"When you decided to leave, did Anne-Marie pursue
you downstairs and challenge you?" Drake pressed.

"No, she was asleep when I left."

"But you have played sex games with Debbie King?"
she asked.

She was right, I did play sex games with Debbie. I
was a dabbler not some committed S&M fetishist freak.
I liked to experiment. It was just a bit of fun and Debbie
enjoyed it. We never did it at her house but when she
came to my flat for dinner, we sometimes played some
kinky games. I'd watched stuff online at uni and then,
when I'd started to use sex workers, I'd got to try it for
real. It was no big deal but I was beginning to see the
police had a narrative: *Turner went back for sex, he tried
to initiate a sex game but it had gone wrong and he'd
strangled her.* Rough sex gone wrong. That was the

motive, it was the thing they had been looking for. It was all mutual stuff but clearly the police had found evidence of this and linked S&M to Anne-Marie's death – at that stage I didn't know what. I didn't know a lot of stuff. But they had their motive, and perhaps the missing money too which was what I had thought they would be asking me about. It was just so hard to 'second guess' their 'lines of enquiry'.

Hinton continued. "Look, it could be manslaughter rather than murder, if it was an accident. When I say 'accident' I mean if you didn't mean to kill her. If you just explain what happened… we might be able to persuade the CPS to accept a lesser charge of manslaughter, how does that sound?"

"But I didn't do it," I spat with mounting frustration. "I did not do it. I did NOT do it!"

"But you do you like sadomasochistic sex games, Mr Turner. You like rough sex. How did Anne-Marie react to that?" This was Alison Drake.

Hannah intervened. "My client doesn't have to answer that question, there is no evidence that he had played a sex game with the victim."

Drake didn't give up. "Was it a sex game that went wrong that then led to an argument? Did you kill Anne-Marie accidentally?" Drake took a photograph out of her folder. "I am now showing Mr Turner a photograph of Anne-Marie's neck."

The photograph was a close-up of her white neck with a red mark across her throat. It was a bit unnerving, looking at a photograph of a dead person – it was the first time I'd ever seen anyone I knew dead.

"She didn't die of strangulation, did she?" I asked.

"Didn't she?" Drake quizzed. "You tell us."

"It's just that in the last interview one of you mentioned a knife. A kitchen knife I think."

Hinton gave me a tight-lipped smile. "So, you were listening despite the 'no comments'?"

"Of course I was!"

Drake tapped the photograph like a teacher to an errant pupil.

"Bringing you back to this photograph, Mr Turner, did you cause those injuries to Anne-Marie's neck?"

"No."

"But you enjoy rough sex?" Drake asked.

"No."

"But you played sadomasochistic games with your ex-girlfriend, Debbie?"

"Yes… but this was different…."

"How different?" Drake pressed.

"It was a one-night stand."

"So, you have no idea how she got the marks on her neck?"

"No."

"Did Anne-Marie at any time wear a short satin dressing gown with black edging and a black tie?" Drake asked.

"No."

"Did you see it hanging up on her bedroom door?"

"No."

"Did you use the tie from her dressing gown to strangle her as part of a sex game?" Drake pursued.

"No."

"Where is that tie now, Mr Turner?" Drake probed.

"I don't know, I've never seen it."

Then it was Hinton's turn. "I am now showing Mr Turner a photograph of the victim's body."

He placed the photograph on the table. It was certainly harrowing. Anne-Marie was lying by the coffee table, her feet pointing towards the kitchen, only one leg was buckled and bent under her. I would have thought it bloody uncomfortable if she hadn't been dead. Her right hand was stretched out and rested on the coffee table as if she had attempted to grab hold of it. Her hair was strewn on the floor. Her cream-coloured negligee with black edging was open and exposed her breasts and pubic area. It was the first time I had seen the garment. Her eyes seemed to stare at the ceiling, blank and expressionless. Her mouth was wide open as if she were about to utter one last breathless cry into the moonlit room. One last cry of life before being shrouded in the darkness of death's finality. There was a small stain of blood on her chest and on closer inspection you could see the crimson syrup smeared across the satin robe.

Hinton must have registered the shock on my face for all he could say was, "Any ideas, Richard?"

I shook my head. "No, none at all."

Hannah placed a consoling hand on my arm.

Hinton slowly removed the photograph and placed it back in his folder.

"So, you have no explanation for the stab wound or the marks on Anne-Marie's neck?"

"No," I said quietly. I was in a state of anaesthetised shock.

"When you went to leave the house, Anne-Marie didn't challenge you in any way? Upset because of something that had happened in the bedroom or perhaps an attempted theft from the kitchen cupboard?"

"No."

"Did you lose your temper with Anne-Marie?" Hinton pressed.

"No."

"Did Anne-Marie upset you in some way?"

"No."

"Did she confront you when you stole the money from the kitchen cupboard?"

"What money? I never stole anything!" I pleaded.

"Was she upset because you had tried to initiate rough sex against her will?"

"No, no, of course not."

"How do you explain Anne-Marie's death then?" Drake countered.

"I can't. I wasn't there."

"Did you argue in the front room? You were trying to leave, she challenged you about something, didn't she?"

"No, I've already said she was asleep when I left!"

Drake wasn't listening. "Rough sex or money, come on, Richard, just tell us what happened in the kitchen and front room of 32, Church Street in the early hours of Sunday, 16th November."

"I didn't do it! I did not do it!" It was so frustrating it was untrue.

Hinton sighed and looked at me with his beady little compound insect eyes. Drake sat with her hands clasped in front of her, covering her pad, as if she were protecting it from my prying upside-down reading eyes.

"OK, so let's look at this period when you left the house. Before that you say you had been to the toilet, you had a headache, although you hadn't drunk much alcohol due to driving. In searching for a paracetamol, you found and I quote 'a condom half filled with cocaine' – is that correct?"

"Yes."

"How did you know it was cocaine?"

"White powder, I guessed that was what it was."

"But you've told us previously that you've never used Class A drugs," Hinton stated.

132

"That's right."

"You went back to bed but still couldn't sleep and so you put your clothes on in the landing and went downstairs, is that right?"

"Yes."

"Then you thought you would get a drink of water and you went to the kitchen, is that correct?" Hinton asked.

"Yes."

"Driving-wise, how far is it from Anne-Marie's house to yours?" Hinton asked.

"Ten, maybe fifteen minutes," I said.

Hinton pounced. "You couldn't wait that short period of time to have a drink of water?"

"It was an impulse."

"OK, so you walk into the kitchen, then what?" Hinton asked. "Talk us through what happens next."

"I opened the cupboard doors, just along from the sink looking for a glass," I said.

"Both of them?"

"Yes, yes, I think so, I can't remember exactly."

"And did you find one?" Hinton fired.

"No," I said, wondering, not for the first time, why so many questions were repeated – I guess to catch me out.

"Did you see anything else in the cupboard? An envelope filled with money for example."

"No."

"Did you find a glass?"

133

"No. I took the cup out of the sink I had drunk out of earlier."

"Did you rinse it?" Hinton asked.

"I might have done, I think so."

"And what tap did you use? Was it the right one?" Hinton asked.

Scarrott, (you will be introduced to him later in this *narrative,* and that's a word my barrister liked to use a lot), would say that this is where I used my 'graduate-educated brain'. I realised in that moment, don't ask me how, but I just did, that the SOCO had fucked up: they hadn't dusted the left tap, the hot tap and by the time they'd realised their mistake the crime scene had been compromised. It was like a light bulb moment. It was a bit of luck. A straw that you grab hold of and clutch on to for dear fucking life. It was like Drake writing 'tapes' not 'taps' – it seemed to be destiny, it seemed to be my way out of the heavy rain that pelted down on me from dark, foreboding criminal justice clouds.

I rubbed my hand through my short hair and fiddled with my mullet. Then I took a deep breath and tried to compose my supercharged, pounding heart. "I'm not sure but it was definitely the hot tap," I said. "The water was warm so I took a sip and tipped it down the sink."

Hinton looked at Drake; they were disappointed, I could see that. The left tap was hot and the right one was cold. I knew in that moment I'd guessed right. Drake had gone back to check my prints on the taps and the left tap had not been dusted! The police had fucked up. Just to reinforce my sense of certainty that I had got a break at long, long, long last, Hinton asked,

"Are you sure about that?"

"Yes, I remember clearly now because the water was so warm, I couldn't drink it," I said, mainly for the benefit of the recording.

"Did you then try the cold tap?" Hinton asked.

"No, no, only the hot tap, I only turned on one tap and it was the hot tap. I used it to rinse the cup out, I remember now (*of course I fucking did, I was on a roll!*) and then for the water." *You're not catching me out on that, Hinton*, I thought. So, I didn't need my 'shirt too long in the sleeve' story after all – the SOCO messing up had given me a better one: I had used the hot tap to get a drink of water and no one could prove otherwise.

The questions went on, of course. They showed me a photograph of the knife block only with one knife missing. Then a photograph of a knife identical to the one missing from the block which was about six inches long and tapered.

"Have you ever seen it? Or one like it?" Drake asked.

"No," I replied.

Then there was the red throw over the back of the sofa; that was missing too. I said I did remember it but I had no idea where it was. Then I was asked about two mobile phones that were in Anne-Marie's handbag. A

135

handbag which, according to the photograph I was shown, was still open on the coffee table.

"Where are the knife, the tie from Anne-Marie's dressing gown, her two mobile phones and that throw now?" Drake asked.

I shook my head. I was now feeling quite confident. "No idea."

"Not at the bottom of the canal?" Drake asked.

"I dunno," I said.

"You passed the canal on the way home," Hinton said.

I agreed I did.

The scenario was becoming clear, Anne-Marie had confronted me over the theft of the money or we'd argued over something, possibly a sex game that had gone wrong, I'd stabbed her with a kitchen knife and wrapped it in the red throw. Then discarded that, along with her two phones and the tie from her wrap, in the canal as I'd driven home (police divers were in the midst of searching the freezing cold water).

"Did you touch anything else before you left?" Hinton asked.

"Only the front door."

"Then what? Explain what you did next."

I paused and took a sip of water which Drake had kindly got me one during a brief interlude. "Look, I've explained all this. I got in the car. I turned on the engine and tried to defrost the windscreen, whilst that was happening, I took out my lenses and dropped them in the foot well on the passenger side. I put on my glasses. The screen wasn't clearing so I got out and scraped it a bit. I was facing up Church Street towards Latimer Road and when I got out of the car, I could see a BMW which was dark blue or black parked further up the street with two men in it. They appeared to be watching me. It unnerved me a bit and so I got back inside."

"Why did it unnerve you?" Hinton asked.

"It was early in the morning, I thought they looked suspicious and they were eyeballing me – or at least one was."

"Then you drove off?" Drake asked.

"Yes."

"What time was that?"

"4.30am – actually probably closer to 5am."

"Oh, for a dashcam," Hinton said. "You won't be surprised to know we've not been able to trace the car. We've checked ANPR on the M4 and no Beamers joined it at that time. Could have used different roads, of course, but we don't know where it was heading, do we?"

It was typical of my luck, a cheap dashcam could have saved me a mountain of trouble, although to be fair, with the ice on the windscreen I doubt if it would have recorded anything of significance. Even so, if the police had had a registration, then they might have been able to trace the car – because if the killer or killers were not from Citi Cabs then they must have been the men sitting in that car.

"Is there anything else you wish to add?" Hinton asked.

"No, that's it," I said.

The interview went on a lot longer than that but I've just given a précis of the more salient bits … or at least things I can remember, this is not a verbatim account by any means. For example, at some stage, I did mention the money and Debbie giving me back some cash in the carpark at the museum, which quickly shut down that line of questioning. You will appreciate I felt under a lot of stress, my heart raced, I had developed a permanent twitch or pulsing just above the right eye and my hands trembled, not through nerves, but just some involuntary spasm that came thundering through my body like a wave washing over a pebbly beach. I was taking pills but I couldn't sleep for long. I was constantly tired and physically and mentally drained. My mind was mired in a deep, unrelenting fog. I feared the policemen's knock, the interview, not being believed, a trial, facing a lifetime in jail…

At the end of the session, Hannah asked for time alone with me. When Hinton and Drake had left the room, she went to her leather bag and extracted a legal aid form.

"Do you want our firm, Breakspear & Venables to represent you? We're happy to act for you in this case,

Richard, but we'll need to apply for legal aid. Or do you have another firm of solicitors who you would like to represent you? If you do, I will pass on today's details."

"No," I said, I was totally deflated. "I'm more than happy for you to take the case."

"Good."

Hannah combed her hand through her fine, light brown hair and eased the form over to me. We sat together going through the various elements. I signed it as well as another form about my personal details, next of kin etc.

After a sleepless night in the cell, I was taken to the magistrates' court in the morning. I was asked to confirm my name and address and the charge was read out to me. I pleaded 'not guilty'.

Hannah represented me in court; there was another solicitor, from the same practice, seated behind her. Hannah looked fresh and breezy, wearing a black, pinstriped skirt suit. She smiled at me as I was brought into the dock cuffed to a security guard. It was nice to know there were people who believed in me, who had my back and would look after me. How defendants represent themselves I do not know. Firstly, you have to negotiate the legal quagmire but more importantly than that is the feeling that someone is doing their best to set you free: without that any defendant would surely be in the pit of despair.

Hannah made no application for bail, which is rarely granted in extremely serious cases anyway, and so I was to be remanded in custody. I was taken down to a cell below the magistrates' court as they had to sort out transportation to the prison where I would be held until my trial. The transport arrived later that afternoon.

Chapter Six

The next stage of my nightmare started on 23rd November when I was remanded in custody for a crime I hadn't committed. I was taken away in a prison van which the lags nickname 'a sweat box' because its freezing cold in winter and as hot as hell in summer, to the prison where I was going to spend my time on remand. We arrived through sliding metal gates, bookended by two small turrets, into a netted compound surrounded by curls and curls of razor wire on top of castle-thick walls. The double-gated entrance led to another double-gated entrance which led to an open space covered by mesh netting: I guess to stop a James Bond style helicopter escape and drones delivering drugs and other contraband. I think there were about six of us taken off the sweat box but I can't be sure as my mind was in a blur. We were taken off the van one at a time and escorted into the 'processing area'. There were CCTV cameras everywhere and guards stood around with Alsatians on leads.

Once inside, we sat around and stared at the floor whilst some youngster in a bloodstained vest kept pacing up and down, swearing, looking to the heavens and shrieking at the top of his voice. Now, I'm no shrink but it looked to me like he had some 'serious mental health issues' going on, and would be the first of many such inmates I would encounter who probably needed psychiatric help rather than incarceration. I tried not to make eye contact with him as he seemed totally unpredictable and extremely volatile. When my name was called, I gave my details and then I was photographed and assigned a prison number. I was given a photo ID card with my name and date of birth on it and told I had to have it on me at all times. My property was stored away in a cupboard box with items listed on a property card. As I was on remand, I was allowed to keep my own clothes which I had to remove. Then I was searched big time, a whole-body search. Turn this way and that, arsehole – the full works. They searched orifices I didn't even know I had and, through the use of a BOSS chair (which is a whole-body metal detector), they did an internal examination too. Next it was the nurse.

"Have you self-harmed?"

"No."

"Do you take illicit drugs?"

"No."

"Are you on any medication?"

"No."

"Do you drink alcohol?"

"Moderately."

"How many units a week?"

"Maybe ten."

"Have you ever suffered from any mental health issues?"

"No."

"Do you have suicidal thoughts?"

Fuck me, yes, yes, yes – who wouldn't have? "No".

I was then assigned a personal officer who was a screw who would be my 'point of contact'. Look, in truth I don't know what order all this stuff took place, my brain was so muddled and addled and sleep-deprived it was all a total fucking blur. I was in a state of complete and utter shock, but I was pushed from pillar to fucking post until I was finally 'processed'.

When it had all finished, I was given bedding and a starter pack containing milk, tea, sugar, shower gel, razors, shampoos and a non-smokers pack with some orange squash and some biscuits. After that I was told I had to buy what I needed from my weekly 'wage'. I was given a phone card and a six-digit pin number and was told I could make one phone call that night for two minutes only. I phoned my sister Kate, who I thought would be sympathetic.

"I don't know what it is with you, Rich, you're always in trouble," she said when I told her the sorry saga.

"No, I'm not!" I protested.

It wasn't quite the reception I'd had in mind or wanted. I felt shit about myself and had hoped Kate would be a sympathetic ear. I thought, maybe I should have phoned Donna instead. The problem was Mum had always been a bit of a cold fish with me, maybe because I reminded her of Dad or because Dad had favoured me over the girls. Mind you, I only had a short time to talk to Kate and after her initial shock she was OK...ish.

Next, I was taken down dark grey corridors to my allocated cell on the first night wing on C. I was allowed to have a shower then it was back to the cell. I completed my menu sheet for the following day's meal (I had missed the evening meal) and then I lay on the thin mattress, with my arm over my eyes. I thought of the terrible turn of events that had brought me to prison awaiting trial for murder and I'll tell you how I felt: FUCKING ANGRY. It burnt me up inside. Ate at me. Gnawed away at me. The injustice of it all. I was seething with rage but without a release. I tried to calm myself down. Tried to take stock but it was no use. I could not stop the random thoughts of violence and hatred that circulated through my head, fuelled by my hyperventilating heart that pumped blood so quickly through my thin veins that I thought any minute I was going to breach like a whale and squirt a deep red ink-like fluid all over the cell.

After a sleepless night, the next day after breakfast I was moved to a claustrophobic, cramped cell with a skinny twenty-four-year-old who I dubbed The Willow Man due to his thin, willowy physique, pigeon chest and pallid complexion. The guy was coming off drugs and was paranoid and neurotic, which didn't help matters. He had *Manchester United* tattooed right across his chest from one pec to the other – a chest, which for reasons better known to himself, he seemed keen to display at frequent intervals. We were on the 'twos' – or the second floor. He was on remand for burglary, amongst other things like breaching an ASBO which had been imposed due to his frequent shoplifting and he was doing cold turkey due to a serious drug habit. He was quite apologetic but kept using the dirty exposed metal toilet and being sick. Of course, the cell reeked. Nice. He had the bottom bunk and I had the top. In the middle of the cell was a window with thin white metal bars across; you couldn't really see out due to the thick glass. If you did manage to look out all you could see was horizontal netting, a mesh fence on super-high posts and razor wire. Under the window was a grey, indestructible table and two chairs all attached (everything in prison is designed not be broken but some of it was and if not broken certainly well past its sell-by date – or should that be 'cell by date'?). At the end of the bunks was the stainless-steel toilet with a screen across to afford at least some privacy (Prison Rule 28 – access to a toilet and personal hygiene including a bath or shower at least once a week, well, I had to read something, didn't I?). On the other side was a washbasin with a metal mirror above it. Next to that, in the corner, was a locker and a pinboard for photos etc. There was a plastic mattress and pillow and the prison issue bedding I'd been given in the reception area (Prison Rule 27 – access to own bedding). Nice of 'em.

In a way it was good that The Willow Man had diarrhoea and sickness as he couldn't see me lying on the bunk with my hand across my eyes as my body pulsated with sobs. I was at an all-time low. Mentally and physically drained. The life had ebbed out of me. I felt numb. Whilst the police were investigating, I thought I had a chance, I thought it was routine, I thought the fucking nightmare would end. However once I was charged, even though Hinton's statement in the paper had indicated they were still seeking information, particularly about the Beamer, I knew they were building a case against me and they were probably just looking to 'eliminate' other 'suspects'. After all, the Crime Prosecution Services or CPS, felt there was enough evidence to charge me. They would instruct a barrister or a QC and his or her mission would be to send Richard Andrew Turner to prison. For life.

In the first week I had to do an induction programme with lots of videos and talks from the chaplaincy or faith team, the drugs team, the medical team, the education team, the probation team, the gym team, Mr T and the fucking A Team: I had to attend the lot. I had a visit from Donna and Kate and that helped a bit. They were shocked to see me and they both held back the tears but at least it was a contact with the outside. At least there were people who still cared about me.

The thing I noticed about prison was the lack of handles on the inside of any doors. Also, it sounds obvious, but the keys: the constant locking and unlocking and jangling of fucking keys like Marley's ghost with his chains in Dickens' *A Christmas Carol*. The other thing was the smell: apparently prisoners used to get free shower gel but now it had to be paid for and that meant there were a lot of smelly, sweaty bodies. There were also a lot of people like The Willow Man who were constantly sick, shaking or had the shits as they came off drugs – not nice when the exposed toilet was in your bedroom. There was one guy, twenties, white, Nike trackie, tatts, crew cut who smelt of urine. Constantly. Whenever it was my luck to be behind him in the lunch queue, I was put off my food by the odour of piss emanating from his every pore, and believe me it's not hard to be put off prison food. He was a bloody hard bastard so I didn't like to say anything about his lack of personal hygiene.

Then there were the rules. There were national rules and local rules for each prison. It was a bit like The People's Republic of Wormwood Scrubs (for example!). I was told that if I contravened any rule, I'd be given two sheets of paper, a DIS 1 or 'nicking sheet' which would tell me what offence I'd committed and what I'd been charged with and another, DIS 2, which would give me information about the hearing or adjudication and an opportunity to write a statement: basically, I'd be hauled off to see the Governor for a kind of tribunal. If I pleaded guilty or was found guilty, I'd lose my IEP status (Incentive Earned Privileges) and I'd go back to basics or I'd lose other privileges.

The Willow Man, when he didn't have his head over the toilet or was sitting on the fucking thing, was quite informative about all that sort of stuff and he told me what to expect. I learnt his name was Ian and he had, in his words,

"Done quite a few tours of duty."

He said that his ambition had been to join the army but he had failed the medical (amongst other things). He'd then got hooked on drugs but he wanted to come off the 'shit' and go straight. He was actually quite a nice lad. Harmless. Led astray. He'd been to a special school, which he'd never really attended, and couldn't read or write. He had drifted into crime as that's what people did on his estate but it was the drugs that had, in his words, 'fucked me up big time'.

"I'd work in a supermarket, warehouse, anything, me, if anyone would have me," he said to me one day.

He was always telling me he was 'no good' at something; whatever he tried he said he was 'no fucking good'. His mother had called him 'the bastard' because she had no idea who his father was. Apparently, she had become pregnant after a one-night stand whilst on holiday in Ibiza and told him she'd only kept him, rather than 'getting rid' because he was 'good for benefits'. She had been 'made up' when he'd been diagnosed as having 'special needs' as it meant an increase in her benefits as he was then classed as having a 'disability'. Then, imaginatively, to increase her 'bens' still further she had become his 'carer'. Some carer, some mother. Children are the key to the benefits door.

The biggest thing for me though was the noise. The reverberation of metal on metal as doors were slammed and locked accompanied by the constant shouting, yelling and wailing of the inmates and the echoes of footsteps on the landings. Then, when something happened the prisoners would give the heavy steel doors a right kicking. During the time I was on remand one of the inmates hung himself on a piece of electric flex at the end of his bed which led to a lockdown, which is when you're locked in your cells for a period of time: the doors were kicked for what seemed like hours. The din was incredible. I've never heard anything like it and shouts too.

"Fucking screws!"

"Kill the fucking screws."

"Murderers!"

Night was the worst time, the clunking of boots on metal stairs, the cries of inmates, the perpetual light (never quite dark so the screws can peer in from time to time and there are strip lights along the walkways; also, the CCTV needs light to be effective). And there's the echoes too and ghosts, for every prison is haunted, for every prison has had deaths: accidental, natural causes, suicide, murder or torture and at night the ghosts roam the corridors and walk ways and landings – there are more ghosts in prisons than there are in haunted castles. But more than that, in some ways at night, the prison came alive as prisoners, ever resourceful, moved stuff between cells. They would 'swing a line' by tearing things into lengths and affixing them with weights like soap or batteries, then they would tie objects onto the them and swing them through the barred windows to the adjacent cell.

I just couldn't sleep. At night I felt a constant pulsating in my left wrist and at the back of my head and in my neck. My heart raced and I often thought I was on the verge of a heart attack. All the pulses in my body seemed to go into over drive; each one Morsing a code to another part of my never resting body – dot, dot, dot; dash, dash, dash; dot, dot, dot – 'get me fucking out of here!' I was anxious all the time and had panic attacks:

my self-esteem and confidence were at an all-time low. When I eventually did drift off, I'd often wake up from nightmares. A recurring one was where the ceiling and sides of the cell were pressing in on me and the cell was gradually reducing in size. I thought I was going to be coffined. I suffer from mild claustrophobia and being confined in a small space didn't do that particular trait a whole lot of favours.

The unlocking was at about 8am. No need for an alarm clock in prison, if you can sleep for more than about three or four hours straight, you're doing well. To think I used to hate the people above me going for a pee in the middle of the night! God, those days were paradise. You'd hear the doors being unlocked further along the landing and know, sooner or later, it would be your turn. The Willow Man and I would go down to the canteen area and get a cup of tea and some cereal from the kiosk and then went back to our cell to eat it. How I wished I was lying in my soft, clean double bed, getting up to a bowl of cornflakes or a slice of toast and listening to the radio before driving over the M4 to work, as I say, paradise. Pure paradise.

My head was full of shit on the outside – what would happen to my flat? My job? My car? I'd think about people on the 'out' and how lucky they were and what they were doing. Then I started to think about other more practical things: direct debits, payments due, bills I hadn't paid. Naïvely, I'd just not considered any of that mundane stuff when I'd been arrested but suddenly, with nothing to think about, it became an overriding burden. I guess it was seeing my solicitor, Hannah, that brought it all home to me.

She greeted me warmly in the consultation room for our 45-minute meeting. It's strange because I think she quite liked me; she used to say I wasn't like her usual clientele, and we used to speak about other things which was great. She liked reading too and wanted to write a book about some of her clients one day but she was ambitious and the 'book could wait' – her ambition was to be 'called to the bar' i.e. become a barrister.

"Good news," she said during our first 'meet up' in the 'lock up'. "My firm, Breakspear & Venables, has got legal aid and we have taken on the case so that means we can start our preparation for the trial."

"The trial?" I said naïvely. "What trial?"

Hannah laughed and tapped her thick wad of papers with a silver pen. "Your trial. The CPS believe there is enough evidence to bring a successful prosecution against you…"

Her voice trailed off. My heart beat like a drum, tat-a-tat-a-tat. I just thought one day (sooner rather than later) a screw would open the door and say,

"Turner, out. The police have arrested someone else. You're free to go."

I buried my head in my hands. A trial. My head pounded as much as my heart beat. I already knew it, of course, but hearing the words, that was the worst thing. *Knowing* I was going to be placed on trial.

"I can't take it," I said. "I'm innocent."

In a warm gesture Hannah placed her hand on mine. Squeezed. She seemed to believe in me.

"Richard, I know it's hard for you but you have to stay strong. We'll get through this, you'll see."

"But I don't want to stand in the dock. I don't want to be cross-examined and accused of something I've not done." My voice rose like an opera singer's on the last notes of an aria. I just felt so, so frustrated.

"We'll mount a strong defence – the evidence is nearly all circumstantial," Hannah said. "Apart from a minor bit of forensics there is no solid evidence linking you to Anne-Marie's death."

"How long?" I asked.

"What? Before the trial?" Hannah asked.

"Yes."

"Well, it'll be next year, probably the spring. The wheels of justice don't move quickly, you're probably talking three months at least."

"Three months? Of this?"

"I'm afraid so."

And that's when I started thinking of all the things on the 'out' – stuff I'd not prepared for on the 'in'.

And there was a lot of time to think. The day was divided into sessions – or a 'sesh' – each one being about one and a half hours long.

153

At 10.30am, the first sesh was over and the mid-morning sesh commenced. Lunch was at 12pm. After I'd queued up for my food, which I'd chosen from a menu sheet, I was banged up for an hour or so which meant an hour of watching TV, lying on my bed listening to music on my MP3 player, falling asleep, reading or just staring at the eggshell blue ceiling (you tell me!) looking at graffiti and daydreaming. Fortunately, I've always been a person who's liked daydreaming, I used to get into trouble for it at school. I remember a teacher shouted at me once.

"Turner, concentrate, you'll never get a job staring into space."

Which had prompted one classroom wag to respond by saying,

"Yes, he will, he wants to be an astronomer."

Concentration has never been something I've been good at but daydreaming – well, that's another matter, I'm a bit like an iceberg: 70% of my life has been lived inside my mind and only 30% in the so called 'real world'. I quickly realised that to exist in prison I needed to escape. Physical escape was impossible (almost) so that meant escaping inside my mind through TV, reading, listening to the radio or music. Some of the other prisoners 'escaped' by getting stoned on spice, weed or other drugs, gaming, gambling, religion and gym work/exercise. For my part I tried to stop gambling whilst on remand – well, I had to try and take some 'positives' from the dire situation I was in.

At around 1.15pm the cell door was unlocked and I was off to the next sesh which was when I could do activities. The Willow Man often disappeared. I found out later that he was being assessed in regard to his mental health issues and was doing some sort of drug rehab: he went to some literacy classes too. Then at 2.30pm it was the mid-afternoon 'moves' where I was more or less free to do what I wanted, if that's not an oxymoron for life in prison. Then at 4pm it was back to the cell. At 5pm it was the evening meal and then 6pm association when I could mix with other prisoners and then 8.45pm lock up until the next morning. The times were a bit different at weekends; the day started about half an hour later: after all you needed a lie in after the heavy exertion of the week.

Wednesday was always a big day as debts were settled with the barons and other prisoners who had leant things. If debts weren't settled it became 'double bubble' whereby the debt doubled each week. If the prisoner didn't pay back the debt it led to 'beefing' or prisoners would get 'jugged' (sugar was added to boiling water and thrown in the prisoner's face). It was always tense on a Wednesday but I did better than most as I had people like Kate, Donna and Mark who'd buy stuff for me and send it in. I got some things for The Willow Man too as he had no one on the outside to look after him. Kate had quite a lot of disposable income and was very generous. You wear trainers all the time in prison so that was something Kate bought for me. If you're banged up it's not your toothbrush you shouldn't forget but your trainers.

I also got to realise that television was a big thing and could cause issues but fortunately The Willow Man was spewing, shitting or spaced most of the time so I had free rein in that regard. Not that I've ever been big on TV, and prefer a book, but in those very early days, I had to wait for Kate and Donna to buy me some books and send them in from the 'approved list' of retailers; fortunately they stocked most of the books I liked but I had to wait for the second visit (I was too distressed during their first visit and didn't know how the system operated) to give them a list of books I wanted to read and wait for them to be bought and posted into me (at my expense). In between times I managed to get to the library and get some books. One was on the kings and queens of England which I learnt by heart. I could have gone on *Mastermind*. I knew all the dates and everything as I used to repeat them endlessly to try to get myself to sleep. Rather than counting sheep I recited the kings and queens of England:

William, William, Henry, Stephen, Henry, Richard, John, Henry, Edward, Edward, Edward, Richard, Henry, Henry, Henry, Edward, Edward, Richard,

Henry, Henry, Edward, Mary, Elizabeth, James, Charles, Cromwell, Cromwell, Charles, James, William and Mary, Anne, George, George, George, George, William, Victoria, Edward, George, Edward, George, Elizabeth.

That little lot would send a raging insomniac off into the Land of Nod.

The other thing I did was write letters. I was allowed one letter a week, in terms of writing paper, envelope and a stamp. However, I was allowed to buy my own to supplement it. Snail mail is not dead in the criminal justice system, far from it, although there was also the prison email service. I was permitted to write to possible character witnesses like Kate, Donna, Mum and others like Claire but not Debbie or Mark or any of The Boys who would possibly be cross-examined about factual evidence in regard to the night in question and the days following it. Debbie's best friend wrote me a letter in which she basically told me that Debbie was OK: she was missing me and hoped I was 'bearing up'.

The letters took my mind off the drabness, the sadness, the waste of time, the utter, utter despair I felt. Alone and hopeless, washed up on the seashore of nothingness. Existing, not living. Day to day. Week to week. Each day the same as the last. The same routines, the same sense of pointlessness and hopelessness. The only changes were negative: someone 'beefing' another prisoner (fighting or arguing), a screw/prisoner stand-off, a big row somewhere. Violence always lurked just under surface and it didn't take much for the fuse to be lit. There was all this pent-up macho anger and aggression, a desire to prove, a desire not to be put down, a desire to move up the pecking older, a desire not to be bullied. If I had had to describe prison in three words they would have been: boredom, bravado and brutality. My father had been violent and although occasionally my bad temper had been known to get the better of me, I tried to curb my aggression and seek solutions not confrontation, but to some inmates confrontation was the only thing they knew. They literally did not have the tools in their toolbox to be able to deal with issues in a reasonable way. I saw a prisoner once berating someone in the kitchen because he'd served him the wrong food; it wasn't that he was really annoyed with the kitchen kid, it was just that all he knew was how to be aggressive when someone had made an honest mistake. Certainly, I wasn't a fighter and that led to a bit of bullying.

"You have to stand up for yourself, lad," one of the older lags told me. "Or you're going to be shat upon."

He was right.

The thing was I wasn't like a lot of prisoners and I got kicked in the shins, they took my food, they spat on me. The funny thing was it was 'nothing serious' I wasn't a target like a paedo or something I was just 'different'. Occasionally, I tried to fight back but it was a nightmare. When a fellow prisoner took my bread roll off my tray one dinner time, I grabbed his wrist and looked at the nearest screw but he just whispered,

"Snitches get stiches," so I released his wrist and let him take my roll. I knew you could never involve the authorities so I just got on with trying to keep clear of the drugs and the violence. I tried to make myself fit in a bit. I enjoyed a joke with the other prisoners and had discussions about football (I wasn't a big football fan but followed it enough to be able to give an opinion, although it led to some piss taking as I got names wrong or didn't know the players – also, being a Millwall supporter meant I was in a minority of one). I'd just respond in typical Lions fashion by chanting our anthem,

"No one likes us, no one likes us,

No one likes us, we don't care!"

I noticed how many prisoners had the scars from self-harming on their arms, cuts from razors that had healed white; their hands and arms were often covered with tatts – my solitary tatt of my Millwall lion was positively lonely in comparison. There were chip nets over each floor to stop suicides or inmates being thrown over, so when you looked at the ground at the pool tables it was just a mass of wire net.

In the first couple of weeks, I completed some forms about my education and did some tests so they could gauge my literacy and numeracy skills. Then I was sent to an assessor. He said to me,

"You're a clever bastard, Richard, more like you and I'd be out of a job."

"Not that clever as I wouldn't be here, would I?" I countered.

He laughed at that. There was no point in saying I was innocent. It was what everyone said.

"You should become a Toe-by-Toe mentor and help other prisoners with reading and literacy skills," the assessor said.

At that time, I was on £35 a week: money to buy phone credits, deodorant, shampoo, books etc. But I applied, and got accepted, on the Toe-by-Toe scheme which was a project sponsored by the Shannon Trust charity to help prisoners improve their numeracy and literacy skills. My pay rose to £51 a week but most importantly it gave me something to do. I enjoyed helping other prisoners and it stopped me thinking of my own dire situation.

Mr Vacarescu terminated my contract on my flat, and my sisters and their partners (Donna had started dating a guy called Wayne) collected all my things. They sold the furniture and TV and moved a few boxes back to Kate's house where they were stored in her loft. I was thirty years of age and my whole life consisted of some cardboard boxes and plastic containers stored in a loft at my half-sister's house. Wayne was a car salesman and he took possession of my Hyundai i20 which he sold on the forecourt, so I was able to use some bunce to pay off some of my more pressing debts. The police had given most of my things back by then though I had no clue what they had kept, apart from the glasses, shirt and trousers and some books. Kate sent some of my things to the prison: the photograph of her, Donna and Mum; the photo of Debs and Dylan camping in the New Forest; books I had requested; my rubber Millwall lion mascot which Dad had given to me when I was a kid which I thought of as a 'lucky charm' and some other bits and bobs that gave me at least some connection to my former life.

I just couldn't believe how messed up my life had become. Every day brought more and more bad news: the loss of my flat, a letter terminating my employment, letters chasing debt. It was just one piece of bad news after a fucking 'nother.

The thing I lived for were the visits. Some prisoners got loads, some got none. As I was on remand, I could have had daily visits but I had no one who could visit me that frequently. It was strange, often it was wives and children but other prisoners would have an endless string of girlfriends – the 'Marks' of the prison system. Donna and Kate were the only people who visited me regularly but they could only visit once a week. My ex-manager at Zorin, Helen, came once, as did Mum, only she spent the whole time moaning about the journey. She had had to get a tube and then a train and it had cost her an 'arm and a leg'. Mum had never taken a lot of interest in me and I knew she was just going through the motions so she could say 'well, I visited, didn't I?' She ended by saying, 'you'll be out soon, have to catch up then,' and perhaps that's what she believed but I knew it could go either way. I didn't like to think about the trial. I just hoped that someone would walk into a police station and say,

"The Anne-Marie case? It was me!" and hold out their hands ready for the cuffs. But life's not like that.

But that's what kept me going, someone admitting to it or else the police finding the real culprit or culprits but I knew, with me on remand, there was little likelihood of the police looking for anyone else. As far as they were concerned, they had arrested and charged the guilty party – because, of course, you're 'innocent until proven guilty' – yeah right! That's why they bang you up first and ask questions *after*!

Anyway, as I say I lived for the hour-long weekly visits from my sisters, Kate and Donna. They always came together, either on a Saturday or on Donna's day off from the hairdresser's which was a Monday. Even if their respective partners came with them, they would not come into the prison, nor my niece and nephews (Donna and Kate felt it would be too upsetting for them to go through all the security checks). I had no visits from Mark, Dave, Matty and Suggo, I think because they were witnesses, though I'm not entirely sure.

One time, during visiting, I was chatting to Kate and Donna when I became captivated by a drop-dead gorgeous blonde with golden skin and model-like make-up. She was wearing tight ripped blue jeans and skyscraper heels and she kept flicking her hair with her crazy, long red fingernails and each time, I'd get a hint of hair spray and perfume. She saw me looking at her and gave me a glossy, cherry-red smile and a wink. The problem was her partner, who resided on 'threes', noticed too. God, he was a beef cake! A muscle-bound hunk who could eat me for breakfast and spit out the bones. He eventually realised 'his girl' had attracted the attention of a prisoner behind and to the side and he gave me a look like a grizzly bear who hadn't eaten for eighteen months and had a red-hot poker stuck up his arse. I could almost feel the warm air from his nostrils as his crate-like chest lifted up and down and he fixed me with his big, brown eyes. Blondie stroked his arm and tried to get him back on track, but I knew I'd overstepped the mark. The Willow Man had said to me once, 'don't fuck around with anyone else's girl during visiting' (having told me how pretty he thought Kate was). His only visitors were his grandparents but they didn't visit him much.

Over the next few days, I was scared stiff. I found out the beefcake was a Russian mobster called 'Mad Vlad' (finding that out didn't make me shit scared, of course!) who ran an extortion and prostitution racket in London (being in prison doesn't stop a true 'businessman'). It was made worse by a fair-haired squirt on 'twos' who'd walk beside me or queue up behind me in the dinner line and say,

"V's gonna get you, nick, nick, nick, nick."

And do this clicking thing with his teeth. All his mates would laugh and that's when I knew I was completely on my own.

He got me one morning when we were on 'moves' – I was lured to a cell and given a beating the like of which you would not believe. His mate stood at the door laughing, whilst another was on the corridor on 'screw watch'. I was punched in the stomach five or six times, kneed in the face and then given a Tyson - (Fury or Mike – you can take your pick) like upper cut to the face which impacted with such force I hit my head on the bedframe. The thing was Mad Vlad didn't say a word during the assault. He just kept pummelling me. All I could hear was the impact of the punches and his heavy breathing. In the end I think a screw must have strolled along the landing as Vlad and the other guy bundled me out the cell, kicked me hard in the back and catapulted me on my way. My head fizzed and I felt pain in so many places: shins, legs, thighs, stomach, side of face, nose (broken), lips, mouth (both of which were bloodied), bruised eye (left), head (back of), it was impossible to process. Of course, he had stamped on my new glasses, which had been kindly supplied by Kate, during the assault and then, very thoughtfully, got a lackey to deliver the pieces to me in a clear plastic bag. I got back to my cell and lay on the bed and didn't appear again all day, telling the screws I was ill – I'd caught a bug.

"Fuck me, you look rough," The Willow Man said without a shred of irony in his voice. And I knew coming from him, I did look rough.

Donna and Kate were due to visit the next day but I had to cancel that and the next visit. I had learnt a lesson though – don't get distracted, look at your visitors and no one else. The Little Runt, who'd kept saying 'Big V's gonna get you, nick, nick, nick' now kept whispering 'ha, ha, ha, he got you' and 'that taught ya, tell the screws and it'll be sugar and boiling wata' – not that there was any likelihood of me telling the screws. Little Runt was obviously Mad Vlad's eyes and ears on twos so I knew not to cross him. Though a small skinny lad he seemed to have a lot of friends and was one of those that giggles, takes the piss and looks for laughs in every single situation. When the poor lad hung himself in his cell Little Runt appeared with a piece of flex and said, 'anyone seen any good hangings lately?' and, 'I've got spare flex if anyone wants to give it a try,' which drew laughter from his immature mates.

When I finally emerged from the cell a screw asked how I'd got my various blemishes so I told him I'd walked into a door which drew a laugh from the assembled crowd in the dinner queue.

In time I recovered enough from Mad Vlad's assault but I knew I had a reputation for being a bit weak so I started to go to the gym where a super-fit Polish guy took me under his wing and showed me the ropes but, of course, it takes years to develop good muscle definition and I'd never really exercised, not ever. Even so, I worked out as much as I could and I got all my hair shaved off (for the price of a tin of tuna) so I had a number one all over.

Slowly, I adapted to my surroundings. One day drifted into another. It's strange how you build up a kind of routine. It's human instinct, you are presented with a set of circumstances so you just adapt to them – I guess it's survival. You have no choice really but the human spirit is such that it tries to make the best of the situation. So that's what I did. I'd get to look forward to the little things like the visits and the letters. Also, the prison employed a 'writer in residence' and I managed to wrangle my way onto the group – it was a fantastic release. There were a few of us in the group and we were taught by a creative writing teacher paid for by a government grant. The teacher, Giles, came in once a week; he was a published author. At first, I didn't say much about my writing experience as I didn't want to appear to have any prior knowledge in front of the other prisoners, but eventually I admitted that I'd been writing since I was a teenager and had had a few pieces published. The other prisoners in the group were actually pretty good but had just not been given any opportunities. I really got on well with Giles and I wrote a piece for him, outside of the group, about prison life, which he liked.

"You could work on this article and send it to a newspaper like *The Guardian*; I'm sure they'd be interested," he said when I spoke to him one day after the group.

"I guess."

"Or you could base a thriller around your experiences."

"I suppose," I said.

"Whatever you do, you need to keep it up, Richard, don't give up," he said.

I tried to write but I felt depressed. I just couldn't believe what was happening to me. The thing was apart from my few visitors, the letters, the Toe-by-Toe and my writing group, I was in the pit of despair. I hated thinking about the impending trial. On one of her visits Hannah informed me that Breakspear & Venables had instructed a barrister called Mr Prentice to represent me. He would visit me once she, as senior solicitor, had compiled our case. She was supported by a junior solicitor called Jermain, who was a young black lad who wore snazzy suits and bright ties.

When Hannah had undertaken the initial work, Mr Prentice visited the prison. He was a probably slightly older than me though not much; he was of medium build with a schoolboy-ish face, collar-length hair and round, gold-rimmed glasses. He said he was very confident that we could mount a strong defence as he felt the prosecution case was built on circumstantial evidence, which made me feel better. Like a top surgeon, Mr Prentice made me feel that the 'operation' would be successful. The case was high profile in its way, an unusual crime which had gained a paragraph or two in the nationals and bit of internet interest. In fact, according to one of the letters I received, someone had posted a poem on Facebook which went like this:

"There was a girl called Anne-Marie,
Who had a fling with Richard T.
He stabbed her and left her for dead
Now he's lying on a prison bed!"

A few days after I first met Mr Prentice, Little Runt assaulted The Willow Man. The Willow Man kind of hung around with Little Runt a bit; they were similar age, had both done drugs and were both on remand for burglary of 'a dwelling' (a house to you and me). Little

Runt saw him as an easy-to-lead, sycophantic follower. It happened in the shower block. By all accounts Little Runt and one of his mates started taking the piss out of the size of The Willow Man's cock.

"You're got a shriveller, bruv," Little Runt apparently said.

"You must need a tea bag string to find it," his immature mate had added.

The Willow Man reacted and threw a few punches, so they grabbed hold of him and laid into him a bit.

It wasn't too bad as assaults go; a few rabbit punches, a headlock and a few whacks in the face, with soap in the eyes first to blind him, that sort of thing. Ironically, when I'd been allocated a cell with The Willow Man, Little Runt had approached me one day and said,

"You mess with Ian and I'll mess with you, you hear what I'm saying, bruv?"

A few nights later I overheard The Willow Man talking to himself on the bunk below. He was telling himself how rubbish he was and how everyone hated him because he was such a 'useless bastard'. I knew Little Runt's assault had affected him mentally and that gave me a resolve to do something about it. Life is about the survival of the fittest. It is the same on the 'out' as on the 'in'. However you dress it up, it all comes down to that and in human terms that means money, mental health and physical health – if you have all three you are top of the tree. Even if you commit a crime, if you have money, you are far less lightly to be caught as the likelihood is you'll commit a 'white collar crime' like fraud which is harder to detect, and law enforcement aren't so geared up to investigate and prosecute as it takes money, time and expertise. Even if they do you can buy your own justice – no matter what the crime – either by paying off your victim or law enforcement or hiring a good defence team that can get you off or get a lesser sentence: an open prison or a community sentence. That's how it works. People will say that justice is equal, fair-minded and blind, but that's an utter load of bollocks. 'Justice' is just a commodity like sex, like washing up liquid, like love, like cornflakes, like friendship, like beef burgers. 'Justice' can be bought and sold and that's why prison is only for poor people. The rich and/or famous buy their own form of 'justice' – a justice where their crimes, however big or small, are matched to minimal or no penalties.

Anyway, I attacked Little Runt in the dinner queue, I just went for him. I hit him on the head with a Millwall brick[1] and then went in fists flaying around like a

---

[1] *A Millwall brick is a tabloid newspaper folded up multiple times to make a hammer – you can see demos on YouTube. It dates back from the days of football hooliganism in the '70s and '80s. The police used to search for weapons on the way into football grounds but they couldn't stop fans entering grounds with their favourite tabloid. However a newspaper, when folded in a particular way, can be quite an effective weapon. My dad, who was allegedly once part of Millwall's notorious Bushwacker firm,*

windmill in a hurricane until I'd floored him. As I say, I'm not much of a fighter and try to avoid confrontation so I went in quick before he could retaliate: kicks, punches, head-butts. It was unprovoked and premeditated. A few minutes of madness in revenge for The Willow Man and 'Mad' Vlad's assault. I did it in the dinner queue because a) I wanted others to see, especially the screws, as I didn't want a prolonged fight and b) I was not as sneaky as Little Runt who had assaulted The Willow Man in the shower block and c) I wanted the other inmates to see I wasn't a 'soft touch'.

I was given a 'nicking sheet' by the screw that witnessed the assault and then, when it was time for the adjudication, I was hauled off to the Governor. I pleaded guilty, of course, and was put back on basics which meant I lost all my privileges like attending the writing group, which was a big loss, and being a Toe-by-Toe mentor.

---

showed me and Maureen's sons how to make one once in Brighton whilst he reminisced about his 'halcyon hooligan days' in the '80s including the infamous 'Battle of Kenilworth Road' when Millwall played Luton Town in the FA Cup in March 1985. He told us that if the police asked him why he had a newspaper in his coat pocket he'd say, 'Fuck me, have you ever seen Millwall play? If you're not reading a newspaper before half-time, you're doing well.' In this case I used The Sun *but other tabloid newspapers are available. Dad's mantra was always, 'Never admit to anything' and 'Never show them you're scared.'*

After the adjudication they moved me to a cell on 'threes'. I think the screws thought that because The Willow Man was a friend of Little Runt it would be a good idea to move me out to stop any further trouble. They said I wasn't coping well on remand and had seen a change in my behaviour: aggressive, depressed and antisocial (not sure how you can be antisocial in prison but anyway that's what they said) so they decided to put me in with an older lag who was also a Toe-by-Toe mentor who I'd seen about the place due to the mentoring we both did. Being on remand meant they had to ask me if I wanted to be moved into a cell with a convicted prisoner (Prison Rule 7). One time I'd seen him with another prisoner and had noticed how patient he was so I said, 'yeah, fine'. So, one day a screw told me to pack up my things and I just followed him upstairs with my stuff.

"Layfette, here's your new cell mate, Turner," the screw said (your first name is never used in prison).

Layfette was a tall, muscular black guy in his sixties. The cell was really clean and he'd made it quite homely. He even had his own bedding which he'd bought. He hadn't had a cell mate for a long while, preferring his own company. He was six years into a thirteen-year stretch (with parole). How did he end up inside? Well, I could tell you but I won't as I don't want him to be identified. He's still on the inside. He had a few jobs in the prison: the Toe-by-Toe, giving help and advice to

172

prisoners, mentoring new prisoners and assisting with the endless forms that have to be completed for absolutely everything. Generally, he was very well liked and respected.

"What's your first name?" he asked.

"Richard."

"I'm Dominic," he said. "Can you name one?"

"What?"

"A Turner."

"'What's Love Got to Do with It'."

He laughed.

"No, not Tina, the painter, J.M.W. Turner."

"I don't know any," I said.

"Well, *The Fighting Temeraire* would be one," Dominic replied. He then showed me round his 'humble abode'.

"I'm Bajan," he said.

"Come again?"

"I'm from Barbados… Bajan…everyone always thinks if you're from the Caribbean, you're Jamaican," Dominic said.

Although Dominic was in his mid-sixties, he looked about twenty years younger.

"Blacks don't crack," he said to me one day. "That's one thing we've got over you whities – we look younger for longer. We don't need no moisturiser to keep our good looks either."

I laughed.

He used to sit on his bunk kicking out his strong legs, pontificating about everything and anything. His bald head glistened in the half light as his heavy-lidded, sleepy eyes wistfully stared out of the window to the world beyond. He told me he was educated at the 'university of life' and he had mostly taught himself although sometimes he had attended prison courses and sometimes evening classes when he'd been on the 'out' but the biggest factor in his education was reading.

"Reading is climbing the tree of knowledge," he told me.

He became a really good friend, we still communicate. He was like a father to me. He protected me too; he worked out in the gym and was muscular. Of course, 'Mad' Vlad was on 'threes' but he knew Dom had my back. OK, I got called 'Dom's bitch' but I could handle that, it didn't bother me at all. The thing was Dom liked to dance and sing so we kinda formed an unlikely duo. The best song we performed together was KC and The Sunshine Band's 'Give it Up'. Dom used to sing to me,

"Everybody wants you,

Everybody wants your love,

I'd just like to make you mine, all mine."

And he'd clap his hands, pirouette and dance like KC in the video and then I'd come in with,

"Na-na, na-na, na-na, na-na-na-na now."

And we'd face each, slightly stooped, heads forward singing, trying to outdo each other with the 'na-na, na-na's' before Dom went into the chorus.

"Baby, give it up

Give it up

Baby, give it up."

Then we'd just fall about laughing, laugher which was often fuelled by spliffs Dom used to roll. He had matchboxes with weed in them hidden all around his cell.

"A bit of whacky baccy will help you calm down," he said one day when I told him about my insomnia and panic attacks.

Up to that point I'd not really smoked dope but was amazed at how relaxed and chilled I felt after a few puffs.

We talked about my case too. Dom asked a lot of questions about it.

"So how did they know it was you that left the club with Anne-Marie?" he asked.

"Social media."

"Not CCTV?"

"No," I said. "That was inconclusive, you can't really see much inside the club and coming out it is mainly the back of me – there could have been other guys who were dressed in a similar way, although the mullet I had at the time was a bit of a give-away."

"And they knew you'd been in her house due to fingerprints and DNA, before you gave your statement I mean?"

"Yes, probably, but they may not have had all the results back except the fingerprints," I said. "They lifted my fingerprints from the coffee cup and various items and, of course, skin particles in the bed etc, so a lot of evidence I'd been at the address which were a match for me on the PNC."

"What about your car?" Dom asked.

"I parked away from the nightclub so they didn't have that on CCTV either, the doorbell stuff was inclusive, no reg numbers. I guess my mates would have told the police I'd left with a girl. They could probably have worked out her movements but because she was on her own, they lost her in the club; she only bought one drink as far as they're aware."

"And you didn't take the money?"

"Fuck me, no," I exclaimed. There was no way I was going to admit to that little sin. Not to anyone.

Being banged up with Dom was great. The Governor, or whoever was responsible, had done a fantastic thing in moving me. When it was my birthday Dom got a very small cake from the kitchen with one candle on it. I was really touched as I hadn't really mentioned my birthday. I talked to Dom about my life, the opportunities I'd wasted, things I'd got wrong… in fact, I opened up to him and told him my life story. It bored me, and I'd lived

176

through it, but Dom had time on his hands and he listened and asked questions but he never, ever judged. He was a good man, Dom, a very good man. So, here's what I told him…

Chapter Seven

I was born into a working class, for want of a better phrase, family. We lived in a small three-bedroom, local authority house in South East London, OK, Bermondsey if you want to pin me down. My dad had an issue with alcohol which led to rows with my mother and domestic violence; he left when I was seven. After my dad left, I was brought up by my mum and two sisters who were five and four years older than me.

My older sister Kate, correction, half-sister (although in truth Donna and I never thought of Kate as anything other than our sister) was extremely pretty with long, blonde hair and bright, blue eyes. She had a very easy-going personality; she smiled and laughed a lot and on the whole people tended to like her. The story was that Dad's best friend had got Mum pregnant and then ran off to work on a North Sea oil rig, as you do, and Dad had stepped into the breach, perhaps relishing Mum's vulnerability. My other sister, Donna, who was actually my sister was the exact opposite. She was plain and had dark hair and was nothing like Kate. She was also far more serious and sensible than her half-sibling, but that being said, Donna also had a good sense of humour. Because they were only born about ten months apart, they were very, very close and always together. They didn't look like sisters (technically they were half-sisters) so people always assumed they were just really good friends. And I mean *really* good friends. Although their personalities were not similar, they seemed to just 'gel' and would talk to each other endlessly, Donna sitting cross-legged on her bed and Kate perched on hers in their shared bedroom. Donna and Kate did everything together and Donna was very much a part of Kate's social group. I guess Donna liked the fact that Kate's playful and somewhat adventurous personality, was a foil for her more serious one whilst Kate liked the fact Donna would perhaps talk her out of some of her more unrealistic schemes. Also, although younger, she would give Kate advice on boyfriends and Kate would give Donna advice on fashion; something for which Kate had a natural flair.

I remember once we were on holiday in Devon and Kate and Donna had a threesome with the barman who worked in the hotel where we were staying, who was by all accounts, a 'ladies' man'. Mum was sunning herself on the beach and I came up to their room during the day to see where they were as I was feeling bored. Their bedroom door was locked and all sorts of noises emanated from inside. I knocked and called to them and eventually a very frustrated voice shouted back.

"Oh, go away Richard, we're busy!" That was Donna.

I heard Kate's wind chime giggle and a male voice and then Kate said,

"Oh, that's just our annoying kid brother."

The male voice said something I didn't catch and I heard my two sisters laugh and then the groaning recommenced. I tried the door again out of frustration but they were not going to open it so I listened for a few seconds as the three of them revelled in the pleasures of the flesh.

Eventually, I walked away and went back to the beach. I sat on a deck chair next to Mum and read a book. That was me. Always on my own. Always with my head in a book. I hated my life and reading was my only escape. I wanted to be anyone other than myself. When Mum asked if I'd found Kate and Donna, I said I hadn't and they had probably walked into town. Mum agreed they probably had. See, I knew even then not to grass people up. Not to talk to people in authority. Kate would have been sixteen, Donna fifteen and I was eleven – it was my first introduction to sex, albeit behind a closed door and the first secret I kept from Mum (possibly).

My sisters mothered me a fair bit. After all there were three females in the family and just me so it was inevitable, I suppose. They often picked me up from school and made tea for me as my mum worked late, odd hours and evening shifts. Mum had two jobs, one in a supermarket and one as a part- time office cleaner which was usually at night. The woman who ran the cleaning company would phone Mum up when someone was off sick or on leave and ask her if she could do a 'few hours'. Mum never refused for, whatever you said about her, her number one priority was 'putting food on the table' and looking after her family. Her motto was 'if there's work, take it, never turn it down,' – she said that a lot.

Although I had few friends at school, I found that having two sisters who were popular gave me a certain kudos. One time, when I was in year seven at secondary school, so aged eleven, I was being bullied. I told Kate who was in year eleven, the last year, and she got her boyfriend at the time to have a 'word' with the bully. Her boyfriend was a black lad called Dwain; bloody hell he was tall, well over six foot and only sixteen. He came up to the bully in the corridor and pushed him up against a wall by his neck. Then he kept slapping him about the head and saying,

"It ain't nice to bully people, do you know what I'm saying?"

Slap.

"It ain't nice to bully people, right, do you know what I'm saying?"

Slap

Result? I wasn't bullied again. Not by anyone.

So that was the family unit, and generally we were pretty happy. My mum, Sandra, was easy-going with a caustic wit and a sharp tongue who had dedicated her life to 'the family'. She managed the budget well and made sure we never went short. Our home life was pretty good with Kate at the centre of a lot of laughter and frivolity. That was until she received a Christmas or birthday card from my dad – her stepdad. As I say, Dad had left when I'd been about seven so I didn't have too many memories of him, apart from him taking me to football, but I knew he'd drunk a lot and was probably an alcoholic. I was also aware that he had served some short prison sentences for violence.

Once, when I was about four or five Mum and Dad were shouting and arguing in the kitchen. I heard a chair scrape back and the table being pushed as well. I remember the sounds; they are hot-iron branded on my brain. Kate and Donna were out and I was on my own watching TV in the front room but not really. I was listening to the kitchen. I was terrified. As the noise increased, I went to the kitchen door. In my naïve, childish, stupid, innocent way I thought I could get them to stop. Mum was up against the sink and Dad had hold of her by her elbow joints. Dad was shouting and Mum was trying to placate him.

"No, John, please, John, no, John."

Dad got in her face like a boxer, forehead to forehead, then he really yelled at her. I was crying and whimpering 'stop, stop' at the kitchen door but neither parent saw or heard me. Then smack. In the face. A head-butt. Hard and fierce and ferocious. Mum screamed. Blood streamed from her broken nose. Dad turned and stomped out of the kitchen: his dark, angry presence loomed over me.

"What the fuck are you screwing at, you little runt?" he hissed.

I moved out of his way. Moments later the front door slammed. I felt warm urine on my trouser leg, it dripped on the floor and soaked into the carpet. I stepped back to the kitchen door. Mum had a tea towel over her lower face – soaked in blood; it seeped through her fingers and drip-dropped onto the floor like water through the ceiling from an overflowing bath. There was blood everywhere, or so it seemed.

"Help me, please, for fuck's sake help me, someone. Help me!" she screamed through breathless, panting sobs.

I ran. Out of the house and down the street, then I turned and went up the street and then I turned again and went down the street: crying, screaming, hyperventilating, my vision blurred with tears. In the end a woman grabbed hold of me and asked me what was wrong. Then moments later Donna took my hand.

"It's OK, he's my brother."

She took me home as I tried to tell her what had happened. I went upstairs and Donna went to see Mum. I felt useless, inadequate, not at the time but later. I couldn't stop them fighting, I couldn't protect Mum, I couldn't help Mum, I hadn't known what to do. It had been left to Donna and then Kate, who arrived home shortly after, to sort things out whilst I lay on my bed, in my damp, urine-soaked trousers (telling off from Mum later) and cried. I am sure the domestic violence, and that incident in particular, triggered my OCD.

Although the domestic violence was often fuelled by alcohol, Mum also said Dad would use the drink as an excuse and he wasn't always drunk when he attacked her. Anyway, he had hit my mother and sisters though never me – or at least not that I can recall. I also had a suspicion that Kate was the victim of sexual abuse but I don't know that for sure. Certainly, she always reacted badly if a card came from Dad. He didn't bother at first but when I was about ten years of age the cards started arriving with an address in Brighton: no appeal to write, just an address and a simple message 'Hope all OK, Happy Birthday/Christmas, Dad.'

Dad didn't 'do' social media (or not that he told us anyway) so there was no way of knowing what he was up to so, to me at least he remained a man of mystery who was occasionally the subject of my daydreams. I thought about what he was like and if he had changed at all and what he did for a living. Being in the digital camera age we weren't a family for albums or printed photos and most, if not all, photos of Dad had been deleted from the computer or from phones so I didn't even have a clear idea of what he looked like. In fact, the only photo I had of him was the one with his foot on a football at the Den but I had discovered that a lot later when helping Mum clear the loft. I used to ask Mum, Kate and Donna about Dad but they just closed me down. The message was clear 'your dad is persona non grata'.

The thing was though that whilst my sisters and Mum hated him, my memory of him was not so tarnished. I recalled how he had bought me a remote-controlled model boat, a yacht, when I had been about five and taken me to a park, which contained a large lake – I suspect it was either Southwark or Burgess Park but I could be wrong. He spent a lot of time showing me how to sail it using the remote-control toggle switch. I remember him being very patient with me. Then he let me have a go at working it whereupon I promptly sailed it to the middle of the lake and capsized it. Dad angrily grabbed the remote from my hand and fiddled with the toggles but the yacht would not respond. He was getting more and more annoyed and, in the end, threw the remote in the bin. It crashed in with a hefty clunk. Then he glared at me and made a fist. For brief moment I was gripped by that whole body fear that only a child feels. I'd seen him hit Mum and thought he was going to wallop me but instead he started laughing. Really guffawing.

"Come on, son," he said. "Let's go home. I won't tell your mother."

And he took my hand and we walked out of the park. He was still laughing.

"Don't ever join the Royal Navy, lad," he said. "Don't ever join the bloody Navy."

He had also taken me to watch my first football matches at Millwall's New Den. I remember I was a bit scared of the 'big crowd' and the noise (that's all relative of course! 'Big' to Millwall is small to other clubs) and my dad being quite reassuring. Of course, I was wearing my navy blue Millwall shirt which had white trim and Dad held my hand and seemed in really good spirits. Loads of people knew him. They kept coming up to him and saying 'hiya'. We even went past a pub, which might have been The Old Castle, I don't know, and someone who was standing outside drinking said,

"Hi, John, is this your junior Bushwacker?" laughed and lit a cigarette.

He seemed very popular and quite charismatic. Going to those matches lived in my memory for a long time. Dad was good to me when he took me to football, he bought me burgers and programmes and souvenirs, like the Millwall lion mascot, and he talked me through the players. He liked the fact I was following in his footsteps; my grandad had also been a Millwall supporter and he was proud of that. He used to say to me,

"You're Millwall 'till you die, son; you're Millwall 'till you die."

So I couldn't understand why, whenever Kate received a card from Dad, she would just tear it up and throw in the bin. Donna and I put ours on the mantelpiece and Mum, of course, never received anything. One day I said,

"I fancy writing to Dad." It was my twelfth birthday and a card had just landed on the door mat.

"No way, ignore him," Kate said. "He's bad news."

"Why?"

"He's a bastard, he beat up on Mum."

Mum intervened. "Your sister's right, it's good that he's finally acknowledges your existence but don't encourage him. He's never given me a penny for any of you despite the CSA chasing him. He's a waste of fucking space. I'm the one that has brought the three of you up all these years whilst he's been boozing and shagging – forget him."

So, I didn't write but it was always there, a shadow in my mind; what was Dad really like? Would I like him? Would he like me? Had he changed at all?

I did suggest it once or twice more but I always got the same rebuke so I didn't mention it again. I left home at eighteen and went to a university in the Midlands (name withheld for legal reasons as they like to say in the legal trade) to study a three-year Film and Media Studies course. Mum (kinda) and my sisters were really proud as I was the first person in the family to go to university.

In the first year I was in the halls of residence. Mum forwarded some birthday cards to me and one just happened to be from Dad: possibly she didn't recognise the handwriting. It had the same message but this time it had a different address in Brighton. Anyway, away from home, and therefore removed from the influence of my mother and sisters, I composed a letter to Dad informing him of what I was doing and telling him I was at university. I hoped he would be proud of me. I don't know what I expected in the way of a response to the long letter, written on my laptop, but what I got back was a short, hand-written note which basically said the following:

'*Glad you're OK, Richard. If you want to meet up it would be great. Can you come down to Brighton? Give me a bell.*'

And there was a mobile phone number. It was hardly the enthusiastic response I had hoped for! Maybe my mum and sisters had been right. I left it a couple of weeks as I just didn't have the courage to phone him. However, one night I had been out drinking with some student friends and, when I returned to the halls of residence, I searched in my desk drawer for Dad's birthday card. It was some weeks after my birthday, but it had been the only card I'd kept; I'd tucked the note from Dad inside. I took it out and, with a pounding heart, I gave him a call on my mobile phone. It was strange conversation as both Dad and I were pissed. It started like this,

"What the fuck do you want at this time of night, you fucking arsehole?" This was the dad I'd not seen or spoken to for ten or eleven years!

"Dad, dad, it's me, Richard... your son."

"Sorry, sorry, I thought it was someone else... didn't recognise the number, see? Anyway, how are you? What ya up to these days, Richard?"

So, we had a stilted exchange. He was walking along the street and at one point called into a convenience store and bought something as I heard the bell ring and him say 'thank you', but the upshot of it was that I agreed to meet him at Brighton train station that Saturday. I was so excited I could hardly concentrate on my lectures. I bought a ticket and texted him the time the train was due in. Dad promised to pay 'any expenses' as I had told him that, even though I had a student rail card, it would 'cost a bit' as trains were 'very, very pricy'.

"Don't worry, Richard," Dad said. "I'll pick up the tab, I'm just glad you want to see your old man again."

So, I took the train to London and then travelled on the tube to Victoria and then got on the Brighton train stopping at Clapham Junction, East Croydon, Redhill, Haywards Heath, Burgess Hill, Hassocks and Brighton.

I arrived about 12.30pm on the Saturday. It was a warm pleasant day and I had enjoyed the train journey. I had been trying to read one of Ian Rankin's Rebus novels but I was thinking about meeting Dad so much my mind kept wandering and I kept missing bits. I reached Brighton station and walked along the platform. I inserted my ticket in the barrier and then I walked to some seats and stood around. I moved to a blue metal pillar and just waited. The station was clean and bright and airy with its conservatory-like roof. It wasn't busy either; mainly students, a couple hugging, others waiting for trains or staring up at the departures board. Orange-overalled Network Rail workmen stood around talking to a cleaner. I gazed around looking for Dad, my heart pounding. The problem was I didn't have a clue what my dad looked like! There were a couple of pop-up type coffee and sandwich places in the middle and a range of shops around the edge. I was tempted to get something to eat but didn't want to miss Dad. Eventually, self-consciously I went and stood under a sign post which pointed to different parts of Brighton. Then I saw an oldish, scruffy man walk in to the station wearing a long tweed trench coat and swinging a green and white Asda carrier bag. His mullet had become white and wild and was part way down his back. He stopped and looked up at the arrivals and departures board. At first, I thought he was catching a train but he glanced at his watch and then walked up to some seats, rested his bag down and started to fiddle with his shirt buttons. Through a process of elimination – our eyes met a couple of times – I approached him. I felt like the journalist and explorer Henry Morton Stanley greeting Dr Livingstone in the African jungle.

"Turner, I presume!"

Only in my case I said, "Mr Turner? Dad?"

He smiled. We shook hands, all very formal and then he gave me a hug and patted my back.

"How are you, son?" he said and I could see, or thought I could see, tears in his eyes.

"OK," I said. "And you?"

"Getting by."

He knew a pub (of course) called Grand Central which was literally just across the road from the train station entrance. It was a tall imposing building with a doomed roof and a semi-circular entrance: it looked a bit like one of the Victorian theatres you see in London. We went inside and Dad nodded to a booth on the right with red seats; the booths were beside a row of windows. He threw his bag on to the bench seat as if it was a towel onto a deckchair.

"What you having to drink, son?" he said.

It seemed so strange to hear that word 'son'.

I said I'd have pint of lager. Any lager.

He walked to the bar and I moved along the vinyl seat to the window end. I drummed my fingers on the table; I felt uneasy as if I was meeting a date for the first time.

The bar was quiet. The walls were covered with beer mats, and a large wooden dresser held spirits and an in-built clock. A chalk board to the side of the bar listed the day's 'specials'.

Dad chatted to the young barman, who leant against some hand pumps. The young lad laughed, then he went off and poured two pints. Dad took a wallet from his jacket pocket; big and brown and old and worn. He pulled a note out and waved it around. He was clearly offering the barman a drink too. The lad smiled, thanked him and shook his head. Finally, Dad returned to the table with the two drinks.

When he had eased down the seat, he told me he knew the bar staff as he disco-jockeyed in the function room – the Nightingale room, I think. He said he had done weddings, birthdays, hen nights.

"It's a good laugh here," he said. "Friendly staff, great function room … I'm always available for a gig. I won't do anything beyond Britpop though. I prefer the '50s through to the '80s."

It was just another thing I didn't know about my dad – he was a part time DJ.

Dad sipped his pint. "Anyway, how you been, son?" he asked.

That word again! I told him about university, my degree course and he seemed genuinely interested. After a while he rummaged in the carrier bag and drew out some rather bent photographs of me (plus Kate, Donna and Mum) when we were young, photos he'd taken which I'd not seen before. They were of us as a family: on a beach, one of Kate on a donkey looking miserable, the family playing frisbee in Burgess Park, and in our house at Christmas, unwrapping presents by the tree. So, we chatted. We ordered some food and I got some more drinks. Dad told me he worked for the council 'doing parks and gardens' which he liked as he was outside most of the time and he lived in a flat in Whitehawk which he shared with his 'lady friend' Maureen.

"It's '50s built, only three storeys high, we're on the top, so don't get no noise from above."

"What sort of music do you like?" I asked, intrigued by his DJ revelation.

"All sorts, '50s through to '70s in the most part – Elvis, Cochran and Buddy." He paused and drank some lager. "The Stones, Bowie, T-Rex, The Who, Led Zep and of course, The Pistols, Clash and punk. But when you're DJing you have to be up for putting on some Abba – the ladies love it and it always gets them dancing. It's the same with Whitney."

He told me he was very proud of his vinyl record collection which he thought was worth a 'mint' as he had 'loads of signed and rare records'.

"Your mother said I should dump my records but vinyl's making a comeback," he said. "I've proved her wrong yet again," he added, sipping his third pint.

We chatted some more and he asked if I ever went to see Millwall and was disappointed when I said I only saw them a few times a year.

"You should follow them, son," he said. "I did, your grandfather did. You'll always be Millwall."

I knew he was disappointed in me.

Even so, it turned out to be quite a good afternoon. We walked over the road and down Trafalgar Street, under the railway bridge and back to the seafront. Then, we took the number 1 bus (I think!) back to Whitehawk. The bus wound up the steep Whitehawk Road to where blocks of flats looked as if they had been dropped like boulders onto the Sussex Downs. The flat Dad lived in was a one-bed affair, with a kitchen, bathroom and living room. It was clean and spacious or would have been it had not been so cluttered with ornaments and cheap knickknacks. Two three-seater blue sofas were butted up to each other to form an L shape and, as you entered, there was a dining room table behind one sofa: Dad's vast record collection covered the wall behind it. At the other end, where the TV was situated, sat a music station with two wall mounted speakers in each corner. I was introduced to Dad's 'lady friend' (as he described her), Maureen. She had come out into the hall, when we had arrived, and had limply shaken my hand. She was, Dad had explained, a divorcee with two grown up sons whom he had met whilst DJ-ing in in the Grand Central.

Maureen seemed very pleased to see me. She said (and I doubt this was true),

"Your dad talks about you and your sisters all the time and wonders what you're up to."

But she wanted me to feel wanted, which was nice. She made some tea and gave me some sponge cake bought from Asda's, and we sat on the sofa and talked some more, with Maureen asking most of the questions. She sat with an ashtray on her black skirt, smoking nervously whilst Dad reclined in the sofa and rubbed a hand through his long white hair. He had changed into red leatherette carpet slippers and his foot moved constantly – I could tell he felt uncomfortable. I got the feeling Dad hadn't told Maureen much about his former life and meeting me was a good opportunity for her to fill in the vast chasms in her knowledge.

"And will we be seeing Kate and Donna in these parts?" Maureen asked.

Dad looked uneasy. He stared across the room towards the large window on the right and a door which opened onto a balcony. The flat had a good view over the Brighton suburbs and you could see the stand at Brighton racetrack in the distance.

"I should think so," I said. "They were both keen to hear how I got on."

"They're waiting for you to report back?" Maureen said. She laughed lightly as a piece of sponge cake hovered enticingly close to her mouth. Her cigarette rested on the ashtray on her lap. "They've sent you in first as the advance party, you'll report back and then perhaps you'll all come down?"

"I guess," I said.

Of course, I couldn't tell her about Mum, Kate and Donna's hostility towards Dad and any potential meeting.

"It would be nice to see them all," Maureen said. "All three of you are always welcome here, aren't they, John?"

Dad nodded.

"Thanks," I said.

"They may not want to see me," Dad said. "It's up to them at the end of the day."

Maureen leant back into the sofa and punched his arm playfully. "Of course, they'd want to see you!"

She looked across to me. "It'd be nice if you all came down, there's so much to see and do in Brighton too if you just want to pop in for a quick cup of tea. We don't mind how long they spend with us, do we, John?"

Dad shook his head.

"I know Sandra cut off all access but no need to take it out on the children. That's selfish in my book," Maureen judged.

Dad didn't want the conversation prolonged so he picked up the remote, which was on the arm of the sofa, and turned the TV on.

"Scores will be in soon, son," he said. "I wonder how The Lions got on? We need to start putting a few results together and moving up the table."

So, I started to visit Dad perhaps once a month or so. I never told the rest of my family, and Maureen didn't ask about Kate or Donna again, I guess he had had a 'word' with her about it. Maybe put her right about a few things; explained that she had embarrassed me and that he knew my sisters would not want to see him.

Sometimes, on the way down to see Dad in Brighton, I stopped off in London and visited a record shop I'd found via Google, which specialised in records from the '50s through to the '80s. I'd buy him an album which he hadn't got which he seemed to really appreciate. However, despite him saying he would help towards the train fare, which was expensive despite my student railcard, he never gave me a penny and the trips put me out of pocket. I told Maureen one day.

"You should ask him, love," she said to me, "I'm sure he'd give you something towards it. He's probably just forgotten. He's got a memory like a sieve."

But I never had the heart to ask him.

I viewed the Brighton trips as the start of my spiral into debt but there was other stuff too and, if I'm being honest, that's probably not altogether fair but maybe it helped me to rationalise my thought process, *no, I wasn't crap with money – I'd been visiting my dad,* we all like to blame other people for our own shortcomings, don't we? The truth was, as a student, I liked to go out and enjoy myself. I guess I was like a lot of students in that respect. Money had been tight at home but being at uni meant I was off the leash and I wanted to have a good time. I didn't get on too well with the people of my own age on the South East London estate where I grew up. Yes, I had friends but they weren't close. To my mind there was a lot of competition plus they didn't like the things I liked, like reading and creative writing. Uni was different, I made some good friends and went out a lot. I drank too much, I spent too much, I enjoyed myself. Or at least as much as someone like me can, which to be honest, isn't a lot. In the moment, yes, long-term, no.

The thing was the other students came from better off families and had more disposable income, and I tried to match them. Sometimes I'd do some part-time work in a pub or supermarket but on the whole my outgoings exceeded my income. Also, at uni I started to develop my interest in writing and went to a writing circle every week. I had written short stories and poetry since my teens but had not really taken it 'seriously'. Certainly, I'd never shown my work to anyone apart from Kate and Donna. The circle was nothing to do with the university but it was something I really enjoyed and, as the other members were better and more experienced writers than I was, I undertook a Writers Bureau correspondence course whilst studying my degree, to develop my writing skills further.

We met, the circle that is, in the attic of an old community building. It was a great little group, about six of us from all backgrounds – a guy who had worked in the car industry, a primary school teacher, an accountant, a care worker, a youth worker: all with an interest in writing. I loved it. We'd take it in turns to bring a pint of milk and chip in for tea, coffee and sugar and make a cuppa and read stories. As a result, I wrote a couple of pieces for an online university mag, which was great. I really enjoyed the writing and the circle was fantastic but the thing was, after the circle, a few of us went for a pint or two or perhaps three in a pub called the Grafton Arms which was just around the corner. We would discuss writing, books and reading, which I loved doing too as it introduced me to different authors and styles of writing. I started to read more widely. The circle was a bus journey from the halls of residents and so I could have a drink without worrying. But again, it was all money. They were all working and I had to stand a round. So the cash was draining. Fast.

In between seeing my dad, studying, undertaking my writing course and writing short stories and poetry, in the second year I started dating a girl called Nicola. She was on the same course as me and we got chatting. We helped each other on one or two assignments, went out for a drink with a group of friends, well… you know how it works out at uni? Friends first, then lovers. I was smitten and tried to spend as much time with her as possible; I bought her presents, wrote her numerous love letters and even a (bad) poem. Then, in a bizarre copy of my sisters being bedded by the barman in Devon, one night I came back early from the writers' circle as it so happened that some of the post-circle drinkers were either absent or couldn't stay after the meeting. I returned to the Halls and I went to see Nicola. Her door was locked and all sorts of noises of a sexualised nature could be heard from within. It turned out she was in bed with a guy called Dan who I knew but was not close to. In fact, my view of Dan was that he was an 'arrogant motherfucker' – nothing personal of course. I had dubbed him 'Danstead', after the airport, God knows why, but he thought he was God's gift and had also bedded another girl I knew, Lucy, who I liked but was well out of my league, as well as quite a few others; so, Nicola was a notch on his bed post, and he on hers.

The next day I challenged Nicola. I remember her sitting on a chair by the desk in my room whilst I sat on the corner of my bed. She said she was '*sooo*' glad I had '*brought things to a head*' (I resisted the temptation to say, 'I thought you'd done that'). She went on to say I was '*too clingy*' and she didn't want a serious relationship and she didn't consider it '*cheating*' as that was '*like… that was like…well, that was like…that was like…that was like…well, male possessiveness*' and the only person she could ever possibly '*cheat*' on was '*herself*' and if I wanted to date or see someone else that was fine by her but she didn't '*do*' '*19ᵗʰ-century male constructs of relationship based, like, as they were, on power dynamics, patriarchy and men treating women like possessions as that was sooo boring and like, so old-fashioned and like...*' The long and the short of it was she was going to sleep with whoever she liked and if I didn't like it, tough. '*Get over it, Rich or do one.*' And '*yes, it had been going on every Wednesday, whilst I'd been at the writers' circle, not that it was any of my male chauvinistic business, of course*' – which kinda begged the question as to why she was going with Dan behind my back but I really wasn't in the mood for a deep, philosophical conversation about sexual conventions in the 21ˢᵗ century.

So that told me. I wanted to tell her I loved her (or thought I did in any case) but decided it would probably make me sound weak and wimpish and '*so, like, old-fashioned* 'so I left it like that, shrugged my shoulders and said, 'OK'. Relationship ended. End of. I didn't date again through uni though. Lesson learnt. Fuck it.

I'm going to hold my hand up here and admit that was when I started to use prostitutes or sex workers or whatever you want to call them. It had started in Amsterdam, a stag night with some mates back in South East London who invited me out with them when I was home from university over the summer in my second year. It was the usual thing. A dare. Well, Turner was always the man to put his head above the parapet. So that was what happened. You probably know what Amsterdam's like; girls sitting in red-neon-framed windowed rooms, sometimes in houses that are three or four storeys high. I tapped on a lower window and a South American beauty with soulful, dark eyes and light tanned skin came to the window and opened it a fraction. The other lads were standing around, hands in pockets laughing and smirking. Of course, the hookers are used to all that: the drunken stag nights, the pissed punters, the voyeurs, the immature comments.

"Looking for business? Or are you just looking?" she asked, raising her plucked-to-a-fine-line dark eyebrow.

"Business, of course," I said.

She closed the small window and pushed open a much bigger one which was all glass and she let me in. The curtain was drawn across and suddenly I was alone with her- the outside world blanked out by the thick, red drape. She was wearing a black, lacy bra which was battling to contain her large breasts- and her matching black mesh panties didn't provide a lot of camouflage either. She smiled at me.

"Are you nervous?"

"A little."

"At least you're not drunk like most of the Britishers," she said, wrapping her arms around me and kissing me on the lips.

"No, I don't drink much," I said, which was probably a lie back then.

There was a new-looking bed or couch with a red plastic mattress and a red plastic covered pillow, no sheets. God, thinking about it now, is this stuff prison issue? Does the Ministry of Justice kit out the brothels of Europe? It wouldn't surprise me. To be honest Claudia's bed (as she called herself – probably a pseudonym) was a lot more comfortable than the ones in prison. As I stripped off, she reeled off prices in Euros. Of course, prostitutes will always try to steer punters away from penetrative sex and towards oral, which is quicker and easier, but that's what I wanted and that's what I got. I paid her and got undressed. She removed her panties and bra and asked me to lie down on the bed cum couch. Then, she went on top, in control. She slid a condom on my erect cock with her versatile, glossy lips and then eased her pussy down on my stiff member: she rocked back and forth, back and forth until I came inside her. About twenty minutes later the curtains were pulled back and I was back on the cobbled canal street, lit with yellow lamps and the white and neon of high framed windows. The bell gables of the tall houses reflected off the ink dark canal which shimmered under the snow-white moonlight. I texted my mates who had disappeared into a bar. They texted back with a name of the bar they were in and some while later (I got lost) I met up with them and returned the all-conquering hero.

"I wish I had the guts to do that," one of my friends said, and that made me feel good. I was brave. I was Richard the Lionheart.

When I got back to university, I Googled local massage parlours and escort agencies. I was spurred on by a conversation I'd overheard in the refectory one day. I had been sitting reading a book on Ealing Comedies, as I was doing an assignment on the post-war British film industry. Anyway, I was eating a pasta bake when I heard some students talking in a booth behind me. One was telling the others how she did some escort work to pay off her student debt, another was on a sugar daddy website. Of course, selling sex in the UK is not entirely illegal, it's just soliciting, pimping, kerb crawling and sex trafficking which are (and some of those activities carry pretty hefty penalties) but as long as the girl doesn't advertise (go figure, as the Americans say!) and she's a free agent there's no issue – after all it's impossible to police the infinite internet: it is awash with escort agencies offering 'in-call' services as well as the more traditional 'out-call'.

Tina was one of the first girls I met. She was a similar age to me with long, blonde hair, bright, sky-blue eyes, skin as soft as rose petals and a lovely, super-white-toothed smile. She gave me a massage.

"If you want extras you have to ask for it, the management don't allow us to solicit," Tina said.

So, I asked. Fuck me, I asked.

After that I visited an escort agency which offered an 'in call' service. That was better. I got hooked. It was easy. Whenever I had a bit of money and some spare time I used to travel to central Birmingham on the train. There I'd meet a girl called Sasha, who might have been Lithuanian, who lived in a modern flat in the centre, above a supermarket. The flat had a pine door with the necessary spy hole. It was clean and modern and always smelt of fresh flowers and her gorgeous Coco Noir perfume by Chanel; I know it was that as I bought her a bottle for her birthday. Sasha was a small, buxom brunette with dark-as-coal eyes, an easy manner and a quick wit. Her long brown hair tumbled down her back like a mud slide which had slipped off the smooth satin of one of the many assorted coloured negligees she wore. She'd totter to the front door wearing her obligatory skyscraper heels. We'd go into her dark bedroom, she'd turn on a bedside light and switch on the radio and then she'd remove her negligee to reveal a basque, bra and matching panties usually in pastel colours. We'd kiss passionately and then I'd get undressed. The bedroom contained two white bedside cabinets, one with a digital clock on top and one with the radio tuned to soft music. On top of that one was various creams and lotions and inside the drawer there were all the accoutrements of the sex trade: condoms, tissues and wet wipes. There was a chair, where I placed my clothes, a white wardrobe and an ottoman with a leather paddle on top as well as cuffs. Sasha always had a white hairband around her left wrist but when we got down to business, she'd fasten her hair into a pony tail.

"You've got lovely blue eyes, Richard," she said one time when she was sitting astride me. I was twenty years of age and she was the only woman who had ever complimented me (that's bollocks but you probably know what I mean). In fact, she flattered me a lot which made me a feel good about myself. She introduced me to the practical side of BDSM (bondage, discipline, sadomasochism for the uninitiated) and a few other things which I enjoyed: we had some good times together. After, if she didn't have to see another client, she'd make me a cup of tea and we'd sit and chat. The sex trade is nowhere near as sordid as you probably think and what I liked about it was that there was no hassle of chat ups and dates and 'will she, won't she'. It was my kind of deal but I got deeper and deeper into debt. I was amazed at how easy it was to get loans and credit. Especially credit cards. I always paid off the minimum and I always got offered more credit and more cards and more loans.

Then one evening, I was out with some friends and one said he'd won a load of money by playing online roulette. He said the gambling companies were always offering free spins and it was easy – register with loads of companies and bet for free. He reckoned he'd won a lot at minimal risk. So, I registered on gambling sites like Ladbrokes and Corals (two different companies back then), William Hill, Betfred, Bet Victor, Paddy Power, Betway, Marathonbet, Betfair and others and used the free spin/bet introductory offers to start to gamble. I won a bit and so I started to upload money. It was so easy, every time I was at a loose end, not writing an assignment or a short story or seeing Sasha, I'd play online blackjack, both live and computer generated (which I particularly liked) or live roulette (both live and computer generated) or sometimes fruit machines on my laptop or phone. It was just so effortless. And, as I always had my phone on me, I would sometimes have a few spins when I was out with friends or during boring lectures. You probably know what it's like. You start with a fifty-pence stake, then move up to a pound but you're only winning multiples of that pound so you move up to £5. That's better. That feels good. You're winning more; it feels like you are making progress and building up your bank. Why not try a ten-pound stake? You do and then you lose... very quickly. Of course, the problem is you start to chase losses. Then when I won, I would go out with my uni mates. I loved 'flashing the cash' and treating my friends to a few pints and a curry but then I'd lose the next night so I'd never really gained from the win. Of course, that was at a time when you could use credit for gambling. The law eventually changed and the government decreed you could only use debit cards for online gambling but at that time I was using credit for a lot of stuff. But I wasn't really an addict. I've not got an addictive personality, unlike my father. I was a dabbler, correction, I am a dabbler. I'm like a butterfly; attracted to the new but I don't stay long on each flower – I move on. It's the same with the S&M, it was never anything serious, it was just something I tried a few times with Sasha. I enjoyed it and that's why I introduced Debbie to it…

But you can see my debt piling up, can't you? What with the escorts – £70 for half an hour and £100 for an hour or thereabouts, drinking with my student friends and my writing circle crew, my Dad trips to Brighton. Then Janet joined the writers' circle; she was a driving instructor. One day we were in the Grafton Arms, after the circle, and she told me how important it was to learn to drive. I had a provisional licence for ID but had never thought about driving. Lessons at £25 a pop were well out of my student league. She offered me a discounted lesson and then I carried on with a few more lessons until I left uni.

I passed my degree. I got a lower second or 2:2, a drinkers (and gamblers) degree as it is known in popular parlance but I came out of uni with debts of £21,000, excluding my student loan. I was twenty-one and deep in the financial mire.

Chapter Eight

But let's put the brake on my financial woes and take you back to Dad. Obviously, Kate, Donna and Mum knew nothing about my trips to Brighton to see him, which continued after I left uni. At first, after graduating, I lived at home whilst I applied for jobs so I stopped seeing him. I managed to secure a temporary job and, with the money I earned, I carried on with my driving lessons and passed my driving test first time: to celebrate I bought (on HP, of course) an Audi TT in a deal with the trader which included the mega high insurance instalments.

Then, when I got my job at Zorin Logistics along the M4 corridor not too far from London, I reconnected with him. Dad understood why I couldn't see him when I was living with Mum, it was just too complicated, he didn't seem to mind (or perhaps care).

One time we went to the horse race track, which was close by his flat, but mostly it was pubs and his place. By then I knew Dad didn't really want to see me, not after the first few visits. When I'd phoned and told him I couldn't visit because I was staying at Mum's house he had just said,

"Oh well, what will be, will be."

I had discovered by then that he had remarried after he had left Mum and had another son, so three children of his own in total, and that son never saw him either. But despite Dad's lacklustre enthusiasm, I kept calling him up, I kept getting on the train, I kept going to see him. The only thing that changed was the journey; instead of having to travel down to London from the Midlands and then getting the tube and then another train to Brighton, it was just a short train journey to Paddington, then the tube to Victoria and then the train to Brighton. From there it was the number 7 bus (I think it was anyway) from the station to the marina and a short walk to his flat or a walk to the seafront and a bus, possibly the number 1, to Whitehawk. Alternatively, I would drive down in my Audi which I hoped would impress Dad.

"Nice car, son," is all he said as I took him out for a drive to Saltdean one day. He didn't even ask if it was expensive or how I could afford insurance. Nothing.

When I resumed my visits, Dad gave up on meeting me at the station and would text me a pub to meet him in. Normally it was the Grand Central, which was close by, or sometimes I would walk down the steep Trafalgar Street and under the railway bridge to The Lord Nelson as Dad had a friend who drank there: that meant there would be three of us rather than two. I would find him by the bar, talking with his mate or else just reading the paper and drinking if his friend hadn't shown up. Always the same.

Maybe I hoped, just maybe, he would acknowledge me in some way. When I passed my degree, he just said, 'that's good, son, it's great to have qualifications, I wish I'd done better at school,' and he bought me a pint of Fosters to celebrate. That's all my degree meant to him, a pint of fucking Fosters. It was pretty much the same when I passed my driving test.

I just wanted him to take an interest in me. Ask me how I was doing, ask me about my drinkers' degree or even about my gambling habit if that's what I had. Anything. *Take a fucking interest in the son you brought into the world, Dad!* I wanted to scream but he didn't or couldn't. As I say, I know he took no interest in his other son, Daniel, and none in Donna and none in Kate (although he did occasionally ask how they were, although never, ever did he ask how Mum was) so why would I be special? Why should I get any different treatment? Well, I was the one that had taken an interest *in him* for a start and travelled to Brighton to meet up (at great personal expense). Even so I tried, beyond uni, to bridge the gap without success and I still occasionally stopped off at the London record shop and bought him an album he didn't have.

Then one Saturday I arrived at the station, walked down to the seafront and took a bus to Dad's flat (as I say he'd given up on meeting me and would either text me the name of a pub or say he was at home). I got there to find Maureen setting out bowls of crisps, salad, plates of sausage rolls, cold pizza, cocktail sausages, cheeses, pickles and crusty French stick as if for a party. There were balloons on the wall, cards on the windowsill and a big banner which read 'Congratulations'.

"Your dad and I are getting married," she announced as she placed a plate of mini-Scotch eggs on the white tablecloth. "You're welcome to stay if you want. John's just gone off to get some more drink from the supermarket."

I noticed she was wearing a blue shift dress, a gaudy, bright gold square necklace and large hooped earrings. She'd had her hair done and looked quite glamorous.

"Thanks," I said. I stayed. I had met Maureen's two grown-up sons, Lionel and Andy, a couple of times at the flat (on one occasion Dad had shown us all how to make the infamous 'Millwall brick') so I chatted to them. They were both tall, thin, wiry lads in their late twenties perhaps early thirties. I think one was an estate agent and the other worked in IT or something. They were friendly enough but laughed and giggled together and told 'in jokes'. I felt out of place. I didn't know anyone; Dad had moved on. Forgotten about his previous two families.

During the evening Mud came on the stereo. The song was 'Tiger Feet'. I was standing close to Dad so I kinda tapped my foot, sang along and sipped some lager from a can as if I was enjoying myself (which I wasn't).

"That's neat, that's neat, that's neat, that's neat, I really love your tiger feet, I really love your tiger feet," I sang. "Mud were a great group," I said.

"They were fucking shit, son," Dad replied in his taciturn way.

"Sorry, I thought they were fucking Mud," I said, trying to make a joke of it. "So, I take it you don't like Mud?"

Dad shrugged his shoulders. "They're alright if you like that sort of thing.... do you want a top up, Sean?" he said to one of his work colleagues who walked close to us, and he wandered off to the table where the tinnies were piled high.

I stopped seeing Dad after that. I wasn't invited to the nuptials. I knew my place and it wasn't in Brighton.

Then, about four months later one of Maureen's son's rung me up.

"Hi, Richard, it's Andy here."

"Who?"

"Andy, Maureen's son, we met at the party, the engagement party a few months back and a few times before that at the flat. I'm just phoning around all those who knew John, your dad, I got your number off Mum, it's too much for her to deal with, having just got married and all that."

"Why? What's happened?"

"Heart attack in Asda. He keeled over in the frozen fish and meals aisle." Then for some unknown reason he added, "Aisle sixteen."

"Dead? You mean dead?"

"Yeah, 'fraid so, sorry to break it to you like this. Can you pass it on to everyone you know your end, who knew him? Cheers."

"What about the funeral?"

"I'll text you the details."

And that was that. The last conversation I ever had with my dad was an idiotic, pointless exchange about the pop group Mud.

I went to the funeral. Dad's ashes were interred at The Downs Crematorium which is part of Brighton and Preston cemetery, just a short drive from his home in Whitehawk. I drove my Audi and gave a lift from the house to the cemetery to a teenage girl I didn't know. In fact, apart from Maureen, her sons and a few others I'd seen at the party I knew no one. It was mainly work colleagues and friends: certainly, there were no relatives that I recognised. It was a long drive up to the small, stone-built chapel. The chapel was a grey affair with a large round window the size of King Arthur's round table and dam-like walls. It stood on top of a snaking road which led through layer upon layer of huddled together gravestones. It was a wet, windy day and it seemed as if even the gravestones were trying to shelter from the elements. Maureen, dressed in black of course, was comforted by her two sons. She never asked about Kate and Donna's conspicuous absence. So we parked up outside and the mourners trawled in through the small chapel doors. Andrew, Lionel, I and a work college of Dad's called Sean, waited outside in the rain as we were 'volunteer' pallbearers. The funeral directors moved the coffin out of the hearse and got it into position for us to shoulder it. We carried it through the chapel doors and down the light blue carpeted aisle. We gently laid it on a large table in front of the altar. For reasons best known to my dad his coffin was piped in (if that's the right terminology) by The King crooning 'Always on My Mind' – part of me wanted to believe it was for me, Kate and Donna. The minister gave a short, considered and well received sermon and then Andy read a poem by the 'Salford Laureate', John Cooper-Clarke, which probably wasn't appropriate but then nothing Dad ever did was.

Dad had wanted to be laid to rest back in South East London and have his ashes scattered over the pitch at Millwall's New Den but he ended up in the neat rose garden just outside the chapel. Maureen planted a rose called 'Remember Me' on Dad's spot and left a memorial in the shape of an open book engraved with suitable words for the dearly departed. My own wreath just read, 'Dad, sorry we couldn't have spent more time together, RIP, Richard.'

I told Mum, Kate and Donna that I'd been to Dad's funeral – I said that one of his new wife's sons had contacted me.

"Good riddance," was Kate's comment.

Mum shrugged and said, "Oh, well. It's a pity he couldn't have been more of a father to you all."

Donna said, "It's sad but not a surprise with how he lived his life – all that boozing and beating up people he was sure to get his comeuppance eventually – it's karma."

Yeah, a heart attack in aisle sixteen at Asda's, Brighton Marina, I thought. *Ashes to ashes. Dust to fucking dust.*

Dad died when I was twenty-four, and that Christmas I drove over to Mum's house to go down to Kate's place. By then she was married to a well-paid City type called Martin, whom she had met in a wine bar in London. They had moved to Surrey where they lived in a four-bed, detached new build. They had one son and she was pregnant with their second child. She worked as a self-employed mobile hairdresser and beautician and had a very profitable business providing grooming services to the affluent of the suburbs. Of course, Kate was personable, funny and good at her job so she'd built up quite a clientele. Donna, in contrast, was a single mother with a daughter called Lili. She lived close to Mum in a two-bed flat and like Kate, she also worked as a hairdresser but for her it was in a trendy unisex salon; you know the type, they are on the High Street, the hairdressers are called 'stylists' and a cut is twice as expensive as most hairdressers.

Anyway, I drove around to Mum's house in my Audi TT on Christmas Day morning (well, I wasn't going to miss Christmas Eve festivities down the pub, was I? And I was dating Claire at the time) and then I drove them all to Kate and Martin's house in Epsom. Poor Donna was squeezed in the back with Lili; not a lot of space in the back of those TT babies, especially with Lili's toys and a bag of presents which wouldn't fit in the boot. Kate had really come up in the world (there was a speedboat on the drive) but Martin was a nice chap and friendly enough. We had a pleasant day at Kate's house before returning to Mum's later that evening. Then, on Boxing Day, I walked to the New Den which was about a mile and a half away from Mum's house, wearing an expensive Crombie, I'd bought in London, with my blue and white Millwall scarf tied and tucked inside. So, I roared on the mighty Lions who unfortunately didn't respond in kind and gave a lacklustre, losing performance. When I came back, I took my coat off and hung it in the hall. Lili was sitting on a bean bag watching TV so I ruffled her dark hair, and she smiled up at me and then went back to watching TV. Donna was in the kitchen making a sandwich for her, nice thick white bread, boiled bacon and mustard.

"Do you want one, Rich?" she asked, "or have you eaten?"

"No, I'm starved, I'd love one, thanks."

So, I sat down at the kitchen table. Mum made me a mug of tea whilst Donna went to work preparing the two sandwiches.

"Nice that you keep your dad's tradition alive of going to football every bloody Boxing Day," Mum said, placing the mug down on the table.

"Well, someone's got to support The Lions," I said.

"At least he's not down the pub till midnight like Dad would have been," Donna said. There was a packet of open cheese and onion crisps on the table: she placed some on each plate and took a handful for herself.

"That's true enough," Mum replied. "Your dad used to get pissed on Christmas Eve and didn't sober up until New Year's Day."

"And don't we know it," Donna added, raising her eyes as well as the bread knife. "I wonder if his new wife ever had the pleasure of spending a Christmas with him?"

"I'd have thought so," I said. "I think they were together a few years. Mind you, he seemed to be doing a lot of DJ-ing in Brighton, so maybe he wasn't drinking so much."

"I doubt that very much." This was Mum. "At least she gets to keep all his crappy records. All in boxes in the loft, our bedroom and the living room, I used to get fed up with them always being under my bleeding feet."

"He'd sorted them out," I said. "They were on shelves across one wall of the flat he shared with Maureen. All in alphabetical order too."

"So, you went back to his flat?" Mum asked.

"Yeah, a few of us went back," I said. "Maureen said I could have some of the records but I've not got a record player."

"That was nice of her," Mum said sarcastically. "It'd be typical of your dad to give you something you can't bloody well use."

"I think she thought I might like to take the records back I'd bought him…"

Mum pounced like a Scarrott on heat (you'll get to understand why I don't care very much for Jonathon P. Scarrott, QC later in this *narrative*).

"So, you've seen him, then? When he was alive, I mean?" Mum exclaimed. "You've seen your fucking father?" Her voice rose like a firework on 5th November … New Year's Eve… Diwali… take your pick.

I had to confess then. At the end of the day there was not much difference between one visit and ten visits, it amounted to the same thing – I'd betrayed her. Mum was distraught.

"How could you? How bloody could you? After all I've done for you?" she yelled at me, sobbing so much she could hardly speak. "You went behind my back! You betrayed me! You betrayed your sisters! You bastard!" She hammered the table, slopping my tea. "How could? How could? … How could you? After the way he treated me and your sisters? I can't believe you'd be so bloody cruel!"

She sat at the kitchen table crying into some kitchen towel Donna had pulled off for her. Lili came running into the kitchen to see what all the commotion was about so Donna took her by the hand and led her back into the living room. She came back and closed the door. Then she sat at the table with her arm around Mum's shoulder. She tried to comfort her. She tried to quietly explain that I'd not betrayed her, but had probably just wanted to see Dad.

I attempted to defend myself.

"He contacted me when I was at uni – he wrote me – he wanted to see me – you forwarded on the letter." My eyes felt damp but I held it together. "I just wanted to see what he was like, for God's sake!"

"You know what he was like. A fucking, evil bastard!" Mum bellowed.

The sandwich Donna had made was now on a plate in front of me. It looked inviting.

Donna stood up and got another piece of kitchen towel. She looked at me and gave me a half smile. Then

220

she raised her eyebrows as if to say she understood. She went and sat back down next to Mum.

"Rich didn't mean to hurt you," she whispered.

"Yes, he bleeding well did," Mum blasted. "He's a bastard just like his dad. I've always said he was a pea in the same fucking pod."

Donna looked at me. I'd scraped back the kitchen chair by this time and got up. I was standing by the door. Donna mouthed 'go'.

So, I opened the kitchen door and went. It was all a bit surreal. I marched back through the living room where Lili stared up at me all wide-eyed and innocent. Then I grabbed my coat and car keys and stormed out to my Audi. I got in but realised I'd left my stuff in my old bedroom. I thumped the steering wheel in frustration. I got out and went back and rang the bell. Fortunately, Donna answered.

"I need to collect my things."

I pushed past her and rushed upstairs. I quickly packed up my overnight bag and some Christmas presents. When I came back downstairs Donna had wrapped the sandwich in baking foil. She handed it to me and gave me a quick hug.

"I understand, Rich," she said, tears in her eyes. "I understand."

I left the house for a second time and drove back to my flat on Petersfield Hill. So, in the end my clandestine visits to see Dad had ended up upsetting Mum, big time, and Dad had never really connected with me emotionally. When I'd wanted love, I'd got Fuck All.

The rest of that Christmas week and New Year I spent with my then girlfriend, Claire, who at least understood why I'd visited my dad. I really liked Claire, she was a complete opposite to Nicola and I genuinely enjoyed her company. We used to walk hand in hand along the canal, went on camping trips and for long country walks until, as usual, I blew it. Why, I don't know, we drifted apart as I wanted more: I wanted to go out with the lads, I wanted to date other girls, I wanted my life to start not finish. I guess, though, it was my one, brief, shining moment – the writers' circle; the nice flat near the centre of town, carefree days with Mark, Suggo, Dave and Matty – going to pubs and nightclubs. Then BOOM – it all came crashing down…

Chapter Nine

"Have you ever been in trouble with the police before, Richard?"

I remember DCI Hinton, who led the murder investigation, asked me that one time when I gave one of my many interviews. I'm pretty sure it was one of the few questions I answered during one of the 'no comment' interviews but it might have been another time. The whole situation was so traumatic from start to finish I'm not really sure what happened when and at what stage so if this *narrative* sometimes seems muddled, confused and repetitive that's the reason why. The police investigation made my head so befuddled I could not think straight and I just drifted along in a somnolent state most of the time. But it was a warm-up question to put me at my ease, he expected me to say, 'no' – which is what I did say! What do you take me for? Of course, I fucking did!

But I had been in trouble with the law before and Hinton knew it. The police know a lot of stuff but they like you to admit it, or at least deny it, which is a tick in their 'evidence against' box. The truth was that when I was arrested, they already had my DNA, fingerprints and mugshot on the PNC (Police National Computer). In fact, I suspect when PC Snot and Hazel Eyes visited that Monday night, they had already matched fingerprints, lifted from Anne-Marie's house to my profile on their super-duper computer.

It was something and nothing really. As I say I'm not a violent guy. Physically I'm probably pretty weedy. I'm shallow chested, skinny and lack muscle definition. I'm not one of those muscled-up hunks that you see on *Love Island* with six-packs and well-toned, tanned and oiled bodies. I'm about six foot and weigh in at about 130 to 140lbs, I guess, or did back then when the arrest for murder took place. Not surprisingly the weight fell off me afterwards and by the time I was in prison on remand I was knitting-needle thin.

The incident with the police had occurred one Saturday. A truck with a winch on top had pulled up on the gravel drive outside my apartment and the next thing I knew my car, my lovely mustard yellow Audi TT, was being winched up on the back! Look, that's not strictly true, the repossession men had given me a last chance to pay the outstanding finance I owed on the car. I asked them to give me a bit longer but they said 'no' and asked for the keys which I handed over and then they set up the winching gear. We'd had a conversation earlier in the week and I had been given until Saturday to get the money so I'd played online roulette and blackjack and when that had failed, I'd realised I'd have to relinquish the car (not that I could ever have won enough to pay off what I owed but it took my mind off the inevitable and I felt I was doing something 'constructive').

As you can imagine there was a couple of burly repo guys over seeing the removal of my car. Well, neighbours from across the street came out and looked down the drive, and others were looking out of windows so, once I'd handed over the keys, I challenged them. To be honest I was a bit upset about seeing my car go west! It was my first car and I was very, very attached to it, also at the time I was dating Claire who loved it.

"Look, can't you give me one more chance?" I asked although I already knew the answer. "Can't you give me one more opportunity to find the money I owe?"

"Mr Turner, you've been ignoring letters from the hire purchase company and now we have instructions to remove this vehicle, you've already informed us that you can't pay."

I rubbed my hands through my short hair and pulled on my mullet. It was a nightmare, but as luck would have it the postman waddled up the drive at the same time, looking quite smug, with a bundle of letters in his hand for the residents of the house.

"I asked my mum to send me some money," I said quickly. "She might have sent a cheque rather than a bank transfer. Can't you just wait a second?"

"The cheque would need to be payable to us and we would need some guarantee."

"It is, it is," I said. "I gave her the details; can I just check, please?"

"I wish you'd told us before, sir. We'd rather take full payment than the car," one of the large, heavily-built repo men said.

Miraculously they stopped the winch. I walked up to the postman and asked for my mail which amounted to a load of junk. I walked away and opened it to buy time. God knows what I hoped to achieve by the little stunt because, of course, there was no cheque but the hopelessness of the situation had suddenly got the better of me. I turned back and said,

"There's no cheque but it might come Monday."

"No, sir, you've had long enough to pay," the repo man said and he pressed the red button on the side of the truck and the winch started again, whirring away and waking any neighbours who had not already been alerted to the proceedings on the gravel drive. As it made its electronic whirl my poor car was hoisted up onto the tow truck, never to be seen again.

I was now standing at the front of the drive looking back at the house where we all lived. I could see my fellow tenants looking out their windows and some using phones to film the incident for social media. This included Juliette who wore a flowery, linen dressing gown and had her head out of the window like her fucking Shakespearean namesake, phone in hand. James' head bobbed up and down behind her as he tried to see the 'action' – I felt like a right loser. To add insult to injury there was a middle-aged couple, Patrick and Sarah, in the flat next to theirs at the top of the house, who were also looking out. I felt riled up. I marched back to the car transporter, my hands were shaking, my temper beginning to get the better of me.

"You can't take my car!" I shouted. "I need my fucking car! How the fuck am I going to get to work?"

"Use the bus, sir," the repo man operating the winch said.

I knew it was a hopeless case. I had been ignoring letters, I had been putting my head in the sand in regards to my mounting debt. I just didn't want to think about it. When my pleas fell on deaf ears, I tried a different tack.

"Please, please just let me get my things from the car," I said. I had gone out with Claire the night before and she'd given me a plastic folder containing some of her short stories and poetry to read and I had carelessly left them on the back seat. She'd not stayed over as she had been on 'earlies.'

Now, I think the repo guy was getting a bit annoyed with me due to my postman antics and he seemed frustrated. I grabbed his arm to beg him to stop but he took it the wrong way and got annoyed.

"Unhand me, sir, unhand me this instant."

I took my hand off his arm. "Please, please let me get my things."

"No, sir, you can do that in the depot, we've given you the details."

"I want my things out of that fucking car now," I said, jabbing my finger at his chest. I grabbed his arm again.

"You can't have them." He aggressively pushed me away. I stumbled back a bit, recovered my footing and got right in the man's face, which wasn't clever. Forehead to forehead. Like a boxer.

"I want my fucking things," I hissed through gritted teeth.

The rest is a blur. The red mist descended and I don't really know what happened but I know I head-butted the guy. Good and hard. There was blood on the repo man's face – not a lot, but it was an 'assault'. Then the police were on the scene and those black stiff plastic cuffs that hold your hands as if one fist is on top of another were placed on my wrists and I was dragged away to a waiting police car. All filmed for social media. Great. I never did recover Claire and my personal belongings from the car. So you see, when I said I'd been taken into the police station's underground carpark three times, you just thought I'd got the maths wrong, but I hadn't, I really had gone into the underground police carpark three times.

I got charged, of course, and when it came up in front of the magistrates' court, I pleaded guilty and got a community sentence: 120 hours unpaid work, a fine, costs and victim surcharge. The repo man, Mr Thomas, had a body camera but that didn't have to be shown as I pleaded guilty to the offence. I quite enjoyed doing the community work which was mainly gardening and I did a stint in a charity shop too and, unlike a lot of people who get placed on Community Orders, I actually finished it without it going back to court. The magistrates said it could have been custodial but they accepted my account that I hadn't meant to head-butt Mr Thomas but had just 'got in his face' and it had got out of hand. The magistrates felt the bailiff had been a bit antagonistic in not letting me get my personal effects from the car, especially as some of them belonged to my girlfriend, Claire, who to her credit, gave evidence on my behalf and impressed the magistrates which I also think helped my corner. Still, I'd learnt my lesson but had racked up more debt into the bargain. I agreed a payment plan with the fines office to pay off so much a month which I paid via direct debit. Did I say I was £21,000 down when I left uni? Well, by my mid-twenties I'd racked up £25,000 and had zero prospect of paying it off. Even so, the 'repo man incident' unnerved me a bit and afterwards I was determined to pare down my debt as far as possible and that's when I started using charity shops and internet sites to buy and sell.

The good news was that Mr Vacarescu, who owned the house, liked me and thought I was a decent tenant. After all, I always paid the rent on time and I was working. When he heard about the repo man incident, he came to see me with his brother. I thought he was going to give me my marching orders but he just said,

"Don't worry, Richard. I understand, sometimes you have to settle disputes with your fists. It's the same in Romania."

And he slapped me on the back and laughed. Basically, he didn't give a toss. The thing was my flat was clean and tidy and after the dispute, during the summer, I would make up a few plant tubs at the front of the house. Mr Vacarescu would purchase the compost for me to do the tubs and I bought the plants, at a discounted rate, from the guy I'd done gardening for as part of my Community Order. Then I watered them throughout the summer as my flat was closest to the front door; it was kind of a quid pro quo for Mr Vacarescu allowing me to stay in the house after my altercation, although I know I didn't have to do it.

I suppose I've always been a bit reckless; it was like taking the money from Anne-Marie's house, an impulse decision. A desire to rid myself of the debt that hung around my neck like an albatross and maybe treat Debbie, ask her to marry me, go to Paris, who knows.

Once when I was about eighteen, I'd been in London drinking with two friends. Later, they had both managed to chat up some women so, after a meal in a Chinese restaurant with five of us rather than three, I'd left the restaurant on my own with half a bottle of wine which I consumed as I wobbled over London Bridge. Then for a drunken reason, I can't really explain, when I'd finished the wine, I threw the bottle off the bridge with the intention of it landing in the Thames. It missed the river, that great big wide expanse in the middle of the bridge, and it hit the road below. I heard it shatter on the pavement and I heard a woman scream. I ran off in the direction of London Bridge station and got a train back to South Bermondsey. Even so, very occasionally I wondered about that incident. It was reckless like the 'repo man incident' as it was labelled in my head at least.

So, I lost my car and for a couple years I travelled on buses and I even bought a pushbike which I rode to work until I got knocked off it by a car that didn't even bother to stop. I wasn't wearing a helmet and cracked my head on the kerb which I think caused me a bit of memory loss and might be another reason this *narrative* might appear to be a bit muddled. The bike was beyond repair, so after that it was all public transport. I quite liked using buses as I could sit and read, which I enjoyed. Eventually, I saved up enough cash to pay a deposit on a cheap second-hand car (the rest on finance, of course)

– a Hyundai i20 – the one I was driving the night I met Anne-Marie.

And that's what I told Dom during those dark, joyless winter nights cooped up in our prison cell. My life story. He would sit on his bed and listen and make comments and in a way, I enjoyed it. It was therapeutic, like seeing a counsellor. Dom gave me a bit of perspective. Helped me appreciate what I'd got, at least before I was arrested. He helped me to see life as not entirely negative which was difficult in a tiny, cramped prison cell but he managed it. He was like an old sage, full of wisdom. He'd always say, 'the child is more important than the adult' and that, 'if you let it, adulthood will just become a postscript to childhood' – I always remember that, 'if you let it, adulthood will just become a postscript to childhood.'

Chapter Ten

With Dom's wisdom, advice and support, somehow I made it through Christmas and the New Year. In fact, I hardly noticed New Year's Eve, or wouldn't have if it hadn't been for the prisoners giving their cell doors a right good kicking at midnight which, I guess, is a prisoners' substitute for fireworks. So, the New Year commenced and I was just awaiting my date with destiny. The start of the trial was scheduled for mid-April. My barrister, or defending counsel, Mr George Prentice and Hannah would sit with me in the consultation room as we went through the case in fine detail. Mr Prentice, as my barrister, would represent me in court being higher up the legal pecking order but the senior solicitor, Hannah, was charged with all the donkey work: putting the case together, talking to me, looking at the Crown Prosecution Service case and generally assisting the barrister. She had some other solicitors and paralegals working for her on the case too.

"The thing they have not really established," Mr Prentice said to me one day. "Is motive. Why would you, having just had sex with Anne-Marie, stab her to death in the front room with one of her own kitchen knives?"

"I guess they're going to say because of the missing money," I said.

"But you didn't take it, did you?" Mr Prentice questioned.

"No, of course not," I lied.

"There's certainly no evidence you did," Mr Prentice said. "Or that it was even there – we only have her housemate's testimony for that and even she can't be certain it was still there at 4am or 5am in the morning or whatever time Anne-Marie was stabbed."

I knew by then there was a red mark on Anne-Marie's neck and that she had been choked (but not enough to kill her – more to restrain) by a black tie from her dressing gown which had subsequently gone missing. She had been stabbed once below the ribcage. It was a very unusual knife wound as the knife had been thrust upwards into her lung. The cause of death was registered as tension pneumothorax which is where the lung is punctured and it floods the organs with air and compresses them. Death can occur in minutes if not treated. There had not been much blood. Rigor mortis had set in by the time her housemate, Lisa X, had found her and that meant it was difficult to determine the exact time of death.

"Her housemate Lisa X is saying that there was a considerable amount of money in that kitchen cupboard. Possibly as much as £10,000 – the proceeds from drug deals. The prosecution claim is that you saw the money when Anne-Marie made you coffee and then sneaked downstairs to steal it whereupon Anne-Marie awoke and came downstairs. She confronted you and you stabbed her."

I knew by then that Lisa X and Anne-Marie were part of a drugs gang. The drugs came out of London and were given to the two women to sell in the local area. Apparently women were better drug dealers than men, so Mr Prentice informed me, and the gangs tended to 'groom' women into becoming dealers by the enticement of clothes, cars, jewellery and money. Although Lisa owned the house, a tenant had introduced her to drugs and she was in 'drugs bondage' to the gang. The dealers, or line holders, never came to her house unless they were collecting the proceeds. They would meet outside of the house: perhaps in a car, a park, a pub or even a nightclub to deliver the drugs to Lisa and Anne-Marie. The house was full of the paraphernalia of drugs dealing: scales, a sheet of paper with weights written on it and letters like D for dark (which is heroin) and W for white (which is cocaine); even the lottery coupons I'd seen on the table were actually being used to take orders. The numbers circled would mean the amount in weight and by the side the W or D meant the type of drug and the initials of the customer.

According to Lisa, the line handlers would send an innocent looking text on the burner phone – the name of a club or a pub and a time like 'Pryzm 10.30' – something which would have no value to law enforcement. Even in the house, the line holders would never mention drugs. The code word was, ironically, 'coffee' meaning 'cash' just in case the house had been bugged by law enforcement, inasmuch as one of them would say,

"Do you want a cup of coffee?"

They would reply 'yes' and the money would be transferred – that was the reason it was easily accessible in the kitchen cupboard.

The gang also had a key to the front door so could enter whenever they liked, hence the bell to warn Anne-Marie and Lisa X of a visit. Once inside the line holders would place a new burner phone on the coffee table and take the old one. That's pretty much how it operated – along with collecting the money, of course.

A nightclub or a bar might seem like strange places to pass on drugs given doormen and CCTV, but Mr Prentice informed me they were ideal because the drugs were usually stored in places a doorman could not search, and once in the club the cameras tended to scan a whole area and would not concentrate on individuals as they would not have an operator. Also often in the darkened club the picture quality was poor, plus if you knew the weak spots of the club's security system then it was easy to escape the cameras. I knew from my own experience the CCTV evidence (which I had imagined would be like a film of me dancing with Anne-Marie and then leaving the club with her) was inconclusive – I could have been any number of people. It was only the back-up of social media and my fingerprints, which matched those on the PNC, which had led the police to my door. My shirt and trousers had revealed partials of Anne-Marie's DNA (but not blood) as had my car, but the police did not have that information until after my arrest. Mr Prentice suspected that a doorman might have been aware of Anne-Marie and Lisa's 'activities' and possibly received a kickback for letting them in and informing them of the many weak spots in the club's security system, which apparently was over ten years old. There wasn't evidence of dealing inside the club. Having been given the drugs Anne-Marie would have gone to the toilet to stash them away. She'd probably hidden the condom filled with coke in her vagina; hence she was keen to go to the toilet when she had returned home, and why she was so horny! Mr Prentice speculated that she might have been keen to have a lift home as she had the coke on her person so I was just a 'patsy' as the Americans used to say – the sex was just a 'pay-off'. Her phone, the murder weapon, the throw, the tie from the dressing gown and the pay-as-you-go burner phone were all missing so there was no way to form a 'alternative narrative' as Mr Prentice liked to say. Boy, did he like that word, *narrative*! He explained to me once that what he meant by that was a consistent, honest story of my actions from the time I'd left my flat on Saturday evening to collect my friends, up until I had legal representation when I was being questioned by the police. This account, he said, should be supported by my character witnesses and previous actions and lead the jury to believe I could not have possibly committed the crime.

"So, it is far more than an alibi for the night in question, it's an account of your actions before and after," Mr Prentice said. "As well as the type of person you are."

His view was that Anne-Marie had been killed due to her involvement in the sale and distribution of illicit drugs and that was the alternative account Mr Prentice was going to present to the jury.

"The police say the mark around her neck came from a sex game you had played earlier," Hannah added. "But that is inconsistent and too much of a coincidence."

Mr Prentice leant back in his chair.

"What puzzles me is this money that Lisa says is missing. If the jury believe Lisa's testimony that there was money in the cupboard awaiting collection, then it really strengthens the prosecution's hand. But you're sure you never saw it?" Mr Prentice quizzed.

"No, never. I didn't know it was there," I said. There was no way I could admit to having stolen the money. If I did, at such a late stage, I really would be staring down the barrel of a *whole life tariff* – I just had to try to blag my way out of it. Also, I was aware that Debbie had covered for me and had given two statements to the police in which she had said she had returned some money to me. I was not allowed contact with her so could have landed her in trouble by changing my story. No, I could admit my sin to no one. No one at all. Ever. (Except here, of course.)

"The key witness is Lisa," Mr Prentice said. "Though she is a prosecution witness she is the only person who can add weight to our account that Anne-Marie was killed due to a drugs dispute, possibly by a rival gang. What we need to do is put forward alternative possibilities. Yes, the prosecution's account, that you took the money and stabbed Anne-Marie, has traction but so does ours. Ultimately the jury can only convict if there is guilt beyond reasonable doubt. Our job is to create doubt. Create alternative scenarios. They don't need to be as strong as the prosecution's, all they need to do is create doubt in the jury's collective mind."

Mr Prentice started to doodle on his A4 pad. I noticed he did that a lot. He'd draw musical staves (he told me once he played the violin in his spare time) or fruit or even faces. He was actually quite a good artist but I realised he did this because he was very frustrated with the lack of a good, collaborated alibi. The fact that I did not have a good *narrative* as he liked to say.

"This is one of the most difficult cases I've ever had to represent," he said.

That made me feel a whole lot fucking better – not!

As Mr Prentice doodled, Hannah picked up the slack.

"Lisa wants to get out of the drugs network and the police will put her in witness protection so she has a good reason for giving solid evidence which will convict you. In addition, she will be on video link with her face obscured to all but the judge so we will never see her, which makes cross examination very difficult. What you say on the stand is crucial, Richard. If you appear to the jury as a credible witness, and there's no reason on earth why you should not, then I think it would be difficult for the jury to convict given the lack of hard evidence." Hannah smiled and patted my hand, "See, I told you, we'll soon have you out of here."

When I got back to my cell I'd speak to Dominic about my meetings with my legal team. I told him that Mr Prentice was finding it difficult to find an alibi for me which would create 'reasonable doubt'.

"Good Lord," Dom said. "It's certainly a mess."

That was the understatement of the fucking year, correction, the decade.

I lay on my bunk staring at the scratched graffiti on the brick wall. My head ached permanently. I was filled with anger, sadness, a sense of betrayal – by who I wasn't sure, it just felt so wrong! I was on remand awaiting a trial for something I hadn't done. I had asked Hannah one day what my chances were of being acquitted.

"It's hard to say, Richard, but I think we have a good case."

A 'good case' was not a good enough case. A 'good case' was not going to get me off and she knew it. I could see by the way that Mr Prentice scratched his head and doodled and leant over the table like a thinker involved in working out some great mathematical paradigm that there was danger ahead. Big danger. Mr Prentice knew he had a difficult case on his hands and the fact his visits had started as quite cheery 'get to know you/get to know the case' with the detail being left to Hannah, and had ended as more frequent visits with him questioning Hannah and me and examining the paperwork in detail, led me to one conclusion: I was a basted turkey ready to go in the oven and the door was open. Even the screws had commented on the number of visits my barrister had made to the prison. There was no doubt I was in trouble. Big time.

I had built up a bit of rapport with Hannah – she liked me and she told me the case was 'interesting' (more so to me, love!). She knew I was innocent but she also knew, as I'm sure Mr Prentice did, that the odds were stacked against us. In fact, one time Mr Prentice even suggested a 'not guilty' to murder but 'guilty' to manslaughter option with an explanation that the stabbing had been accidental.

"It's only one stab wound, not a frenzied attack," Mr Prentice had said. "You could give an account that I'm sure the prosecution would accept to avoid a long, lengthy and costly trial which could go either way."

I had hammered the table. "But I'm innocent! I'm innocent, for God's sake! Don't you people understand that for fuck's sake?"

By that time we had full disclosure from the CPS so we knew exactly what we were up against.

The biggest problem was that police were simply not looking for anyone else. I was the chief suspect. And if they were not looking for anyone else, unless the murderer or murderers killed again using the same MO, then it was touch and go whether or not a jury would acquit me. I was in a pit of despair. One day I was talking to Hannah and Mr Prentice when Hannah left the room to get some coffees served, as always, in white plastic cups.

"Sorry, I couldn't remember if you wanted sugar," Hannah said, putting the cup down in front of me. "So, I brought you a sachet and a spoon."

I thanked her, poured the sugar in, stirred it and picked up the cup. My hand started to shake as if I had

242

Parkinson's and I started to cry. I put the cup down and Hannah leant over me and mopped up the split coffee with a tissue.

"It's alright, Richard," she said and I sobbed even more. I don't know what set me off, just the normalness of it all, someone getting you a coffee, someone being nice to you but I bawled like a baby. It was all out there. On the outside. Beyond the prison walls. That was life. This was death. Hannah sat down beside me; her dark tights stretched and released static as she crossed her legs. She placed a comforting hand on my shoulder. I knew she believed me, believed I was innocent.

"It's all too much," I said. "I don't want to be inside. I don't want to be locked up!" I covered my head with my hands.

"Not long now, we're soon have you out," Mr Prentice said. He tried to be reassuring but I knew, we all knew, there was a *possibility* that may not be the case. More than a possibility, a *probability*.

I don't know if Mr Prentice or Hannah told the prison staff about how I was feeling because I was taken to the doctor the next day. The screws escorted me to the ground floor and into a small room with a couch, a desk and a chair. The doctor sat at the desk looking at some notes. He gestured for me to sit down, whilst the screw waited at the open door. He asked me for my prison number: everything in prison is done by your ID card so I showed it to him.

"Do you experience suicidal thoughts?" the doctor asked. He was a pigeon-like grey-haired man who had come out of retirement to take the prison job part time; I guess he felt he was doing his bit for the community. It was a thankless task dishing out pills for depression, anxiety, insomnia and addiction. They monitored medication carefully and you had to collect your daily dose from a hatch every morning. It was supposed to stop you overdosing but some still managed it.

"Of course I do," I said, "I could be banged up for years and years and years."

"Quite, quite, I can see that would be depressing, have you got a trial date?"

"Yes. April."

"And you're charged with murder?"

"Yes."

I could see his brain working, '*this man has deprived another human being of their life and now squirms at the sentence that might be imposed.*' He, of course, like the screws thought I was guilty. It's strange but no one in prison thinks anyone else is innocent. Screws, other prisoners, other staff members; they all believe if you're banged up you've done it – even if you're on remand. The only person I met who wasn't like that was the prison chaplain. But I guess I was the same. I'd see new prisoners and say '*what are you in for, mate?*' rather than '*what have you been charged with?*'

The doctor looked at his notes. "I see your blood pressure is good and you're generally in good health. Do you smoke or drink?"

"No, to the smoking, I used to consume a moderate amount of alcohol."

"How much?"

"Eight to ten units a week."

"Problems sleeping?"

I nodded my head. I started to feel emotional. "That's the worst time, there's so much noise and I can't sleep properly and when I do my head is…"

"Oh well," the good doctor said. He wrote for a while and then he looked up. "I'll order some antidepressants, that should keep you going and a pill to help you sleep. You're to be given one with your lunch and one for dinner."

"Thanks," I said.

Then in a moment of macabre humour he added, "Don't worry, you can't OD on the pills they're herbal." He smiled at his notes.

They didn't work. I was still depressed and I still couldn't sleep. I say they didn't work but they did in a way because I was able to trade them. There was a guy in the kitchen who managed to get tins of tuna so I swapped my pill allowance and some other bits my sisters sent in for tuna and other kitchen 'surplus'.

The only reason I managed to keep going was because of Dominic. Ultimately it was Dom who gave me a 'fighting spirit'. He was a good laugh too. We did our singing and dancing together and he told an entertaining story. He was one of those people who are genuinely clever, someone with an intelligence that is rare and intuitive. Look, at the end of the day anyone can study, pass exams and get qualifications – it's just a question of regurgitating what you've been taught, but Dom was a thinker. One time he said to me,

"Why don't UK prisoners get recognition for helping da fucking environment?"

"How do you mean?" I said, completely lost.

"Well," Dom said. "You think about it. We're locked in here, we can't travel, we can't fly, we can't go out no place so our carbon footprint must be many, many times lower than ordinary folks on da outside, see what I mean?"

I agreed I did.

"Also," Dom said, warming to his subject. "There're economies of scale, isn't that so? We're all banged up in one place rather than thousands of different houses and flats and we're all eating similar shit food."

"True."

"So why don't that David Attenborough and all those crazy eco zealots go around to all the fucking British prisons and give all us UK prisoners a big fat pat on the back and a 'thank you very much, sir' for saving da fucking planet? Why don't we get no awards from them environmental groups?"

"I don't know," I said.

"I tell you for why, Richard my man. It's always the ordinary folks that have to make da sacrifices, never da rich. The world is just a rich persons' playground. Look at them Hollywood stars: the Hollywood Bleaters I call them. Just around the corner from Hollywood is South Central LA. Who does the most damage to the planet?"

"Hollywood, I guess," I said.

"You're right a million times over, Richard my man, so who bleats and complains all the fucking time about the environment? And says we should do this thing and do that thing and change our way of doing things?"

"Hollywood stars."

"Right again, Richard my man. The Hollywood Bleaters. Not them poor, black and Hispanic kids in South Central LA, they'd never say nothing about the environment but they're the ones that have to make all the fucking sacrifices to keep the rich flying and travelling here and there and everywhere and spending their mega bucks. It's always the poor that have to support and pay for the fucking rich."

"It's true," I said.

"But at least sometimes they plant a fucking tree."

Then he lay back on his bunk and he started to laugh in that wheezing, creased-eyed way of his.

"They plant a tree and that stops da fucking Antarctic ice from melting. That's what they do, they plant a fucking tree."

And he laughed some more.

"At the end of the day, it don't matter what anyone says, you can't change human nature," I said.

"Ah, but you can, Richard my man, you can. You have to believe you can," Dominic said. "You have to believe you can."

We certainly had some crazy, crazy conversations like that – sometimes fuelled by a shared spliff. We'd also discuss books we'd read. One time he saw me reading a Stephen King novel.

"You should read Chester Himes. He's the real deal, he was sentenced to twenty-five years hard labour in the States for armed robbery and started to write in prison."

Dom was right, as usual. I managed to get *A Rage in Harlem* from the library, it was great; a really good, light-hearted read.

On another occasion he was lying on the bunk bed reading a worn copy of Victor Hugo's *Les Misérables*. He asked me if I'd read it. I said I hadn't but I had seen the musical: I'd taken Debbie to see it one Saturday in London.

"Was it good?" he asked.

"Fantastic, Debbie loved it. She went on about it for ages."

I remember waking up the following morning and finding her sitting up in bed reading the programme.

"Most people think it's about the French Revolution," Dominic said.

"Yeah, that's right." I replied. "I think we did when we saw it."

"But that ain't right. It's actually about the communes in Paris following the Franco-Prussian war in 1870 and the vacuum caused by the defeat of Napoleon 111," Dom said.

Don't get me wrong, he was a lovely, lovely bloke but he did like to air his knowledge a bit. Still, he was my number one support whilst I was on remand and he probably saved my life. I say probably...but if I'm totally honest... he did.

"You lack self-confidence and self-belief," he said to me another time.

"That's always been my problem," I said. "I've low self-esteem."

"You need to believe in yourself, Richard," Dom continued. "You're got a lot going for you."

"What, in here?"

"You'll get out, have faith in your brief Richard, my man. The evidence is all circumstantial. The CPS hate these sorts of trials. Nothing solid, nothing to hang a case on. The CPS is in love with DNA. They wank over it. Yours is all over Anne-Marie's house but not on the murder weapon, which ain't nowhere to be seen. Apart

249

from the blood spots on your glasses they've got nothing. Nothing."

"So why have they got me here?" I asked.

"There's no one else," Dom said. "And they've got to pin it on someone. The police and the courts don't care about right and wrong or innocent or guilty, it's all about the conviction, that's all it's ever been."

Which was exactly what I'd told Debbie all those months earlier. A conviction for the sake of a conviction. A tick in the 'caught' box. Case closed. Innocent or guilty? Who cares?

Talking to Dom was like counselling, the mistakes I'd made he reframed, the negatives he made positives. I started to feel better about myself. He was respected in the prison too; he was one of those prisoners who people either ignored or were friendly towards: I suppose in part because he was older, and that meant I didn't really have any problems with other prisoners.

In fact, the only 'negative' was a prisoner called Carter who I dubbed Snidey Bastard. He was friendly to my face but I knew I couldn't trust him. He'd come into our cell and ask how I was doing and pretend to be concerned but he was constantly talking to the screws. I don't know if he was a pick-pocket on the outside but he 'lifted' my silver pen; you remember the one Kate had given me for my birthday that Hazel Eyes had had her watchful eye on? And some other things my sisters had sent in. Dom told me to be wary of him, 'trust no one and believe nothing,' he always said.

In between talking, reading and having deep philosophical discussions Dom showed me all the amazing things you could cook in a kettle (he knew people in the kitchen and managed to get 'surplus' with the aid of my pills and some other bartered goods). He showed me how to make instant noodles, tuna and pasta, tuna and baked beans on toast but best of all he gave me a fighting spirit. I started to think about a change of career, *when* I was found 'not guilty' and was released. I was determined to get a job helping prisoners with literacy skills; maybe through a prison charity or something. Dom thought I would be really well suited to it, especially given my experiences. He used to say to me,

"Come on, Richard, the best form of defence is attack; attack them, don't let the bastards bring you down. Fight the system." And he would clench his fist and punch my shoulder. "Fight the system, fight the system." He would grit his teeth and punch me harder and harder. "Fight the fucking system. Fight the fucking system. The system is wrong but it paints itself as right."

He mentored me, taught me, coached me. Sometimes he was hard on me but it was what I needed. I felt like Tyson Fury, the Gypsy King, preparing for his next world heavyweight bout. He laid into me, pretending to be the prosecutor. He got me to answer question after question after question so that my *narrative* was word perfect. When I saw Hannah and Mr Prentice, they were surprised at the change in me. Mr Prentice said to me one day.

"You've really rehearsed this but you need to sound natural."

I smiled and looked him in the eye. "Don't worry, Mr Prentice, when I'm in the dock I'll be so natural you won't believe it."

"Oh, I hope you are, Richard, I hope you are," he said, and smiled broadly. He knew that Richard A. Turner aka Rat was prepared to go into battle.

Back in the cell I'd sit on my bed or on a chair and tell Dom about my trips to see my legal team.

"I think you're going to do it, I really do," Dom said as he slapped me on the back. "I'm going to miss you, Richard, promise to write."

"I'll write and visit, Dom, don't worry about that."

By that time the days had rolled into late March and the weather had got warmer and lighter. If I stood on a chair, I could see the hazy grey tower blocks in the unreachable distance engulfed by a white puffy cloud. For some reason an annoying little ice cream van started to park just beyond the prison walls. It would play its stupid 'Match of the Day' or 'Greensleeves' jingles. I don't know if the driver did it to wind the inmates up. Maybe someone was banged up who'd murdered his daughter or something but the prisoners would shout out 'give us a Cornetto, mate' or 'make mine a Magnum,' in the end he was told, by the staff, to 'do one' (I guess more politely).

As the trial date approached, I asked Kate to buy me shirts, shoes, socks, ties and suits. I said I would need five sets of each. She had already told me that she had discussed it with her husband Martin, and he had told her that she could 'spend whatever she needed to' so I looked presentable for the trial. Kate had excellent taste and I knew she would get me well kitted out. My hair had grown back by then and was no longer a crew cut. The mullet was gone and my hair was neat and tidy. I looked respectable.

Spring arrived and then it was April. The cold, dark months of prison despair were over, the evenings were lighter, the clocks had sprung forward and I felt it was time for a new beginning. I spoke to the prison chaplain about the Bible and the resurrection of Christ. I'd never really studied religion at school but found it really interesting; even if you didn't believe, and I was beginning to, the narrative was just incredible. The Biblical stories were fantastic and the Bible was a book I could read without returning it to the library as a bunch of Evangelicals had donated a pile to the prison which were just gathering dust in the chapel. That meant the chaplain was more than happy to hand one out to anyone who showed an interest. A lot of prisoners convert in prison, mostly to the Islamic faith. What the deadheads in the Ministry of Justice don't understand is that religion gives a sense of *purpose* and *meaning* without which the soul of man shrivels and dies.

Two pigeons built a nest outside our window. Dom and I christened them Martine and Luther (Martin Luther King, get it?). We could hear them cooing in the morning and evening. I used to drop bits of bread onto their nest from our window, which was actually a punishable offence as pigeons were classed as vermin. Even so, some prisoners would catch them and dye them football colours so when they flew around the yard they could look up and say, 'that's my pigeon – he's an Arsenal supporter'. They'd also attach empty tuna cans to their feet so they clanked around on the roof. One time our cell was spun (searched) and I dropped some cannabis resin onto the nest to get rid. Poor old Martine and Luther were as high as kites!

But things were looking up and not just for our two pet pigeons. I was feeling happier. More confident. Of course, we had had full disclosure from the CPS well before then and I knew exactly what we were up against…

For a start the police had interviewed the staff at Citi Cabs due to my statement, and the fact they had seen a cab on CCTV which appeared to be following my car. Anyway, they had traced the driver and interviewed him because he was a witness: why he had followed me would come out in the trial so I will leave that for now.

The most important disclosure, however, and the one which sent me into the pit of despair I described earlier (*sorry* I withheld information!) related to a 42-year-old ex-Afghan vet from Sunderland called Fusilier Simon Ricoh – but known to everyone in his regiment as 'Sunderland' Simon. He had suffered PTSD after witnessing his colleague being blasted into a thousand and one pieces after he'd stepped on an IED in the Helmond Province of Afghanistan. Blood, flesh and brains had been splattered across Simon. On his return to Blighty, 'Sunderland' Simon had beat up his wife and children who had escaped to a refuge before Simon had been evicted from the family home by the courts, thus allowing his wife and kids to move back home. After that Simon had drifted around, returning briefly to his old regiment who were based on Salisbury Plain to see his 'best mate' who was still a squaddie. He had fallen out with him after a drunken row over a bag of chips which had resulted in a fight. Then he had gone off the radar for a bit before he had drifted into our town, by which time he was down on his luck, homeless and without a friend in the world.

Now my friend Simon could not believe his luck when one fine morning he put his hand into a council bin to see what waste food there was, and emerged with a dirty, white envelope filled with money! There was a

God! The voices in his head were right after all! God existed and had chosen him to carry out a very, very important mission – go to the nearest Wetherspoons and get absolutely bladdered. Fortunately, Simon threw away the white envelope (the envelope would have had my dabs on it but not the loot which I'd never even got time to count bar removing a few notes from the middle) so that was something the police didn't ever need to know about.

So, one cold, overcast Tuesday morning (18th November), Simon made his way to the Lord Rochford and, at 9.32 in the morning, bought the first of many refreshing pints of lager, along with a large cooked breakfast and an extra round of toast. I'm not sure what time a bunch of builders arrived at 'The Roch' in their mixture of high-vis jackets, tabards and dirty jeans but it fair to say Simon had had a right old skinful by then. He was leaning against the bar buying yet another pint when one of the builders made a comment to his workmate that he'd had to move away from the bar because the man beside him (Simon) suffered 'one or two personal hygiene issues'. Simon overheard the remark and being an ex-squaddie and a former member of the distinguished Royal Regiment of Fusiliers wanted to defend his dignity.

"What the fuck do you mean by that?" Simon said, standing as upright as the bar would allow.

The builder turned. "Wasn't talking to you, was I, mate?"

Now this builder was a rather large, middle-aged type who he could handle himself as well as a pint. However, he had learnt enough about life to understand that a fracas in a pub, especially one you went to for your breakfast every morning along with an endless stream of free coffee, was not a good idea so he had a good handle on diplomatic withdrawals from such incidents without losing face.

"No, but you were talking a-fucking-bout me, my mate," 'Sunderland' Simon blasted.

"I was talking about that gentleman there." The builder pointed to a grey-haired, dark-suited man with a walking stick and heavy framed glasses who carried a wobbly pint which slurped down his grey woolly jumper. The old man turned, shook his head, pushed his thick glasses up his nose and moved away.

"He smells," the builder said and tried to involve 'Sunderland' Simon in the joke. But Simon was having none of it.

"You're taking the fucking piss, my mate," 'Sunderland' Simon said.

The builder tried another tack. He moved closer to Simon and said, "Calm it down, alright." He put his hand on Simon's shoulder. "We don't want any trouble."

He looked at one of the members of the bar staff who was watching the incident. He wanted it to be seen that he was the peacemaker. He wanted to ensure his crew would be served a hearty Wetherspoons breakfast in the morning.

Simon stumbled forward. "You'd better watch your fucking lip or I'll give you a knuckle sandwich. You like hospital food, do ya?"

The builder tried to defuse the situation again – this time he was prepared to lose face. "Sorry, mate, I meant, no offence." He took his hand off 'Sunderland' Simon's shoulder and held it up.

Unfortunately, his mates could see good sport and were laughing and one, a young lad in his early twenties who was fresh-faced, clean-skinned and a handsome devil wanted to claim kudos with his older workmates. He held his nose and said in a hoity-toity voice.

"I say, old chap, there's an awful pungent smell around here."

Boy, did his workmates laugh! But a few seconds later the twenty-two year was digging bits of beer glass out of his scarred-for-life face as he collapsed on the floor, screaming his head off in abject agony. His hands and face were covered in a rich creamy, crimson sauce which seeped across the dark, wooden floor causing three women at a nearby table to jump up as one and join the young builder in a shrieking, panicking fit.

The peacemaker builder was quick to react with a heavy, hard fist to 'Sunderland' Simon's face.

'Sunderland' Simon rocked back. It was like an explosion. Suddenly he was transported back to Helmond. It was like the IED all over again. The high-vis jackets were Afghan garb and the tabards Afghan dress and he was back in a war zone. He over turned a chair and then swept glasses from a table. Fusilier 'Sunderland' Simon went into battle. People were screaming and trying to get out of the pub and the bar staff were calling,

"Police! Police! Police! Call the fucking police!" to no one in particular because about twenty mobile phones were out of pockets and bags and pulled off tables, and numbers were being frantically pressed. Nine, nine, bloody nine.

"Police, ambulance, fucking quick! The Lord Rochford!"

Then the three remaining builders went on the attack too and Simon, assailed on all sides, lashed and slashed and fought like a man possessed. It took four police officers twenty minutes to restrain him.

So, Simon was in custody (ironically at the same time I'd given my voluntary interview on the Tuesday night) charged with assault and affray. A body search threw up a rather interesting question.

"Where the hell did you get all this money?" DCI Murray asked 'Sunderland' Simon.

There was approximately £10,000 in total when it was counted.

"I found it in a council bin."

"A likely story," the detective laughed heartily. "Do you think I just came up with the fairies? Who did you steal if from?"

Of course, it just so happened that Lisa had told the police whilst giving her initial statement on the Sunday, again something I knew nothing about till the disclosure, that a large sum of money had been taken from the house. Apparently, it was usually stored in the kitchen cupboard (where no one would think to look, of course!).

Simon Ricoh was charged with GBH (Grievous Bodily Harm) and affray. The police confiscated the money until they could find its rightful owner, but unfortunately DCI Murray wasn't great at communicating with his colleagues (who I got the feeling didn't particularly like him; you'll see why later). So, following an early morning 'not guilty' plea in the magistrates' court they sent poor Simon to an approved premises, what was formerly known as a bail hostel, to await his day in court. Belatedly DCI Hinton heard about 'Sunderland' Simon's antics and the money and naturally linked it to the Anne-Marie case. He and DI Drake drove to the approved premises so they could interview him but, unfortunately, 'Sunderland' Simon had absconded before he could be questioned any further about the provenance of the money and exactly where he had found it. As there was no sign of the envelope and my prints were not on the money, it was difficult for the police to make a forensic connection to the MacDonald case. However, they looked at hours and hours of CCTV and found footage of me walking to the writers' circle and stopping at a bin briefly. It was impossible to say what I'd thrown away but nonetheless it was evidence they were determined to use against me.

So that's got you up to speed before we move on to Section Two.

SECTION TWO: THE TRIAL

Chapter Eleven

M r Prentice told me that before the jury were sworn in, he was going to attempt to get the judge to dismiss two pieces of the prosecution's case during the case management stage prior to the trial. Firstly, the fact that I'd played BDSM sex games with Debbie, as he thought the idea that Debbie and I enjoyed such activities in no way indicated that I had a predilection for violent or rough sex. The prosecution was going to try to establish a link between that and the attempted strangulation of Anne-Marie with the tie from her dressing gown. Mr Prentice felt the link was tenuous, to say the least, and the other issue he wanted the judge to dismiss was the 'bad character' application, made by the prosecution, in regard to the mild assault on the chap who had repossessed my Audi TT.

On both counts Mr Prentice failed.

So, on a warm, sunny April day I was led from my cell to another room on the ground floor which had a full-length mirror. A screw dropped a big cardboard box on a table and waited by the door whilst I took out the first of my new suits. I got changed in front of the screw for there is no privacy in prison. I pulled on a lovely new white shirt (box creased for want of an iron). Then I put on a navy-blue suit, a matching blue tie and new black shoes. It felt so, so good to wear new, clean clothes again. I slapped on cheap aftershave, applied hair gel and I felt superb. Lastly, I pocketed my rubber Millwall lion mascot that Kate had sent in when my flat had been cleared; it was a lucky charm and was in my trouser pocket throughout the trial.

When I looked at myself in the mirror, I looked good. I felt like I was going to the office again. I was transferred to the court in a sweat box and placed in a holding cell down below the dock. Eventually, I was handcuffed to a security guard and led up to the dock where the cuffs came off. The clerk asked me to confirm my name.

"You have pleaded 'not guilty' to the charge that sometime between 3am and 7am on Sunday, 16th November you did unlawfully kill Anne-Marie MacDonald contrary to common law, do you wish to change your plea?"

"No," I said.

I was then taken back to the cell whilst the jury were sworn in.

The rest of the first day I sat in the cell whilst legal arguments went on above my head. Literally.

Eventually, on day two I was taken back to the dock and the trial-proper commenced.

The judge was an elderly grey-haired buff; mind you that might just have been the wig. Anyway, with my writer's hat on I dubbed him 'El Hombre'. El Hombre means 'the man' in Spanish and he was 'the man' who would ultimately decide my fate.

El Hombre said a few words to the jury. Basically, that it was for the prosecution to prove their case 'beyond reasonable doubt' and it was not for the defence to prove my innocence, merely to rebut, or undermine, the prosecution arguments. They did not need to offer alternative explanations, merely to explain my actions in the context of the case put forward by the prosecution.

"Remember," El Hombre said. "You are not the police. It is not your job to determine who killed the victim and why. It is your job to decide whether or not the defendant, Richard Andrew Turner, killed Anne-Marie MacDonald. That is all."

After the judge's opening remarks to the jury the prosecution put forward their argument. What is called a 'skeleton argument' in the legal trade, a brief synopsis, if you like, of what will come later. And here you will finally meet Jonathon P. Scarrott, QC, representing the

Crown in the form of the Crown Prosecution Service. He was a large, rotund man with strands of grey hair protruding from under his short white wig and with a mole on the side of his nose. He wore the garb of a QC: a silk gown, court coat and waistcoat whereas Mr Prentice wore the outfit of the barrister, i.e. the black robes, white shirt, jabot or bib and necktie in a bow and the 18th century wig.

Scarrott outlined the prosecution case which was that I had gone back to Anne-Marie's house, having met her at a nightclub. We'd had sex during which I'd played a game of strangulation with her dressing gown tie (*nice!*) and prior to that, when she'd made me coffee, I'd realised she had some money stashed in the kitchen cupboard and I'd stolen it in the night. Anne-Marie had woken up and come downstairs tying her robe and caught me in the act of theft. We'd argued and I'd pulled a knife out of the knife block and stabbed her once just below the rib cage but with the knife thrust upwards and piercing her lung, causing tension pneumothorax. Possibly, he accepted, (*nice of him*) I did not mean to kill her but had just meant to scare her enough to get her to move out of my way so I could exit the property. I had then had the presence of mind to wrap the knife in a red throw which had been over the settee which had, according to her housemate Lisa, gone missing, and rifle through Anne-Marie's handbag which was on the coffee table, and remove from it two mobile phones: an iPhone and a cheap burner phone. I had then wrapped all of the items in the throw, along with the tie I had used earlier for my strangulation game and placed the bundle in a plastic carrier bag. The prosecution case being that I might have given Anne-Marie my number which she'd put it into her phone, so I wanted to make sure it went missing. Then on the way back to my flat I'd ditched the carrier bag containing said items, possibly in the canal that I'd passed or I had disposed of it elsewhere. Job done. Case sorted.

Then, on the Monday after I had been quizzed by the police, I had panicked and thrown the money in a bin on the way to the writers' circle. Of course, it would have assisted the CPS if they could have had had the collaboration of Mr Simon Ricoh about where he'd found the money but unfortunately for them 'Sunderland' Simon was nowhere to be found (an advantage of being homeless). Mr Prentice then stood up and outlined the defence skeleton argument in somewhat briefer terms, stating that the prosecution case was 'guesswork' and 'circumstantial' and I just happened to be in the 'wrong place at the wrong time' – *you can say that again, Chaffinch, you can say that a fucking 'gain!*

The prosecution always leads, they are presenting the case after all, and it is for the defence to rebut the prosecution's arguments. So, the first days were taken up with the statements from the police officer who had been called to the address at approximately 4.40pm on Sunday afternoon when Lisa had returned from seeing her parents in Hull, and the pathologist. The court was also played the distressed 999 call and if you had a sick sense of humour, and mine possibly verges on it, the call was fairly amusing with the 999 call handler constantly repeating,

"Yes, but is she still breathing?"

And Lisa X responding, "No, she's been dead for ages. What bit of that don't you understand?"

"Yes, but please try and check for a pulse."

Lisa X was frustrated. "Look, there's no point, I can see she's been dead for hours."

I guess the court heard her distressed call to give a bit of credence and background to the whole proceedings. Then it was the turn of the pathologist. He told the court about the position of the body: it was lying between the coffee table and the settee with the legs pointing towards the kitchen (photographs shown – the jury had them in their packs). The wound, which was just below the rib cage had been caused by an upward knife thrust piercing her lung (photographs shown). The cause of death was said to be tension pneumothorax: this is where there is a large hole in the lung which causes a build-up of air in the surrounding areas which compresses other organs. The time of death was put at sometime between 3am and 7am which meant by the time the body was discovered, rigor mortis had set in, which then makes it difficult to

267

accurately determine the exact time of death. The pathologist also confirmed the fact that my DNA was on Anne-Marie's body and the fact we had intercourse (undisputed) and that there were marks on her neck consistent with 'mild strangulation' (photographs shown) but that had 'almost certainly not' killed her.

Next up was the SOCO, who reported that my fingerprints were on a mug in the kitchen bowl and the front door etc as well as on various door handles. They were also on the kitchen and bathroom cabinets but not on the satin dressing gown Anne-Marie had been wearing when she had died. On cross examination by Mr Prentice the SOCO admitted he could not be sure if I had used either tap because the fingerprint evidence was 'inconclusive'.

"So, my client could have used the hot tap, if for example, he had wanted a drink of water?"

The SOCO admitted I could have.

The first three witnesses had basically given facts and there hadn't been a need for Mr Prentice to cross-examine (bar establishing, in a roundabout way, that the hot tap had not been dusted for prints) but the fourth witness was crucial to our case and the prosecution's; Lisa X, Anne-Marie's landlady. Lisa X gave evidence via a video link, with a screen across which meant only El Hombre could see her. This was because she was in a witness protection scheme as the Met Police were intending to use her as a witness in a drugs trial which was due to start later in the year. It was clear Lisa wanted to escape the tentacles of the drugs gang and, in return for her testimony, her name was going to be changed and she was going to be moved out of the area – in other words she was going to go into witness protection. It became apparent she wasn't the sharpest knife in the block, which is probably totally the wrong phrase to use in the circumstances. It transpired that she had moved down from Hull to work in sales and been able to buy the house due to an inheritance. Various lodgers had lived with her to help pay the mortgage. Then she had become aware that one lodger was involved in drug dealing. Rather than asking him to leave Lisa X had stupidly started using drugs herself. She had become hooked; the other tenants had moved out and she had lost her job. She had found herself indebted to the gang, in drugs bondage as they say. The drugs gang had kindly agreed to pay her mortgage and bills for her in return for a little dealing and free lodgings to anyone they felt could do with a roof over their heads. So in effect, the drugs gang had taken over the house; what's termed 'cuckooing'. Normally there were quite a few people living at the address on a temporary bases but Anne-Marie had been moved in permanently as a support to Lisa X. The two women were easy to control, but by all accounts were desperate to escape the clutches of the malevolent gang. Lisa X and Anne-Marie were never allowed to chain the front door or lock it from the inside as the gang had keys and could enter at any time, hence the bell on the door handle to warn them of a visit.

Lisa X explained how Anne-Marie had come down to London from Scotland and had worked as a waitress, then she'd met a guy at a party. He had lavished gifts on her and had given her money and eventually offered her a better job out 'in the sticks' (or 'going OT' as it's termed) so she had been moved to the house where Lisa lived and became another cog in a drugs network out of London to various distribution points across the country. The line went from importers, to regional wholesalers, to brokers, to runners. Anne-Marie and Lisa X were brokers with their own network of street dealers and regular users who they'd text when a new supply of drugs arrived. According to Lisa they had a widespread network of users. Everything worked by texts to burner phones which were frequently replaced: pick-ups, collections and the like were all arranged by text, usually on a fortnightly basis. They then distributed the drugs to the runners: the 'street kidz', often under the age of sixteen, on mopeds, e-scooters or pushbikes who would sell on the street and were often arrested or attacked by rival gangs when they ventured into the wrong areas. There was no CCTV on the doorbell just in case the police raided the house and discovered it and, due to the number of parked cars up the road, it would have been difficult for any doorbells to record anything of note from the opposite side of the road. The dealers never brought drugs directly to the property just in case it was under surveillance. They only ever collected the money from the house, which gave them an opportunity to reinforce the power they held over Anne-Marie and Lisa, and to provide them with new phones (they would replace the SIM cards and redistribute them to other houses they 'owned'). Apparently, Anne-Marie had been expecting a collection that weekend. Lisa said that she and Anne-Marie were both scared of the visits and sometimes they were 'slapped about a bit' or 'keyed' if they'd not made enough money. Different people came to the address each time. Always in twos. Sometimes they recognised them, sometimes they didn't. She didn't know when a text would arrive on a burner to say they should be ready with the money but Lisa said they were always nervous when they received a text to say a collection was to be made.

Scarrott, of course, gave her an easy ride. He talked to her about her involvement in the drug gang, questioning her in such a way as to make her appear a victim. Lisa X was quizzed about the drugs paraphernalia found in the house: the scales, the cutting equipment, plastic drug bags and wraps, lists marked D and W and the lottery tickets with the circled amounts and initials. The police search had only found a few rocks of uncut crack cocaine and a plentiful supply of dope. She confirmed she wanted to 'get out of it' and 'get a life' and she was sick of being beaten up and 'shat on' by 'fucking everyone'. Of course, all this was accompanied by behind the screen tears and I could see that El Hombre looked a bit concerned. He was obviously in two minds about whether or not to have a recess (which he would have done in open court) but knowing how fragile tech can be and the fact it might not be so easy to reconnect to the court cameras, he allowed Scarrott and Mr Prentice to carry on. I almost expected the usher to pass Lisa X a virtual tissue.

It was a different story when Mr Prentice stood up to cross-examine her. We knew she was a key witness and we wanted to construct an alternative *narrative* that Anne-Marie had been killed by the drug dealers who had come to collect the money. So, the prosecution had a narrative 'there was definitely money in the kitchen cupboard awaiting collection' and so did we 'the drug dealers had killed her', but why? If the money had been there, and they had taken it as usual, what would have been the point in killing someone who Lisa admitted was 'great at distributing drugs to all sorts' – it just didn't make sense. The drug dealers wanted money, not dead bodies and police attention, and with Anne-Marie and Lisa they had a good industry going (Lisa X even admitted she took drugs back to Hull with her to distribute to dealers in that city when she went home to see her parents).

I wished I'd come clean about stealing the money right from the start but if I had that would have fitted the prosecution's *narrative* and I would have been staring down the barrels of a life sentence. I just seemed to be in a total fix.

Mr Prentice pressed Lisa X hard about the money; was it really there? Lisa was certain it had been there on Saturday morning but admitted she could not be sure that it was still there at 4am on Sunday morning.

"The money could have been collected earlier on Saturday, could it not?" Mr Prentice urged. "Before Ann-Marie went out for the night, for instance?"

Lisa agreed it could have. But that didn't really help my case as I was with Anne-Marie that evening and she had been very much alive.

"Are you sure there was money in that kitchen cupboard?" Mr Prentice quizzed.

"Yes," Lisa X replied. She wasn't sure how much but £10-12,000 sounded 'about right'. She could tell as soon as she had seen Anne-Marie's body that the money had been taken, as the kitchen cupboard doors were wide open and she could see things had 'been moved about a bit' and it was a 'right mess'. Also, plastic carrier bags had been pulled out from the recess on top of the washing machine and were 'strewn all over the kitchen floor'. She admitted that her first thought had been, 'that it was the drug dealers that had done it.'

Mr Prentice tried to question her on rival gangs but she wasn't aware of any.

"We have it pretty much stitched up… I mean the drugs gang…" she said.

"But what about threats? Has anyone ever threatened you or Anne-Marie?" he asked.

"Yeah, plenty of times, we've had loads of threats."

"But recently?"

"No," Lisa X said. "Things were going good."

"Things were going good." Mr Prentice hummed under his breath and sat down.

Not for me they weren't.

Lisa X spent about a day in the virtual witness box and at the end of it I could see we were no further forward. Mr Prentice did his best; he tried to put it to Lisa that Anne-Marie and the drug dealers had got into an argument but Lisa said that was 'highly unlikely' as there were normally two men visiting and they were 'well hard' and both she and Anne-Marie had been 'walloped' or 'keyed' multiple times by them so they knew not to upset them. It was all very depressing. I just had nothing to support my case: the kitchen knife that had been taken from knife block, her mobile phone, the burner (Lisa said that she thought Anne-Marie would have had the burner phone on her constantly) and dressing gown tie had all gone missing from the house, along with the condom loaded with cocaine from the bathroom (Lisa didn't know about that but might have been covering her own back) and the throw off the settee, which all meant there was no evidence of anyone else being in the house and no forced entry.

At the end of the day, I was transported back to my cell and had a debrief with Dom. I lay on my bunk and stared at the ceiling whilst I talked to him. Lisa X had been key to our case but we had been unable to get her to admit there was even the slightest chance that members of the drugs gang, or possibly a rival gang, had killed Anne-Marie. I felt a sense of hopelessness. I was lost in a fog of my own making. I felt angry with myself. I just could not believe what a fucking mess I'd got into. It was so tragic as to be untrue.

The next day it was the turn of PC Snot and PC Hazel Eyes (better known as Price and Tanner) to take the stand. They had undertaken the routine enquiry on the Monday evening when I had denied ever having met Anne-Marie. Again, the prosecution led the cross-examination.

"Was the defendant a suspect at that time?" Scarrott asked.

"No," PC Price, or was it Tanner, I was still unsure – said. "Although we had reviewed the club CCTV it was inconclusive. He was about the right height and build and the defendant had a mullet haircut at that time but CCTV can be difficult to determine body size, particularly if the individual is walking away from the camera, as was the case here or is with a crowd of people, which is also the case as others were leaving at the same time. The CCTV evidence in the club was also of poor quality and difficult to make a positive identification but there were some similar features."

"To the defendant?" Scarrott asked.

"Yes, sir."

"Why then did you want to talk to him? I am sure there must have been hundreds of young men in the club that night," Scarrott said, a fist to the side of his body, his black gown pushed back. His neat white wig fitted perfectly on his elongated head. I had a suspicion he powdered his face to give a more 'natural' effect.

"Exactly so, sir," PC Snot said. "The young man in question had been mentioned on social media. Apparently, someone knew his friend," here he consulted his notes, "a Mark Reed – and someone had put on social media '*saw Anne-Marie leave with a friend of Mark Reed's* so that gave us a heads up."

"And you interviewed, in the slackest sense of the word, all this Mark Reed's friends?"

"Yes, sir," PC Snot said. "And some others who were of interest as well."

"And what did the defendant say?" Scarrott asked.

"He denied ever meeting Anne-Marie but did admit he'd left the club on his own and he admitted he had been on his own in the club for some time."

"And the others?" Scarrott asked.

"The others, a Mathew Froggatt, Dave Smith and John Sugden, all said they had been together at the bar. Fortunately, the CCTV at the bar was of far better quality and we were able to verify that this was indeed the case."

"So, that just left the defendant without an alibi?" Scarrott said.

"Indeed so, sir, yes."

Then PC Hazel Eyes took the stand, and said I'd appeared interested in the case despite denying all knowledge of having met Anne-Marie. Apparently I'd seemed nervous and on edge. She recounted the story of the pen and how I had anxiously pressed it up and down.

"No more questions, Your Honour," Scarrott said and sat down with aplomb.

Mr Prentice didn't have any questions to ask either of them. Next up was DCI Hinton who was the SIO.

"At what stage did the defendant become a suspect?" Scarrott asked.

Hinton lifted his head and looked Scarrott in the eye. "Well, here's the thing, we lifted fingerprints from where Anne-Marie lived, 32 Church Street and a number of particles of DNA in the form of skin cells and also fibres. The most interesting prints were on the coffee cup. There was possibly a match on the PNC to the defendant so we went to his address to bring him in for an interview based on that as well as the CCTV evidence and social media. Unfortunately, the prints on the coffee cup were a bit smeared as the victim had also held the cup so they were not conclusive and the DNA and fibre evidence took longer to process. However, when we arrived at his address, the defendant said he had prepared a written statement which he described as a 'confession'."

"Did he indeed?" Scarrott said, raising his eyebrows. "And what did this so-called confession say?"

Hinton smiled. "Well, he admitted that had met Anne-Marie and gone back to her house; they had had sex and then he had left the house."

Scarrott then took Hinton through my other statements: the verbal collaboration to written statement, the two 'no comment' interviews and the last interview following my arrest. Hinton kindly pointed out a number of inconsistencies and discrepancies in all my testimonies.

"Have you ever come across a defendant who has, when he is not a suspect, denied everything, then in his first voluntary interview, when he is a suspect, co-operates with the police and even gives them a typed statement which he refers to as a 'confession' and then, in the second and third interviews, when asked to clarify a few minor points gives unhelpful 'no comment' interviews but then comes back for more, when arrested, and gives a further interview? Have you ever met such a suspect in your long and illustrious career, DCI Hinton?"

Hinton folded his arms and smiled smugly. "No, sir, I must say the defendant exhibited rather bizarre behaviour from start to finish. Normally the first interview is likely to be 'no comment', if the interviewee is so minded, and when the police present more information, supported by additional evidence, there might be a desire to explain. In this case the opposite happened and then, once arrested, the defendant seemed to have a yearning to get things off his chest as it were."

"And why do you think that the defendant chose not to help the police with their enquiries, to then help the police with their enquiries, then not to help the police with their enquiries and then finally to help the police with their enquiries again?" Scarrott asked.

Some members of the jury laughed and there were titters in the public gallery. I wanted to stand up and say *'it wasn't like that for, fuck's sake, I listened to legal advice, I shouldn't have undertaken the voluntary without a solicitor'* – but it was too late. It was all too late.

Hinton placed his hands in front of him. He was wearing a new black suit, he looked like the father of the bride at a wedding – he was just missing the carnation. His hair had been cut and I'm sure his shoes were polished to army parade levels.

"I can only imagine the defendant felt he could get us off his back, so to speak, by giving a voluntary interview and the written statement and when that didn't work, he gave us the run around, two 'no-comment' interviews and then another interview in which he tried to elaborate a bit more, which is all very contrary behaviour."

"And whilst not establishing his guilt would that perhaps suggest to you, DCI Hinton, with your thirty years of exemplary experience, that the defendant had something to hide? Would it not suggest that the defendant, to use popular parlance, was 'running scared'?" Scarrott asked.

"Indeed, so, yes, sir," Hinton said. "Right from the get-go I felt the defendant was not being as open and honest as he might be."

Of course, Hinton's testimony was accompanied by interview footage from the various interviews I'd undertaken. In each I moved uneasily, tugged my mullet and seemed to prevaricate, pause and hum and ha (God, I never realised I did that so much!) as I tried to give a very good impression of Mr Guilty.

Scarrott then took Hinton through the other lines of enquiry, Citi Cabs and Mr Simon Ricoh.

"Unfortunately, he had absconded from the approved premises before we had an opportunity to interview him but it seemed likely that his story about discovering the money in the council bin was genuine. After all there was no forced entry at the victim's house and why would he randomly select that particular premises to rob? He would not know about the money after all. He had a criminal record in regard to an incident of domestic violence but nothing in regard to theft or burglary and there was no evidence he was a drug user."

"If he'd not have absconded from the approved premises, it might have given you an opportunity to interview him about the provenance of the money and which bin he had found it in, is that correct?" Scarrott asked.

"Yes, it is. Regrettably, by the time myself and DI Drake became aware of the money and the fracas in the Lord Rochford, Simon Ricoh, or 'Sunderland' Simon as he's known, had absconded so we were unable to ascertain which bin he found the money in or indeed to seek clarification of his movements and whereabouts on the night of Saturday, 15th November and the early morning of Sunday, 16th. All we knew was that he sometimes slept in a park which happened to be fairly near to the victim's house."

"Thank you, DCI Hinton, most enlightening. That will be all," Scarrott said and, with a wave of his gown, sat back down.

Mr Prentice stood up. He cross-examined Hinton at some length, asking him to speculate on why I might have answered some questions in the way I had and whether or not I might have been nervous and scared by the whole process. Hinton agreed that was one explanation but it did not explain some inconsistencies in the statements nor – in his words – 'the strange way I had gone about things.'

He also probed more deeply into 'Sunderland' Simon discovering the money in a bin and then absconding from the approved premises.

"Although you have stated in your previous testimony that it is likely the money was found in a bin, as Mr Simon Ricoh said in the statement he gave to DCI Murray, and that you felt you could rule him out as a suspect, it is also true, is it not, that there are none of my client's fingerprints on the money?"

"That's correct," Hinton stated.

"And I assume the money has now been thoroughly examined?"

"Yes, it has," Hinton stated.

"Would that be unusual? No fingerprints I mean?" Mr Prentice probed.

Hinton smirked. "Well, it depends if the defendant wore gloves."

"But another explanation might be that he did not touch the money at all, is that not the case?"

Hinton agreed it was but in typical police style there was a qualification. There's always a qualification. "It's a reasonable assumption but we can't rule out the possibility that the defendant wore gloves at some stage."

Mr Prentice bristled. "You seem to be suggesting, DCI Hinton, that my client wore gloves when he entered and left the Pryzm nightclub on the Saturday night: the CCTV evidence would seem to contradict that view."

Hinton looked on edge. "No, I'm not saying that but he may have put them on later."

"In the evening?"

"Yes."

"So, my client had gloves on his person when he entered the victim's house but he only put them on *after* he had opened the kitchen cupboard?"

"I suppose not," Hinton croaked.

"So, there were no gloves?"

"Possibly not," Hinton finally conceded. "But the victim's housemate, Lisa X, stated that the money was in an envelope."

"But there's no evidence of that either, is there?" Mr Prentice stated. "I mean the envelope has not been found, has it?"

"No," Hinton agreed.

"So, we cannot know that for sure, can we?" Mr Prentice pressed.

Hinton conceded that the police only had Lisa X's word for it that the money was in an envelope. Fortunately, when she'd been cross-examined she had been very vague about the dimensions and the colour of any envelope, even admitting that the money might have been in a 'plastic bag'. And fortunately, there was no mention of an envelope at all in Simon Ricoh's statement.

Mr Prentice let a whisker of a smile slip across his face. Whilst Hinton was on the back foot, he managed to get an admission from him that the police could not be completely certain of 'Sunderland' Simon's innocence as they had been unable to corroborate his story about the provenance of the money and his whereabouts on the Saturday night and Sunday morning.

DI Drake gave a similar testimony.

The final witness for the prosecution that day was Mr Iqbal from Citi Cabs. He said I had come to the minicab office in an 'aggressive and threatening manner' on 22nd November. He explained that the cab company had stopped taking fares from Anne-Marie and Lisa X as Anne-Marie had been in a relationship with one of their drivers and had supplied him with drugs to distribute around town. They had sacked the driver but were suspicious of the activities that went on at the house and that was why they often followed her if they saw her out and they didn't have a fare. They were aware as well that the former driver, who was a brother of one of the current drivers, was 'still in a relationship with Anne-Marie' and when the Citi Cab driver had seen me with Anne-Marie leaving the club, they thought she was cheating on him. Prior to Mr Iqbal's testimony, the driver that had followed us answered a few questions but as his English was limited and a translator was required, he only confirmed the fact that he had indeed been the driver of the minicab that had followed me – Mr Iqbal provided the substance.

The following day started with the testimony of Detective Inspector Murray. He had interviewed 'Sunderland' Simon Ricoh who had been placed in an approved premises until his trial and done a 'runner' a couple of days later. Murray was a complete arsehole, I nicknamed him Yul Grinner, after Yul Brynner. Whilst I had respect for Hinton and Drake – they had both been very professional and courteous and I knew they had only been doing their jobs – I had none for Murray. He thought he was a stand-up comic and this was his fifteen minutes of fame, never mind that a young woman had been murdered and I was staring down the barrels of a life sentence. Murray was a large, bald-headed bastard with an irregular laugh which led his shoulders to go up and down like Muttley in the *Wacky Races*. Boy, did Murray enjoy a good belly laugh! He told the court about 'Sunderland' Simon's encounter with the builders in the Lord Rochford with requisite jokes about beer (*I didn't know the beer in Wetherspoons was so good people had to fight over it*) and how he'd been waiting six months for his extension to be built due to a shortage of builders.

"No wonder," Murray said. "They're all in the Rochford."

In fact, here is a selection of one-liners from the 'Yul Grinner Joke Book'.

(About homeless 'Sunderland' Simon) "£10,000? He could buy a lot of sleeping bags for that – and maybe he could even run to a tent."

"I thought the council was in debt? Well, if they emptied the bins a bit more regularly, they'd have had a nice little windfall from time to time."

"Maybe the person who left the money in the bin was drunk and thought they were depositing it in a bank."

He stated that when 'the character' called 'Sunderland' Simon ('I guess they nicknamed him that because he came from Sunderland' – was yet another of Murray's 'witticisms') was arrested he had had a large amount of money 'on his person' (in his pocket to you and me) which, he had said, he had found it in a city bin. It didn't seem to matter that 'Sunderland' Simon was no longer available to give evidence, for one of Murray's many, many talents was the ability to mimic a Wearside accent which he did with great self-assurance as he repeated, reading from his notes, what Simon had said.

What entertainment DCI Murray was! He drew many laughs from the jury and the public gallery and that spurred him on to greater forays into his comedic routine.

Of course, he was being grilled by a very serious Mr Scarrott QC, who was stony-faced and as unamused as Queen Victoria. In fact, it was the only time in the whole trial that I was actually on Scarrott's side. He asked

Murray to clarify where Mr Ricoh had said he'd found the money.

"In a council bin, sir," Yul Grinner said.

"Which bin?" Scarrott enquired.

Yul Grinner shrugged his shoulders, laughed like Muttley and then bared his horse-like white teeth.

"No idea, sir, the council are guilty of fitting numerous litter bins around the pedestrian area to combat litter pollution, and one yellow or concrete council bin looks much the same as another. Now the IRA have stopped their campaign of terror on mainland Britain the litter bin is once again a fashionable town centre accessory."

I could see that Scarrott was absolutely fuming; his large chest went up and down like an airbed that was being inflated. He looked as if he was almost struggling to breath and had to take a sip of water. I thought if he got close to Yul Grinner, he'd be liable to thump him.

"This court has no interest in the antics of the Irish Republican Army, DCI Murray," Scarrott said, "I asked you a simple question and you have responded that you have no idea which bin the money was placed in, is that correct?"

"Yes, sir."

"So, when you interviewed this individual, Simon Ricoh, you didn't think to question him about the specifics of which bin he found the money in?"

"No, sir," said Grinner, "To be honest I thought it was a tallest tale I'd ever heard in my life and it didn't seem significant at the time."

"It didn't seem significant," Scarrott repeated. "So, it could have been any bin in the pedestrianised area of the town centre?"

"Yes, sir," Grinner said as he wiped his sweating head with a handkerchief and then, unable to resist a joke, he added, "I suspect it was the bin by the bank."

And this is where he threaded in his 'pissed bank depositor' joke.

El Hombre gave Grinner a piercing look.

"I would thank you, DCI Murray, to treat the court with a good deal more gravity and less hilarity."

"Yes, Your Honour," Yul Grinner said, still smiling. El Hombre was not going to get the better of Murray; Murray was here for a laugh and all jokes would be repeated ad infinitum to his police colleagues. This was his moment to shine – and not just his glistening, bald head.

Scarrott continued. "Thank you, Your Honour, a timely intervention."

He then paused as he was apt to do.

"So, DCI Murray," Scarrott continued. "You didn't try to investigate the man's story, knowing another man was being questioned for murder which might have been linked to the possible theft of some monies of a similar amount?"

"We didn't know that at the time, did we, sir?" Murray countered with a broad smile and a shrug of the shoulders. "Simon Ricoh was arrested for assault and affray, that was the charge we put to him, the money was another matter."

I could almost see Scarrott's look of despair; fortunately, 'Sunderland' Simon, being a thorough sort of chap, had looked in many a council bin before he had hit upon his monetary jackpot. CCTV showed him taking things out and dropping them back into pretty much every council bin along the pedestrianised zone. You just could not tell in which bin he had found the money. It could have been the one I could be seen (possibly) dropping something into, but it might not have been. Snookered!

"Where's the money now?" Scarrott asked in almost resigned disbelief.

"We confiscated it until we could find its rightful owner," Grinner said.

"I suspect you communicated this to DCI Hinton, knowing he was investigating the murder of Anne-Marie MacDonald?" Scarrott asked.

"Not right away," Grinner shrugged dismissively. "What with shift patterns and one thing and another it was a couple of days later."

"So, you informed DCI Hinton a couple of days later?" Scarrott repeated.

"Yes, sir," said Grinner. "We then married the two cases together."

"And then what?" Scarrott asked.

"I believe DCI Hinton and DI Drake drove to the approved premises to interview Mr Ricoh but he had absconded."

Scarrott took his glasses off and wiped them with his JPS initialled white handkerchief and repeated, "he had absconded."

I could tell what he really wanted to say was, '*Are you for fucking real, Murray? No wonder the police are so fucking incompetent with arseholes like you in their ranks*', but, not surprisingly, he resisted the temptation.

"So," said Scarrott, "Mr Simon Ricoh is probably sunning himself in the Bahamas now. No more questions, your Honour." There were none from Mr Prentice either. Things were starting to look up. For the first time in a long time, I had a smile on my face. A smile almost as broad as Yul Grinner's.

And that was the prosecution case all wrapped up! Of course, there was far more to it than what I have recorded here. Scarrott fleshed out his 'skeleton argument', called other witnesses, made the 'circumstantial' appear 'factual', but I want to move on to the important stuff – the defence – and the parts of the trial I can remember all too clearly. So, by the third, or was it the fourth day or even the fifth, of the trial, I can't rightly remember now, Mr Prentice commenced the rebuttal. Finally, I was able to stand in the dock and Mr Prentice went through my evidence. I stood with my hand in my right pocket, gripping my Millwall FC 'lucky charm' lion.

Mr Prentice started off slowly. He talked about my upbringing and my family make-up: the fact I was brought up by a single mother and had two older sisters and that I was the first member of the family to go to university.

"So, you did well to get two A-levels and got to university?" Mr Prentice asked.

"I like to think so, yes," I said.

"And you got a Lower Second in Film and Media Studies which is quite a hard course, so I understand," Mr Prentice said.

That led to general mirth from the public gallery and a titter from the jury. Even El Hombre smiled, such was the contempt in which such courses were held.

"And where did you study?" Mt Prentice asked.

I gave the name of the university in the Midlands.

"Umm, a fair trek from South East London. So, at eighteen, you left home and had to make your own way in the world?"

"Yes."

He then asked me about my time at university, friendships, the course, my interest in writing… and my high level of personal debt.

"It shows you're a person who can apply yourself and are self-motivated," Mr Prentice continued. "Am I right in saying that, throughout your time at university, you received no financial support from your family?"

"Yes, that's right."

"Would you say that was an unusual situation?" Mr Prentice asked.

"Yes, very, most students did receive financial help from their families but my mum never had much money so it was hard for her."

"And your father? He left when you were seven and he never contributed to your upkeep at all?"

"No. My mum never received a penny from him despite the CSA trying to track him down. He told me at one point he was declared bankrupt and they gave up after that."

"I see," Mr Prentice said. "The CSA was replaced by the Child Maintenance Service, I believe?"

"Yes, that's correct but it was the CSA when we were children."

Mr Prentice continued. "So, you had to work at various times, perhaps when other students were studying?"

"Yes, I did part-time jobs in supermarkets and pubs whilst I was at uni," I said.

"And perhaps that explains why you were tempted by online gambling, is that not right?" Mr Prentice asked.

"Yes," I replied. "I was lured by the appeal of easy money, but it never works out like that, does it?"

"Indeed not," Mr Prentice said. "But if a young lad, away from home, has a friend who has won some money, it's not surprising you'd be tempted to give it a go; given you were short of cash, is that not the case?"

"Yes."

"And, I believe, it is quite easy now with phones, tablets, laptops etc – you can gamble pretty much anywhere and at any time, is that not right?" Mr Prentice asked.

"Yes, that's correct, but I wasn't addicted," I protested.

"No one is saying you were, no one is saying you were," Mr Prentice said. "I am just saying that an eighteen-year-old, away from home for the first time, wants to keep up with his friends, sees one of them win some money, and he tries it too, nothing unusual in that."

Then he asked me about my dad. How I'd re-established contact with him whilst at Uni and had gone down to Brighton to see him.

"It's a fair trek from the Midlands to London and then to Brighton, how did you travel?"

"By train or National Express coach."

"Expensive though?" Mr Prentice mused. "Particularly by train?"

"Yes, the coach was quite a good deal, but the train was very expensive. I had a student rail card, but it was still a lot of money."

"Did your father ever give you any money towards the trips? After all, they were at his behest."

"No."

"So that was all from your own pocket?" Mr Prentice asked.

"Yes, sometimes, on the way back, I would get the train from Brighton to London Bridge and then take the train to South Bermondsey to see Mum as well as Kate and Donna if they were around. They thought I'd just come down from the Midlands. I'd stay one or two nights depending on whether I had any lectures on the Monday morning; if not I'd travel back then – to kill two birds as it were."

"Indeed," Mr Prentice said. "A good use of time."

Next Mr Prentice questioned me about my life post university – my administrative job in South East London on the twelve-month temporary contract and then at Zorin Logistics. I told him how I liked the job and had stopped looking for another opening even though the pay wasn't great.

"But whilst employed at Zorin you passed the threshold for paying back your student loan and had to pay back how much exactly?" Mr Prentice asked.

"Nine percent, so about £500 a year," I said.

Mr Prentice then asked about my relationship with Debbie and my creative writing. He questioned me a lot about that: what I had published, the fact I had completed a creative writing correspondence course as well (whilst at uni) and joined a couple of writers' circles. Mr Prentice seemed to like that.

"And you write poetry too?" Mr Prentice asked.

"I have been known to pen the odd bit of doggerel," I said.

The court laughed, even El Hombre tittered. Mr Prentice was stitching together his famous narrative like a patchwork blanket, and I felt it was going well. I felt I was presenting as a good and credible witness. That's what I thought anyway.

Next, we moved on to Anne-Marie.

I explained how I had met her in the Pryzm nightclub and gone back to her house, we had had sex, I'd had a headache, I had gone to the toilet, opened the bathroom cupboard door and seen a condom part filled with cocaine after which I couldn't sleep so I had got dressed and gone downstairs. I'd felt thirsty so I had gone to the kitchen to get a glass of water. I had looked in cupboards for a glass but couldn't find one so I had used the mug I had drunk coffee from earlier. I had used the hot tap by mistake and tipped the tepid water away and then I had left the house.

I had denied knowing Anne-Marie on the Monday because I had been alarmed by the police presence in my flat. Also, I hadn't wanted my ex-girlfriend Debbie finding out I'd cheated on her; I knew from social media a woman had died and thought it might be Anne-Marie.

"What happened next?" Mr Prentice asked.

"What when the police left?" I asked.

"Yes."

"I went to my writers' circle."

"And where and when is that, Mr Turner?" Mr Prentice asked.

"In meeting room 3 in the public library every Monday at 7pm."

"And how did you normally get to the library?" he asked.

"I'd walk from my flat down an alley which leads between houses and shops onto the pedestrian zone. I'd then walk through the town, normally stopping at a fast-food restaurant en route; the library is at the far end."

Mr Prentice smiled. "I see." He consulted his notes. "But this particular Monday, 17th November, you missed out on the burger and went straight to the library, why was that?"

"I had been held up by the police visit."

"So, you walked straight to the library and as you walked through the pedestrianised zone you would have passed any number of council litter bins?" Mr Prentice asked.

"Yes, probably."

"Do you recall dropping anything into any of the bins as you made your way to the library?" Mr Prentice asked.

I shook my head. "No, not as I can recall."

"So, you don't know if you dropped anything in a council bin?" Mr Prentice pressed.

"To be honest, I can't, but that doesn't mean I didn't drop a tissue from my pocket or something in a bin; it's hardly memorable, is it?"

"I'm sure it's not. In fact, I don't suppose many of us would recall throwing rubbish in a council bin," Mr Prentice said.

Next CCTV was shown to the court of man who looked remarkably similar to me (*my God, it was me!*) strolling through the town centre, wearing a black leather jacket and carrying an umbrella. I had a black folder under my right arm. The image showed me stopping by a bin, after which it was a little blurred as the umbrella had obscured the image from the closest camera but I seemed to place my folder on the rim of the bin and then I moved off. Of course, the rain and moisture didn't help picture quality either.

"Does that person look like you?" Mr Prentice asked.

I agreed it did. I also confirmed that the black leather jacket looked like the one I had been wearing, I had been carrying an umbrella and I would have walked past the bin at approximately the time the CCTV had recorded which was shortly before 7pm.

"You stop by it and you might be throwing something in the bin, is that not the case?" Mr Prentice probed.

"I might be," I agreed. "I don't really recall what but that certainly seems to be the case."

Mr Prentice looked at me through his little round glasses which magnified his small eyes. He was a young man making his way in the legal profession. I knew this was a big case for him. A challenging case against a top, well-respected QC like Scarrott. There was almost a twitching smile on his face. He knew we were doing well.

"Explain to me what happened the next day, Tuesday, at work," Mr Prentice asked, turning a page over in his file.

I told him how I had been worried, confused and upset about the police visit and I hadn't been able to sleep. I had always got on well with my line manager, Helen Glover, so, the next day, I had gone to seek her advice.

"And what did she suggest you do?" Mr Prentice asked.

"She said I should make a full statement. She suggested that I write it up and take it to the police station."

"And that's what you were doing when DCI Hinton arrived to ask if you wanted to come to the police station to undertake a voluntary interview, is it not?"

"Yes."

"You referred to the statement as a 'confession', why was that?"

"I dunno. It was purely a slip of the tongue," I said and then added, "I'm not used to police procedures and it just seemed to be what people said... in movies and such like... I guess I was a bit naïve."

"Precisely so, so moving on, did you have any hesitation about giving a voluntary interview?"

"Absolutely not, no."

"And although it was given under PACE, so you were entitled to legal representation, you waived that right, didn't you?"

"Yes."

"Why?"

"I had nothing to hide. I wanted the police to know I was innocent so they could concentrate on catching the real killer or killers."

"So why, on the next two occasions did you give 'no comment' interviews?" Mr Prentice asked.

"That was on the advice of my brief. I felt very uneasy about it so, when I was arrested, I told my new solicitor I was desperate to tell the police everything I knew to help them catch the killer or killers."

"Yes, very good," Mr Prentice said. He took a sip of water and surreptitiously eyed the jury. Were they buying it? I had given an account of my seemingly inconsistent behaviour regarding the interviews.

Next Mr Prentice took me through the other interviews right up to the time of my arrest, concentrating on certain aspects: the bloodstains on the glasses, my dabs on the kitchen cupboard, the Beamer that had been parked up the road when I'd left Anne-Marie's house. Finally, he dealt with the topics El Hombre had refused to accept as 'inadmissible': the prosecution's insinuation that I had a penchant for 'rough sex' and then the assault on the repo man, or bailiff as he was referred to in court. First, he dealt with my relationship with Debbie, and I accepted we had played consensual sex games but they had never involved the restriction of airflow by applying pressure to the neck which some people find gives heightened sexual arousal.

"So sometimes you play some mild BDSM games at your flat but sometimes you'd cook Miss King a meal or sometimes you'd have a takeaway and watch a movie, it's no more or less than that?"

I agreed it wasn't.

Then he had to deal with the assault which had occurred when I had been twenty-five or six, I'm not sure exactly now.

"How would you describe that assault?" Mr Prentice asked.

"It was an accident," I said, "I felt embarrassed because the other tenants were looking out of their windows, and some were filming my car being removed on their phones. I got annoyed, I loved that car – it was my first car and I was really attached to it. I didn't want to lose it but knew it would be taken away. Also, some of my ex-girlfriends' things were on the back seat and I was unable to take them out. The magistrates felt the men from the repossession company had been high-handed and had antagonised me by not allowing that simple request. I didn't mean to head-butt the guy."

That brought a laugh from the public gallery and jury, even Scarrott smiled.

"Before that incident had you ever been in trouble with the police?" Mr Prentice asked.

"No," I said.

"Nor after it?" Mr Prentice asked.

"No."

"And records show you completed your Community Service without any issues?" Mr Prentice stated.

I said I did.

"In fact, the probation report described you as a model offender, is that not right?"

"Yes."

"You did gardening, didn't you?"

"Amongst other things."

"And isn't it true you got on so well with the gentleman who provided plants to the community groups and old people's homes that you supported, that he allowed you to buy plants at a discounted price for tubs at the front of the rented house you lived in?"

"Yes, it is."

"Thank you, Mr Turner, that is all from the defence."

After Mr Prentice had sat down it was the prosecution's turn to cross-examine me. I disliked Jonathon P. Scarrott, Queen's Counsel from first glance. He was a bumptious, egotistical toad. He looked at me as if I was something on his shoe. I was clearly guilty, and I was wasting everyone's time by not admitting it. His shock of grey/white wavy hair protruded from beneath his white wig as if it was a matching outfit. His watercolour blue eyes were set on a pale aubergine-shaped face. He was dressed in the QC's robes, of course, underneath which I could see the trousers of an expensive grey suit. He wore a Rolex on one wrist and a gold chain on the other. Scarrott didn't need any Apple watch to tell him when to get up and move around and monitor his activity – he knew *exactly* when to move, *exactly* when to pounce. Like a lion in the savannah, Scarrott was one of life's predators.

So Scarrott stood, paused (silence was a large part of the Scarrott game) and whilst the court room waited, Scarrott said nothing. He was centre stage, and he was in control. I was to realise he was a man who had cultivated the art of silence. Then finally he spoke, deep, clipped, assured.

"Mr Turner, why, when the police first carried out a routine check at your address on the night of Monday,

17th November did you deny having ever met Miss MacDonald? Any explanation?"

I was ready for this; I had rehearsed it with Mr Prentice, Hannah and Dom.

"I...I...felt nervous and anxious. I had cheated on my girlfriend and I didn't want her to know about it," I said.

"Speak up," Scarrott said. "I don't think the jury could hear you."

I was surprised he hadn't address me as 'boy' and I was shocked he felt my voice was quiet as Mr Prentice had had no trouble.... But then again it was just a tactic. It was to knock me slightly off balance, like the silence, it was all done to unsettle me.

"I felt nervous and anxious," I almost shouted.

"And the rest of it, what else did you say?" Scarrott asked.

"I had cheated on my girlfriend, Debbie, and didn't want her to find out," I said.

Scarrott appeared to be looking at his notes. His voice echoed through the chamber, loud and clear and resonating. "Ah, yes, you had cheated on your girlfriend and didn't want her to find out. And are you still in a relationship with Miss King?" Scarrott asked.

"No," I said.

"Did she terminate the relationship or did you?"

"She did."

"Can I ask why?" Scarrott asked.

"She didn't like the fact I was implicated in a murder; she had a young son, you see…"

"Implicated," Scarrott repeated. "Strange choice of words. And could I suggest that perhaps she didn't like the fact you had cheated on her?" Scarrott waved his reading glass, hand on hip, staring directly at me with ice-cold, hard, emotionless eyes.

I blushed. I didn't know if any of Debbie's friends were in the public gallery or not, she was a witness so she had to remain away from court until she had given her evidence.

"No, that's right, who would?"

"Who would, indeed, Mr Turner? Who would indeed? It's right your nickname is 'Rat', isn't it?" He paused. "Because of your initials I mean, Richard Andrew Turner," Scarrott continued.

"Yes, it is," I said.

That drew a titter from the jury which developed into full blown laughter across the court. Scarrott had achieved two things: he had the jury on his side and he had made me look like a love rat. Round One. Seconds out. Next round, pin the murder on him.

"I want to question you some more about that Monday when you were first interviewed… no, no that's the wrong word… you were spoken to by the police… routine… but first of all I am going to take you back to the night of that fateful Saturday in November. Step by step, in as much detail as possible, if you don't mind."

Scarrott smiled, deep and rich and dark. He knew I couldn't mind. I wasn't here to mind. I had to give evidence. I was a murder suspect. I was fighting for my life.

So, once again I went through what I had told Mr Prentice and every now and again Scarrott would intervene and ask for clarification, but I told the story. True and unabridged. Bar the money, of course.

"Do you normally wear contact lenses, Mr Turner?" Scarrott asked.

"Yes."

"And what type are they?"

"Daily disposables."

"Daily disposables," Scarrott hissed. "Does that mean they should be disposed of each day, before you go to bed for instance?"

"Yes, that's correct."

"So, you wouldn't normally go to sleep in your contact lenses?" Scarrott asked.

"No," I said. I was puzzled.

"Have you ever?" Scarrott asked. "Gone to sleep in them, I mean?"

"I may have nodded off once or twice or when I've been drunk but I try to avoid it and I'm normally pretty careful."

"Would you say that nodding off, having a quick nap, going to sleep in your contact lenses was a rare or common event, Mr Turner?" Scarrott pursued.

I shrugged. "I don't really know."

"Come now, Mr Turner. Answer the question – rare or common?"

"Rare, I guess."

"And can you remember, when you entered Anne-Marie's house were you wearing glasses or contact lenses?" Scarrott asked.

"Contact lenses."

"Are you sure?" Scarrott pressed.

"Yes."

"So, you never took your contact lenses out before you entered the victim's house? In the car before you drove to her home or perhaps outside her house?"

"No."

"So, you weren't wearing glasses when you entered Anne-Marie's house?"

"No."

"So, if we take your previous answers to their logical conclusion on this occasion – Saturday 15th November – you *did* fall asleep in Anne-Marie's bed, for some hours whilst wearing your contact lenses."

Bugger, I thought, *the slimy toad has caught me out*.

"Yes, that's right," I said.

Scarrott punched home his winning advantage. "But just for the sake of clarity, that would not be something you would normally do. Indeed, it is something you have described as being 'rare', as ordinarily you like to take them out before you go to sleep?"

"Yes," I said, deflated.

"So why was it different on this occasion, Mr Turner?" Scarrott paced very slowly, and sometimes turned, like a pendulum of a clock, hypnotic.

"I forgot to take my glasses into the house with me." The truth was when I'd parked outside Anne-Marie's house I was unsure how the evening would end. Anne-Marie had seemed to go a tad cool and I thought it would look a bit forward to collect my glasses from the glove compartment.

Scarrott repeated what I had just said very slowly and deliberately. Then he said,

"Would another explanation perhaps be that you did take your contact lenses out in the car, put on your glasses on and wear them into the house?"

"No."

"How do you account for traces of Anne-Marie's blood on those very same glasses?" he asked.

"She cut her finger on an advertising card given out by the doorman at The Pryzm, I told her I had some plasters in the glove compartment – she must have moved my glasses."

"Did she find any plasters?" Scarrott asked.

"No."

"But there were some in your glove compartment, weren't there?" Scarrott questioned. "I am now asking the jury to look at the photograph numbered C36 in their packs and I'm showing it to the defendant. You can see a box of plasters positioned at the front of your glove compartment, can't you?"

"Yes."

"Not hard to see, are they? How do you account for the fact the victim didn't find them?"

"She didn't look hard enough."

That caused a moderate level of mirth in the public gallery.

"Convenient, isn't it, Mr Turner?" Scarrott said.

"What is?"

"That Anne-Marie cuts her thumb on a piece of paper the very same night someone thrusts a knife into her lung."

Mr Prentice was on his feet, infuriated. "This speculation is quite out of order," he said. Scarrott smiled in that sarcastic way of his; once again he had made his point but there was a cut on Anne-Marie's finger, there were pathologist photographs to prove it. She'd put her own plaster on it when she'd gone to the toilet for about three hours.

"She did cut her thumb, there was a photograph shown earlier – she had put a blue plaster on it," I said. I felt on edge.

"Thumb or finger?" Scarrott questioned.

My heat vibrated like an overstruck gong. I felt anxious, suddenly I couldn't remember. I tried to think back to the photographs but they had been shown days earlier by the pathologist. My mind went blank. "I'm not sure now."

"Come now, Mr Turner, this slight mishap happened in your car and you can't recall whether she cut her thumb or finger?"

Just to emphasis the point Scarrott raised his thumb and then his finger as if I didn't know the fucking difference.

"Thumb or finger?" Scarrott repeated.

"I can't remember," I answered. Then it came to me. "Actually, I think it was her finger, I don't know why I said thumb."

"You're right," Scarrott said. "It was her index finger. A fifty percent chance and you guessed right. And that happened in your car? This cut to her finger?"

"Yes."

"On an advertising flyer, a piece of card or paper?"

"Yes."

Scarrott looked at me. Waved his glasses with a flourish. "But it was only a small abrasion and may have happened earlier that day, before she went out for instance. And, as has been established, it was in fact, her own plaster on her finger. After all she was unable to find one of yours despite searching your glove compartment for plasters which were, in fact, there." He paused. "So having cut her finger on a piece of card that has gone missing and being unable to find plasters that were at the front of your glove compartment she sucked her finger till she got home and then ran to the toilet, with her handbag, and reappeared, sometime later, with a plaster on said finger, is that correct?"

I nodded. "Yes."

"So, you are now in the house with Anne-Marie, what did you do during her extended trip to the toilet?"

"Nothing, I sat on the sofa."

"Come now, Mr Turner, that's not strictly true, is it? Didn't you send a text to your erstwhile girlfriend saying how much you missed her and loved her and how you were now home and you couldn't wait to see her later in the day – it now being Sunday?"

I took a deep breath. "Yes," I said.

"Members of the jury, you will see a transcript of that text labelled exhibit TC05 in your packs. But does my version cover the essential elements, Mr Turner?"

"Yes, it does."

Scarrott paused and looked at his notes.

"When Anne-Marie eventually returned to the living room and made you a cup of coffee did you go into the kitchen?" he asked at last.

"No."

"Where were you? Can you remember?"

"Sat on the sofa," I said. "But I did get up to look out the window and saw the Citi Cab minicab outside."

"Oh yes, the Citi Cab," said Scarrott. "And Anne-Marie came and joined you and she appeared nervous?"

I said she did. Then we talked through the exchange, how she had come up to me, drying a mug, and had then gone back to the kitchen a short while after.

"Did you, at any point, go and stand at the kitchen door?" Scarrott asked. "Lean against the doorjamb perhaps?"

(*Yes, that's exactly what I did.*)

"No, definitely not. I was sitting on the sofa the whole time. Apart from when I got up to look out the window."

"How do you account for a fibre from your shirt on the frame of the kitchen door?"

I had all this rehearsed. "Anne-Marie called to me when the coffee was made and I came to the door to collect my mug, perhaps I leant against it, I don't recall."

"And were the kitchen cupboard doors open or closed when you collected your coffee?"

"Closed."

"So, you didn't happen to clock (*it's strange how barristers and QCs pepper their speech with colloquialisms, I guess they pick them up from their clients*) the fact that there was a large sum of money in the kitchen cupboard?"

"No."

"So, you had your coffee and then what?"

I described in pornographic detail how Anne-Marie and I had had sex twice. I'd woken a few hours later with a headache probably induced by dehydration and the noise of the club (here I made the court chuckle with a joke of my own, saying I was too old for nightclubs), saw the cocaine in the bathroom cabinet, gone back to bed, been unable to sleep so I'd got up, got dressed on the landing and gone home, having first gone to get some water from the kitchen due to my persistent headache and dry throat.

"How far were you from where you live?" Scarrott asked.

"About three miles."

"Estimate an approximate travel time for me," Scarrott requested.

I shrugged. "I would say it was about a ten-to-fifteen-minute drive, no more."

"The drink couldn't wait until you were home?" Scarrott asked.

"I guess, but it was an impulse thing, my head was killing me, my throat was dry, I needed some water."

"So, you walked into the kitchen? Did you open any cupboards?" Scarrott asked.

"Yes," I replied.

"Can you remember which ones?" he pressed.

"The one to the far left of the sink, I think... and perhaps the right one too."

Scarrott handed me a photograph, having told the jury to turn to the corresponding exhibit number in their packs. "Does that look like the cupboard?"

"Yes," I said. I could see the grey powder covered with black marks left by the SOCO where they had dusted for prints. "That's the cupboard."

My heart trembled and my hands felt clammy. I wiped them on my trousers. I tapped my foot constantly. *Concentrate, concentrate, concentrate*, I told myself.

"So, you opened it and what did you see?" Scarrott asked.

"Nothing in particular: the jar of coffee, bottles of tomato sauce, cans of beans, vinegar, jars, the normal really... oh and lots of those Knorr sauce sachets."

"But no envelopes containing money?"

I shook my head. "Not that I can remember."

Scarrott spun his reading glasses as if they were fucking helicopter blades. "And then what?"

"There were no glasses so I closed the cupboard. I saw my mug, I mean the mug I had drunk coffee from earlier, in the washing up bowl so I picked it up, rinsed it out and poured some water from the tap into it."

"How did you recognise it being the mug you had used formerly?" Scarrott asked.

"It was red and had 'keep calm and carry on doing something'.... I don't remember what... on it."

"So, you picked it up?" Scarrott asked.

"Yes."

"You poured water into it? What tap did you use the left or the right?"

My heart started to beat faster and faster. This was a crucial question. I put my hand in my pocket and held my lucky charm, the Millwall lion Dad had given me. I knew the cops had fucked up and not dusted the hot tap but suddenly, in the heat of the moment, my mind went completely blank, and I couldn't remember what I'd told Hinton and Drake! My head was as empty as my bank account by payday. For the life of me I couldn't remember which side it was on. I took a punt. "The right one I think… it was the hot tap anyway; the water was warm so I tipped it down the sink."

Scarrott got the usher to pass me a photograph of two chrome taps about six inches apart. He cross-referenced it to a photograph in the jury packs. The old-fashioned type, not mixers.

"Does that photograph refresh your memory?"

Of course, neither tap had my dabs on because I hadn't touched any tap but which one had I told Hinton I'd used? For God's sake! *Come on, Rich*, I told myself, *think, think, think, fucking think, man!* I had rehearsed this so many times, even trying on a similar shirt (the police had the original one I had worn on that night, which, incidentally, I never saw again – like my trousers) and trying to see if I could turn on the taps in my rented flat with my shirt cuff, but in the nervous tension of being cross-examined I couldn't remember, my foot tapping quickened and my heart pounded like an overactive piston. I gulped, I knew hot and cold taps

314

weren't always in the same positions. I thought about my flat and Debbie's house... *you used the blasted things every day*. I closed my eyes.... *Calm, Rich, calm, take a deep one...*

"It was the left... definitely the left..."

"You sure."

"I'm sure."

It was like Clarkson or Tarrant on *Who Wants to be a Millionaire?* And that draining music as they say, '*Mr Turner, you've just won yourself one million pounds*' but all I got was a defeated shuffling of papers from Scarrott. The SOCO had fucked up, there were none of my dabs on the cold tap (naturally if you wanted a drink, you would use the cold tap even if you turned on the hot tap first by mistake) and for some reason they had not bothered to dust the hot tap. Too late now, I'd landed a punch of my own on Scarrott and the prosecution, and I felt on cloud nine. Round two to Turner, seconds out.

"So having aborted an attempt to clear your head with a drink of water you left the house?" Scarrott said.

"Correct."

"Yet just a few minutes earlier you were desperate for a glass of water. You've said, and I quote, '*my throat was dry and my head was killing me*' – then, seemingly you abort the mission to have a drink of water simply because you turned on the wrong tap!"

Scarrott was on the ropes, but he was still landing blows.

"As I say it was an impulse thing, when the water was hot, I just thought, 'sod it, I'm not far from home, why am I doing this?'" I said, feeling buoyed up.

Scarrott looked up at me, his arrogant face pockmarked with menace. "So, you then do what most normal people would have done in the first place which is to leave the house, should they be so minded, drive home and then partake in a fresh glass of water and perhaps a paracetamol or two in the comfort of their own home, is that what you eventually did when you got home, Mr Turner?"

"Yes, it is."

"So, perhaps saying your throat was dry and your head was killing you was a slight exaggeration, was it not?" Scarrott swiped.

"Yes, I guess I could have hung on," I accepted.

"Ten minutes to home, Mr Turner, drive fast, on quiet, early morning roads and it's half that time. Not that I'd advocating breaking the speed limit." (*Laughter all around*) "So, you could have waited, couldn't you?"

"Yes."

"So, what was the *real* intention of this trip to the kitchen, Mr Turner?" Scarrott asked. He was not giving up. He perched on the table, almost as if was about to sit on it, his dark robes draped around his legs like the wings of a sleeping bat.

"I've told you, to get a glass of water." I felt angry, frustrated.

"Come now, Mr Turner, you expect the jury to believe that?" He turned back to his notes.

"Yes, it's the truth, why wouldn't they believe it?"

Scarrott looked at me and smiled without revealing his teeth. "Why wouldn't they indeed, Mr Turner, why wouldn't they indeed."

He looked at his notes again and turned a page in his folder. Taking his time. Using his black reading glasses as a bookmark. Time was crucial to the great inquisitor.

"Where were your shoes?" he asked.

"In the hall."

"So, after going to the kitchen, you walked back into the hall, slipped into your slip-on shoes and left the house, is that right?"

"Yes."

"And did Anne-Marie wake up? Ask you why you were leaving? Perhaps wonder why, having spent the night with her, you had decided to terminate the pleasure before breakfast?"

"No, I never saw her, I was careful not to make a noise."

"Careful not to make a noise," Scarrott repeated. "You had had your fun and so like the Sir Lancelot you are, you thought it better to leave the house as quietly as possible, like a cat burglar, one might say."

The jury tittered. Oh, Scarrott was good, you had to hand it to him, he was putting those subliminal messages out there. *Cat burglar*, Scarrott was first-rate at putting sub-conscious thoughts into the jurors' heads.

"And did you by chance leave any notes, any contact numbers, any wishes and desires to see Anne-Marie again?" Scarrott asked.

"No."

"Any thank you notes, a little billet-doux expressing your undying love for her, even if it was for less than six hours – a little like a mayfly." The court laughed at that, Scarrott held them in the palm of his hand.

"No, nothing," I said. I felt embarrassed, awkward.

"Did you, at any point during the night, exchange phone numbers, for example?" Scarrott inquired.

"No."

"She was, simply put, a one-night stand, a notch on your bedpost."

"And me hers," I said.

The jury liked that; I could see some of the women smiling. It was only a jab but I had landed something on Scarrott.

"Perhaps so; did she show any interest in wanting to see you again?" Scarrott pursued.

"No."

"So, you walked out into the cold November night, sorry, early morning, and walked over the road to your car?" Scarrott said.

"Yes."

"Did you see anyone else on the street?" he asked.

"No, but when I scraped ice off my windscreen, I thought there was a black or dark blue car – a Beamer – parked further up the road with someone in it. It was facing my car."

"A what?" El Hombre asked.

"A BMW, Your Honour," Mr Prentice piped up, half raising to his feet.

"Oh, I see," El Hombre said. "Carry on, carry on."

"If the jury will look at exhibit C37 in their bundles they will see a map or plan of Church Street and the position of the two cars."

A copy of the exhibit was passed to me.

"Is that your recollection of the position of your car relative to this mysterious BMW? You are facing up Church Street towards Latimer Road and the BMW was facing down it towards High Street West?"

"Yes," I said. The exhibit was a neater version of Hinton's artwork.

"So, you got into your car and then what?" Scarrott asked.

"My eyes were really tired and sore so I took my contact lenses out and put on my glasses – I always put them in the glove compartment if I'm going out for the night."

"Very meticulous of you," Scarrott mocked. "And you dropped said contact lenses in the footwell on the passenger side of the car?"

"Yes."

"And when you got into the car you didn't drop anything else on the floor on the passenger side?" Scarrott asked.

"Like what?"

Scarrott turned as he spoke so he was addressing the whole of the court, almost a pirouette. "Oh, I don't know how about a plastic supermarket carrier bag containing a bloodstained knife, a tie from Anne-Marie's dressing gown and two phones wrapped in a red throw… and perhaps an envelope bulging with notes?"

I huffed, "No, of course not."

Mr Prentice was on his feet. "Your Honour, this line of questioning is pure speculation. We have already established that my client never saw the money in the kitchen cupboard, if indeed it was still there, and he has said when he left the house Anne-Marie she was still alive."

"I agree," Judge Nicholls aka El Hombre said. "Do you have any further questions for the defendant?" he asked Scarrott.

"Yes, indeed I do," Scarrott said. He looked at his papers as if he were about to read a question, but it was already in his head. Again, it was the game of the pregnant pause, the silence. He was like a bowler, and I was like a batsman at the crease. He delayed his run to make me feel nervous, ill-at-ease. To add to the silence that now fell upon the court room he replenished his glass of water. All anyone could hear was the pouring of water and the jug being placed back on the dark wooden table. Oh, how he liked to be the centre of attention, to hold the court in the palm of his hand. After a sip of water, he changed tack.

"You're a person, Mr Turner, if I may say so, who is not devoid of intelligence. Educated, I believe, to degree level. You're not the usual suspect. In fact, you are well read and I believe, from the list of books you have taken out of the prison library, the books sent into prison by your sisters, Kate and Donna, and from the books that were on your bookcase in your flat, you enjoy detective novels. Indeed, you write short stories yourself, don't you?"

"Yes, yes I do," I agreed.

"And do you write in a similar genre?"

"Yes," I said.

"Do you have ambitions to write a novel at some stage in your life?" Scarrott asked.

"Yes, I'd love to write a book, a thriller, but it's really a hobby. I'm not very good at writing, I could never make a success of it."

"So, you don't see it as a career option?" Scarrott asked. "I'm familiar with the names Agatha Christie, Dorothy L. Sayers and Raymond Chandler and the like." The jury laughed. "You don't imagine you'll be like one of those greats of the murder/mystery genre one day?"

"No, no, not at all, it's like playing the piano or painting a picture, it's just a hobby. It's something I enjoy, that's all."

"But that being said," Scarrott mused, "you do take it quite seriously, don't you? I mean you have completed a Writers Bureau course in creative writing and you have been a member of two writers' circles. That's the case isn't it, Mr Turner?"

"Yes, it is."

"So, I would suggest there is a hankering after a dream?"

"Maybe. It's good to have dreams."

"My, my," Scarrott said, turning around so the jury got to see the full eloquence of his wig-framed face. "I wonder if these somewhat mundane proceedings will one day become the subject of a book?"

A hum of laugher reverberated around the court.

"A very boring one," I jabbed. I leant on the brass rail of the dock. For the first time I was enjoying myself, relishing the cut and thrust; maybe that was Scarrott's intention, to get me to relax, for suddenly he went in with an upper cut.

"Perhaps, so," Scarrott said. He was warming up to make his point.

"You are intelligent and you are capable. You learn and you absorb knowledge. You're a person well versed, albeit mainly through fiction, in police procedures, aren't you?"

"Yes, I suppose I am."

"One of the books found in your flat was entitled 'A Writer's Guide to Police Procedure' and another was a factual book about the criminal justice system, have you read them both?" Scarrott asked.

"Yes, yes, I have," I said.

"And would it be fair to say you used highlighter pens and marginalia so remember the 'best bits'?"

I was confused. "Sorry, you've lost me there."

Scarrott gave that non-toothed grin again. "Oh, marginalia – simply notes in margins, something you did, Mr Turner, isn't that, right? Something students of a particular subject often do? Or at least did do in a pre-computer age."

"Yes, that's right," I said.

"And you watch documentaries on crime, don't you?" Scarrott added.

"Yes, it interests me," I replied. "It helps with my writing."

"And your computer reveals many Google searches on police practice and procedure... some of them following the events of 15th November... is that not right?"

"Yes... yes, it is."

Scarrott filled his lungs with air. "I suspect you have a leaning towards the sly, Mr Turner," he said. "If we return to my questions some ten minutes before about the explanation for the blood on your glasses, I suggest that you may have picked up on the fact that Anne-Marie had cut her finger, and hey presto, you have an explanation for the blood on your glasses. What a clever man you are, Mr Turner, and straight out of the pages of one of those thrillers you love to read."

"That's not the case," I said trying to control my breathing, I was feeling angry again. "I was not wearing my glasses when I entered Anne-Marie's house."

"We only have your word for that, Mr Turner."

"We only have your word that I was," I said, thrusting back at the arrogant pig.

Scarrott paused (again). I like to think I rattled him because he said, "Ah, but I'm not the one standing trial for murder, am I?"

I could see the white wig of my barrister shaking with annoyance, Scarrott was getting under his skin and mine. Big time.

Fortunately, El Hombre intervened.

"I would thank counsel to bear in mind we are here to consider facts. Not speculation. Not insinuation, but facts. It is a fact that there was a plaster on the victim's finger. That is not disputed. When the Scene of Crimes Officer gave his evidence (*here El Hombre looked through piles of paper to try to find out the SOCO's name before finally giving up*) he showed a photograph of the defendant's glasses which had two particles of blood on them, one on the arm and one on the lens. Forensics informs us that is Anne-Marie's blood. That

324

is a fact. The defendant has provided an explanation. The jury must decide whether that explanation is credible."

Apparently worn out by his little speech, El Hombre sat back in his high red chair. "Do you have any more questions for the defendant?"

"I do have some more questions, but I wonder if we might reconvene after lunch?" Scarrott said.

So, we broke for lunch which for me was a processed sandwich and an orange drink in a carton on a tray in the cell below the dock. Mr Prentice and Hannah came to see me; they said how well I was doing. They didn't feel Scarrott had made any significant inroads into my testimony.

"After lunch he's going to take your through the days after 15th November: the first police enquiry, your denial about knowing Anne-Marie, your first voluntary interview but they're got no murder weapon and apart from the blood on your glasses, which you've explained, there's nothing to link you to the crime, only the fact you were in the house close to the time of the victim's death. It's all circumstantial and in my opinion the threadbare nature of the CPS case is showing through." Mr Prentice walked up and down the cell as he spoke, his hands clasped behind his back. "That's why the CPS has brought in a top man like Scarrott. But you're doing well, Richard, very confident and self-assured. Keep it up."

Hannah stood at the door and smiled. Quickly. Our eyes met. Briefly. I wanted to believe that she liked me, but did she? Maybe in that instance I saw our disparate lives. She was twenty-nine, highly educated, personable, successful, ambitions and I was two years older, a failure, mired in debt and stuck in a prison cell on a murder rap.

That afternoon I was back on the stand.

Scarrott puffed out his chest and started again. His black gown fell about him. I bet his lunch hadn't been an egg and cress sandwich on stale white bread.

"Let's take you back to Sunday, 16th November and you go to an aircraft museum with your then girlfriend, Debbie King, and her son, Dylan. Is that correct?"

"Yes."

"Who drove?" Scarrott asked.

"I did."

"In your car?"

"Yes."

"So, you get to the museum, who paid for the entrance tickets?" Scarrott asked.

"I did."

"Can you remember how you paid?" Scarrott enquired.

My heart started to race. "Yes, by cash," I said, wringing my clammy hands.

"Cash indeed," Scarrott said looking at his notes, which were on the table; he pressed them with one finger. Beside him was a thick-as-a-Bible folder with little orange tags on the pages, and Mr Prentice had the same; not for the first time I thought about the huge cost of such trials and how much preparation had gone into it. "Can you remember how much it cost for two adults and a child?"

"About £50."

"Actually, £56.75 but not far off. Did you buy anything else that day?" Scarrott questioned.

My mouth felt dry, I started to gulp. I needed some water, but I couldn't bring myself to ask for it. "A model plane which was a present for Dylan and the meal in the cafeteria."

"What did the three of you eat, can you remember?"

Scarrott was looking at something on the table – I knew it was a reproduction of our receipt from the restaurant.

I paused; my heart was thumping, my polished shoe tapped on the wooden floor of the dock. I put my hand in my pocket and played with my Millwall lion mascot. I rubbed its smooth contours. The cut and thrust confidence of the morning was over but I knew I needed to remain calm. I needed to concentrate. To focus.

"Dylan had a burger and chips; I had a chicken and leek pie and Debbie had a salad."

"Any drinks?"

"Yes, Dylan had a can of something, Debbie and I shared a pot of tea," I said.

"Good," Scarrott said. "Your memory is excellent… at times."

Scarrott poked his glasses towards me. "Do you remember how much the meal cost?" he asked.

"Not exactly, about £30?"

"Umm…not far off… £28.60 to be exact. How much in total did this little excursion to the museum with Miss King and her son cost?"

"About £100," I said.

"About one hundred, umm, you're in the right ball park, £94.34 to be exact," Scarrott said. "That's including the small gift for Miss King's son."

I shrugged. "OK, I'll go with that."

"And how did you fund this trip out with your ex-girlfriend and her son, Mr Turner?" Scarrott asked. As he spoke his cold watercolour blue eyes never left me.

"I paid for everything using cash," I said. God, my mouth felt dry. I was desperate for a drink. My hands were clammy, I rubbed them on my trousers again, I wanted to loosen my tie; my collar seemed too tight.

"Everything was paid for using cash," Scarrott repeated. Very slowly. He paused. "If the members of the jury like to turn to exhibit C38 in their bundles they will see a copy of Mr Turner's bank statement for the period in question. You will see the last cash withdrawal, on the afternoon of Saturday 15th November was for £30 at a cash machine in the town centre. I would suggest that that was to pay for the night out, am I correct?"

I gulped. "Yes, you are." Then I did something that Mr Prentice and Hannah had strongly advised me not to do, I carried on and I answered more than the question I'd been asked. "I always have cash when I go out for fear of losing my bank card, although I have that on me too."

"I see," said Scarrott. "You are a very well-prepared man, Mr Turner; glasses in your glove compartment, plasters too for the accidental cut, and cash just in case you lose your bank card. You are a person who likes to think ahead. To prepare."

"I like to think so." I tried to pay attention and listen hard to each question. My life depended on it.

"Did you spend the £30 on Saturday night?" Scarrott asked.

"Yes."

"So, if the £30 had gone on Saturday, Mr Turner, can you please tell the court where this mysterious money, which had morphed into £100 by Sunday, appeared from? Do you have access to a magic money tree? If you do, perhaps you wouldn't mind informing the Chancellor of the Exchequer."

The court laughed at that one. I held my sticky hands behind my back and wrung them continually.

"No, sir," I said, fuck knows why I suddenly called him 'sir' but I was feeling so nervous it was untrue. I could feel perspiration on my collar. "I lent Debbie some money, she was short one month, what... what with being a single mother and all, money... money doesn't go far, and... well... she paid me back in the carpark before we went into the museum."

"Did she indeed," Scarrott said with malevolent cunning. "How much?"

"£150, I think."

"I see and being the Sir Lancelot you are, you then blew, to use the popular parlance, about £100 on a trip to the museum? A treat for your girlfriend's son, Dylan?"

"That's right."

"Don't you think it would have made more sense for her to pay for the day's outing and perhaps deduct a contribution from what she owed you if you wished to donate to this jolly?"

"That would have been one way to do it, yes" I said, "but when we go out, she likes me to pay for things, she prefers it that way."

"Oh, we really are living in the 21st century, aren't we, Mr Turner? Your former girlfriend who lives on her own, looks after her son and lives perfectly independently still likes to feel the macho urge (*he said this with a deep quiver in his voice*) of a man paying for her when she goes out." And to emphasis the point further Scarrott made a Freddy Mercury type thrust with his right hand.

That brought laugher from all sides of the court, and even a sly smile slipped up the side of El Hombre's mouth, for like the late Queen frontman Scarrott was a performer *par excellence*, and I knew that having ducked and dived and bobbed and weaved for a bit now he had had his lunch he was on the offensive with some accurate punches. Scarrott continued.

"Members of the jury, if you look at the top right of exhibit C38 again you will see it gives an overdraft limit of £200 and if you look at the next exhibits in your packs you will see other bank statements belonging to Mr Turner marked C38a, C38b and C38c – I'm sure you are all familiar with bank statements – you will notice Mr Turner's often show a deficit, isn't that right, Mr Turner?"

"Yes."

"How much debt, may I ask, as a ballpark figure, have you accumulated in your somewhat short life?" Scarrott was waving those blasted glasses again – I wanted to stick them right down his throat... or up another orifice.

"Including my student loan?" I asked.

"With or without, it's up to you?" Hand on one hip, Scarrott swished those fucking glasses through the air like a conductor in an orchestra.

I took a deep breath and said softly, nervously. "I'm not totally sure but I think around thirty thousand, excluding the student loan."

Scarrott took a deep intake of breath, whistled and said as slowly and rhythmically as a train pulling into a station, "£30,000, that's nearly £1,000 for every year of your life – if my maths is correct."

A wave of tittering laughter washed over the audience, sorry, court; as I say you had to hand it to Scarrott he was good, he played the jury like a concert pianist. Every word, every sentence, every silence, every joke, cold and hard and calculating. His trick was, and I guess this is true for all barristers and QCs, not to explain. To leave things hanging, not to make too many insinuations or judgements. When he was cross-examining me, I could see Mr Prentice frantically making notes. He wanted to intervene and say the questioning was irrelevant, but he knew that was not the case, it was very relevant to Scarrott's *narrative* (as Mr Prentice would say). Very relevant indeed.

"And can you tell me what some of the companies are on the bank statement – they appear quite regularly."

He handed bank statements to the clerk who got the usher to hand them to me. I really was sweating now, I started playing with that bloody lion again.

"LC International, William Hill, Betfair, Paddy Power, Bet Victor, Marathon Bet, Sporting Bet, Betway, Vegas Casino, Betfair – I occasionally play online roulette, poker, blackjack and fruit machines," I said.

"Occasionally?" Scarrott questioned.

"Well, three or four times a week – I started it at uni."

The jury laughed at that one.

"I see, and do you ever win?" Scarrott asked.

"Yes, sometimes."

"But overall you're down, in gambling parlance?" Scarrott said.

"That's correct."

"By how much?"

"I don't rightly know, I don't keep records, but a lot."

Scarrott gave me a closed-lipped smile. A crocodile's smile, "two figures, three figures… four…"

"Four, I guess."

"So over £1,000?"

"Yes."

"Close to £10,000?"

I shrugged. "I honestly don't know, I would have thought less than that."

"You would have thought but you don't know. Guess for me. Come on, Mr Turner, you're an educated man, make an educated guess, how much money have you lost over the years playing online casino games?"

"About six or seven."

"Six or seven thousand," Scarrott repeated. He paused. Checked his notes. "You seem to have spent your somewhat short life with money worries, Mr Turner, is that not the case?" Scarrott asked.

"Yes."

"And have those worries ever led you to steal?"

"No."

"To commit fraud?"

"No."

"Try to make an illicit quick buck?"

"No."

"Come now, Mr Turner, I'm sure you've been tempted. £30,000' worth of debt, excluding a large student loan, no prospect of owning your own property, the picture is bleak, isn't it, Mr Turner?"

I felt riled. "Well, it's not as rosy as yours on your inflated salary and gold-plated pension."

The jury and public gallery took a collective intake of breath. I enjoyed that one. The worm had turned. Even El Hombre raised an eyebrow. Scarrott pushed back his bat cape – sorry, gown – and stood with both hands on his hips. He stood like some latter-day Goering inspecting a squadron of Luftwaffe bombers about to blitz London. He puffed out his chest. He looked proud and conceited. He raised his chin and inhaled. He was almost saying, '*yes, I'm paid a lot of money but look at me, I am worth it. I tuck up murderers so you can sleep safe at night and I'm going to put this bastard away too.*'

"Indeed so, Mr Turner, indeed so." He continued. "But you do admit to being heavily in debt?"

"Yes."

"Mr Turner, I will now take you through Monday, 17th November and beyond…"

He then pressed on with more regular questioning, questions I had already answered to in my submission to Mr Prentice and practised endlessly with Dom.

Why I had driven back past Anne-Marie's house on the Monday on the way home from work?

Why had I said I didn't know Anne-Marie when I was first spoken to by the police?

Why I had I called my statement a 'confession'?

Why had I taken my trousers to the dry cleaners?

Why hadn't I replied to Matty's text, sent mid-afternoon Monday, enquiring if the girl who had been killed was the same girl I had met at the Pryzm nightclub?

Lastly, he brought up the assault on the bailiff who had come to repossess my Audi TT. I would have thought he would have asked me about that when he questioned me about my money worries but Scarrott liked to keep me on my toes; move back and forth through his *narrative*.

"You have given an account which makes you sound like the victim; you were challenged and you reacted. At the time you said to the police '*a red rage came over me and I just lost it*'. Is that what happened when Anne-Marie confronted you over the theft of the money from her kitchen cupboard?"

"No, she didn't confront me and I didn't take any money," I said.

Scarrott snorted. "But you do admit to having a bad temper?"

"When I was younger, yes, not now."

"But you assaulted the repossession man, a Mr Thomas, when you were twenty-five, that's only five or perhaps six years ago."

"Yes, but I've changed since then. I'm calmer now." But the truth was I had never been particularly bad-tempered or violent, it was a one-off incident.

"That's all from me, Your Honour."

So, after two and a half days of being cross-examined by Scarrott and gently coaxed by Mr Prentice I was free (to go back to prison and then back to the dock the following day).

The trial continued the following day, of course. Kate was next up, looking demure in an A-line white skirt and pink blouse with a pussy bow. Her blonde hair had been layered and fell about her shoulders. Mr Prentice took her through our family life. The fact our mother, Sandra, and her stepdad, John, had argued a lot and sometimes arguments became 'heated.'

"When you say heated, Mrs Webster," Mr Prentice asked. "Can you elaborate?"

"My stepdad… well, he sometimes hit Mum."

"Sometimes?"

"Well, frequently, there were a lot of rows."

Mr Prentice clarified that her stepdad was in fact my and Donna's dad.

Kate explained how she and Donna had 'mothered' me. Apparently, when Mum and Dad had been 'arguing' she had taken me upstairs to the bedroom she shared with Donna and they had closed the door and played games with me. Also, they used to wake me up, if Mum and Dad were fighting, and take me into their room. I had slept in either Donna or Kate's bed as they hadn't wanted me waking up and being frightened. Apparently, one time they had heard me crying, so they had taken preventative measures. Kate said that she and Donna had always looked after their 'kid brother' and were very proud that I had gone to university. She admitted that our mother favoured her and Donna but she still loved me 'just the same' but perhaps 'didn't show it as much.'

Next, Donna gave a very similar testimony but she did not spend very long in the witness box as she was heavily pregnant.

So that was that. A bit of character and background. Kate and Donna did well and I saw El Hombre and jury warm to them. Even Scarrott was perfectly charming when he cross-examined them both, keeping his tiger-like claws well concealed. He told Donna that he would not place her under any undue stress and he would ensure the cross-examination was not prolonged due to her pregnancy.

They both knew, of course, about my altercation with the repo man and that I had seen Dad. Donna was more understanding on that subject – she said I'd not told anyone because I knew Mum and Kate wouldn't like it but that she understood the reasons. Kate said she was totally mystified as to why I'd want to make contact with him, after all, she didn't know her dad. In addition, having seen how badly he had behaved towards our mum and her and Donna, she wondered why I'd want to 'pander to him'.

Next up was Claire Stratton, my ex from the writers' circle. Mr Prentice wanted to take her through the Monday night when we had met at the library. Claire stood in the witness box looking slightly ill at ease. Her long, light brownish hair fell down her back. She was wearing blue jeans (I'd never seen her wear anything else) and a white smock top over which, probably for the benefit of the court and to look vaguely smart, she had chosen to wear a garish black and gold waistcoat. She looked over at me and gave me a glint of a smile. I wondered where she thought my moral compass was now pointed. Under questioning from Mr Prentice, she said on the Monday night, I'd appeared 'normal' – relaxed even. I had read out a short story which the other members had thought was 'pretty good'. She said the only unusual thing about my behaviour was that I had not gone for a drink afterwards as I 'always did'.

"It was Rich who set up the inner circle – we used to call ourselves The Writers' Revolutionary Committee, a bit stupid really – but Rich was always first to the bar.

He was always quick to get a round in – people liked him."

"Who else was in your Writers' Revolutionary Committee?" Mr Prentice asked.

"An IT guy called Kev… Kevin; Terry who is a history teacher, Brian – who works in retail but behind the scenes – personnel I think; Shelley who is a nurse and Penny who works in the library we meet in – she's a librarian."

"So that was your little group?" Mr Prentice asked. "And what did you discuss?"

Claire shrugged. "What we'd written, other members' stories, sometimes we'd take the piss – sorry – take the mickey out of some of the old members."

"And the defendant? How did he fit in?"

"Very well. He was very well liked and his stories were good on the whole. He wrote some duff ones, but what writer hasn't done that?"

"Just so, Miss Stratton. So, every Monday, after the circle, you basically went for a drink?"

Claire shrugged. "Yes."

"Always the same group?"

"Yes, but sometimes Shelley was on duty or Terry was marking so I'd say the regulars were me, Rich and Kev… and perhaps Penny – Brian drifted in and out."

"I believe you have had a relationship with the defendant?" Mr Prentice asked.

"Yes, that's right," Claire said.

"And that was a sexual relationship?"

"Yes."

Mr Prentice paused, looked at his notes. "Did he, the defendant, at any time suggest anything which you might be describe as kinky or deviant?"

"How do you mean?" Claire asked.

"Spanking games? Bondage? Games where he was dominant, perhaps enjoying what's loosely termed 'rough sex'?"

"What like Fifty Shades?" Claire asked.

"Yes, exactly like that."

"No, never," Claire said. Then added. "It sounds exciting though."

The jury and the public gallery laughed.

"That will be all, Your Honour. Thank you, Miss Stratton."

Next it was Scarrott's turn. He cross-examined her about the writing genre I liked.

"He liked crime," Claire said. "It seems funny really but he liked to write murder stories – crime thrillers – his favourite author was Ian Rankin. He'd read most of the Rebus novels but he liked – I'm not sure of the author's name, I think it's Peter James too – he said he was lighter, also, he liked the Brighton connection because of his dad. He was quite well read."

"The Brighton connection?" Scarrott asked.

"Yes, the central character in the Peter James novels is a Ray or Roy Grace, I think, and he's based in Brighton, Rich liked that."

"I see," said Scarrott, "you must forgive my ignorance on such matters, Miss Stratton. As one who, you might say, earns a living from other people's nefarious activities, I must say when I relax, if I'm not reading legal papers, I prefer to avoid reading crime thrillers and watching crime dramas on TV. You might say I wouldn't know my Rankin from my elbow."

El Hombre smiled at that one and again the court tittered. When Scarrott had finished his cross-examination Mr Prentice called on my landlord, Mr Vacarescu. He said that I was an excellent tenant and that he'd never had 'no trouble' from me. I always paid my rent on time and in the summer, I fed the birds and, having done some gardening as part of my Community Order, made up some tubs at the front of the house with plants I obtained from a supplier I knew, which I watered as I was downstairs.

At the end Mr Prentice said, "That's all from me."

Scarrott had no questions for him.

Next up Mr Prentice called Mark, Matty and Dave who gave evidence about the night of the 15th November. Matty and Dave both said they had seen me with a girl who they now knew to be Anne-Marie (Mr Prentice felt Suggo would not have been very creditable but that Mark, Matty and Dave presented well. It helped give the appearance that I was a regular guy out with my friends who had been caught up in an awful maelstrom of bad luck). They were questioned about the social media too; their contact with me via text and the WhatsApp group; the messages that had gone back and forth and the text Matty had sent which I'd not replied to. I hadn't seen them following the incident, so their evidence was limited. Though Suggo had sent a WhatsApp message, in typical Suggo style, which was read out to the court by Scarrott when he finally got to his feet and cross-examined Mark.

"Did you receive a message, within your WhatsApp group, by someone named Suggo which read: '*You were supposed to fuck her not kill her?*'"

Mark agreed he had seen it.

"It was directed at the defendant, wasn't it?" Scarrott asked.

Mark agreed it was.

"Why do you think that was?" Scarrott pressed.

"He's an idiot," Mark said. "Suggo, not the defendant."

The court room tittered with a gentle wave of laughter.

"I meant why did this character known as Suggo send such a message to the defendant?"

"I don't honestly know."

All three were asked about my relationship with Debbie, and they all said I really liked her and we were

342

well suited. Apart from asking Mark about Suggo's message, Scarrott had only a few minor questions for them about social media: when they had learnt of Anne-Marie's death and how, that sort of thing.

Next it was my ex-boss, Helen Glover. She looked very professional in a black business suit. I must say I had butterflies in my stomach seeing Helen; for some reason her presence in the witness box unsettled me. It was a reminder that I had lost my job. That I would never work for her again. I felt embarrassed, an idiot, a fool. The job wasn't great but at least it was a job. Now at thirty-one years of age I'd have to start again – and that was the best-case scenario.

Mr Prentice coaxed her through some questions about the company, what Zorin did and my role in it. How long I had been there and how long she had line-managed me. She was a good witness, very creditable. She said she regarded me 'very highly' as an employee and that she had always found me to be 'honest and trustworthy' with an 'excellent' sickness record. She said she was aware of my debts but she thought I was 'doing my best' to pay them off. She said that, unfortunately, the company had been forced to terminate my employment when I had been remanded in custody as, although the Ministry of Justice guidelines stated that those on remand should not lose their jobs, a post was being made redundant and the company had felt they should give it to that person rather than let them go. She said she hoped I would find a new job and she would be 'very happy' to write me a reference. Then, Mr Prentice moved on to the conversation I had had with her on Tuesday, 18th November, after the police had visited on the Monday evening. Helen said the police visit had 'shaken me up' and I had sought her advice.

Scarrott was quite charming towards her and just had a few points of clarification about my conversation with her on the Tuesday.

Then it was Debbie's turn to take the stand, Mr Prentice had left her to last on purpose. El Hombre, perhaps with a feeling of foreboding about the magnitude of her testimony, adjourned proceedings until 11am the following day, even though it was still early in the afternoon. So, I was driven back to prison in the sweat box. I was led to my cell for an extended debrief with Dom who was fascinated by the case. He liked a blow-by-blow account and even wrote notes and offered suggestions (I sometimes think he wanted Mr Prentice's job and felt if he had been representing me, he would have done things differently). The debriefs helped crystallise events in my mind for the record I have tried to recreate here.

Chapter Twelve

My ex-girlfriend, Debbie King, was a witness for the defence, of course. It was strange seeing her again. Her black hair had been restyled into a sophisticated bob and was now collar length. She wore a grey skirt and matching black jacket over a purple turtle-neck jumper. As she went into the witnesses' box, I noticed she was wearing high-heeled black court shoes. I knew the clothes were new. Seeing her I felt a sense of sadness and of sorrow at the thought I would probably never date her again. She looked over at me and our eyes met, filled with longing and hope and questioning.

She was very nervous so Mr Prentice asked her some simple, easy questions to try and put her at ease. He asked her where she worked and about her son, that sort of thing. She kept giving me darting, furtive looks as I sat in the dock, especially when Mr Prentice asked about our relationship. She said it was 'great and that we got on really well'. Then he asked her about my relationship with her son, Dylan. Debbie became tearful as she answered. She said that it was good and that, in fact, I was the only boyfriend that she had ever had who had treated Dylan like part of the family and 'included him' in things we'd done. I had taken them camping in the New Forest, which Dylan had loved, and I had taken them both to their first professional football match at Millwall's New Den. Debbie admitted she'd not enjoyed it much but Dylan had talked about it for ages afterwards and subsequently I'd taken him to see Millwall play Reading at their ground; she hadn't come on that trip. She said Dylan was 'very attached to me' and I often bought them both presents. She told the court how I had bought Dylan a remote-controlled boat which the three of us had taken down to an artificial pond or mini lake in a park to sail which he'd loved. Apparently, Dylan asked about me and why I didn't come around 'no more' and she had tried to explain where I was as she believed in being honest with children but that it was 'difficult' because Dylan thought 'prison was for bad people', at which point she took a handkerchief from her handbag and dabbed her tearful eyes.

Then Mr Prentice asked about our sex life – again Debbie said it was good. He then asked her if we ever played any sexual games. Debbie confirmed that we had played some consensual spanking games and I had tied her up which she had enjoyed; in fact, she said she had suggested it originally (*which I don't think was strictly true*).

"Who initiates such games?" Mr Prentice asked.

"Sometimes me and sometimes Richard," Debbie said. "We always do it at his flat when Dylan has a sleep over or my best friend babysits…. sometimes after a meal."

"And you liked that?" Mr Prentice asked. "Going to my client's flat, I mean?"

"Yes, it is… was… clean and tidy; he was a good cook, and we had a nice time together."

"And during the twelve months you were together has my client ever placed his hands around your throat? Has he attempted to strangle you as part of a sex game?"

"It was thirteen months," Debbie corrected. "And no, never."

Mr Prentice paused. "Thank you. Now take your time, I'm now going to take you through the events of Saturday, 15th November. Please, have some water if you wish."

Mr Prentice paced up and down whilst Debbie was given a white plastic cup by the usher. She took a sip. Mr Prentice wanted to ensure she was calm as it was going to be an emotional rollercoaster ride for her.

He started by going through the telephone conversation I had with her on the Saturday evening before I'd gone out for the night, the text messages I'd sent (which he read out) about how I was missing her and loved her and the messages she'd sent back. She looked on the verge of tears and it wasn't helped by El Hombre who suddenly sparked into life and said, after the last one, "Just for clarity that was sent from the victim's house?"

"Yes, Your Honour," Mr Prentice said.

Debbie sniffed and started to cry. I buried my head in my hands and looked at the polished wooden floor filled with its dark knots.

When I looked up, I saw the usher handing Debbie a box of tissues.

Then Mr Prentice moved on to the Sunday. Debbie said I had picked her and Dylan up from their house and taken them to the museum.

"So, you stopped in the carpark, did anything happen then?" Mr Prentice asked.

"What do you mean?" Debbie asked.

My heart and head pounded. *What the fuck would Debbie say?*

"Well, did you give the defendant anything?" Mr Prentice gently coaxed.

"Oh yes," said Debbie, suddenly remembering. "I gave him back the money he'd lent me."

Cue a big sigh of relief from the dock.

"How much, can you remember?" Mr Prentice pressed.

"Not exactly. £100, maybe 150."

That was good, excellent in fact. Debbie had come to my rescue, her lovely brown eyes kept seeking me out. The tears had gone and there was even a hint of a smile on her face. For some strange reason I felt mildly aroused. *If I ever get out*, I thought to myself, *the first think I'll do is drop down on one knee and propose… if she'd still have me.* Things were looking up.

"So, you gave the defendant cash. Do you tend to use cash a lot?"

"Yes, I like cash. I don't have a credit card and tend to draw out a lot of money when I get paid and use cash for most things," Debbie said. That was even better, as it was true and, as Mr Prentice would say, it added to my *narrative* and as I would say, the best lies are built on a foundation of truth.

"Yes, yes we can see that from your bank statements. I have two or three months' worth of statements here, not in the bundles." Mr Prentice said. "Would you mind if I shared them with the prosecution and the members of the jury?" he asked.

Debbie shook her head.

"Your Honour?"

El Hombre looked at Scarrott, who rose slightly and shook his head.

"No, no carry on, we all accept that Miss King likes using cash," El Hombre said. "No need to prove it."

"I'm grateful, Your Honour," Mr Prentice said. He paused.

"Miss King, do you recall why the defendant lent you money?" He pressed the top back on his ink pen, moved it to his left as if he wanted Debbie's eyes to follow it.

"Yes, I was short one month. Sometimes it's hard to make ends meet. I had some unexpected bills and Richard... well, he's always been very generous."

"Indeed," Mr Prentice said. "And the museum? My client then showed his generosity by using that very same cash, the cash you had just given him, to pay for the day trip to the museum: the admission, the meal in the canteen, a present for young Dylan... that's correct, isn't it?" Mr Prentice turned a page over in his notes, I could see the orange tags, sentences highlighted and pen marks where changes had been made to the typed script.

"Yes, that's right."

"When you went out, Miss King, with my client, was it normal for him to pay – for drinks, admissions to cinemas and museums and meals etc? You didn't 'go Dutch'?" Mr Prentice asked.

Debbie seemed to grow in confidence. "Richard paid. He mostly used debit or credit cards which was easier. I liked that. Even if we did split the bill, I'd often give him money from my purse before we went out or at the end of the evening. I liked him paying for things."

God, I loved her. I felt I'd been losing a sporting contest and suddenly I had victory in my sights. We were giving the prosecution a right royal trouncing. I folded my arms and let a murmur of a smile form on my lips. *Get out of that, Scarrott, you arrogant, conceited bastard*, I thought. Debbie had ridden to my rescue and her testimony was just so, so sweet. She was a star. A superstar. A megastar and I loved her so, so much.

Lastly, Mr Prentice dealt with the advertising flyer from the Pryzm nightclub.

"You found it in the footwell of the car, didn't you?" She confirmed she did.

"And was there anything unusual about it?" Mr Prentice asked.

Debbie mentioned the blood and that she had thrown it in a bin before we had entered the museum.

"Where was the bin?" Mr Prentice asked. "Can you remember?"

"Close to Richard's car at the far end of the car park."

God, I loved her even more!

"That will be all, Your Honour."

Mr Prentice sat down and turned and smiled at me as did Hannah. The tide was turning in our direction. Our counsel had the upper hand. DCI Murray's testimony about 'Sunderland' Simon had shown that there was no proof I'd put the money he'd fished out, in a bin (nor, indeed, that the money had come from Anne-Marie's house) – no forensics or CCTV. And apart from the blood on my glasses (which I had explained) there were no forensics linking me to Anne-Marie's murder; a fibre on the door jamb was nothing, I'd explained that. Surely, the jury would conclude that there was 'sufficient doubt' (by the fucking bucketful) about the prosecution case to find me 'not guilty'. For the first time in six agonising, nightmare months I was feeling optimistic and my God, if got acquitted, I'd make it up to Debbie big style. I'd buy her anything, take her anywhere, never, ever cheat on her again. Fuck me, I'd be loyal. No, if I got out every Saturday night would be spent indoors watching whatever she wanted to watch on TV or if I went out it would be with Debbie for a meal or to the cinema or something. No to nightclubs. No to pubs. No to meeting my mates. Those days were well and truly over. I had learnt my lesson, big time. I'd behaved recklessly and, yes, I had been stupid. Bloody stupid. But by God, I had learnt my lesson. And then some. Never again. Never ever again.

"We'll adjourn for lunch now," El Hombre said.

I looked at Debbie, caught her eye and gave her a huge smile; she smiled back and was it my imagination, but I could have sworn she winked at me. Just a small, subtle wink. But there was no mistaking it – there was love in those big, doleful brown eyes, there was love in those eyes. There was love… there was love… there was love…

I rose, beaming. A feeling of tingling ecstasy cascaded through my body. The exit door was starting to open. Soon I would be walking free, victory was in sight. I was beginning to awaken from my nightmare which had started with a one-night stand and a desire to rid myself of at least some of my crazy, colossal debts.

As the jury and all the court staff trawled out, I was handcuffed to a Serco security guard. I was taken back to the holding cell below the court where another tray was pushed through the door. This time it was a ham and mustard sandwich and another carton of juice (always apple or orange). I ate hungrily, suddenly my appetite had returned and I started to use Dom's reframing techniques to think positively about my situation and how I could use it to good advantage by working in prisons; perhaps even teaching creative writing like Giles. There were suddenly opportunities, not closed and locked doors. I could, as Dom had suggested, reframe this nightmare experience into a positive to help others and have more sense of purpose in life: prison had taught me a lot – none of it intentionally.

There was a Zebedee-like spring in my step when I entered the dock that afternoon. When the cuffs were taken off, I rubbed the lion mascot in my pocket for luck and sat back down. After the court had settled, Scarrott took to the floor to cross-examine Debbie. He started off quite gently. Like Mr Prentice, he asked about her upbringing and former marriage, the fact she was a single parent, her job, her son and then he moved on to our relationship. She repeated the same *narrative* she had told Mr Prentice. Then he asked her about the night Anne-Marie had been murdered, the contact I had had with her via text messages, as we went into the nightclub and then, back at Anne-Marie's house, when I had led her to believe I was back at my flat. Debbie answered clearly and confidently, her earlier nerves and upset seeming to be a thing of the past – after all she had known for a long time that I had cheated on her. Then, Scarrott took her through the Sunday visit to the museum. Again, Debbie replied that she had returned some money to me whilst in the car: money that I had lent her some time earlier.

"We've heard that you like using cash and you don't have a credit card, why is that, Miss King?" Scarrott asked.

"I find it easier to budget with cash, when it's gone it's gone."

Scarrott let a thin wisp of a smile momentarily quiver on his upper lip. "When it's gone it's gone," he repeated slowly, almost quietly. "When it's gone, it's gone." He paused. "Yet, I should imagine it must be hard being a single parent with ever-increasing bills to pay: council tax, utilities, food, rent and then there's clothes, shoes and toys for your eight-year-old son."

"Nine now," Debbie corrected. "Yes, it is."

"And sometimes you find yourself a bit short?" Scarrott suggested

"Yes, yes, I do." Debbie rubbed her forehead.

"And does Dylan's father contribute to his son's upkeep?" Scarrott asked.

"No," Debbie said. "He did do once but I've not had a penny for years, despite the Child Maintenance Service writing to him. He has a new family now and is not interested in me or Dylan."

"You get Family Tax Credits?" Scarrott asked.

"Yes, yes I do."

"But even with that benefit on the whole money is tight and you have to watch the pennies, what with price hikes, food price increases, energy bills and the like," Scarrott said. "Is that a fair assessment?"

"Yes, yes, it is," Debbie said.

"You've spoken about a very enjoyable camping holiday in the New Forest with the defendant and your son – do you have many holidays, Miss King?"

"No, I… I… can't afford them."

"So, when you went camping in the New Forest with the defendant that was your first holiday in how many years?"

Debbie shrugged. "Four, maybe five."

"And how did it rate, this holiday?"

"Dylan absolutely loved it."

"And you?"

"It was fantastic to be away from home but I would have preferred a hotel."

Scarrott smiled warmly. "I'm sure you would, Miss King, I'm sure you would. Who suggested the camping holiday in the New Forest?"

"Rich," Debbie said. "He'd been camping with his previous girlfriend and had all the equipment at his flat."

"And he paid?"

"Yes."

"Just as he tended to pay when you went out?"

"Yes, mostly."

"It would have been difficult for you to take your son on holiday, is that not the case, Miss King? Even camping in the New Forest?"

"Yes, that's right."

Scarrott turned to his notes. "And that's perhaps one reason why you quite like the defendant to pay for, for want of a better word, pleasures, activities, trips out etc, is that not right?"

"Yes, it is," Debbie stood with her hands clasped in front of her. My heart raced. My stomach rumbled. I tapped my foot constantly and listened intently. She was keeping to the story, she sounded convincing. She sounded good. Of course it was all true, which helped matters.

I looked down at the wooden floor, closed my eyes, placed my hands together and I prayed: *please, God, if we can just get through this. Please, God, help me, God, if we can just get through this. Please, God. Help me, God. Please, God, let me go free. Please, please, God, release me from this ordeal.*

"And at other times you may be a bit short because of an unexpected bill or something which is unforeseen and not budgeted for, is that correct?" Scarrott asked – he almost seemed to be on her side.

"Yes, that's right," Debbie said. Her voice was clear and confident.

I looked up. Captivated.

"It happens to the most careful budget planner: the dripping tap, the boiler breaking, the washing machine leaking, a problem with a computer, a school trip, something unexpected which eats into your budget," Scarrott said.

"Yes, yes, that's right," Debbie answered.

"And that's a reason, perhaps, why the defendant might lend you money?" Scarrott asked.

"Umm, that's right," Debbie nodded, her hands at her side now: she seemed to be relaxed and was answering the questions with self-assurance.

Come on, Debs, come on, I urged internally. *Come on, Debs, do it for me, get me out of this fucking shit hole.*

"Not for anything special, just basic household expenses." Scarrott was staring down at his notes, as he did so chewing the arm of his black plastic reading glasses.

"Yes, that's true," Debbie said.

"And that's what happened on Sunday 16th November. The defendant had lent you some money and, in the carpark, prior to entering the museum, with your son sitting on the back seat of the defendant's car, perhaps watching proceedings and anxious to get into the museum, you went to your handbag, took out your purse and said 'here's that £100, or maybe it was £150, I owe you'. Is that correct?"

Debbie smiled. Quickly. Nervously. "Yes, it is."

"So, you picked your handbag up off the floor and took out your purse?" Scarrott reiterated.

"Yes, that's right."

"When you bent down did you notice anything else on the floor? The Pryzm adverting flyer for example?"

"No."

"The defendant's contact lenses?"

"No."

"So, you took up your handbag, placed it on your lap and went to your purse. Then you just handed…" Scarrott hesitated. Smiled. Waved his hand. "You explain, Miss King, I don't want to put words into your mouth."

Debbie suddenly looked ill at ease. "Yes… well… I had the money folded over in my purse and I just gave it to Rich."

"Did the defendant ask how much?"

"No."

"Had the defendant asked for the money to be returned to him?"

"No."

"So, sorry I am putting words into your mouth again, but you just said, 'here's that money I owe you'?" Scarrott quizzed.

"Yes, exactly that."

"And what did the defendant do with it?" Scarrott enquired.

"He took his wallet out of the inside pocket of his leather jacket and put it inside."

Well done, Debs, I thought. The CCTV from the museum entrance had shown me getting the money out of my wallet which was in my inside jacket pocket.

"And can you recall why you owed the defendant the money?" Scarrott asked.

"Not exactly. Not for one thing in particular, Rich gave it me over a period of time, I had some spare money so I returned it to him." Debbie blushed, blew up her fringe.

"So, you must have kept a record?" Scarrott asked.

"How do you mean?" Debbie responded.

"Well, to know how much you owed the defendant."

Debbie looked at El Hombre, clearly starting to feel uncomfortable. She moved uneasily in the witness box. "I suppose I did, but Rich was never too bothered about money, and I just returned what I felt I owed him."

"What you felt you owed him," Scarrott repeated. "Is that why you're not sure if it was one hundred or £150?" he asked.

"No, it was £150," Debbie said, sounding sure of herself.

Great, I thought, *well done, Debs, we've got Scarrott on a fucking string.*

"You are aware, of course, that not answering my questions truthfully is an act of perjury which, in itself, is a criminal offence and could be punishable with imprisonment?" Scarrott said with menace.

Debbie suddenly appeared very nervous. She moved from foot to foot and went red in the face.

"Yes, yes I am," she said. She breathed uneasily.

A seething El Hombre intervened. Debbie had clearly made a good impression on him. "I would remind counsel that it is for the judge in any proceedings to make declarations about possible perjury and not for the prosecution to tell the judge how to do his job!" he thundered. "In this case I find Miss King to be a compelling witness who is answering your questions to the best of her knowledge and ability. I find the tone of the prosecution to be one of threat bordering on intimidation. I would request that you desist!"

That told Scarrott!

"Miss King, please ignore what has just been said to you and accept my sincere apologies on behalf of the court," El Hombre continued.

The usher passed Debbie another cup of water. She smiled. "Thank you, Your Honour."

Fuck me, we really did have the bastard Scarrott on the run! Life was looking up; life in that moment was good. Better than good. If I hadn't been next to a security guard I would have got up and left the court there and then; the jury were going to find me 'not guilty'. No question. The nightmare was nearing its end. The nightmare was nearing its fucking end! YES! Elation rolled and pumped and pulsed and fizzed through my body. Soon, I would be walking down the steps of the court and back out onto the street. A free man! Mr Prentice would read a brief prepared statement to the press about my ordeal and how the police should never have arrested and charged me! My God, there could even be compensation for the mental anguish and physical stress the police and CPS had caused me. I would ask my solicitors, Breakspear & Venables to put in a claim for compo – I might even be able to clear my debts!

"Sorry, Your Honour," Scarrott said at last. "I did not mean to be in any way threatening or intimidating to Miss King, and I did not mean to overstep my brief. I merely wondered if there was anything she had said that she perhaps wished to clarify, add to or change?" Scarrott paused. "Before we go on, I mean."

"Well, it didn't sound like that to me," El Hombre said, leaning back in his chair. "And I'm sure I speak for the rest of the court and the witness. But please proceed."

"Thank you, Your Honour," Scarrott said. "Miss King?"

Debbie looked confused. She sipped some water. "No, no, nothing." She sounded uneasy. "I've told the truth."

"Thank you, Miss King," Scarrott shuffled his notes. "When did you notice the Pryzm advertising card or flyer?"

"As I got out of the car."

"And you picked it up?"

"Yes."

"And you have said you noticed there was blood on it?" Scarrott pressed.

"Yes, yes, that's right."

"Where did you discard the card or flyer?"

"The closest bin."

"To the defendant's car?"

"Yes."

"I believe the defendant had parked some way from the entrance even though there was a lot of space in the carpark."

"Yes, that's right."

"Why was that, Miss King?" Scarrott asked.

She gave a tight-lipped smile. "I don't really know... I think he feared people knocking their doors into his car so he didn't like people parking close to him."

"Didn't he, indeed."

Scarrott then asked questions about paying for the museum, the meal etc. Then he moved on to questions about our sex life and the BDSM games we'd played – all of which Mr Prentice had covered. Once again Debbie said that we had had a healthy sex life and I had never attempted to asphyxiate her during foreplay. Then Scarrott dropped a great hunking bombshell.

"Are you aware, Miss King, that the defendant has cheated on you in the past?" Scarrott asked.

For some reason Mr Prentice hadn't dealt with this when cross-examining Debbie or me, so it left it wide open for Scarrott. I think he felt that the fact I had cheated with Anne-Marie was enough and an earlier incident of infidelity was not relevant. It was a mistake. A huge mistake.

Mr Prentice moved uneasily in his seat; he wanted to get up. To intervene. I looked at the wooden floor of the dock. I didn't want to look up but when I did, I saw Scarrott had my orange diary open on the desk in front of him.

"Members of the jury, if you would like to turn to exhibit C40 in your packs it is a facsimile of an entry from the defendant's diary dated April of last year. You were in a relationship with the defendant at that time, weren't you?"

"Yes, yes I was," Debbie said, dabbing her eye with a tissue.

He passed a copy of the exhibit to the clerk, who passed it on to Debbie.

"I won't embarrass you by reading it out in open court but does it not indicate to you that the defendant has been unfaithful to you in the past?" Scarrott asked.

El Hombre moved forward. Perhaps feeling the need to show he favoured neither one side nor the other, he said, "I am sorry for the embarrassment this might cause to Miss King, but I think this diary entry needs to be read out in court; after all has the defence had sight of it."

Mr Prentice rose slightly. "Yes, Your Honour, we are aware of the diary entry."

Scarrott flicked the offending page with his fingers. "It is only brief, Your Honour. Diary entry of Saturday, 6th April – 'met Sarah in The Crazy Horse and got talking, Mark and I had met her and her friends a few weeks back. I ended up back at her place having endless sex – Mark got off with her friend, Rachel.' "

"I didn't know he was like that," Debbie sniffed, and started to cry again. She patted her eye gently with the tissue to avoid smearing her mascara. "I really didn't." She started to sob and scrunched up the tissue.

The clerk passed her a box of Kleenex.

"Take a few minutes," El Hombre said. "We'll adjourn for ten minutes whilst the witness composes herself."

But before the court could rise Scarrott jumped in with an Oscar Wildean-type quip,

"I believe Your Honour, that the defendant might now be thinking that a diary is best kept unkept."

"Yes, very good," El Hombre said. He rose.

"Court rise," the usher called.

El Hombre smirked as he shuffled out of court; he liked that one and so did the jury who stood as one. If nothing else the trial of The Crown versus Richard A. Turner had provided a huge amount of entertainment; most of it emanating from Scarrott, and little did I know that Scarrott had more ammunition in his arsenal. In fact, he'd not really unleashed his big guns. For there was no doubt about it, Scarrott was good. Too bloody good. I rubbed my damp hands together and wished I could be taken back to prison for a debrief with Dom. The optimism of the morning and early afternoon had started to wane.

When the court returned Scarrott delivered the killer question. He was so arrogant he had his back to Debbie when he asked it, one hand placed on his hip, exposing his barrel chest. Imagine the French guillotine, imagine your head resting on the wooden block and then Scarrott, the black hooded executioner, releases the rope…that blasted piece of super-sharp metal is sliding towards your neck and you can do nothing about it…

"Remind the court again, Miss King," he said. "How much is your overdraft?"

Debbie was momentarily nonplussed; she had never mentioned an overdraft.

"What overdraft?" she said, frowning.

Scarrott gave a toothless smile. "I'm sorry, I assumed you had an overdraft, Miss King. Most people have. The defendant has. I have – even on my somewhat inflated salary. I'm sure most members of the jury have too but you do not have an overdraft, Miss King?"

"No, I've never had one." Debbie looked at El Hombre but he was just as perplexed as she was.

Scarrott faced her now, still with his hand on his hip. "But you could have one, after all, we've seen that you manage your finances admirably. You receive a regular monthly salary, you budget well. You bank with," here Scarrott consulted his notes, "NatWest, I believe. I am sure they would happily provide you with an overdraft facility."

"I suppose." Debbie blew up her fringe again, like me she was feeling the heat. "I've banked with them for years, they're a good bank, very helpful, but I don't want one."

God, Scarrott was like a snake in the grass – a big, thick, slimy python slithering over to its prey and Debbie just didn't see it coming…

"Why is that?" Scarrott asked. "If I may make so bold as to pry into your private financial arrangements."

Nothing's private in court and Scarrott knew it, of course he did, he was a top QC. The best. Probably.

Debbie was still confused by the line of questioning. "I like to live within my means, I manage my finances well. I budget and I save and try to make sure I'm never in debt."

The snake had struck. Its fangs had punctured flesh. There was blood. Two neat pin pricks.

"And, as you say, you use cash because 'when it's gone it's gone', is that not right?" Scarrott asked, pressing home his winning advantage.

Debbie nodded and whispered an, "umm".

I wondered, in that moment, if she realised the trap she had just walked into, or did she even care after hearing my diary entry? But she was lost in the moment, mesmerised by Scarrott's hypnotic questions, caught up by his flattery, his praise of her; for a moment I was forgotten. She was enthralled by Scarrott's quiet, complimentary manner and bewildered by his line of questioning. She was lost...

Mr Prentice was itching to get to his feet, to say something, anything – that the line of questioning wasn't relevant but it *was* relevant and Scarrott knew it. He continued to quietly attack.

"As Mr Micawber said in *David Copperfield*, *'Annual income twenty pounds, annual expenditure nineteen and six, result happiness. Annual income twenty pounds, annual expenditure twenty pounds nought and six, result misery.'* It might be said that you would have more of an appreciation of Mr Micawber's pearls of wisdom than say the defendant, who lives in a perpetual state of debt, does he not?"

Debbie shrugged. "I suppose so, yes."

Scarrott took a deep breath and said almost too quickly, "So, to sum up, Miss King, you don't have an overdraft, you prefer using cash because you have more control over your outgoings, and you don't possess a credit card. Would that be a fair assessment?"

Debbie cast an anxious, furtive glance in my direction. No smile this time.

"Yes," she said, "that's right."

"That'll be all, Your Honour." Scarrott sat down, drawing his gown out over his fat thighs as he did so.

"Do you have any further questions for the witness?" El Hombre asked Mr Prentice.

Mr Prentice stood up. "No, Your Honour."

I was taken back to the prison that evening in the pit of despair. Part way through the day I had felt so close to being acquitted it was untrue, yet by the afternoon the tables had once again turned and I was facing the possibility of a life sentence for a crime I'd not committed.

The following day I was taken back to the court. I wore the same suit as I had on the first day – the navy blue one. When I'd left the prison cell Dom had patted me on the back but even his words of advice and encouragement had worn thin. The thought of being incarcerated for the rest of my life, lying on a paper-thin plastic-covered mattress and pillow in a bunk bed with the constant, odious smells and the metallic din, was just beyond anything I could imagine. It was an awful world of dark days and darker nights.

So the sweat box, containing one small cell of misery, transported me back to the court. A few cameras went off as the Serco van drove into the court compound; I guess the press were there waiting like vultures ready to pick over my hopeless bones for the trial was nearing its conclusion.

Chapter Thirteen

The following day the summing up commenced. The prosecution always leads – after all it is their case so Scarrott took to the floor. This is, in essence, what the great orator said with my bits in italics. Interestingly during his final remarks, initially at least, Scarrott was often less of the showman and more of the considered, intelligent QC painstakingly stitching the prosecution tapestry together – until his thunderous conclusion.

"You will, of course, have your own opinions about the defendant (*but whether you have or not I'm going to tell you exactly what you should think of him*), he has, after all spent two and a half days giving evidence. He is intelligent, he is articulate, he is bright, he is sharp. He is also a gambler with his eye on the main chance. We have heard of his debts and his online gambling habit; he likes the spin of the roulette wheel, he likes the electronic fold of the cards in blackjack and poker, the electronic clunk, clunk, clunk of the fruit machine. Miss King, his trustworthy and sensible and stable ex-girlfriend, says she hated online gambling and urged him not to do it but the defendant saw it as the only way to pay off his debts. The only way, mark you. Not by hard work, nor by diligently saving and not going out and enjoying himself but by gambling. The defendant wants his cake, of course, like many others do but there is always a day of reckoning, there is always a day when bills must be paid, when, to use a colloquialism, chickens come home to roost. So, who is the enigmatic defendant? I ask you, members of the jury: who is Richard Andrew Turner?"

Scarrott paused to allow my name to ring around the hallowed court building. I almost expected the fat pig to give a blast of that old football chant, *who are you? Who are you? Who are you?* But he was silent. He was always silent. After a while he went on. Robe pushed out, glasses in hand.

"Criminal practice puts you in touch with every single facet of human life: the arrogant mega-rich, who think they are above the law, to the poor who perhaps steal or commit crime through what they perceive as necessity, to all those in between. The old to the young. The clever to the stupid. The opportunist to the career criminal, the psychopath to the mercy killer. So where does Mr Turner, the defendant, fit in? He is clever, certainly, he is enigmatic, certainly, but he is also a gambler, a risk taker, a chancer who chances his arm chatting up women in the hope he won't get caught by his girlfriend – you will, of course, remember his apt nickname, Rat? But at the same time, he plays the role of the caring, doting boyfriend. He is a chancer who ignores letters from debt companies in the hope they will go away, a chancer who lives for the day, for pleasure, a hedonist, always first at the bar with a note in his hand or a debit card ready to swipe. And where has that 'pleasure principle' got him? Deeper and deeper and deeper into debt. You will, undoubtedly, be familiar with the Shakespearean quote from *As You Like It*,

'All the world's a stage,

And all the men and women merely players;

They have their exits and their entrances,

And one man in his time plays many parts,'

"And that, members of the jury, is who the defendant is – an actor. A man who plays many parts. Many roles. The looks between the defendant and Miss King, even to my somewhat jaded, twice-divorced eye, seemed genuine enough, affectionate even and the defendant has a lot to thank Miss King for – something I will elaborate on in due course. But whilst Miss King presented as nothing more and nothing less than she appeared in the witness box, the opinion I have built up of the defendant is that he is a man who plays many parts. A man who puts on many masks: to his boss, the elegant and articulate Ms Glover, to his male friends, the lad about town – up for a good time – we met Matty, Dave and Mark; to his landlord, Mr Vacarescu, he plays the part of the perfect tenant, preparing tubs of plants during the summer; to his writing circle buddies, remember he created the Writers Revolutionary Committee, a small band of drinkers who met after the main circle, he plays yet another part. To the women who become casual acquaintances, like Miss MacDonald, and most of all to Miss King and her son. I am not saying that the defendant is a fraud, we all play out many parts at different times, as the Bard so rightly recognised, but I come back to my central question: who is Richard Andrew Turner?"

Scarrott did that helicopter thing with his glasses again – how I hoped the bastard would take off and disappear like the insect he was. He looked down at the table to where his notes lay.

"The defendant likes the stability of a regular relationship with a home-loving woman who clearly dotes on him despite his infidelities. He likes being with Miss King, likes her son but at the same time he plays the part of the single man, he admires his lothario friend, Mark, who is at least single when he is pursuing his frequent, sordid conquests. But how does Mr Turner repay this kind, loving, affectionate woman? He cheats on her on a number of occasions. I have quoted his diary entry in regard to a Sarah, and I am sure there are more. I suspect the defendant is beginning to think that a diary is best kept unkept (*he'd used that one before but obviously liked it so much he'd decided to recycle it*) for surely these encounters would have remained a secret, but for the fact that the defendant likes to write things down, it's in his DNA."

Scarrott waited, allowed the jury to absorb his words of wisdom.

"You will, members of the jury, draw your own inferences from what you have heard in court but is Mr Turner the nice, friendly, intelligent man who is in a financial pickle because of bad luck and circumstance? Ask yourselves, why is the defendant in the dock? (*Here Scarrott pointed at me with his fucking glasses just in case the jury had forgotten who the fuck I was*) Why is he here? I will tell you why, he took the biggest chance in his life and it went disastrously wrong."

Scarrott paused, looked at his notes. "Oh, I'm not here to make the defendant out to be a cold-blooded psychopath, maybe there is an explanation for the death of Miss MacDonald and perhaps if the defendant had chosen to admit the offence there may have been a possibility of a manslaughter verdict. It may have, after all, been unintentional but because he is a chancer, a risk taker, a gambler, because he is cavalier and reckless, he has chosen to spin that wheel of fortune to take a chance on a 'not guilty' verdict, without a thought to the cost and hurt to the family of his victim or of Lisa, her housemate or landlady, who appeared via video link, or indeed for his own family and friends who have had to put up with the ordeal of appearing as witnesses."

Again, Scarrott allowed his words sink in.

"But now we have a picture in our minds of the defendant as an enigmatic chancer, let's go back to the night of Saturday, 15th November. The defendant meets Anne-Marie in a nightclub, they go back to her place. At some point prior to entering her house he takes his contact lenses out and puts his glasses on. He enters the house. She offers to make him a coffee. He stands against the kitchen door jamb – there is fibre from his shirt on the jamb, don't forget. So positioned, he can easily see into the kitchen. Anne-Marie opens the cupboard doors and she opens the very cupboard that contains an envelope with £10,000 or thereabouts in it, to take out a jar of coffee. Of course, we cannot be certain that the money was still there but does it not seem likely that the men Anne-Marie met in the night club, who possibly gave her a new supply of drugs, were also the men who were due to make the collection? Does it not seem likely, as the defendant has testified, that perhaps there was a car waiting at the top of the road, that perhaps the drugs gang, or line holders as they're termed, were waiting for the defendant to leave the property before making their presence known? We can only speculate but what we do know is the defendant says 'not me, guv, never saw it' – he sat on a sofa whilst the coffee was being made, staring into space. Do we believe that explanation? Really?"

Again, Scarrott paused, sipped some water, and looked at El Hombre and the jury.

"The defendant then went upstairs with Anne-Marie, they had sex, they played a game where he wrapped the tie of her dressing gown around her neck. Of course, the defendant had no thought for poor Miss King at home alone with her young son. Indeed, earlier in the evening he had sent her a text implying he himself was home and he was missing her – a text sent whilst he sat snuggled up with the victim on her sofa."

He walked up to the jury.

"Let's just imagine ourselves in that situation, shall we? The defendant has a mountain of debt. £30,000' worth of ever-increasing debt excluding his student loan. Credit card companies and loan companies are chasing him. He admitted, in his testimony, the amount of debt worried him, that it caused him sleepless nights. He has seen the money in the cupboard. He knows, for he is not an unintelligent man, that the money is the proceeds of crime. He has worked out that Anne-Marie is involved in some way in selling drugs. He goes to leave the house. Then he thinks, 'wait… there is money in that kitchen cupboard' and being the chancer he is, he sneaks back into the kitchen, knowing that he can pay off at least some of his spiralling debts. Maybe treat Miss King: take her somewhere nice, perhaps he sees it as penance for the appalling way he has treated her."

A male voice in the public gallery shouted, 'he bloody needs to' which raised a laugh from the jury.

"Silence in court," El Hombre said and looked suitably stern.

I could see Scarrott was pleased with the interruption

"We know he opened the kitchen cupboard doors for his fingerprints are on them, and he has admitted that he did, indeed, open the doors whilst searching for a glass. His explanation is that he was thirsty and wanted a drink of water. You will, of course, draw your own conclusions about that particular story."

Scarrott paused.

"Anne-Marie wakes up, she comes downstairs, she confronts the defendant in the kitchen. She would have known only too well the implications of not having the money available for the drugs gang – a good hiding, maybe worse – so she would have challenged him. Maybe the defendant was scared. Imagine that scene in the kitchen, if you will? The one, fearful of the consequences of the money being taken, the other with his hands on an envelope which was literally stuffed full to bursting with cash. He is desperate to escape. The defendant panics. He grabs a knife from the kitchen block. Maybe he hopes to frighten her but Anne-Marie, as we know from her landlady's testimony, is feisty and brave. She does not frighten easily. He pokes the knife at her but rather than backing off she comes at him. Maybe he gets angry; he is after all someone who lacks self-control, as was seen when a gentleman came to exercise his lawful right to reclaim the car he'd failed to pay for. The defendant's reaction was to assault him."

Scarrott stopped to ensure his last sentence was remembered.

"Seeing him so angry, maybe she does back off into the front room, but she'd want that money back. They argue, he stabs her with one fatal blow below to the ribcage, upwards into her lung causing an explosion of air to burst onto her vital organs and incapacitate them. There's very little evidential blood but there are traces on the defendant's glasses. Blood he claims was the result on the victim cutting her hand on a card given by the doorman at the Pryzm nightclub. I grant you such flyers were being given out that night but the management has said take-up was low and the CCTV is inconclusive (*again!*) as to whether Anne-Marie took one (*I seem to remember people behind us*). Once again, the defendant's testimony is supported by the reliable Miss King who says she saw the Pryzm advertising card in the footwell of the defendant's car and picked it up and threw it in a bin. And what of his trousers? Why not just place them in the washing machine rather than take them to the dry cleaners?"

Scarrott paced up and down and, as he did so, he gesticulated: then he stood in front of the jury, like some US Presidential candidate who had just take to the stage.

"I have said the defendant is clever. Bright. He likes writing. He is widely read – he devours the novels of Ian Rankin and Peter James and avidly reads each new title. He likes detective stories. You will remember he had this book in his bookcase."

Here he held up a book I had bought called, *A Crime Writer's Guide to Police Practice and Procedure*.

Honestly, you could not make it up! If this story wasn't true no one would ever believe it! It is unbefuckinglievable! Scarrott started waving the fucking thing around as if it were a Millwall 2001 Cup Final flag.

"Maybe having stabbed Anne-Marie, he pauses as he makes his getaway. All is quiet. Then the defendant uses his graduate-educated brain to think. Think like the characters in all those detective novels he reads. He is forensically aware. Of course he is. Most people are nowadays. He knows the most important thing in any murder investigation is the weapon. Take that away and the police are on the back foot. As quick as a flash he pulls it out of the wound. It has his fingerprints on it, of course. He looks around for something to wrap it in – the most convenient thing is a thick, red throw over the settee so he wraps the knife in it. Then he thinks of Anne-Marie's phones – which continually send out electronic signals. The defendant explained how Anne-Marie spent a long time in the bathroom and she had taken her handbag. What would her phone reveal? Text messages? Fortunately for the defendant, we have no evidence that she sent any; still he couldn't be too careful, perhaps she had texted her friend, 'met a lovely, charming guy called Richard, going to spend the night together,' he didn't know, did he? Maybe he had given her his number earlier in the evening, despite his denials, maybe she knew his surname. Maybe someone will call or text Anne-Marie determining the time of death. He knows her housemate or landlady, Lisa X, is not due back till late Sunday afternoon. He knows this because the victim had told him and he has admitted it in his own statement, so that gives him time. Rifling through her handbag he finds not one but two phones. There are no fingerprints on her bag but is it not likely that the quick-thinking defendant used a carrier bag or placed some other item over his hands to ensure no prints were left? He decides to take them both – how can he be sure which one she used? And what about the black satin tie from her dressing gown? He played a game with her earlier in the evening when he tried to asphyxiate her as part of a sex game for, despite his denials, the defendant does have a predilection for rough sex: internet search evidence, which was deemed inadmissible, shows us that it is indeed the case. The tie had his fingerprints on it. He wraps all the items in the throw. Then he thinks he should put it in something. He spies the plastic carrier bags roughly pushed into the recess above the washing machine next to the sink. He pulls one out and places the

380

throw containing said items inside. He leaves the house. He drives home and as he drives, he realises he is driving parallel to the canal. He stops. He makes his way to the canal and throws the plastic bag which contains the throw, knife, phones and dressing gown tie into the canal, perhaps weighing it down with something heavy like a brick. A diver search did not reveal the phones or murder weapon but as you can imagine such a search could take a very long time as there are at least three miles of canal between Mr Turner's and Ms MacDonald's house. And of course, there was no evidence that the items had been despatched to the bottom of the canal, only speculation, for of course he may have got rid of the evidence in a different manner, we can't be sure, but what I place before you is a possible scenario."

I thought Scarrott was going to sit down but he hadn't finished.

"Some might say (*the defence in other words*) that Anne-Marie was killed by a drugs gang. The imaginative defendant has helped concoct a story of cocaine in the bathroom cupboard and they (*the defence*) will say that a drugs gang killed Anne-Marie, but why? If the money was there in the kitchen, why kill the goose that lays the golden egg? So, what of a rival gang? The witness, Lisa X, didn't seem to know of any other drugs gangs operating in the area and surely it is too much of a coincidence that one should enter Anne-Marie's house, with no forced entry remember, on the very night the defendant leaves it. No, I would submit to you, members of the jury, that if you believe that the defendant," here Scarrott pointed at me again just in case they had forgotten who the fuck I was since the last time he'd pointed at me, "if you believe he took the money then he killed Anne-Marie. It may very well be that the first people who discovered her body were the men in the BMW, in other words the drugs gang, or line handlers, but they did not kill her. If they came across the victim, they would have probably left her for her housemate to discover later in the day, being the type of people who are callous to the core. But I ask again why would they kill Anne-Marie if they had come to collect money and that money was in situ?"

Scarrott paused again to allow the jury to let his words to run over them like water over rocks, slowly, subtly eroding them. He looked at his notes, sipped some clear tap water and then he started again.

"So let us turn to the Monday," Scarrott announced. "The defendant knows, for he is an intelligent man, that the hours and days following a murder are the most crucial for investigators so, when the police visit, he stalls. It is purely routine, don't forget he denies knowing or having met Anne-Marie. He knows he will, in the vernacular, eventually be fingered – after all he has already seen his name linked with Anne-Marie on social media, something his phone tells us he was actively checking throughout the day at work. Indeed, on the Monday morning the defendant had posted a WhatsApp message to his group called 'The Boys' in which he had boasted of his sexual conquest but he had not named names. Later in the day, Suggo, posted a rather crude WhatsApp message and his friend Matty had texted him with the message, '*is this girl who has been killed the girl you left the club with?*' The defendant doesn't reply to either message because, of course, he knows it is. Yet he denies it to the police. Then, fearing the money will link him to the slaying of Anne-Marie, as surely it would, he discards some of it. How much did he keep, who knows? But what we do know is that a person named Simon Ricoh finds that very same money in a council bin. Anything else is simply beyond coincidence. £10,000 found in a council bin and approximately £10,000 stolen from a property, what are the odds on that money not being the same?"

Scarrott picked up a pen and wrote something on his notes.

"We know that money was found at some time prior to 9.32 on the morning of Tuesday, 18th November when Mr Ricoh purchased the first of many pints of beer from the Lord Rochford public house. And we know that the defendant walked past many council bins on his way to his writers' circle on the Monday evening, after the police visit. We also know that the defendant stopped at a bin, rested his folder on it and possibly threw something in it. Now, members of the jury, cast your mind back to a time when you have dropped something in a bin; a tissue from a coat or trouser pocket, for example. The chances are you deposited said item whilst passing without even breaking stride whereas the defendant can clearly be seen, on CCTV, stopping at the bin and resting his black folder on it. Was the money inside? Did he perhaps tip the folder up and let it slide into the bin? The CCTV is unclear but the defendant, who at times has remarkable powers of recall, does on this occasion remember throwing something in a bin when prompted by the CCTV evidence."

Again, Scarrott fell silent. He eyed the jury as he walked towards them.

"Now I'm not saying at this stage the defendant did not panic. I'm not saying he did not regret his actions of the Saturday night or Sunday morning but what I am saying is the chancer, the gambler, the wheel spinner was once again acting a part, playing games, trying to distract and confuse. And how else does he do that? On the Tuesday he gives a voluntary statement to the SIO, DCI Hinton, having spent time on his own computer trying to cobble together a somewhat believable account of his actions. For let us not forget that the defendant is a story teller, a weaver of lies, a fabricator, whether it's to his wonderful, placid and compliant ex-partner, Miss King who has stuck by him, or his friends or even his family from whom he hid the awful truth about his clandestine trips to see his brute of a father for many years whilst he was at university and beyond."

Scarrott stepped back to the table where his file rested and waited.

"The defendant is a man who has lived his life by deceit and dishonesty and when cornered he has lashed out physically. We have heard of his altercation with the gentleman who tried to reclaim his car, but I am also aware of another such incident in prison, where the defendant assaulted a fellow remand inmate. My information is the assault took place in the dinner queue against a smaller, weaker individual – a model prisoner indeed – who the prison authorities have said was certainly not the instigator. In fact, the assault was entirely unprovoked and the victim has spoken of his utter, utter disbelief as he'd tried to assist and befriend the defendant when he had first arrived at the prison gates. That is how the defendant repaid that prisoner's kindness."

Unbefuckinglievable.

Scarrott carefully placed his pen down on his notes and continued.

"But more pertinently he uses that graduate level brain, that thinking brain, that intelligent brain to think of routes and pathways out of danger. And that's what he did that Monday night – he put the money in the bin and by Tuesday he had his story concocted. He spoke to his manager, what of it? He got on well with her, he ran the story past her, used her, as he used Miss King, as he knew both women would be good and creditable witnesses if he were to ever stand trial and so it has proved."

Here Scarrott got a crisp white handkerchief from his trouser pocket and, leaving it folded into squares, he dabbed his dry, flaky brow; I could see the embroidered *JPS* in the corner.

John Player Fucking Special – I didn't smoke but sitting in the dock listening to Scarrott I could have happily chain-smoked my way through a packet of twenty.

"So, alas, I come to Miss King, the agreeable Miss King who struggles to bring up an eight- or nine-year-old son on limited means and with no family to support her and with an erstwhile, feckless ex-husband who offers nothing in the way of financial or emotional support. Then she meets the defendant, they form a relationship. It is hardly Romeo and Juliet but he is caring, loving, outgoing – when he is with her, for surely that is just another character the defendant plays. When not with her he is one of the lads, out for a good time and an easy conquest with no thought of the hurt it may cause Miss King. And so he finds himself, to use the vernacular again, 'in a spot of bother' – so what does he do? He asks Miss King, who he has cheated on, let us not forget, to take the witness stand and lie for him. To lie under oath. To commit perjury. To risk imprisonment and separation from her eight- or nine-year-old son for the sake of some cock and bull story he has concocted. Miss King has told us that she manages her finances well, that she doesn't even have a credit card or an overdraft; she has said she likes to use cash because when 'it's gone it's gone' – a good fiscal maxim, and one I am sure financial guru Martin Lewis would be proud of."

That raised much mirth from the court. Even El Hombre smiled. Scarrott, the comedian, sending out subliminal messages.

"So, are we truly to believe, members of the jury, are we truly to believe, (*here Scarrott became animated and started pointing and wagging his finger like Hitler at Nuremburg*) that this woman, this paragon of financial probity has to rely on handouts from a man who plays online gambling games and who has amassed debts of over £30,000, which he has not an earthly chance of ever repaying? A man who has had his car repossessed. A man who has little control over his income and outgoings! Yet he would have us believe he is Miss King's knight in shining armour! He is the man who rides gallantly to her rescue when she is short of a bob or two! He is the man who keeps the wolf from her financial door. He is the man who says, 'here, have my spare £100 or was it 150'!"

Scarrott pointed at me in the dock.

"I give you, members of the jury, Miss King's Sir Galahad."

The court loved that, lapped it up, boy did they laugh! Of course, with his references to chivalry he was subtly reminding the jury that I had cheated on Debbie and that, in fact, I was the complete opposite of a noble knight of old. I rubbed my hands through my short hair and looked to the floor so no one could see my moist eyes. I knew the trial would be hard, but I had never expected what Scarrott unleashed – I never expected a complete character assassination. But Scarrott hadn't finished.

"In addition to the money there is, of course, the Pryzm advertising card and the paper cut. It is noticeable that in none…. I repeat none… I repeat again… none…. I repeat again… none…. of the defendant's many statements is there any mention of Miss King finding the advertising flyer in the footwell of his car, when they parked at the museum, and then discarding it in a bin en route to the entrance (*I'd been so fixated by the money I'd forgotten all about it!*). A bin that is so far from the museum it just happens, very conveniently, not to be within range of CCTV. So, once again Miss King comes to the rescue of the defendant, perhaps by dint of her own enterprise. For not only did she notice the card in the footwell on the Sunday but she picked it up, registered blood on it, don't you know, and then kindly consigned it to a bin before entering the aircraft museum – it's all there in the two statements she gave to the police. I have to say a lot gets dropped in bins in Mr Turner's world."

The jury tittered with laughter.

"So, members of the jury, if you think the defendant stole that money from Anne-Marie's house, I say again the only logical conclusion is that he stabbed her to death when confronted. The only logical conclusion. The evidence is overwhelming. He has a penchant for rough sex. He was at the house at the time of the murder. He opened the kitchen cupboard doors where the money was stored. He had traces of blood on his glasses. He sent his machine-wash trousers to the dry cleaner. He checked his phone constantly on the Monday. He failed to reply to messages concerning the victim, yet he drove back past the victim's house. He had the money in his possession at some point on Monday evening. He described his first statement as a 'confession' and when he had the opportunity to tell the truth, he deliberately prevaricated and misled the police not on one but on multiple occasions. So, I say to you, members of the jury, find this man guilty and remove a calculating killer from our streets."

And with that theatrical flourish Scarrott finally sat down and shut the fuck up.

Not surprising Mr George Prentice had the after-lunch shift. Again.

And this is, as far as I can remember, what my barrister said.

"Members of the jury, my learned friend has concentrated a lot on the character of my client portraying him as having a dark and devious side which must inevitably mean he is guilty of murder, but we are here to examine the facts of the case and that means you cannot possibly convict my client on the evidence presented by the prosecution. There is a scenario, I grant you, which is as the prosecution sets out, that my client, having seen the money in the kitchen cupboard tried to steal it, was confronted by the victim and perhaps, in an effort to escape, killed her. But what evidence is there of this? A speck or two of blood on a pair of glasses my client kept in his car and which he claims are a result of the victim cutting her finger on an advertising flyer given to her as she left the Pryzm nightclub, and the fact he took his trousers to the dry cleaners on the Monday as he drove to work – but that is unlikely to hide blood residue when forensically examined and his trousers have been. Result? They are clean."

That raised a titter of laugher. Mr Prentice continued.

"The same is true of my client's car which has been forensically examined: what has it revealed? Nothing of any interest! Of course, Anne-Marie's fingerprints are in the car and fibres from her coat, he gave her lift home after all, but there are no traces of blood, no fibres from Anne-Marie's house. Nothing! Yet when faced with this startling lack of evidence what does the prosecution do? Merely concoct an alternative scenario. The witness, known as Lisa X, has said that plastic carrier bags from Tesco's and the like were stuffed in the recess on top of the washing machine and when she returned home, they were strewn across the floor. Conclusion? The prosecution says that my client placed all the items in a carrier bag before exiting the house. But where is the evidence for this? There is, remember, no murder weapon and, as my learned friend has admitted, without a murder weapon the police are on the back foot, to use his own words."

Mr Prentice paused, turned a page over.

"So, what happened in that house between midnight and maybe six or seven in the morning of Sunday, 16th November? The death of the victim is thought to have been sometime between 3am to 7am – a wide window – for the body was not discovered for another ten to twelve hours when Anne-Marie's landlady, Lisa X, arrived home at approximately 4 or 4.30pm. She is unsure as to the exact time but whatever time it was rigor mortis had sent in which makes it more difficult to determine the exact time of death. The call to the emergency services was recorded at 4.36pm. So, we don't know what happened. We can't know what happened. It could have been exactly as my client describes. Why is his version of events any less plausible than the prosecution's? He left the house and went home only to be questioned about whether he knew the victim on the Monday. He felt frightened – who wouldn't? He knew he had had a sexual relationship with the victim and he knew he might well be a suspect. Hence his anxious conversation with his line manager, Ms Glover, and his attempt to put things right by writing a statement."

Mr Prentice turned to a tagged page in his folder.

"Other scenarios are equally as valid: the defendant didn't shut the door properly and Mr Ricoh – who disappeared from an approved premises don't forget – crept in, found the money and killed the victim when challenged. Another, perhaps more likely scenario, is as Lisa X has said, she and the victim were involved in the sale of illicit drugs; the money was due to be collected and perhaps there was a dispute over the amount raised. You have heard the witness known as Lisa X say the line holders assaulted them if they didn't earn as much as they thought they should have: that could have happened in this case, only it went too far. Unfortunately, due to the covert way in which these criminal gangs operate, Lisa X has no idea as to the possible assailants. She says they rarely saw the same people twice and many were sent to do the bidding of the drugs barons. But did the police follow up on any of these scenarios? Of course, they didn't! They might have questioned Mr Ricoh further if he hadn't absconded and they might have probed more deeply into Citi Cabs, as my client had suggested, as they had followed him and Anne-Marie back to her house. She presented as being anxious and worried by them and had been, or still was, in a relationship with one of the former drivers; was he questioned? Did they follow that lead? Perhaps, but not in any great depth. My client did his own detective work and questioned Citi Cabs but obviously they were not going to reveal their true intentions. My client has spoken about the condom filled with cocaine in the bathroom but my learned friend doubts the validity of that story, if it were ever there it has gone missing, so he concludes it wasn't there at all but I would remind him that the victim and the Lisa X were drug dealers. Drug dealers normally have stockpiles of drugs."

The court laughed; another one over on Scarrott. Mr Prentice waited whilst he eyed the jury.

"My client gave a voluntary interview as he wanted to clarify matters following the police visit and then one or two 'no comment' interviews, as that was what was advised by the duty solicitor. Then, when arrested, he once again wished to 'set the record straight' so he gave another interview, despite the advice of his second solicitor not to do so. This all suggests to DCI Hinton, the SIO in charge of the case, that my client was the guilty party and further lines of enquiry were closed down: whether it was Mr Ricoh who goes under the nickname 'Sunderland' Simon or drugs gangs or Citi Cabs. Such a blinkered approach can only lead one way – up a cul-de-sac to a miscarriage of justice."

Mr Prentice paused to let his words sink in. I felt he was doing a good job, in his quiet way he was just as effective as Scarrott – well perhaps not.

"On the Monday, my client denied knowing the victim. He has explained the reason for this; he did not want to upset his girlfriend, Miss King, and, as I have already said, he felt panicked and worried about the suddenness of the police visiting his flat when he wanted to go to a writers' circle. As to the money being placed in the bin, what evidence is there of this? A hazy CCTV image of my client walking past a bin, resting his folder on top and possibly dropping something in it. Excuse me, are we all now to be accused of throwing the proceeds of crime into council bins whenever we threw a toffee wrap or fast-food carton away! Such a scenario is ludicrous."

Here there was a murmur of laughter around the court, not as much as Scarrott achieved but still a murmur.

"Where is the evidence? Show it to me! I say to the prosecution on this, and on so many things they have singularly failed to evidence their case against my client. Where is the witness Mr Ricoh to fully explain where he obtained his great wad of cash? Nowhere to be seen! Are we to believe the story of a homeless itinerant, who assaults people in pubs and then absconds from an approved premises, over my client who holds down a job and has a loving family? You have met his sisters

Kate and Donna who have spoken with genuine warmth and affection about their younger brother. Yes, he is reckless with money but he is basically honest, loving, caring and fair-minded."

Mr Prentice looked over to the jury.

"My God, if we started imprisoning all those who were irresponsible with money many millions would be incarcerated – the whole of the current government amongst them."

That raised a laugh from the jury and the public gallery. Even Mr Prentice could tell a joke. He turned a page.

Every sinew of my body was strained as I concentrated on his speech, I put my hand in my pocket and gripped my lion mascot. I was fixated by his words, urging him, willing him, praying that he would strike a home run; that somehow his closing remarks would breed uncertainty in the jury. Mr Prentice continued.

"So, Mr Turner attended the writers' circle," he said. "He, by all accounts, presented as his normal, happy-go-lucky self. He read a story, he joked, he talked about the previous night's TV, the only thing he didn't do was go for a drink after nor mention the police visit. On returning home he phoned Miss King and confided in her about the police visit and told her he missed her. She said he sounded 'upset' perhaps because he had cheated on her and was feeling remorse. Yet, she herself said the defendant was to her knowledge a loyal and trustworthy boyfriend, who got on well with her nine-year-old son, taking him to his first football matches and both of them on a camping holiday to New Forest, with the defendant buying most of the treats; she said it was a very enjoyable holiday, the first she had had for many a year. They also went out for days; on the Sunday, he took them both to an aircraft museum as her son had wanted to go to one, being at an age where he is fascinated by planes. She claims the defendant treated her really well. Miss King liked that. Her ex-husband had, in her words, done 'nothing' but 'slob about all day lying on the sofa and the watching football on Sky or BT. She moaned at him and eventually he left her and went to live with another woman who he had apparently been seeing behind her back."

Mr Prentice looked down to where his notes lay on the table.

"My client liked to take Miss King out for meals or cook meals for her at his flat, or maybe they'd go to the cinema together or even to the West End to see a musical – another first for Miss King. She says she liked going to his apartment when her best friend was babysitting Dylan or he was on a sleepover as it was always clean and tidy and the defendant was a 'good cook'. She said she liked the fact he was always coming up with ideas of where they could go and things they could see and he would include young Dylan in the plans. They played kinky sex games, so what? It was for mutual pleasure and Miss King said the defendant never touched her in a violent way and never tried to strangle or asphyxiate her even as part of one of those games."

Mr Prentice stopped briefly to pour water into his glass but unlike Scarrott he continued to talk as he did so.

"His manager, Mrs Glover, too has spoken highly of my client; he was in her words 'trustworthy, smart, punctual and eager to please' he wasn't particularly ambitious but 'he got on with the job without fuss', 'he had few days off sick' and he was 'well liked in the office' having an easy sense of humour and a pleasant manner with staff and customers. His friends too say much the same. A people person. A person with empathy and sympathy."

Mr Prentice stood in front of the jury.

"The prosecution has made much of the defendant's debts and give this as a reason why he might be tempted to take the money in the kitchen cupboard but the defendant claims he never saw it and even if he had, does that fit the profile of the caring, people person who takes his girlfriend and her son away on holiday at his own expense? Is such a man likely to plunge a knife into the heart of a woman he barely knows, let alone one he has just slept with? Surely, if the prosecution claim is correct, and he had been challenged by the deceased about the money he would have merely thrown it down and run off. The idea that he would grab a knife from a knife block and plunge it into the victim's chest is simply absurd."

I have to say I was feeling a lot better about things. Mr Prentice walked back to the table and sipped some water. He looked down at his notes. I could see Scarrott frantically scribbling away, God knows why. Hannah turned and smiled at me. I gave her a discreet thumbs up. Mr Prentice had quietly manoeuvred the bombastic Scarrott onto the ropes. Mr Prentice continued.

"Yet my learned friend paints a picture of a cold-blooded killer who, once he has stabbed the victim, possibly by accident, and caused her death, has the presence of mind to wrap the knife in a throw from the settee, take two mobile phones from her handbag on the coffee table, ensuring of course he leaves no fingerprints and then the tie from the victim's dressing gown, as he had played a game where he tried to asphyxiate her earlier in the evening, and he is aware there maybe fingerprints on it! Having just killed the victim! Come on, please! This scenario is beyond belief let alone beyond reasonable doubt. It is in the realms of fantasy. I would think, in the cold aftermath of a fatal stabbing, the murderer might feel slightly panicked, might feel remorseful, might feel scared knowing what he faced in terms of punishment. But here the prosecution gives my client all the characteristics of a cold and calculating killer."

Mr Prentice paused and looked at the jury. Eyeing them slowly and deliberately.

"For members of the jury, does not the scenario my learned friend suggests take a degree of cunning and deviousness that most average people, faced with the shock of a dead body, and knowing they have caused the death, would not be able to muster? And for all the negative insinuations the prosecution has laid at my client's door, where is the evidence that he is criminally minded to such an extent? Members of the jury, my client is a normal, average man – yes, one who has made mistakes, yes, one who is flawed, but not one who is cold and calculating. Not one who murders for money or for any other reason."

Mr Prentice started to pace up and down, his notes forgotten. He had just been warming up but now he got into his stride. Mr Prentice was an excellent brief. The best. He became agitated and animated and he set about the self-important Scarrott with some deadly combinations of punches but first he stopped, paused, leant on the table like an exhausted, breathless long-distance runner. Then he straightened up and launched an all-out salvo on Scarrott and the CPS. He held his arms aloft,

"But wait. Let us just stop here and concur with the prosecution's scenario."

Across the court there was a sharp intake of collective breath.

"It is, let us imagine, exactly how my learned friend says it is. My client did steal the money, my client did stab Anne-Marie, my client did then have the presence of mind to cover his tracks. He did discard the incriminating evidence, possibly in the canal, possibly elsewhere."

My heart was flapping like a fledgling's wing. I tapped my foot, I felt nervous energy roll through me. I knew this was the moment of truth. This was the home run.

"So, my client has the money from the kitchen cupboard on his person," Mr Prentice continued. "He has killed Anne-Marie, possibly not intentionally. He knows, for as my learned friend says, he is not an unintelligent man, that he is likely to be questioned by the police... members of the jury, do you not think my client would have come up with some plan? Some way of *hiding* the money? Do you not think he would feel he should not use it for a few days or more? If my client is, as my learned friend suggests, devious and calculating and forensically aware, surely he would know *not* to use the money straight after the murder. Surely, he would be aware that the three times he allegedly used the money; at the museum, at the fast-food restaurant and at petrol station would leave a digital and CCTV footprint? Such a scenario stretches to the realms of incredulity which are then strained to breaking point when the last act in this drama is considered: the disposal of the money in a council bin! Let us all just reflect on that for one moment…" Mr Prentice paused, "he wanted that money, he killed for that money and yet by the Monday he casually drops it in a council bin!"

He threw his hands up.

"I say again, it is beyond belief! Surely if my client is as artful and devious and cunning as the prosecution alleges, that money would have been well hidden by Monday night; perhaps in the garden, perhaps in the storeroom at the back of his shared house which has been thoroughly searched, perhaps at Miss King's house, perhaps in one of the tubs he so diligently made up for his landlord, which were still filled with soil. But why would such a calculating individual throw the proceeds of a crime, during which had committed murder, away?"

Mr Prentice walked back to the table and sipped some water.

"Members of the jury, is my client guilty of murder? Of course he is not! It is ludicrous to think that having taken the money he would not hide it rather than throw it away. The prosecution case is fantasy and fabrication built upon threadbare evidence and circumstances which place my client in the victim's house before the victim was murdered. Surely my client can't be committed on such flimsy evidence. Members of the jury, to find my client guilty would be a gross miscarriage of justice. He was in the wrong place at the

401

wrong time – that is all. That is all. Let my client go free and release him from this terrible ordeal."

And with that Mr Prentice sat down. El Hombre looked at the clock at the back of the court room.

"I thank counsel for their closing speeches. We will adjourn until 11am tomorrow when I will commence my summing up. Then I will ask the jury to retire to consider their verdict."

"Court stand," shouted the black-gowned usher.

Once against I was placed into the white Serco van and transported back to prison. I had a near permanent headache (with no hope of any paracetamol as I wasn't around for the meds queue although Dom managed to get me one or two), and my body shivered, I had a tic above my right eye, my mouth felt dry and I was permanently tired. I returned to prison each day after the trial to rubbish food and more sleepless nights but at least it was over…ish.

The next day I wore a grey charcoal suit with a faint check, matching waistcoat, shirt and tie. It was the suit I'd worn on the second day of the trial (I'm counting from the time I was actually in the dock). I wanted to look smart for the summing up and the verdict. I just hoped the jury didn't retire for too long. Once again, I was taken up the wide steps to the dock, past the white brick walls and into the wooden dock skirted by brass rails. I looked up at the gallery and saw Kate. She wore a flowered dress and plain blue jacket, her husband

Martin, had his arm around her shoulder – I wondered who was looking after the two boys? Donna was next to her, dressed in a purple maxi dress, her hands resting on her enlarged, pregnant stomach: it was strange because there was a man next to her who I assumed was her new partner, Wayne. I had never met him, only read about him in letters, it was one of a hundred things I'd missed out on whilst I'd been banged up on remand. I smiled at them both and Kate blew me a kiss off the palm of her hand and smiled. I could see Mark too, the row behind; his arms were folded, he looked serious and, for once, there wasn't a girlfriend by his side. I searched out Mum and Debbie but couldn't see either. I wondered if Mum was babysitting Kate's boys and Donna's daughter – that was probably it. She'd probably said,

"You two go, I'll look after the kids."

At last, El Hombre came in and the usher shouted 'all stand'. We stood until he had bowed and taken his seat. The rest of the court sat whilst I remained standing.

"You may sit down," El Hombre said to me and waved his hand like a Roman emperor.

"That's good of him," the obese security guard said under his breath.

El Hombre cleared his throat and began to speak.

"Members of the jury, you are here to decide a very simple matter – did Richard Andrew Turner murder Anne-Marie MacDonald? That is all. In my view both the prosecution and the defence have been too ready to

403

provide you with speculation and theories which might or might not fit the facts but scenarios never killed anyone and you should discount notions of drug gangs and Mr Simon Ricoh and the thousand and one other scenarios that you have been erroneously presented with during the course of this trial. If you find the defendant 'not guilty' then the police will find the real culprit or culprits."

"Some hope of that," my friendly, walrus-like security guard said.

"That is not your concern," El Hombre continued. "Your concern is whether there is enough evidence to convict the defendant of murder beyond reasonable doubt. The prosecution case, simply put, is this. There was money in the kitchen cupboard, a considerable amount of money, the proceeds of crime, but we only have one witness that confirms this, Lisa X, and you, the jury, must decide how creditable she is as a witness. They, the prosecution, claim the defendant stole the money and was confronted by the victim. In the fracas that resulted the defendant stabbed Miss MacDonald once. They accept he probably did not mean to kill her. Then he took the tie from her dressing gown, which he had used earlier for a sexual game, her phones which may or may not have been in her handbag which was on the coffee table and, of course, the knife and then wrapped the items in a red throw which was over the sofa: he then placed them all in a carrier bag and then exited the property. There is no collaboration of this. However, the prosecution point to the fact £10,000 was found in a council bin – surely it is too much of a coincidence to think that two amounts of money, of roughly the same amount, went missing and were found at the same time. The man named as Mr Simon Ricoh, whom DCI Murray was apt to mimic, collaborates that part of Lisa X's story, to some extent, however it was remiss of the police not to have properly interrogated Mr Ricoh in regard to which bin the money was found in – if indeed Mr Ricoh found the money in a bin as he alleged. The two cases should have been joined up at an earlier stage which would have provided DCI Hinton an opportunity to probe into the origins of the money and the story Mr Simon Ricoh told DCI Murray. Mr Ricoh could then have been properly eliminated as a possible suspect. Just to allow him to be bailed to an approved premises, where he absconded, is careless in the extreme and is something I shall be addressing with the Chief Constable."

Yul Grinner was for the high jump.

El Hombre paused and looked at his notes.

"But what of the defendant?" El Hombre said. "He denies ever seeing the money, in which case he could not take the money, and he denies throwing anything of any worth in a council bin on the Monday night. However, the prosecution claims his monetary transactions on the Sunday, when he took Miss King and her son to an aircraft museum, on the Monday when he visited a fast-food restaurant, and on the Tuesday, where he bought petrol were out of his normal routine. On each occasion he used cash. You must decide, as a jury, who you believe. But you are not here to decide who took the money, if indeed anyone did. You are here to decide whether or not the defendant murdered Anne-Marie MacDonald. The evidence against him, as the defence have said, is not strong and in the most part is purely circumstantial. Indeed the only forensic evidence, apart from the blood traces on his glasses, for which an explanation has been proffered, are the fingerprints on the kitchen cupboard doors – so we know he opened the cupboard doors where the money was stored, if indeed it was there. We also know, at some point, he leant against the door frame of the kitchen door. There are fibres from his shirt to prove it – so he could have seen the money, if indeed it was ever there, or it may be that he leant against the door jamb when collecting the coffee the victim had made for him, as he has said. The defendant's explanation for opening the kitchen cupboard doors was that he was desperate for a glass of water and he opened them in the hope of finding a glass, but why not just go home, a ten-minute drive or less and drink some water at home? And why, when he used the hot tap instead of the cold did he not just simply turn on the cold tap if he was so thirsty and in urgent need of a drink? You must decide if these aspects of the defendant's story are believable. Unfortunately, we can't be sure if he used the hot tap as the forensics have proved questionable. But remember, there's no murder weapon; there's no tie or belt from the victim's dressing gown, there are no mobile phones and the throw from the settee has gone missing too. We can see, by traces on the defendant's mobile phone, that the timings he gives more or less accord with his own testimony although unhelpfully Mr Turner's phone did not ping or page any masts on his way home. He says the battery died, so we can't be certain as to when he left the property. Likewise, Anne-Marie's phones both seemed to have stopped transmitting during the early hours of Sunday morning. That is why that particular evidence has not been used."

El Hombre paused. He looked at the jury like a parent looking at his errant children – were they still listening? He threaded his fingers and moved forward in his seat.

"Members of the jury, it is for you to look at the evidence and decide if there is sufficient evidence to convict. Remember there is very little linking the defendant to the murder evidentially. His car has been forensically examined and, although there are traces of Anne-Marie's DNA in the defendant's car, as result of giving her a lift home, there is no blood or any fibres from her house. The prosecution claim he may have hidden the evidence in a plastic carrier bag, having pulled one out from above the washing machine, but this is pure speculation because such carrier bags littered the kitchen floor as you have seen in your court packs when you were asked to look at photographs of the kitchen."

El Hombre took a deep breath and started again.

"Whether or not the defendant did take the money is not the key point here – he has not been charged with theft. He is not here to answer accusations that he took money from the kitchen cupboard. No, he faces one simple charge; did he kill Anne-Marie MacDonald and you, as a jury, must decide whether or not there is enough evidence to convict him of that crime. Of course, his DNA and fingerprints are all over the house, he had gone back to her house and had sexual intercourse with Miss MacDonald, he has touched various things in her house but that doesn't mean he killed her."

I have to say I was feeling buoyed by the good judge's comments – I told you El Hombre was the man! I was almost smiling. I folded my arms and started to relax. How could the jury possibly convict me? But he hadn't finished.

"Of course, the defence present a picture of an honest, hardworking individual who just happened to have run up a large amount of personal debt and who just happened to have an altercation with a man who came to reclaim his car and just happened to launch an unprovoked assault on a fellow prisoner in the dinner queue whilst on remand. I feel the defence is being slightly duplicitous in their representation of the defendant as honest, caring, hardworking young man whom bad luck has dealt a terrible hand, but even so that does not make him a murderer."

El Hombre stopped and looked at his notes.

"I have to say I found his former manager, Ms Glover, his ex-partner, Miss King, his sisters and even his friends very creditable witnesses, and it is noticeable that Miss King stated she managed her money well yet on the Sunday, the day of the murder, the defendant had a sum of money on him which he claimed was given to him by Miss King in payment of a loan he had made to her earlier. I am sure you will reach your own conclusion about the veracity of that story."

Here El Hombre stopped and looked long and hard at the jury.

"Now whilst I have told you to discount the money – the defendant is not being tried for its theft after all – I feel it may be relevant to the case in this respect. Why has the defendant consistently denied taking it, if indeed he did? If he did take the money and didn't kill Miss MacDonald, why not just own up to that fact? Why not just admit that lesser crime? A crime, indeed, for which he'd face no sanction for it has never been mentioned or pursued by the police as a crime. Why not admit he threw the money in the bin on the Monday after he was spoken to by the police, and that meant Mr Ricoh did indeed find it and spent some of it in a pub called the Lord Rochford, which in turn led to a confrontation with some workmen. That is something which you must ponder. For surely it would have been in the defendant's best interests to tell the truth. Innocent people tell the truth. That is a fact. Those with something to hide do not. That is also a fact. It is in all our interests to tell the truth. So that is another point to consider; if the defendant is not telling the truth, then why not? What is he trying to hide? Is his involvement as innocent as he would have us believe?"

El Hombre sat back in his high red-backed chair like a king on a throne.

"I must say I have found some of the defendant's answers a little too well-rehearsed and well-prepared, as if he has, whilst on remand, practised his responses. Does an innocent man need to practise? Does it indicate that the defendant does indeed have something to hide? These are questions you must ask yourselves for I would suggest that the truth never needs to be rehearsed."

El Hombre leant forward again and addressed the jury as if they were the only people in the court.

"This is a very difficult case. A very difficult case indeed. However, the view I have formed of the defendant is that he presents as a man of intelligence, well capable of quickness of thought. A man who might well be able to think like the character in one of the short stories he likes to write or the crime detective novels he reads so avidly, when presented with an unexpected situation. After all he knew there was no likelihood of being caught in the house for several hours, unless of course the drug dealers or line handlers visited the property, and he was not to know that. As to the money in the bin, you might be tempted to agree with the defence's claim that it is fanciful and ludicrous that someone who had gone to such lengths to cover his tracks would then just throw away a wad of cash, but I would remind you, members of the jury, that people under extreme stress behave in a haphazard and chaotic way which is not logical. Also, he may have had feelings of remorse. It is well known that when people have committed terrible deeds, they often wish to distance themselves from the act, and the money was a continuous reminder. However, he may have kept a small amount back and felt that the financial transactions on the Monday and Tuesday were too small to be of any significance and that is why he continued to use the money. So, it may be that having taken the money and killed Anne-Marie accidently, the defendant did panic on the Monday night after the first police enquiry at his flat and that, in turn, led him to discard the money. After all he has admitted he was scared and worried by the police visit. Why was that? That is something you must ask yourselves. It was only routine after all and his friends and even his ex-girlfriend, Miss King, who were also visited by the police, have said in their testimonies they had no such qualms.

411

"In conclusion, I would submit that you apply the evidential test supported by reasonable inferences from the circumstantial evidence. If you feel the evidence is purely circumstantial then you must, in all conscience, acquit; if, on the other hand, you feel the evidence – the cold hard facts, if you like – support the circumstantial evidence then you must decide if there is enough to convict beyond reasonable doubt. I leave it in your capable hands. Retire now and consider your verdict."

So that was El Hombre's summing up, I was hoping for a direction to acquit but it wasn't to be. I was taken back to my cell, a sparse, white brick, rectangular room of misery with its high window threaded with black metallic strips and the obligatory hard bed. Hannah and Mr Prentice came to see me.

"How are you, Richard?" Mr Prentice asked sombrely.

I was seated on the bed. "I don't know how I feel anymore," I said. "Sometimes I think I'll be acquitted but at other times I'm not sure."

"I know, it's frustrating," Hannah said. "It could go either way but I think we hold a strong position. I think George gave an excellent closing statement."

I noticed a smile exchange between the two; Hannah obviously admired my barrister. He was what she dreamed of becoming. And, in the fullness of time, inevitably would.

"You should be acquitted but you can never tell with juries," Mr Prentice said matter-of-factly. "If they take a long time, it means there's a lot of discussion and there's a difference of opinion in the group and you're probably more likely to be acquitted; if it is short then it is likely they all agree which means it could go either way. But whether it is the right decision or not you won't know until you're back up in the dock."

"Great," I mused, sitting on the bed, my head in my hands.

Of course, it was going to take a long time. I knew it would. Nothing in my life has ever been easy, if there's bad luck to be had then I've had it. By the fucking bucketful. The jury weren't able to reach a verdict by the end of the day so they were sent to a hotel for the night. That meant I was transported back to my prison cell. My future would be decided on the following day.

SECTION THREE: THE VERDICT

Chapter Fourteen

It was about midday when the jury had finally reached a decision. I had just finished off a cheese and tomato sandwich and a carton of drink. The same walrus security guard from the day before hooked me up to the cuffs and I was taken the short distance to the wide steps that led up to the dock. I felt a bit like a footballer walking out at Wembley for the Cup Final. My heart was racing. Blood pulsed through my body. My stomach churned. Back in the holding cell I had gone to the toilet continuously. The whole experience was made worse as I had nothing to read and nothing to do but worry. I felt a tug on my wrist and realised Walrus was on the move. He slowly padded up the stairs with me one step behind. It had all started on 15th November and it was now late April – over six months of anxiety and chaos for a one-night stand. But it could get a whole lot worse. A hell of a lot worse.

I reached the top of the steps. This time I could not look around to acknowledge my sisters and their partners and any other friends who were sitting in the public gallery. I just felt too anxious and I knew it would make me emotional: in the next few minutes, my fate would be sealed.

The Walrus led me into the brass-rail-framed dock and pushed a red seat down for himself. He seemed to forget, or more likely didn't care, about the fact that I was attached to him and when he moved, I moved. My arm was momentarily painfully tugged. With my left hand I tried to manoeuvre the seat down: I sat down with a hefty plonk. The Walrus looked smug.

"Sorry, forgot to detach you," he whispered. He removed the cuffs.

His dark moustache barely covered a slight smirk as if he wanted to stay attached to me. He wanted to take me back downstairs into the holding cell rather than see me go free. I was, in his eyes, guilty no matter what the jury's verdict. The fact of being in custody and on trial was enough to confirm my guilt. For he, of course, like the police and all the law enforcers was an expert and he knew, he just *knew* no innocent person was ever accused of anything. Never. Ever.

"Court rise," called the black-robed usher.

At last, El Hombre filed in and the Walrus and I stood up. El Hombre bowed his head, his white wig contrasting momentarily with the red of his gown. He took his seat.

"Please sit," the usher said.

"The defendant needs to remain standing," the clerk said. I moved to the front of the dock. My heart pumped frantically. My pulses seemed to be in overdrive mode. I clasped my hands behind my back and continuously threaded my sweaty fingers.

"Could the foreperson of the jury please stand?" El Hombre asked.

A woman in her mid-fifties with straw blonde hair, a thin mouth and small silver-rimmed spectacles stood up. She looked nervous, rather terrified in fact.

"Have you reached a verdict upon which you all agree?" El Hombre asked.

"No," the woman said. "We can't agree."

"Have you reached a verdict in which ten of you agree – what's called a majority verdict?" El Hombre asked.

"Yes," came the reply.

My skin tingled and I felt dizzy. I tapped my foot. I put my hand in my pocket and played with my plastic lion. I thought I was going to faint. I looked to the floor. Held the bridge of my nose. Pushed my glasses up.

"Therefore, do you find the defendant, Richard Andrew Turner guilty or not guilty of the unlawful killing of Anne-Marie MacDonald at some time between 3am and 7am on Sunday, 16th November last contrary to common law."

And then came the simple response. A soft 'guilty' whispered on the air like a butterfly's wing yet so loud it reverberated around the court and grow lounder and louder, guilty, guilty, guilty...

I heard a howl of, 'no!' and a woman burst into hysterical tears – probably Kate or Donna. Possibly both. I heard someone else shout, 'no, no, no.'

Then someone else started sobbing.

Yet I stood stock still like a sentry. Emotionless. I had rehearsed this in my head – being found guilty, I mean, and I knew what I was going to do: stand tall. Show no emotion. I wasn't going to let the bastards see they'd won.

El Hombre stared at me with cold, piercing eyes.

"Mr Richard Andrew Turner, you have been found guilty of the murder of Anne-Marie MacDonald. I will hear a victim impact statement and then you will be sentenced following a pre-sentence report, perhaps next week."

"Yes, Your Honour," I said for reasons best known to myself. I was shaking and constantly wringing my hands. I was unable to comprehend the word I had just heard, *guilty, guilty, guilty* bounced around my head like a squash ball being hit against the walls of a court. I pushed my glasses up my sweaty nose again; my face was hot and sticky. I was hyperventilating. Surely my fucked-up life hadn't come to this? A lifetime in jail?

The doors of the court opened and an obese woman wearing a mauve woollen coat drove in, operating an electric wheelchair with a lever to the side. Behind her was a slim, gaunt man wearing a white shirt with black trousers and a bootlace tie. He had greased back hair and a pitted face. As he approached the front of the court he turned and looked at me and mouthed,

"Scum."

It was all I needed; Anne-Marie's mother was an invalid. I never got to know who the other man was – a brother, an uncle?

Mrs MacDonald had a soft Edinburgh accent. El Hombre took a fatherly, friendly approach to her. He smiled and apologised to her for the ordeal she had been put through and expressed his gratitude at the fortitude she had shown. Then the usher asked her if she was alright? Did she need water and tissues? She held up her own box in reply.

"I'm alright, thank you, dear," she said. Then she opened her handbag and took out a folded, handwritten note. The man she was with bent over the wheelchair and the two conversed for a minute or so. I guess he was asking her if she wanted him to read it. The answer was 'no' because she started to read with shaky hands and tearful stops. It was the history of her lovely daughter who, it transpired, had got involved with some unsavoury types in Edinburgh when she had moved from Leith. Then she had moved down to London with a boyfriend.

"She was such a wee girl going to such a big city," Mrs MacDonald said. "I was worried sick for her, for you hear such stories of child abusers and drug addicts and muggers and terrorists and drug dealers and all sorts of bad people living in London, so you do. And all my worst fears were truly well founded, so they were, for poor Anne-Marie was killed by this brute."

She explained how Anne-Marie was lost without her father who had died when Anne-Marie was twelve. This, Mrs MacDonald felt, had sent her daughter 'off the rails' – she'd been permanently excluded from school and 'used to hang around with some older men' and generally 'mixed with the wrong types'. However, according to Mrs MacDonald, she had tried to 'better herself, so she had' and had gone to London with her boyfriend who had then deserted her. Apparently, she had been really pleased when Anne-Marie had told her she had been offered a room to rent in a friend's house. Mrs MacDonald said she had been shocked to find out (*during the trial*) that the house was being 'run' by a drugs gang. She said her lovely daughter would not get involved in anything like that unless she was coerced. Then it came to me.

"I will tell you this much, Judge, that man, if you can call him that, who stands in the dock, well, in killing my lovely daughter he killed me too. He plunged a knife into my heart, so he did, for what I am now without Anne-Marie?" and here she sobbed for Scotland as Bootlace Tie Boy comforted her by rubbing her shoulder and her back. "I am just an empty, empty shell, so I am, Judge. I want my daughter back!"

God, it was heartbreaking to hear. I just stood staring down at the floor, trying to conceal the fact that my eyes were moist. I was shaking, trembling, quivering but I tried to hold it together. I played with that plastic lion in my pocket. I felt for her, I really did. If one of my sisters had been murdered, I'd have jumped into the dock and pummelled the bastard. It was a nightmare.

At last, the Walrus attached the cuffs and tugged me back to the holding cell. I must admit I was relieved to get back into the cell and hear the key turn in the lock. I was left on my own and glad of it.

They had to sort out a bed for me in a local prison (local to the court). I was told I'd be moved to a Category B or dispersal prison where I would complete my sentence. They said the prison could be anywhere in the country, although they would try to ensure I was close to home.

As soon as I was on my own all the emotion and the tension of the last six months exploded out of me, my face folded in great sobbing tears. I threw the plastic Millwall lion across the cell – some lucky charm that had proven to be! Then I sat on the bed, took my glasses off and just cried and cried. Hannah and Mr Prentice came to see me.

"I don't know what to say, Richard," Mr Prentice said sheepishly. "I don't know how they could have reached that decision."

I responded angrily. "I bet you say that to all the clients you fucking pot, Mr Prentice."

I dabbed my eyes with some toilet tissue I'd pulled out of the holder.

"We did our best. Juries can be very fickle. But they should convict on the evidence and the evidence was wafer-thin."

Hannah was standing at the door, looking trim and professional in her navy-blue skirt suit and black high heels. I sniffed, blew my nose. Why couldn't I be like her? Why couldn't I be successful? Why was my life so fucked up?

"We'll lodge an appeal, Richard," she said. "I'll make a start on it over the weekend."

Her voice sounded weak, lifeless; I knew she was shocked by the verdict.

I stood up. It must have been a bright, sunny spring day for the light streamed through the dirty, frosted and barred window, creating a dark shadowy cross on the cell floor. I stood under the warm sunbeams, my back to them both. I let the tears roll down my face and then I scrunched up my face, bowed my head and lifted my arms as if mimicking an aeroplane: I let the rays of light wash over me. Then Hannah was beside me; she placed her hand on my shoulder and the spell was broken.

"I'm so, so sorry, Richard. But we'll appeal."

She gave me a hug.

Mr Prentice looked at his watch. "We'd better be going; the train back to London leaves in thirty minutes."

"I'll lodge that appeal," Hannah said softly, lifelessly. "I'll make a start on it as soon as I can. This weekend in fact."

So, I was left on my own, pacing the room. Then, I sat on the bed and started crying some more, "Oh, Debs, don't leave, don't leave me." I pushed an old bit of toilet tissue in my eyes but I couldn't hold back the torrent of tears. I was deflated and defeated.

Chapter Fifteen

Eventually, I was placed in a sweat box and locked into a cubicle. Then I was escorted along the M4 to London. It was late evening and the earlier sun had turned to torrential rain. Vehicle tyres splashed on the tarmac and I could hear the incessant hiss of the spray. I sat on my hard seat leaning forward like a praying mantis, deep in thought. The window was tinted but frequently the car lights would flash a streak of white and then red all fuzzed up by the wet and the moisture and the tint of the almost opaque glass. Here was a tin box and inside it was Richard A. Turner – convicted murderer. I rubbed my eyes with my fists, I'd cried so much no more tears would come. I felt sad, I felt angry, I felt frustrated, I felt despair – it overwhelmed me and it ate away at me like some gnawing cancer. I could see that a mixture of bad luck and my own stupid, stupid, stupid decisions had led me to my current predicament. I guess in some ways I was resigned to it. I'd woken up from so many nightmares with the word 'guilty' ringing in my ears – this was just one more time.

But the thing is, and here's the rub, I'm just a normal guy, I'm the same as you, I really am! I've hurt people I shouldn't have hurt but I've helped people too. I've tried to be honest and caring and empathetic and on the whole I have been. Yes, I've been an immature idiot too but why was that? Low self-esteem? Insecurity? A lack of love? Who knows? I didn't have the best start in life with my dad's drunken, violent outbursts and with him leaving the family when I was seven and then rejecting me when I was older. That hurt a lot. But I was brought up by my sisters, Donna and Kate really. My mum provided the material support but they provided the emotional care and I'm grateful to them for it. They gave me a better start in life than I could have expected and I know I had a better childhood than many others. I'm just so sorry for how it's all turned out. I'm sorry for how I've treated them. I'm sorry for my mum too in a way, she didn't deserve this.

All my life, I've hoped, I've dreamed that things would come right. That I would be a lucky man, that something would fall into my lap, that a chance encounter, a twist of fate would lead me to a good life. I don't mind working; I'm not lazy, not really, but I've just wanted a break, something to go right, not wrong but every time I've rolled the two dice, I've got a couple of ones instead of sixes.

We all know about the success stories, the people who 'make it'. We all hear the glib 'positive messages' and 'positive affirmations', all trite and meaningless but puked out like sick into a bucket at every training session and every TV programme that deals in that sort of meaningless crap. But what about me and people like me? People with fucked-up lives? People who've made wrong decisions? Not bad people but people who've made mistakes, got things wrong? Turned right when they should have turned left and left when they should have turned right until they've ended up in the centre of the Maze of Hell with no way out. What about those people? Does anyone care? Where's our second chance? Where's our opportunity? Where's our chance to make amends?

There is no black or white, there is no male and female; there's just success and failure and that success or failure is grounded in childhood. Most people in prison, both male and female, have experienced bad and worse than bad childhoods. You will say, no doubt, that some classes, groups, races, genders have a more difficult route to success and that may be true but when it's achieved the journey is immaterial. There are winners and losers and pretty much everyone who you don't have personal contact with, is a success, and even some of your personal contacts might be – like Mark and Kate for me. But on TV, in the music industry, entertainers, sports stars, TV presenters, TV reality 'stars', vloggers, bloggers, influencers, creatives, entrepreneurs, no one meets people like me who've fucked up. Who've made mistakes, who've got it wrong. No one.

I've never had good days. Not really. I've had snatches of happiness but I've never walked in the sun. I've never achieved what I wanted to achieve, I've never become what I wanted to become, I've never got it right. I've made mistake after mistake after mistake after mistake after mistake until finally I've fallen...

Why did I make so many mistakes? Why did I get so much wrong? Why did I make so many bad and worse than bad decisions?

I can't answer that.

So, I was transported along endless lengths of back tarmac to a castle in the sky, where it was hoped, by me and least, and I'm sure by Anne-Marie's mum, and uncle or whoever it was in the bootlace tie, that I would die, and sooner rather than later. I believed in capital punishment. For myself.

It was late when I arrived at my new prison home. It'd been a long day and a bloody tiring one too. Emotionally and physically, I was exhausted, wrecked. I was the only prisoner to arrive and the check-in was easy enough although the same ludicrous, rigorous routine was applied to me by tired, disinterested prison warders. I was assigned to a cell where my snoring cell mate had the top bunk. I had my prison issue kit so I got undressed – I now had the standard issue track suit-style grey prison uniform. I cleaned my teeth and went to sleep. First night. No longer on remand. Convicted. El Hombre would sentence me later but it would a whole life tariff, that was mandatory, it was just a question of whether he made any recommendations.

A few days later I was transported to another category B prison, somewhere in the south of England and a week later I was finally sentenced via video link: I was too far away to be transported back to court (and there was a risk of me losing my lovely Cat. B bed). El Hombre recommended a minimum of fifteen. It could have been worse, I suppose. He took into account my previous good behaviour and the fact I probably hadn't meant to kill Anne-Marie – it was not premeditated. By then I was numb to it all. I'd ceased caring. I'd ceased feeling. Fifteen? Twenty? Twenty-five? Thirty? What difference did it fucking make?

When I'd finally got to a phone, I managed to phone Debbie for ten minutes. I was using the payphone on the landing with a queue of prisoners behind me and she was sobbing and I was trying not to cry. She blamed herself but I told her not to. Afterwards I wrote to her and told her to forget about me (although with a tad of inconsistency I said I still wanted to stay in touch) and just concentrate on bringing up Dylan. And, well, a few letters later she took my advice on board and wrote;

'Look, Rich, I can't go on, not like this. I can't write, it's too painful. I need to think about Dylan, he can't see his mummy crying all the time. Every time I write or you write I'm upset for the rest for the day and it's not fair. It's not fair on Dylan. I need to be there for him. Please, please forgive me.'

Apparently, she'd met a police officer who had taken her for a coffee during the trial, I don't know if there was anything in it; if it was the reason for her 'Dear John' letter or not. I don't know. I don't care. Mark mentioned it when he drove down to see me with his latest girlfriend, whom he introduced as Ruth. She wore a red satin blouse over the top of grey leggings and her well-manicured nails were frequently pressed to her open neck as she constantly fiddled with a thin gold chain. She sat next to Mark and she could not take her wide, blue as summer sky, eyes off me; not because she fancied me in anyway but she was probably mystified by the lack of devil's horns sprouting from the top of my head. I imagined that Mark had casually informed her that one of his 'besties' was currently 'serving time for murder' and did she want to 'visit him' en route to a weekend away? Mark told me they were booked into a 4-star hotel in Brighton. Acquaintance with a convicted killer would probably add to Mark's 'bad boy' image and his womanising prowess.

How the system works is that you are not eligible for parole until you admit the offence (if you don't admit it, you can't be 'rehabilitated') and I was never going to admit the offence. Never. But, of course, you know by now that I did kill Anne-Marie.

Inadvertently.

Look, if I'm totally honest I'm not entirely sure that I saw her talking to two men in the nightclub; after all she meant nothing to me then so why would I remember it? She was an attractive girl but not stunning. It may just be a false memory, my brain trying to create a story – one of Mr Prentice's famous *narratives*. It's the same with the Beamer, it was definitely parked up the road, it is a common enough car after all, and there were two men in it, but were they watching me, as I thought, or was it just my guilty conscious? Frightened that I'd be fingered for stealing the money – not by the police but by a drugs' gang? So, I really don't know. It could have been my overactive imagination grabbing at straws which were slipping and sliding through my grimy fingers. The cocaine in the bathroom cupboard was there though, I saw that, in the condom. Of course, I was trying to escape and my senses were alive; my imagination was in overdrive, adrenalin was pulsing through my body, but that's the only thing I'm sure about.

Mr Prentice kept saying we needed a 'narrative' and that's what I tried to give him. I tried to create a story to get me out of the great big fucking hole I'd managed to manoeuvre myself into. It didn't work, of course – well you know that. But what if the men in the car, parked at the end of the road, were watching me? Well, this is my theory about what happened. Of course, the men might have visited after I'd left the house and might not have seen me at all, in which case, with a little adjustment, the same scenario (a word hated by El Hombre – *scenarios never killed anyone*) holds true.

Two guys, the line holders, came across from London to collect the proceeds of the drugs deals. Anyway, they saw Anne-Marie had a visitor so they waited. They were not very happy. It was cold and it was late. In the end they saw me leave and entered the house, wearing gloves of course – they had a key remember. Anne-Marie woke up as the little bell jingled. She came downstairs, trying to tie up her satin dressing gown but otherwise naked. Maybe this time she knew the guys who had come to collect the money. Perhaps they were the ones she had seen earlier in the nightclub, if they were indeed there and it wasn't just a figment of my feverish imagination. The men might have said something about having to wait around in the freezing cold whilst she was being fucked senseless and that they were not all that happy. Maybe Anne-Marie deflected that one. Now they wanted the 'coffee'. Quickly. So, she padded into the living room in bare feet, and then into the kitchen and opened the cupboard. Her mouth fell open in shook. Fear rose through her petite frame. She punted around a bit in the cupboard, moved sauces and other condiments. No money. She realised immediately that I'd taken it.

"Oh, fuck, he's taken the money!" she exploded. "He's only gone and taken the fucking money!"

Imagine the two gang members that were in her house – built like brick out-houses, well-muscled up, probably steroid junkies. Intimidating. Angry. Ruthless. Dressed in black. One of the gang members pushed past Anne-Marie and looked for himself. Anne-Marie backed into the living room. The gang member in the kitchen was furious. He grabbed a knife from the knife block. Perhaps he thought she had given me the money to hide and split later, possibly he thought that rather than a one-night stand I was a regular boyfriend – yes, I think that's it. I think he thought I was a boyfriend. Remember it's a world in which no one trusts anyone, everyone is suspicious, everyone is a potential grass.

Maybe he asked her where I lived,

"I don't know, I met him in the Pryzm, all I know is his name's Richard."

"You lying bitch!" the gang member shouted. "Tell us where the fuck he lives or you get shanked."

Anne-Marie was terrified. "I don't know, I honestly don't know."

As she stepped back the other gang member grabbed the tie from the night gown she wore and pulled it back through the loops. Then, holding the middle of the tie he placed it around her neck, crossing his hands as he did so to ensure it was tight around her throat. I imagine he then pulled her head back and placed his mouth to her ear. He spat,

"Where's the fucking money, bitch? Just tell us where the fucking money is."

"Where's your boyfriend live?" the first gang member shouted as he poked her with the knife.

Anne-Marie screamed,

"I don't know, honestly, I don't know. Get off, you're hurting me."

The second gang member pulled the black satin tie tighter around her neck. Tighter. Tighter. Tighter.

"Just tell us where the money is and we'll go and collect it from your boyfriend. Where does he live?" The first gang member prodded the knife at her as he spoke. The second gang member jerked her head back.

"I don't know, honestly, I don't know," Anne-Marie said with mounting terror.

"Lying bitch. Tell us where the fucking money is!"

The thugs would have been scared too as they would have had to deliver the money further up the food chain, maybe they'd done a few collections already. You get the picture.

Anyway, kitchen gang member lunged at Anne-Marie as if he was going to stab her, whilst Anne-Marie was being dragged backwards by the other gang member who held her by her neck. She had her hands to her throat trying to release the tie. Then what I think happened was that the gang member that was dragging her back bumped into the back of the sofa just as kitchen gang member lunged at her with the knife. Remember he's a big unit, six foot something, so the top of the sofa came up to his bum cheeks. He fell back, over the top of the sofa, bringing Anne-Marie down with him just as kitchen gang member stabbed her with the knife. As she fell the knife penetrated Anne-Marie below the rib cage – an upward stab wound piercing her lung. The other gang member was over the sofa by this time, with Anne-Marie on top of him. His head rested on the coffee table and his legs spread over the back of the sofa. He released Anne-Marie who rolled onto the floor. Perhaps the knife was pushed further into her body as she crumpled in a heap onto the carpet between the sofa and the coffee table. Hence the strange upward thrust of the knife, which even the pathologist report described as being an 'unusual stab wound'. Her right-hand rested on the coffee table, with her left leg buckled under her. The pathologist said that, with a collapsed lung, she would have died in minutes. The red throw, which had been pulled off in the melee, lay on top of her. I imagine then the kitchen gang member grabbed his mate and pulled him back up over the sofa.

"Fuck me, what just happened?" he said when he was back on his feet.

"I think we've killed her."

The kitchen gang member then pulled out the knife with the red throw. His mate had the tie from the dressing gown in his hand and he placed it on the throw.

"Quick. Get the phones."

Her handbag was still on the coffee table so they took out the phones. Then they removed the batteries to stop them pinging or paging or whatever phones do whenever they see a mast. After, they quickly searched the house. Maybe the coke in the bathroom cupboard had been there before and Anne-Marie hadn't collected it in the nightclub but either way they took it and anything else that could be of interest to the police. They wrapped it all up in the throw and put that in a plastic carrier bag they found in the kitchen, one of the ones stuffed in the recess on top of the washing machine. There was an elderly neighbour next door and he and other neighbours said there was always a lot of noise from the house and 'comings and goings at all hours' so they took no notice. One gang member stayed in the house for a little longer whilst he did a final 'sweep' and clean up whilst the other gang member walked down Church Street and onto High Street West with his carrier bag full of goodies. He walked off around the corner (an insomniac had reported to the police that a man dressed in black walked by her house carrying a carrier bag in the early hours of the morning) and continued to walk along the High Street West until the gang member who had stayed in the house collected him in the Beamer: they then drove back to London on A roads.

So that's my theory. It's as good as any, and of course, I know more than most about all this, but listening to the evidence, I think that's what happened. The pathologist said Anne-Marie could have fallen back onto the sofa whilst escaping a lunge from me but my theory explains the marks around her neck too. Once I had denied taking the money, I'd placed myself in a double bind: if I admitted it, I would have become a hostage to the prosecution and the later I admitted it the more of a hostage I'd have become. Also, I could possibly have landed Debbie in trouble, as I'd asked her to lie for me. Then there was the small matter of Mr Simon Ricoh, aka 'Sunderland' Simon discovering the money in the council bin, which I was not aware of until the CPS disclosure – that was totally unexpected and really torpedoed my defence. However you looked at it I was in a Catch-22 situation. Hey, actually, I'll add that to my list of books to read, Joseph Heller, a nice meaty tome too, that's good. I wonder if the prison library will have it? Probably not.

In the early hours of Sunday, 16th November my whole life pivoted on one simple action. I did the dumbest thing ever. As I stood in the hall looking at my slip-on shoes, I could have left the house. I didn't. I thought about my gigantic debt. I thought about buying Debbie a present and taking her to Paris on the Eurostar (she'd always wanted to go) and maybe getting engaged. And I thought about leaving. But, as Scarrott correctly observed, I was a gambler, a chance taker, a risk taker; I saw the wheel of life spinning and the little white roulette ball trickling into the rim. Spinning. I had a chance. I made a decision. I gently pushed open the living room door and walked towards the galley kitchen.... Well, you know the rest of the story...

POSTSCRIPT

So, I'm banged up. I won't say where or how long I've done already but it's for life. I joined the Toe-by-Toe again and help other prisoners with literacy skills which I really enjoy and this time I've managed to become a library orderly. I've also managed to get a job in the kitchen which has really enhanced my IEP standing. And of course I have to work too, for wages well below the minimum wage, and at the moment we're making cabinets.

Letters are a big thing in prison, it gives you something to do so, if I'm not helping other prisoners, I write my own. I wrote to Dom, enclosing a letter which I asked him to read to The Willow Man, who is illiterate, but he replied saying he was 'no longer with us' – whether he meant dead or moved, I don't know. He did not elaborate – the prison service is very suspicious of prisoner-to-prisoner letters. Dom knew not to say too much. I asked him if he had a new cell mate, he said he didn't. I also write regularly to Kate and Donna and

Mum (who responds briefly) and Mark (who responds but letters are delayed and brief) and Claire (who writes me great long letters – she's the best!). In one she said, '*I saw you tip that envelope, which I now know was filled with money, into the council bin; it was a good job I was never asked about it, because you know I wouldn't lie, Rich!*'

Slowly, I adjust to my new life behind bars. That's all you can do, try to forget about the outside world, as much as possible, and concentrate on your new reality. A reality so far removed from what you wanted, what you wished for, what you ever foresaw in your wildest nightmares it's untrue. But all you can do is isolate and insulate, that's the key, isolate and insulate. Nonetheless it's hard. You wouldn't believe the noise and that smell that really gets to you. It's difficult to explain but it gets under your skin, fills every pore and sinew of your body. It seems to enter your inside and emanate from the inside to the out and no amount of washing can clean it off.

I've continued my Bible studies and I've started to go to the chapel again – it gives me something to do on a Sunday and I find it peaceful. It is a quiet space where I can be reflective. But whilst those on the outside pray that God will, in some way, spare them cancer or some other terrible, incurable illness that they or a loved one might have, I pray that I will get a terminal illness. I want to die but I don't want to be the author of my own demise. No one can blame you for being ill. I'm not worried about 'clearing my name' and bollocks like that. I've got no name to clear. I'd love to write to El Hombre and say '*you know that fifteen you gave me? Well, I'm going to be out soon. In a wooden box. It's terminal. Bysie-bye*'.

I like talking to the chaplain, he's a really nice man. As I say, I've continued reading the Bible, which I enjoy very much. I love the stories and I know if I don't die, I'm going to have to let Jesus Christ into my messed-up life. Possibly.

The Bible gives me something else to read because the thing with prison is it is just so fucking boring. Some say prison is a 'holiday camp'. OK then, show me the rides and the slides. Show me entertainment that's not beefing and fights and quarrels and inmates squaring up to each other or screws; show me any part of prison that meets that definition. You can't, they can't. Being in prison is a way of life so far removed from the 'normal' as to be devoid of anything you could even loosely describe as living your life… it is, as it says on the tin, 'serving time.'

Every day is a bad fucking day.

And because you have a lot of time on your hands, you inevitably think about people on the 'out' getting on with their lives, their careers. Getting on with their jobs (however menial they might be), going on holiday, buying cars and houses and phones and all sorts of tech and going to the latest release at the cinema and going out for meals and screwing and drinking and praying and partying and seeing friends and having children and watching them grow up and looking after elderly family members and visiting family and friends and having family times together and Christmases and birthdays and get-togethers at home or in restaurants.

Then I think about my family – I try not to think too much about them as it makes me depressed but I always come back to them. Mum growing older; Kate working part time as a mobile beautician and hairdresser, married to her City broker husband Martin, with two boys who I'll never see grow up. Donna, who has two children, Liam and Lili, and who has married Wayne who I've never met. I think about my niece and nephews and how I must appear to them – the black sheep uncle in prison. I think about the fact I will never be a father or a grandfather too. And so, and so on and so on.

On Saturday nights I think about going out with Dave, Mark, Suggo and Matty. I know Mark is still the same lothario, up for a good time. Although, by all accounts he's met someone he's quite fond off and she's moved in with him: I'm not sure if it was the same girlfriend who came with him on the prison visit. Suggo and Matty are going off on holiday together to Greece. Dave's met someone at work and is going to get married.

Then, every Monday night I think about the writers' circle meeting at the library. I lie on my bunk bed and imagine myself leaving my flat and walking down the alley between the shops and then through the pedestrian zone with my folder under my arm containing my short story, a pen and some blank paper. I picture myself going to a fast-food restaurant and buying a burger and fries whilst I read through it. Sitting at a stool by the window, making notes, underlining words to emphasise, maybe making a few last-minute, revisions. I'd see other members of the group walk past – John with his shuffling walk, wearing the fawn jacket he wore all year round and Edna, who wore long skirts and walked with a stick: she used to interject her stories with asides explaining what she meant! I think about Claire and Kevin and Penny and the rest of our little crew I dubbed The Writers' Revolutionary Committee, and how we'd go for a drink afterwards in the Queen of England. We'd chat about the other members, take the mickey, have a laugh, Claire and I central to the piss-taking activities; such simple pleasures.

Then I think of the inside. Nothing. Endless days of nothing. Nothing to plan for or to hope for, no weekends away, no holidays, no evenings or days out at theatres, cinemas, restaurants, football, rugby, cricket or whatever sport flicks your switch, museums or even shopping in shopping malls. I used to hate it but now I'd give my eye teeth to have the opportunity to take Debbie and Dylan to Reading Gate Retail Park again. There's barely any difference between weekdays and weekends

– more visitors perhaps, a slightly different routine. So here I am. Banged up. In my thirties. Mid, late, early, it doesn't matter – one mistake on a night out.

Sometimes I think about Hannah and Mr Prentice representing other cases (never heard a bird about any appeal) moving on, me forgotten – a defendant potted – that's all.

I found a guy on the out – I call him the Mayo-man[2]. He's an amateur writer sort, probably wants to be some big shot. Like I once did. Never met him – he's never even visited and he could be a fucking dickhead for all I know but, anyway, I started to correspond with him and he agreed to edit and publish my story. After a few letters back and forth I started writing this on a word processor: it has to be written on a memory stick which is returned to the screws so they can review it, if they want. Hence, that's what I've been doing, writing this and as I say, he'll compile it into a book for me. So, if some of it is repeated or don't make a lot of sense, or I've got facts wrong, well, for one thing I can't check stuff with no internet and for another my head was all over the place from the time of the first police visit to my final incarceration. The reality is that for six months or more I lived in perpetual fog which means memories might be skewed and blurred and unreliable. But I have done my best. All I can say is that I have done my best.

---

[2] *This section has been left in at Richard's request.*

The Mayo-man said he'd publish the book via Amazon KDP. We debated putting my name on the cover too but, of course, Richard Andrew Turner may not be my real name! I wanted the book to be called 'My Fucked-Up Life' but the Mayo-Man said that even if I spelt it 'My F**ked Up Life', with two asterisks, Amazon would not publish it. He said 'The Defendant' was better – more accessible.

So that's what I do. I write. Slowly I pull the story together so at least it'll be out there. I asked the Mayo-Man about money, Royalties if you like. How we were going to split the profits?

"Don't worry, Rich," he said in one of his letters, "it'll make fuck all. You'll be lucky to sell twenty-five copies – everyone's self-publishing these days and no one is interested in your life."

No one is interested in your life.

That hurt me a lot because I knew it was true. Even so, the Mayo-man can be bloody blunt at times. Anyway, you're not supposed to make money out of crime, ha! ha!

Writing this makes me think of a real old film called *Kind Hearts and Coronets*. I like old films for my sins. I studied them at uni on my pointless, worse than useless, waste of time degree course which added to my mega-pile of debt and led me to make contact with my pointless, worthless, waster of a father. I won't ruin the story but basically, it's a black comedy made by Ealing

Studios in 1949. The central character is Louis D'Ascoyne Mazzini, played by Dennis Price. He kills members of his family to get an inheritance and title he believes is rightfully his. All the family members, both male and female, are played by the genius that was Alex Guinness – to my mind the greatest cinema actor who ever lived. Anyway, when the film opens poor old Louis is banged up and awaiting trial for murder (*know the fucking feeling, Louis!*) and to pass the time he is writing his memories which then morph into the film as a flashback. In one scene Louis and his girlfriend Sibella, played by the husky-voiced Joan Greenwood, are sitting by an open fire in his apartment when she says,

"What would you say if she (*a love rival*) asked you about me?"

Louis replies, "I'd say that you were the perfect combination of imperfections. I'd say that your nose was just a little too short, your mouth just a little too wide. But yours was a face that a man could see in his dreams for the whole of his life. I'd say that you were vain, selfish, cruel, deceitful. I'd say that you were adorable. I'd say that you were – Sibella."

Sibella says, "What a pretty speech."

To which Louis says, "I mean it."

And Sibella replies, "Come and say it to me again."

The reason I mention that is because one time Debbie was around my flat and we were watching that film – *Kind Hearts and Coronets*. She was stretched out on my

444

three-seater sofa with her head on my lap looking up at me. She wasn't really watching the film (which being in black and white she found a bit boring) but she heard that speech and she gazed at me with those big, brown eyes of hers and she said,

"Make a speech up for me, Rich."

So, I said to her, touching her nose and lips, and combing her dark hair off her forehead. I said this, straight off the bat without really thinking about it.

"Did we touch like children touch?

And did we kiss like lovers kiss?

And did we snog like the Frenchmen snog?

And did we screw like rabbits do?

And did we say?

'I love you."

Debbie giggled in that pretty way of hers and I could see her eyes were moist.

"No one's ever said anything like that to me before, Rich; will you write it down for me?"

I said I would but like so much in my life, I never did, 'till now.

So that's it. That's the story. My fucked-up life.

Oh, I almost forgot, there's a small coda to my tale. One day I was in the exercise yard when a big, deep, anonymous voice behind me croaked,

"Where's that fucking money, Rat?"

End

For my previous please visit my website www.colinmayo.com or follow me on Twitter @**colinmayo9** or on **Facebook.**

About the Author

Colin was born in Croydon and now lives in Hertfordshire with his wife, Jane. Educated to degree level he has done a variety of jobs in between very long bouts of unemployment. His jobs range from an NHS and university administrator; a credit control clerk; barman (multiple times); day porter in a Devon hotel; supermarket cashier; motorcycle despatch rider; postie; postboy; British Gas salesman; trainer and truancy officer – during which time he has lived in Slough, Stoke-on-Trent and Middlesbrough; currently he works in education. Creative writing has always been a passion of his since his late teens. He has completed a variety of writing courses and has joined numerous writing circles. Over the years, he has written novels, articles, short stories, plays and poems and has been fortunate enough to have had a few pieces published, including a number of articles in *Best of British* Magazine. He has previously self-published a thriller, *Deadman's Roulette,* a book of poetry, *Hen's Teeth* and a play, *Shocked to Fame.*

Acknowledgements

No man is an island and no book is written in complete isolation, I would like to thank the following for their friendship, time, patience, skill and expertise: Mark Halsall; Sharon Weigall; Julia Gibbs and Three Shires Publishing. I would also like to acknowledge and give a huge "thank you" to Noel 'Razor' Smith for his foreword and insights into prison life: he was the first person to read and comment on a draft of this book which then allowed me to revise it and place this published, and hopefully much improved version, before the public. I would also like to thank the following for their reference materials, these being the excellent webs sites that offer support to prisoners and their families: Inside Time; The Prison Reform Trust; The Howard League for Penal Reform and Doing Time as well as Carl Cattermole for his highly informative and entertaining book Prison: A Survival Guide. In addition, there are many other sites and prisoner blogs which have proved invaluable in assisting my deep dive into the criminal justice system. I would also like to extend my gratitude to Julia Horobets who designed the cover for this book and all my previous books. Julia lives in the Ukraine. Enough said. Lastly, I'd like to thank my wife, Jane for her constant love, loyalty and support.